THE WAY INTO
CHAOS

Book One of The Great Way

Harry Connolly

RADAR AVE
PRESS

Interior art by Claudia Cangini
Map illustration by Priscilla Spencer
Cover art by Chris McGrath
Cover design by Bradford Foltz
Book design by The Barbarienne's Den
Copy edited by Richard Shealy

Printed in the United States of America

PRAISE FOR THE BOOKS OF
HARRY CONNOLLY

The three novels of THE GREAT WAY

The Way Into Chaos
The Way Into Magic
The Way Into Darkness

"Connolly pens one hell of a gripping tale and kicks Epic Fantasy in the head! Heroic in scope, but intimately human, and richly detailed. *The Way Into Chaos* intrigues and teases, then grabs readers by the throat and plunges them into desperate adventure related through the experience of two extraordinary narrators. The story never lets up as it twists and turns to a breathless finish that leaves you crying for the next book of *The Great Way*. Fantastic!"

—Kat Richarson

"One hard-hitting, take-no-prisoners, breathtaking holy moly of a book."

—C.E. Murphy

"Complex world, tight action, awesome women as well as men; Connolly was good right out the gate, and just keeps getting better."

—Sherwood Smith

TWENTY PALACES

CHILD OF FIRE

GAME OF CAGES

"*Game of Cages* is a tough, smart, unflinching urban fantasy novel."

—Andrew Wheeler

"This has become one of my must-read series."

—Carolyn Cushman, *Locus Magazine*

CIRCLE OF ENEMIES

"An edge-of-the-seat read! Ray Lilly is the new high-water mark of paranormal noir."

—Charles Stross

"Ray Lilly is one of the most interesting characters I've read lately, and Harry Connolly's vision is amazing."

—Charlaine Harris

SPIRIT OF THE CENTURY PRESENTS: KING KHAN

"An exuberant romp that distills all the best of pulp fiction adventure into one single ludicrously entertaining masterpiece."

—Ryk E. Spoor

BAD LITTLE GIRLS DIE HORRIBLE DEATHS AND OTHER TALES OF DARK FANTASY

"Connolly writes tales of magic and mystery in more modern times incredibly well. His work reminds me a lot of Tim Powers or Neil Gaiman. I highly recommend this collection."

—Jason Weisberger at *Boing Boing*

For Lloyd Alexander, who turned me into a reader of fantasy.

THE WAY INTO
CHAOS

THE EN—

KAL-M—

THE
WASTES

TEMPEST
PASS

LAKE
WINDMARK

TH—

SPL

SALTSTONE

WHITE CA—

DEEP
STON—
LAKE

FREEWELL

BENDERTUK

GERR—

ESPILETH

BESCOS
SEA

SIMBLIN

W—

RE OF
DDUM

QORR
VALLEY

SHELTERLANDS

WEEPS

FORT
PISKATOOK

FORT
SAMSIT

FORT
AARILIT

TOWN

RD

EAST
FORD

THE STRAIT

INDRECA

GRIMWOOD

WITT

PERADAIN

BAY OF
STONES

RIVERSHELF

ER LANDS

BY PRISCILLA SPENCER

CHAPTER ONE

Without his armor, Tyr Tejohn Treygar thought he must have looked like a man disgraced. It was ridiculous, of course; by Festival custom and royal decree, everyone went without armor today, even the guards at the gates. Still, he felt odd as he strode into the morning chill onto the promenade of the Palace of Song and Morning in the soft, slipper-like shoes Laoni had bought for him. His steps were so quiet, he felt like a sneak thief.

The queen wanted to speak to him. Again. Tejohn had not been and would not be officially summoned to the throne for an audience, but she was not a woman who would ever let anything rest. What's more, he would never hide from her—not ever.

However, if he happened to be away from his chambers in the early parts of the day, he could hardly be blamed if her servants didn't think to look for him on the lonely northern end of the promenade.

She found him anyway, of course.

"My Tyr Treygar," she said as she approached, her attendants arrayed behind her like a wedge formation. "You must be chilly out here in just your shirt and waistcoat."

He bowed. "I'm not accustomed to normal civilian clothes, my queen, let alone Festival clothes. But I'm sure I will be more comfortable when the sun has been up a while."

She glanced at the gray sky with disapproval. It had drizzled overnight and would begin again soon. "Morning in the Morning City. Great Way, but I am looking forward to summer." She stepped to the wall beside him and stared off into the distance, just as he had been. Her own waistcoat was made of deep red cloth woven with golden threads. Not the latest fashion, as he understood it, but still beautiful. During the Festival, even the queen wore pockets. "It will be nice to have a few days of sunshine. The mountains are so lovely in the morning, when we can see them."

The Southern Barrier—which was north of the city but bore that name because there was another range even farther away—was sometimes visible in the morning mists. At least, that's what Tejohn had been told. His vision was too short to see the thatched roofs of the city beyond the walls. Not that such things mattered to him.

The queen looked sideways at him, a sly smile on her face. Queen Amlian Italga wasn't a beautiful woman, but she was intelligent, clever (not the same thing, as Tejohn had learned long ago) and relentless. When she wanted something, she didn't give up until it was hers. The king may have been a bit of a fool in some ways, but he'd passed over the most beautiful women in the empire to choose her for his second queen. It was the wisest decision he'd ever made.

Which meant there was little peace for those who did not give her what she wanted.

"Have you thought about my proposal, Tejohn?"

He bowed again. It was always good to bow when you were about to disappoint royalty. "I've thought about little else, but I can not do it." She scowled but did not interrupt. "I'm not being obstinate, my queen. I have worked many hours on this, but it is beyond me."

The queen crooked her mouth as if she were addressing an obstinate child, never mind that Tejohn was three years her elder. "Beyond you? I think we both know that isn't true." With a lazy flick of her wrist, she gestured toward the sky cart flying westward over the city, streamers trailing behind.

Tejohn studied it as though her gesture had been a command. It was a large square wooden cart with spoked wheels. Mounted above it were the two obsidian-black disks that lifted it free of the ground.

The metal underarmor had been removed, of course, as had the rows of shields along the sides. The cask holders, designed to drop lit oil into holdfasts and other enemy camps, now bore nothing but colorful streamers. It, too, had been stripped of its armor, and it looked as odd as he must have.

Martial displays were forbidden during the Festival. The Evening People didn't believe in conquest.

Tejohn sighed. The Gift that created the carts—and the tremendous advantage they gave the empire in the fighting on the frontiers—existed because of him and the song he'd written. And no one would let him forget it.

"I was a young man then," Tejohn said softly, "and fresh to my grief. Now I'm old. I have a wife and children again. My home is a happy one."

The queen sniffed. "Well, that would certainly not make a very moving song." Tejohn was tempted to disagree, but of course he didn't. "And you aren't *that* old. The Evening People will be here for ten days. Are you *sure* you couldn't write a sequel? Or just perform the same song again?"

It had been years since the corpses of Tejohn's first wife and son had flashed through his memory, but they came to him then—and with them came the familiar urgency to take up his spear and start killing. "I could never revisit that pain, and you should not ask it of me."

If his rebuke offended her, the queen did not show it. She squeezed his hand briefly, then stepped back. "You must feel this very deeply to speak to me that way. Tejohn, my friend, please accept my apology. Song knows you've always been good to Ellifer and me, and to Lar, too—not that he deserves it. We have other singers and playwrights; the king and I will have to be satisfied that our legacy will include some lesser form of new magic. Will Laoni and the little ones be joining us?"

"Laoni has taken Teberr and the twins to East Ford, to visit her cousins. They're still so small . . . "

The queen wasn't fooled by that, but she let it pass. "I should go. There's so much to do. Tejohn, after the Evening People return to their home, the city will be bustling for a month at least, and we expect the scholars will have a new Gift to argue over. . . . I believe I have some messages to send to East Ford. Would you be willing to deliver them for me? And wait a month for the responses? Lar is full-grown now; I'm sure he can practice in the gym without you for a while."

If only he would. But there was no need to say it. Tejohn and the queen both wanted the prince to redirect his energies toward his martial training and away from his . . . other pursuits. "Thank you, my queen," Tejohn said. "It would please me greatly. Thank you."

Queen Amlian smiled and turned away. "Just be sure Lar is in his place today and that he's sober. He's not planning to sing a bawdy song, is he? It seems I heard a rumor to that effect."

"If so, I will do my best to dissuade him." Tejohn took his leave. A chill drizzle had begun to fall, and he returned to his room first, to put on the long black coat his wife had made for him. The whole city would be wearing bright reds and yellows—even blues, for those wealthy enough—but for the man who wrote "River Overrunning," Laoni thought it best to wear something somber.

After that, he put on the polished bronze bracers. He wasn't permitted to carry a spear or shield today, but the weight of the metal on his forearms was reassuring.

Tejohn had just refused the queen. She could have punished him in a hundred ways, including taking away his honorary title, but she had shown him kindness instead. She understood. *Grateful am I to be permitted to travel The Way.*

At the end of the last Festival, the leader of the Evening People had stared at Tejohn with those terrible golden eyes as though he'd wanted to take Tejohn's soul home with him. As if he hadn't already taken too much. *We will meet again*, Co had said. Tejohn had dreaded it ever since.

Tejohn hurried through the palace. It didn't matter. If Co hoped to feast on another piece of Tejohn's grief, he would be disappointed by the simple, decent life the soldier had created for himself over the past twenty-three years. And Tejohn was prepared to hide his pleasure at that disappointment very carefully.

It was time for Lar's lesson in the dueling gym, but of course he wasn't there. An allowance could be made because of the Festival, but the truth was that Lar often made excuses to be absent from Tejohn's sword and spear lessons. In fact, he'd skipped so many over the winter that it was just about time to bring it to the king's attention. Again.

Colchua Freewell was there, of course, along with the Bendertuk boy, Timush. Nothing Tejohn had done could discourage them from sneaking into the gym, and eventually, Lar had convinced his father to grant them full access. The first day that Tejohn had been forced to teach the use of weapons to a Freewell and a Bendertuk had almost brought him to the brink of treason, but he had done his duty.

They stopped their exercises to bow to him formally, to show the respect every student owed their teacher. He kept his expression carefully neutral, nodded in return and walked out.

Tejohn went crossed the tiny southern gate yard to the south tower. When Lar wasn't in the dueling gym, he was either still abed—and drunk—or he was playing at magic at the top of the Scholars' Tower.

Not that the yard was really a yard any more. There was so much foot traffic in the palace that no grass could grow in the yard except in ugly patches, and it had so bothered old King Ghrund that he'd ordered it covered over with scholar-created pink granite. Everywhere Tejohn turned his head he saw the same blurry pink color, broken only by the darkness of windows, barrows, and people.

Inside the Scholars' Tower, Tejohn's left knee ached by the time he was halfway up the stairs: too many battles, too many years on the road, too much sparring. Not that the medical scholars seemed interested in relieving him of the pain. Someday soon, the twins would be old enough to join him in the gym, and Tejohn could send them on missions like this. It was one of the privileges of parenthood to make your children run errands for you.

Until then, he laid his hand on the mottled pink and black stone blocks—he could only see the detail when he was this close—and trudged upward.

On the last flight of stairs, he could hear Lar and his friends inside, playing with spells they already knew by heart.

Tejohn knocked loudly. There was another pair of loud impacts inside the room, then the sound of desultory cheering. After a short while, the prince called, "Enter!"

Tejohn did. Prince Lar stood at the center of the room. He was wearing his spellcasting robe, which was rough white cloth with a set of odd symbols down one side. Beside him stood Cazia Freewell. She was a talented scholar, having already learned just about every spell the tutors were willing to teach her by the age of fifteen. She was also sly, secretive, and too often in the library. Her elder brother Colchua might have been reckless and proud, but Tejohn thought this sneak had been born to treachery.

Little Jagia Italga, the king's nine-year-old niece, was also wearing her robe, but she stood well back against the wall. Possibly she had not learned this spell—or any spells. She was still so young.

"My Tyr Treygar," the prince said, pushing his long black hair out of his face. "I almost didn't recognize you without your cuirass. You look . . . almost human. In size, I mean."

The Freewell girl turned away to hide her laughter, but Pagesh Simblin and Bittler Witt laughed openly. In all likelihood, they had been the ones offering the halfhearted cheering. Neither had the interest or inclination for magic, and the Witt boy was hopeless in the gym, doing little more than complain about pains in his belly. Pains no scholar could relieve.

And Tejohn didn't know what to make of the Simblin girl—well, she should surely be called a woman now, since she was older than the prince. However she had no interest in magic, marriage, or anything at all that he knew of.

Not that Doctor Twofin hadn't tried to teach them all, per the prince's wishes and the king's indulgence. He was a better tutor than Tejohn had ever been; the weapons master had humiliated himself by asking the old scholar for advice on more than one occasion. But a teacher can do as little with an unwilling student as a blacksmith can do with a fired clay pot.

Out of habit, Tejohn confirmed that Doctor Twofin's cheeks were dry. Of course they were. The old tutor was the only scholar Tejohn could bring himself to trust, even partially.

"I'm sorry, my Tyr Treygar," Lar said immediately. He wore a mischievous smile that had been charming when he was twelve, but on a man of seventeen made Tejohn want to knock him to the floor. "My jest was not intentional."

The prince was a bad liar. "My prince, you are late for your lesson in the gym."

"Do you see?" Lar asked. He gestured toward the wall. A dozen cloth-covered hoops had been pinned to a wooden wall with iron darts nearly a foot long. This was the prince's favorite spell. "I like to think little Caz and I are becoming genuinely dangerous." He turned to the Freewell girl. "Don't you agree?"

She beamed up at him. "We're at least at the level of a nuisance.".

"Oh, I've been a nuisance for years," Lar answered, and the young people laughed again. They always laughed, even when the jokes weren't funny. Tejohn wished he had some of that easy charm, but he didn't have the knack.

He glanced back at the wall of targets. The ribbons tied into the loop at the back end of each dart were brightly colored, almost as though they'd been made for the Festival. Those darts the prince—and other scholars—used were heavier than arrows and, depending on the skill and sanity of the spellcaster, deadlier than anything that could be shot from a bow. But there was one advantage that an arrow had that no scholar's dart ever would: they were shot by soldiers.

"See?" The prince gestured toward the pinned hoops. "Why should I practice dueling in the gym when—"

Tejohn suddenly rushed at him, springing across the distance between them in a few long strides. Lar was startled, then raised his hands to begin a fire spell.

Of course, the prince didn't have time. Tejohn slammed a shoulder into him, upending him onto the wooden floor and kneeling atop him. Then he seized the young man's scrawny neck.

An iron dart flew between them, striking hard into the wooden floor. Tejohn spun toward the source, and saw the Freewell girl glaring at him, preparing another spell.

CHAPTER TWO

"ENOUGH!" DOCTOR TWOFIN SHOUTED. HE RUSHED AT CAZIA, AND THE furious expression on his face froze her with terror. The sharpness of his voice had already disrupted her spell gestures, but he clasped her hands to be sure. "My dear, you don't need to protect the prince from his own weapons master and bodyguard. Never cast at this man again! Do you understand?" The old teacher's voice became high and shrill.

Doctor Twofin had the authority to bar Cazia from the Scholars' Tower, and he would do it, too. The idea made her sick. She looked down at her feet and said, in a carefully miserable tone, "I understand. I'm sorry, Tyr Treygar."

Old Stoneface Treygar stood without replying. He gave her a look full of cool hatred, but she was used to that. Of all the Enemies in the palace, he was one of the most obnoxious.

Lar tried to roll to his feet but got tangled in his robe. He fell to his knees, prompting Jagia, Pagesh, and Bittler to laugh. For once, Cazia wasn't in the mood to join in. "Caz, you're not supposed to kill him *after* he's assassinated me," Lar said. "Mother and Father couldn't have questioned him then. Am I correct, Tyr Treygar?"

Stoneface didn't answer, so Doctor Twofin answered for him. "That's correct! Have you been neglecting your other studies to come here, my prince? If you have, I'll bar you from the library and the practice room."

Lar was startled. "You can't bar me from parts of my own palace. I'm the prince!"

Doctor Twofin was highborn, the sixth son of some minor Fifth-Festival mountain tyr, and he was less intimidated by royalty than most. "You just try me."

Lar stepped back and raised his hands to placate the old tutor, laughing. "I promise! No threats needed."

Out of the corner of her eye, Cazia saw Stoneface scowl. He probably thought Lar should stand up to his teacher—or threaten him—but he played those games. Cazia turned away to slip out of her robe, but she kept Treygar in her peripheral vision. She'd had a lot of practice keeping an eye on Enemies without seeming to.

Doctor Twofin wagged his finger at them. He was forever wagging that finger. "You have practiced enough for one day already. Remember, do not practice your magic—"

Lar finished the sentence with him. "—unless we are in this room with you. We've heard it a thousand times, doctor."

"You'll hear it a thousand more, my prince. I won't have you going hollow under my tutelage. Think of the consequences!"

Cazia thought of the consequences every day: Lar would never become king. Twofin would lose his head. Cazia would lose her fingers like Doctor Whitestalk, if she was lucky, and she almost certainly wouldn't be. And there was always the damage that hollowed scholars might do.

The prince's thoughts were on other subjects. He turned to Treygar. "Tell me, my tyr: Is that how you slew Doctor Rexler?"

Stoneface looked directly at Cazia, so she had to turn her back—just for a moment—as she hung her quiver of darts on a peg. Apparently, this Doctor Rexler had something to do with her . . . or with her father. Treygar said, "Your mother the queen has asked me to accompany you to the Festival today, my prince."

"I hardly think I need a bodyguard to meet the Evening People. From the stories everyone tells, they never offer more than a cutting remark."

"That's true," Treygar said, "nonetheless . . . "

"Nevertheless, she wants me to be sober."

"She does, my prince. Is it true that you plan to sing a comedy?"

"Yes!" Lar exclaimed, as though he'd been asked this question a hundred times. "But it is not a bawd, I promise you. There are no mighty warriors, no wizards, and no overenthusiastic lovers, Song knows."

Pagesh spoke up from the bench against the wall. "The Evening People don't care for comedies, do they? I thought they liked sad songs."

Everyone glanced at Stoneface, and Cazia noted how uncomfortable that made him. Interesting. "It's true," Doctor Twofin said. "The more they appreciate our performances, the more powerful the spell they give us. The nail-driving Gift they offered after the Tenth Festival was seen as a rebuke for that event's emphasis on slapstick and farce."

A flush of annoyance ran through Cazia. "And yet, look what we've made of it." She gestured toward the darts and hoops on the wall. They'd spent the whole lesson on that spell—well, on the somewhat-altered spell humans had created from it. It wasn't as useful as the other Gifts, but it was the most fun. How could people call it a rebuke?

"Quite," the doctor said in his high, unsteady voice, as though she was missing the point. "However, the stone-breaking spell after the eleventh has made copper and iron commonplace within the empire. Not fifty years ago, the only soldiers with iron cuirasses were generals. Am I correct, Tyr Treygar? Now every soldier but archers wear them."

"Every soldier but archers and fleet squads," Treygar droned. "And skirmishers. Also, the iron has been largely replace by Sweeps steel now. But you're correct, doctor. It made a huge difference at Coldwater Falls." He shrugged. "According to the reports."

Doctor Twofin seemed proud of Treygar's approval for some reason Cazia couldn't fathom. She'd never even heard of Coldwater Falls before.

"I don't understand," Jagia said, looking up at their faces one after another. "I thought the Evening People gave us gifts."

Pagesh took the little girl's braid and tickled the bottom of her chin with the end. Pagesh smiled at her; the older girl was always kind and even-tempered, but she only smiled for Jagia. "We just call them that, little one. Gifts. But in truth, it's more like a speck you toss into a mummer's wooden bowl after a song. A cheap coin to show your appreciation."

"I don't think that's fair," Bittler said. He turned his watery gaze on each of them, hoping someone would take his side. "It's more of a trade, isn't it? We put on a Festival of art and athletics for them, and they teach us a new spell."

Pagesh dropped Jagia's braid and gave Bitt an even look. "It's only a trade if both sides get to negotiate."

"She's right," Lar said. "As usual." Pagesh bowed her head to the prince. He smirked and nodded back. "For the next ten days, we will make every effort to please the Evening People so that they will grant us whatever reward they see fit."

"But why?" Jagia asked. "Why do they come here at all?"

It was a question Cazia had never thought to ask. She turned to the doctor, waiting for his answer.

"Well, erm, you see . . . " Doctor Twofin looked a bit flustered. "The

Evening People are a proud people—and potent, too—but they have their limitations. Er . . . " The old scholar looked as if he was dancing around a sensitive subject.

"Magic is physical," Old Stoneface said, and Cazia thought he had never been more worthy of that nickname than when those words were coming from him. "Break rocks, start fires, suppress fires—all of that is a way of magically pitting your will against the mundane world. But a spell can not make you fall in love. Magic can not make a person weep for the enemy he has slain. It can not change a person's mind, or convince them to take up spears for their homeland, or fill their heads with dreams of glory and wealth in distant lands. Songs, plays, even athletic games, can do all this. To the Evening People, this is a magic in itself. One they have no talent for."

"Quite," Doctor Twofin said a little nervously.

Treygar stared intently down at Jagia as though they were the only two people in the room. No honorary title or fancy clothes would ever hide the fact that he was a commoner at heart. "That is everything I know about it, Miss."

"Doesn't that make you a kind of scholar, too?" the little girl asked. "Your song was a kind of magic to them, so that should make you a scholar to the Evening People, right?"

A tense silence filled the room. Only a nine-year-old girl—and the royal niece—would dare to broach the subject of Stoneface's horrible song. The old soldier did not betray any loss of temper. He just solemnly shook his head.

"Oh. Well, thank you for answering my question," Jagia answered politely.

"I am pleased to offer whatever I knowledge I possess to the prince's cousin."

Hmph. Cazia was the prince's cousin, too, but she hadn't gotten any lessons from the old bully. But then, Jagia's father had never tried to seize the crown.

Bitt opened his mouth as though he wanted to continue debating the point, but closed it again. Either he was especially unwell this morning or he knew the argument was a lost cause. Little Jagia reached over and took his trembling hand gently in hers, and they smiled at each other.

Lar hung his robe on a hook. "Tell me, my tyr, do you think the Evening People would be impressed if I wore the battle helm and spiked shield father gave me?"

Stoneface's answer was wary and unpleasant. "Shield and helm won't protect you from the Evening People's disapproval."

Cazia didn't like that punch line, so she supplied another. "And no armor in the world would protect you from your mother's."

Even Doctor Twofin laughed at that, but not Stoneface. When Cazia noticed the look he gave her, she felt a little sick. The queen had always been distant but respectful to her; while Treygar wouldn't personally rush to the throne room to tattle on her, he would probably make sure she heard about the joke somehow.

Cazia bit her lip. No matter how careful she was about the way she spoke in the palace, she was never careful enough.

"I must return to my rooms so Quallis can change my clothes," Lar said. "Do you mean to accompany me, Tyr Treygar?"

Stoneface's tone was icy. "I do, my prince."

"Excellent. If a jar of wine should get too near me, you may throw yourself upon it."

"Colchua would do that for you," Pagesh said from the bench. "And kill the jar, too."

But no one laughed. Stoneface had squelched their mood.

Lar lightly touched Cazia's shoulder. "Caz, thank you for practicing with me today. Please take Pagesh to her rooms and help her find a dress for the Festival that doesn't have grass stains on it. Bittler, find Col and Timu. They're probably dueling in the gym and they're likely to need a dunking before they dress up. And try to eat something."

Bittler laid a half-starved hand over his belly and nodded.

Treygar opened the practice room door and followed the prince to the stairs.

As the door swung closed, Cazia felt a chill run down her back. Old Stoneface might have been the prince's bodyguard and weapons instructor, but he was the king's man. It was no secret that Lar's parents were afraid that he might play a prank during the Festival. The Evening People were easily offended, and the Festival itself was a sort of mummery that the entire city of Peradain put on to please them. And Lar . . . He still had a boy's impulse to call out hypocrisy when he saw it.

She loved him. Not that she wanted to hold his hand or feel his kiss, no. She was a fifteen-year-old girl, and she had reached the age where she noticed the way many of the palace guards looked in their crisp uniforms. She couldn't help but notice them.

However, as the daughter of Tyr Freewell, if she got too near, the guards were more likely to spit on the ground between them than offer her a kind word. It simply wasn't safe to do more than glance at them from afar. Servant girls with debt tattoos on their wrists were more free to talk and laugh with boys than she was.

No, she loved Lar the way she would love a second older brother, a friend, and her prince. She'd been brought to the Palace of Song and Morning as a baby and had grown up alongside him. All of his circle, with the exception of little Jagia, were the children of traitors, and the only truly safe place for them was beside the prince. She loved him because he was her better, yet he treated her with kindness and protected her from the worst of the bullying. Someday, when their fathers' generation had left The Way, her older brother Colchua would be the new Tyr Freewell, and she would be running things inside the Scholars' Tower. King Lar Italga would have no subject anywhere in the empire more loyal than her.

Today, she couldn't help but worry. Would his parents prevent him from singing this song he'd prepared in secret? King Ellifer was a decent sort—for a king—so she didn't believe he would kill his own son. Not like the Italgas of years ago. Still, the stakes were so high. Maybe he would have Lar locked away?

And who better to arrest the prince than his own bodyguard?

No. Cazia couldn't leave the prince alone with the Stoneface. Not today. She laid her hand on the hidden latch.

Pagesh noticed and recognized immediately what she planned to do. The older girl stood. "Well, it's time we got ready," she said, then spilled a quiver of iron spikes onto the wooden floor.

The terrible noise made Doctor Twofin cry out and rush toward her. At the same moment, Cazia pulled on the latch, opening the secret panel, and slipped inside, taking care not to snag her skirts.

The panel closed behind her, blocking out all light. She found the ladder just where it was supposed to be, then started down.

It wasn't a true ladder—the builders of the Scholars' Tower had inserted this secret passage along the stairs, and it had apparently been easier to gouge deep foot- and handholds in the stone than attach a real ladder.

She made her way down with confidence, even though it had been months since she'd last used it. When she'd been Jagia's age, she used to come here just to sit in the dark, away from the petty cruelties of the kitchen staff or the snide challenges of the palace guard. There were few hiding places from her Enemies, and no one even seemed to know it was here.

But when she was thirteen, she'd almost gotten caught slipping out of the lower hatch, and now only used it when she had to.

After descending a while, she came to the stairs. The passage was so narrow, she couldn't turn around easily, but she knew the way. The secret stairs matched the broader public stairs on the other side of the wall, and eventually . . .

She heard Lar's voice just on the other side of the wall. Perfect. She stopped to listen and, standing silent in the darkness, she couldn't help but smile. She loved spying on people. Loved it. The only thing that made her feel more powerful was casting spells.

"Tyr Treygar, I wish you could be kinder to my friends."

Treygar's answer was noncommittal. "Yes, my prince."

Cazia descended quietly to keep up with them. She heard Lar sigh. "I would command you to smile at them once in a while, but I fear it would shatter your stony face."

"I am not as fragile as that, my prince."

She heard their footsteps stop, so she did, too.

"My Tyr Treygar," the prince said. He genuinely sounded annoyed. "I have lived with these people my entire life, and not one of them was alive when Tyr Freewell and his allies moved against my father. This new generation has been treated with respect by my royal parents and with kindness by me. Whatever crimes the Witts, the Simblins, the Bendertuks, and the Freewells have committed, my friends are blameless. I would prefer you treat them so."

"I do, my prince."

"You do? It seems to me that you are short with them at every opportunity."

"My prince, if I thought them guilty of crimes like the ones their fathers committed, I would have already struck through their necks, dropped their heads into their families' holdfasts, and dumped their bodies into the Sweeps for the alligaunts."

Cazia wasn't grinning anymore, but she was still glad to be there, spying on her best friend and the bully who tutored him at weapons. *I know you better than you know me.*

"These words do not please me," Lar said. A king would have said that with anger or would have made it feel like a threat, but Lar sounded sad and helpless. She couldn't help but feel a familiar twinge of sorrow for him; he was too good a person to have to deal with bullies like Treygar and the world they'd made.

Treygar said, "I have sworn my service to your royal parents: they have my life, my honor, and my duty. So do you, my prince. However, my thoughts and what little wisdom Fury has granted me remain my own. Your cousins might make fine palace playmates, but their families—their names—will call to them. They live here as hostages, not guests. They will not forget that, even if you have. When the time comes for them to choose, *you* may be sure of their loyalty, but my duty requires me to be watchful."

"I have not forgotten why they are here. I won't allow myself to forget."

"Then remember also that, if I had not slain Doctor Rexler and broken the guard at Pinch Hall, you would not have ventured onto The Great Way, with all its featherbeds and jars of wine, and Colchua Freewell would be prince now."

For some reason, Lar laughed. "Col would make a much better prince—and king—than I ever will."

Shocked, Cazia stayed perfectly still while the footsteps receded down the stairs. Did the prince really think her brother would make a better king? Sadness suddenly filled her so full that tears welled in her eyes. Lar should never say such things aloud, especially not to a killer like Tyr Treygar.

Fire and Fury, Lar needed a bodyguard to protect him from himself.

Cazia went down the stair more slowly, not wanting to hear any more and all too aware of what would happen to her if she emerged from the passage with tears on her face. Pagesh, Bittler, and Jagia's footsteps passed and faded. At the bottom of the stair, she slipped through another panel into a disused map room.

It was empty. Perfect. She crept out from behind the shelf of scrolls and walked quietly toward the propped-open door at the entrance. She peered through.

Doctor Whitestalk, sitting at a desk near a window, glanced at her without interest. The scholar had a sparrow laid out before her and she cut it open to expose its innards. Cazia watched her pick something out of the body—a tiny organ, obviously—with her thumb and index fingers. Those were the only fingers she had left. She'd gone hollow years ago when she was barely older than Cazia herself, but without her fingers, she could no longer cast spells. All she could do was consult with other scholars, when she felt moved to talk.

According to rumor, she'd been a medical scholar before she'd become a wizard and she had used her healing magic to create terrible *things*. No one would specify what those things had looked like, but Cazia's imagination ran wild.

A young woman in a pale robe approached Doctor Whitestalk, her posture deferential. Although Doctor Twofin had never explained why, scholars who had gone hollow had a special insight into spells and spellcasting, which they shared with the tower on rare occasions. It was enough to keep them off the gallows, whatever their crimes.

Instead of responding to the young woman's question, Doctor Whitestalk lifted the bird's organ to her mouth and touched it to her tongue. Her expression was flat, devoid of any human emotion. Her cheeks were streaked with tears.

I won't have you going hollow under my tutelage. Think of the consequences!

Shuddering, Cazia stepped through the doorway, only to have someone seize hold of her ear. It was Doctor Winterhill.

"What have I told you," he said in his dull, blubbery voice, "about creeping about in my map room? I won't have you smudging my work, you little sneak!"

"The prince gave me permission," Cazia said, trying to act as though having her ear nearly pulled off the side of her head wasn't painful at all.

"Bad enough you are permitted in the tower at all," Winterhill insisted. "No Freewell in all of Kal-Maddum has permission to study the imperial maps. Now get out before I have Twofin ban you."

He shoved her toward the yard. The other scholars sat glowering at her, so she lowered her head and hurried after Pagesh and the others. Even inside the Scholars' Tower she had Enemies. For now.

Bittler had already left the girls and headed toward the gym. Cazia watched as he hunched his shoulders and took a circuitous route to avoid a cluster of palace guards.

For all the good it did him. One of the guards threw a pebble at him. They all laughed as Bitt winced and clutched at his upper arm.

They weren't supposed to be doing that anymore but there was little anyone could do to stop them. If Bitt complained about the guard—or if Cazia complained about Doctor Winterhill—they would simply lie about what happened, and their superiors would never take the word of a traitor's child over one of their own. They had all learned that lesson while they were young. As the prince, Lar should have had the authority to put a stop to it, but somehow he didn't. No one seemed to take him seriously; Cazia still wasn't sure why.

Things would be awful for a month afterwards—they would find wet linen in their beds, scorching amounts of salt in their food, and grubs in their rooms. It wasn't worth striking back.

The truth was, the Palace of Song and Morning was very large, but the only safe spaces within it for her were inside the circle of her friends with Lar, or in the practice room with Doctor Twofin. Even her tiny chambers were Enemy territory.

In her room, the fire had been lit and a bowl of bread and salt cheese set beside her bed. The maid—never "her" maid, not considering how often the girl searched through her things for Song knows what—had laid out Cazia's new green dress with beautiful white swirls at the sleeves and hem. While Cazia washed and changed, the maid returned and laid out a white scarf and a string of tiny blue gems to tie back her hair.

Since trade had opened up through East Ford again, blue had become the current thing, but Cazia thought it would be too showy for a *hostage*, even though the stones had been a gift from the prince himself. So it was green and white for her, with a white hat made of stiffened linen to protect her face from the rain. The gems she wore hidden underneath. It didn't matter to her that no one else would see them. In fact, it made her enjoy them more.

It was still early when she hurried to Pagesh's room. As expected, Pagesh and Jagia were frantic to be ready for the start of the Festival. Jagia was all in red and gold—a beautiful combination that made Cazia want to change immediately. Pagesh emerged from her bedchamber in a red-on-white dress embroidered with rose petals that was so unlike her usual mud-stained robes that Cazia actually gasped.

"You both look beautiful," Cazia said.

Pagesh made a face. "Girl clothes. They always bring out the marriage proposals."

At nineteen, Pagesh had been fending off suitors for years. She was Tyr Simblin's only acknowledged child, and King Ellifer wanted Simblin's heir to marry someone loyal to the empire. Pagesh herself wanted to spend her days in the garden—she had little interest in anything else—but the queen had made it clear that she would soon be returning to the Simblin holdfast, and that she would be bringing a husband along.

Cazia honestly felt sorry for her. Only a year before, Cazia had asked the queen for permission to stay at the palace when Colchua returned to the family holdings. She planned to devote her life to studying in the Scholars' Tower, and the Enemies who worked there would have no choice but to accept her. She would *make* them.

It had been a risky thing to say, she learned later. Queens were trained as scholars—in limited ways, but still—and Cazia's lineage put her in line for the throne behind Lar, Jagia, her own brother, and Ellifer's brother and sister.

However, Queen Amlian had understood she wasn't interested in sitting on a throne. She was learning to read, to set things on fire, and to hit targets with her darts. At the end of this Festival, there would be a new Gift to play with; whatever it was, Cazia wanted to be part of it. If the Italgas could give her that, they would have her utmost loyalty even before Lar was crowned.

Pagesh said goodbye to her maid with a kiss and they hurried into the hall. Bittler, Timush, and Colchua were already waiting for them. All three looked handsome in the king's gray and red. Even Bittler, almost.

Col made a fuss over their dresses in his half-mocking way, although of course he was gentlest with little Jagia. To Pagesh, Timush said quietly, "You look wonderful, but I think I prefer you in those muddy field clothes." She did not smile nor did she look at him. She only stared silently at the floor. For his part, Timu accepted her silence as a kind of distance between them that he did not know how to cross.

On their way to the courtyard, one of the servants contrived to tip over a bucket of dirty water as they passed, but Cazia had been watching for it and hopped out of the way.

"Oh, *excuse* me, miss!" the girl said, unable to disguise the sneer at the corner of her mouth. "And you in such lovely clothes."

Cazia and Pagesh both glared at her with enough hatred to kindle a flame, and the girl retreated down the hall.

Enemies everywhere.

As they rounded the next corner, Col started joking about the Evening People and Lar's song. Like everyone around them, they'd talked all their lives about putting on a show or doing some sort of crazy mime at their first Festival, but nothing had ever come of it.

Except with Lar. The only one who knew anything about this song of his was Col, and he wouldn't say a word.

Their bootheels scuffed the pink stone as they hurried through the empty halls.

CHAPTER THREE

Lar's valet had laid out three suits for the prince to choose from. While Tejohn stood against the wall and waited, they discussed each at length. Eventually, the prince combined two, choosing a bright red linen coat with a green-and-yellow-checked shirt. Tejohn wouldn't have dressed a clown in those colors, but the prince could do as he liked. He always seemed comfortable with his choices, even when he made them sober. The queen wouldn't like it, but she had asked him to make sure the prince arrived sober, not fashionable.

Eventually, they made their way into the main courtyard. Controlled chaos was a kindly way of describing the work being done there, and the king and queen were in the thick of it.

"My prince! There you are!" Kolbi Arriya raced up the stairs and clutched at the prince's sleeve. She was the king's shield bearer, which had once been an honorable position for a talented and well-born young warrior, but in these luxurious imperial times had become a counselor and royal secretary.

She scowled at the prince's clothes, then at Tejohn. Kolbi herself wore the Italga gray and red, although her clothes were rumpled and soaked through with rain, sweat, or a combination of both. She would not be joining the royal family at the dais looking like that. "You know where to go, my prince? Be sure to let Sincl know if you want to sing first, last, or somewhere in between. He will accommodate you." She rushed breathlessly toward the food tables without waiting for a response.

Lar laughed, then stopped at the top of the stairs and looked out over the throngs of people. The king covered his face with his hand and turned away in irritation at something one of the chief servants was telling him; the queen stepped in smoothly to resolve the problem. Lar seemed to find the whole thing amusing. "Twenty-three years between Festivals. Do you think my bride will do as well?"

Lar was betrothed to the daughter of the head chieftain of the Indregai Alliance. The girl lived inside the Morning City and was as much a hostage as the Freewell children. When she came of age, they would marry, forging a peace with the people of Indrega and allowing some troops stationed in East Ford to be relocated to the turbulent west.

Tejohn could not help but notice that the prince had asked if his bride would organize the Festival as well as his parents, as though he himself couldn't be bothered. "I have not met her, my prince."

"She's a terror. Only twelve years old and already thinks she's sitting on the throne."

Tejohn nodded politely. Typically, no foreigners would be allowed inside the walls of Peradain at all. She and her retainers would be locked up for the next ten days in her big, comfortable house with a watchful guard all around. She would not get within five hundred feet of the Evening People until her marriage was consummated and she'd proven herself loyal to the empire. If that was even possible.

Tejohn gestured toward the royal dais. "Perhaps we should take our place."

"Not up there," Lar said, then began moving through the crowd toward the yard below. "I want to wait in the pen with the other singers."

"My prince—"

"Not now, my tyr!" Lar was unexpectedly fervent. Almost fierce. "This . . . production my parents are putting on may please the Evening People and it may please the merchants and generals and scholars and . . . and everyone. But I am here as a singer. I will sing my song—which is not a bawd, I assure you—and then I will find a jar of wine and do as little as possible for ten days."

Tejohn studied Lar's expression. For this, he finally shows some spine? "My prince—"

"After my song, I will no longer need a chaperone and you can go where you please, but right now, you will come with me to the singers' pens. I'll wait there, just as you once did."

They crossed the courtyard and entered the winter garden at the north end of the yard. Singers and musicians, most of them looking ill-rested and underfed, lounged on benches or sat beside the evergreen shrubs. It was obvious none recognized the prince, because none thought to jump up and offer him their seat. Lar didn't seem to notice; he moved to the wall overlooking the courtyard and dais.

Sincl found them by the rail and solicitously arranged for the prince to sing the last song of the day, at his request. One of the musicians began to nervously pluck at his lap harp, and Sincl rushed toward him to give the man a sharp kick. Tejohn was glad to see his back; the performance master was a jittery, sweating, nervous wreck.

Down in the courtyard, the tents had been erected long ago, and most of the commotion now centered around the food tables. Servants arranged identical delicacies on each of the six tables: sourcakes, onion soups, pickled compote, leaf rolls, wet rice, and more. The Evening People did not eat animal flesh, so for the rest of the Festival, there wouldn't be a roasted chicken breast, boiled snake, or stuffed lamb's heart to be had for any amount of gold anywhere in the Morning City.

Palace guards came through the garden, searching the singers for weapons. Their commander was named Kellin and he was an old friend of Tejohn's. They were of an age, often playing cards or sparring in the gym. He seemed on the verge of asking a question, if only he could think of a way to say it.

Tejohn knew what the question would be and he didn't think he could bear to hear it. "I'm here as the prince's guard," he said abruptly. "I have no song to sing."

Kellin nodded, looking a bit disappointed. Never a man for frivolous words—or serious ones—he clapped Tejohn's shoulder, bowed to the prince, and moved on. When his men had finished, they moved on to the actors in the next garden.

"Col!" Lar called happily. The prince's friends swarm around them. The Freewell girl was there, and so was her older brother; Bittler had indeed brought him, but he hadn't convinced them to wash. Still, someone who didn't know them would have though them respectable.

Lar and the Freewell boy embraced as though they hadn't seen each other in months. Tejohn hated to admit it, but Colchua Freewell did look more like a prince than Lar Italga: his face was broad and handsome, his smile bold. "We couldn't let you make a fool of yourself without us to jeer from the crowd!" Colchua said.

"Thanks, Col," The prince answered. "I can always rely on you."

"Nervous?" The Bendertuk boy asked, grinning.

Lar nodded *yes* while he said, "Absolutely not. Why should I be?"

They laughed and talked about inconsequential things as a shadow passed slowly over them. A flying cart circled above the palace. It settled down on top of the Scholars' Tower and, judging by a flurry of movement Tejohn could barely see, discharged a few men before floating away again.

The Freewell girl broke away from the group and stood beside Tejohn at the garden rail. The dais where the king and queen would stand was below them in the courtyard. It wasn't proper for singers, actors, mimes, and clowns to stand on higher ground than the royal family, but the portal would open down there, in the usual place, so the rightful order had to be upended. Merchant families, palace servants, notable scholars, and honored guests lounged on balconies, or leaned out windows, or sat on the edges of roofs or promenades.

But there were no tyrs in attendance. Not the loyal ones, not the treacherous ones, none of them.

"Those men down there are palace guards, aren't they?"

The Freewell girl pointed to a line of men standing fifteen feet behind the thrones. Each held a tall pole with a different colored streamer attached. "Those are athletes," Tejohn answered, trying to keep the irritation out of his voice. There weren't supposed to be any guards or soldiers in the yard when the portal opened, but of course, Kellin also had a duty to protect the king and queen. "They'll be competing in the games."

"I recognize them." If that was true, she had sharp vision, and that made him even more suspicious. It wasn't rational, but few important things were. "They aren't carrying weapons, though, are they?"

"The Evening People can sense weapons, so no, the athletes are unarmed."

"Then why . . . Oh! They're each holding a pole and streamer, and I'll bet there's a sharp metal point at the bottom, right? A spear point?"

Tejohn wondered if she was trying to goading him somehow. "The metal tip allows the pole to be set into the ground. They are not weapons."

"Right," she answered. "And those skull-crackers you're wearing on your wrists are just jewelry."

There was a sudden flash of light, and a sound like far-off lightning. Tejohn jolted upright, startled. The portal was opening, and soon the Evening People would appear.

The servants who were not supposed to be in the courtyard rushed into the palace. Everyone else hurried to take up their positions, even the king and queen. The scholars, "athletes," and servants accompanying the royal family—and even the scholars were considered royal bodyguards, although Tejohn was careful not to show his opinion on *that*—assumed postures appropriate for welcoming respected guests. In the garden, the singers, actors, and other wastrels pressed against the rail, crowding around the prince and his entourage for a proper view.

The flash of light returned, and the disc appeared. It hovered in the air on its edge like one of Twofin's hoops, and the surface was like a pool of water with bright sunlight reflecting from it. At first, it looked larger than Tejohn remembered, almost as wide as two men lying heel to crown, but no, it was the same.

The Freewell girl shifted position, and he realized she was in a perfect position to fire an iron dart at one of the Evening People as they came through. Tejohn tensed, ready to slam his metal bracer onto her collarbone if she drew something from her sleeve or began to cast a spell, but her hands never left the railing.

He looked back down at the dais. Nothing happened. Tejohn realized he was holding his breath, and exhaled. Had it taken so long for Co, the leader of the Evening People, to step through the last time? He wondered if he misremembered the events of that day, now a generation gone.

Then there was a terrible sound, like an animal roar mixed with a man's scream. Before it faded, monsters charged through the portal onto the dais.

Chapter Four

Without any warning, a creature burst through the portal, bounding onto the stone dais and sniffing the air. It was as large as a mountain bear, but its frame was almost human. Its long arms and legs both ended in monstrous hands, and it was covered with pale purple fur.

It roared at them, displaying the fangs of a grass lion.

Cazia glanced up at Treygar, absurdly hopeful that she would see him smiling as though this was the most normal thing in the world, or maybe a prank they played on the young folk every Festival, but he was gaping in stunned surprise like everyone else.

Someone screamed. The beast glanced around the dais, roared again, and launched itself onto a scholar. The man fell back as the creature sank its fangs into his arm, then tore it from his shoulder.

Panic erupted in the courtyard. Bear men began pouring through the portal like water from a leaking bucket. Guards in civilian clothes charged forward in a line, swinging their bracers at the creatures' heads.

But the monsters knocked them flat like they were rag dolls. Men and women screamed as the creatures bit into them. More beasts bounded over the line, landing directly in plumes of fire erupting from the scholars' hands.

The creatures fell back from the wall of flames, letting the scholars advance. Could the scholars push them back through the portal? *If only I could be down there with them, defending the king and queen.*

Then one of the beasts lifted a guard over its head and threw him into the jets of fire. He struck two scholars, knocking them completely off the dais. Beasts charged through the gap and swarmed the scholars from all sides, tearing them apart with their teeth and claws. Goose bumps ran up and down Cazia's whole body and she suddenly felt lightheaded.

Servants, merchants, performers, all of them mobbed the gates or jammed the entrances to the palace in panicked mobs. Screams came from everywhere.

The king stood between the queen and the creatures, swinging his heavy chair in a powerful downward stroke. At the same moment, a jet of bright fire shot from the queen's hands, so focused that it cut one of the creatures in half. The long spears of the so-called athletes in the yard suddenly thrust through the confusion, stabbing into the monsters surrounding the king and queen. A scholar, wounded but still alive, created a huge stone block—bigger than any Cazia had ever seen—between the royal couple and the beasts.

It didn't matter. One of the bear men, though punctured with three long spears, knocked the king aside with a swipe of its claw. He fell into the surging mass of creatures. The queen stepped backward, fell off the dais and landed on her neck.

"MOTHER!" Lar screamed. Cazia saw the shock and anguish on his face. For a moment, the pain was so clear in his expression that he looked as if he had been murdered, too.

Treygar grabbed hold of him to stop him running out of the garden into the melee.

Cazia realized she had been frozen in place, watching the chaos and brutality as though it was just a mime. The king had vanished. The queen lay still in the dirt. The creatures bounded from the dais into the yard with the speed and grace of grass lions, running down those too slow to have escaped. Cazia had to do something. Anything. She was in danger. *Her friends were in danger.*

"My prince," Treygar shouted, "we must retreat!"

"I can help!" Lar shouted back.

"*We* can help!" Colchua said.

"NO!" Cazia shocked herself by the force behind her response.

"My prince, we are overrun! *You must withdraw!*"

Timush and Pagesh grabbed Lar's arms as though they were about to drag him away. Cazia heard scuffling on the stone below the railing and began the motions for a flame spell of her own. Out of habit, her hand motions helped bring out the correct clarity of thought, the colors, the swell of emotion the spell required.

One of the beasts reached the top of the railing, pulling itself up and roaring. Cazia finished just in time, feeling the flame rush from the space between her hands into the creature's open mouth.

Treygar spun, moving much faster than she would have thought possible for such an old man, and slammed his bracer down on the creature's head.

The beast's gray blood splattered over them both. *These creatures are full of magic. I can feel it.* For one absurd moment, Cazia was overwhelmed with dismay over her ruined dress, then she glanced over the rail. The creature was still plummeting to the paving stone below, but two more were climbing up.

She turned back to the others but didn't have to say anything. Her brother seemed to read her mind. He and Timush grabbed the ends of a stone bench and lifted.

Treygar grabbed the prince's arm again. "No!" Lar said. "I can't abandon everyone!" Colchua and Timush dropped the bench over the railing. Painful yelps and heavy crashes followed soon after.

"Lar!" Cazia shouted at him. "Stoneface is right! Do what he says or you're going to get us all killed!"

Treygar pointed at Pagesh. "You're in charge of the little girl! Let's move!"

Pagesh scooped up Jagia, who immediately burst out crying. The courtyard was filled with screams, prayers, and monstrous roaring. Treygar began to run eastward through the garden, heading toward the promenade and the graveyard menagerie. Did he plan to go into the palace and escape through the Sunrise Gate?

"Stop!" Cazia called. "We can't go that way; they're already inside the palace. We have to go there." She pointed toward the Scholars' Tower, pulling Lar and the others after her.

Treygar didn't argue. He pushed forward, letting the young people run ahead. Col and Timush led the way, sprinting toward the tower door. Lar ran just behind them, with Treygar close on his heels. Pagesh was a strong runner, but not when she had a hysterical child to carry. Treygar glanced back at her, clearly worried, but he didn't pause to help. Cazia ran last, regretting her decision to wear this big, beautiful dress and ignoring her hat when it blew off her head.

I am running for my life inside the Palace of Song and Morning.

This was happening. It was happening right now. Cazia almost stopped to look around; she'd just seen the king and queen murdered, and she might be next. This was a moment for histories, songs, and plays, and she was actually living it. She felt strangely detached and incredulous.

The servant girl who had tried to dump dirty water onto her feet—an Enemy—ran by them, her eyes wild with terror.

"Don't you shut that door!" Col shouted. A weedy-looking scholar was pushing the heavy door to the Scholars' Tower closed. His eyes bulged in terror, and for a moment it seemed he wouldn't obey. Treygar shouted at him, and he hesitated long enough for Colchua to throw his shoulder into it and fling the door wide.

"To the top!" Treygar yelled. Good. He'd already figured out why Cazia had chosen the tower. A pair of frightened old scholars demanded someone Explain Everything Immediately, but Timush shoved them aside. They all ran for the stairs.

"Bar that door!" Cazia yelled back at them. Doctor Whitestalk's desk was empty. "Shutter the windows!"

"Wait!" Pagesh shoved Jagia into Cazia's arms. Her eyes were wild and a little sad. "I'm going to find Zilly." She sprinted out of the tower, shouting, "Bar the door behind me!"

One of the old men slammed the door and threw the bolt. Lar, Col, and the other boys had already vanished up the stairs. No one but her and Jagia had seen Pagesh go. Zilly? It took a moment for Cazia to remember that was the name of her maid.

Jagia's face was uncomfortably close to her own: the girl had stopped crying, but she looked pale and stunned.

Cazia set her down. "Can you run?" She nodded. "Go! I'll be right behind you."

"My prince!" a voice farther up the stairs shouted. "What can we do to help?"

The girls caught up with the others in the administration chamber, and Cazia was the last to push inside. The speaker was Doctor Warpoole, the Scholar Administrator for the entire empire. She was more of a functionary than a spellcaster, but she had been formidable in her younger years. Cazia didn't much like the woman but she hoped to be her someday, or at least serve the empire in her place.

Two other young women sat at desks beside her, styluses in hand. They looked utterly stunned. Cazia knew their names—Ciriam Eelhook, Barla Shook—but she had never spoken to them. They were Enemies, and right now, they were terrified.

Lar looked at Cazia blankly. Great Way, he'd just seen his parents die.

"The Evening People did not come through the portal," Treygar said. "We've been invaded by some kind of monster. The king and queen were lost within moments. The palace is overrun and the prince must be flown out of the city at once!"

Doctor Warpoole spun on her heel and yanked on a braided cord beside her desk. "That will summon the cart. What else can I do?"

"Can you shut the portal?" Cazia blurted out.

"Alas, child, I don't think I can."

Cazia yanked a quiver of iron darts off the wall and tossed it to the prince. He caught it and, as if shocked out of a trance, slung it over his shoulder. Cazia took down a second quiver, then a third.

"Those are relics," Barla said, "Tyr Cimfulin Italga used them in the Clearing of Shadow Hall."

Cazia had heard that story, hadn't she? Something about a scholar soldier and a swarm of giant spiders. "Lar and I are his descendants," she said. It occurred to her that she had campaigned for one of these clerk positions last fall, but Shook had been chosen instead. "Let's say we inherited them." She slung the quivers over her shoulder.

Treygar started pushing Lar toward the stairs. "Uncover your mirror, doctor. Tell the commanders stationed outside the city to arm themselves. Then—"

There was a loud boom from the bottom of the tower. The creatures were trying to batter their way in.

"Go!' the administrator yelled. "Barla, send an alert to Beddalin Hole and have them spread the word. Ciriam, you're with me."

Treygar had already herded the prince up the stairs, with Colchua shoving Timush and Bittler after. Cazia had been left in charge of the little girl again.

Barla and Ciriam exchanged looks. One had been ordered to flee with the prince and one had been ordered to stay behind, but the shocked expressions on their faces were identical.

Cazia pushed Jagia up the stairs; Ciriam and Doctor Warpoole followed. Cazia heard the cloth being yanked off the mirror behind her, but she did not look back. She did not want to see Doctor Shook's expression again.

Cazia and Jagia ran upward, passing one empty floor after another, not daring to pause long enough to do more than glance through the narrow tower windows at the chaos below. The rest of the tower seemed empty; everyone had gone down for the Festival.

There was a sound of shattering wood from below, followed by roars of flame and screams. Ciriam shrieked, "Hurry! Hurry!"

The muscles in Cazia's legs burned, but the thunder of heavy footsteps below urged her onward. Jagia started to flag as they came near the practice room; Cazia was tempted to scoop the girl up, but she knew that would be slower still.

There was another scream from below, a woman's this time, and much nearer. Doctor Warpoole, who was bringing up the rear, barked, "Don't look back!" and Cazia knew she wasn't talking to her.

The last few flights of stairs were made of wood and the noise of their stamping was oppressive and alarming. They might as well have goaded the bear-things to chase them. "Almost there," Cazia said to Jagia. "Keep going." For some reason, offering encouragement to the little girl made her feel stronger. It gave her hope.

She heard Treygar shout from the effort of throwing open the heavy trap door. It slammed against the roof with a boom that echoed through the entire tower. The grunts and roars and heavy treads on the stairs below grew louder and louder. Treygar ran out of the top of the stairs into the gray daylight, and the Prince stumbled out behind him, wheezing and clutching his sides. Col, Timush, Bittler, then Jagia and Cazia and the two scholars all spilled onto the slab roof. Bitt fell to his knees, wheezing and pale. Cazia and Col raced around to the far end of the trap door and lifted it.

"Not yet!" Doctor Warpoole yelled. She started a spell Cazia had never seen before: her gestures were elaborate and unusually constrained. What was she doing? Then she pushed her palms outward as she exhaled, and a plume of green mist billowed down through the trap.

The wooden stairs dissolved like snow thrown into a boiling pot. One of the beasts leaped upward into the daylight, fanged jaws gaping. The moment it entered the mist, the fur and flesh of its face boiled off its skull. Its bloody bones fell into the gap made by the missing stairs and it disappeared down into the tower.

Doctor Warpoole nodded at Cazia and Col, but her brother was the only one to shoulder the heavy door into place. Cazia could only stare in shock.

That was not one of the Thirteen Gifts. Doctor Warpoole, the scholar administrator for the entire Peradaini empire, had just cast a wizard's spell.

The trap slammed into place and Timush threw the bolt home. Then he grabbed Cazia's elbow. His black hair was matted with sweat. "Where's Pagesh?"

There was a floating cart fifteen feet from the edge of the tower. It wasn't large—a six-person design, at best, but the single black disk above it was huge. It would be fast, and it would fly high.

However, the driver looked at them with blank, terrified eyes. Tyr Treygar shouted orders for the man to pull into the dock to let them aboard, but he didn't respond. The driver seemed to be frozen in shock.

Timush's huge, dark eyes were just as wild and sad as Pagesh's had been before she ran out of the tower. "Out there. She—"

"WHAT?" He yanked her arm painfully, spinning her around. "You left her behind? How could you leave her behind!" His face was right beside hers as he screamed, and she could see the patch of pimples on his forehead.

"Pagesh abandoned us!" Jagia shouted. "She left us all alone!"

She left to save Zilly, Cazia almost said. *She chose to risk everything to save her rather than flee to safety with you.* But she couldn't say that to Timu. Everything was already too awful. Cazia yanked her arm out of his grip. "Jagia loved Pagesh as much as you did. Maybe you two should look after each other."

"Oh, this will not do," Doctor Warpoole said. She stepped up to Cazia and lifted both quivers over her head as though taking a sharp knife from a child. She gave one to Ciriam and, as she slung the other over her shoulder, drew out a long, nasty-looking spike.

The driver may have been terrified out of his wits, but he knew better than to defy a scholar with a quiver full of darts. He angled the cart so that it floated toward the tower deck.

Cazia ran around the perimeter of the tower, looking down the sides. Three beasts were climbing the pink stone wall. "Clerk!"

After receiving a nod from Doctor Warpoole, Ciriam ran to Cazia's spot on the western end of the tower. "Ciriam, right?" Cazia asked, immediately remembering that she should call her *Doctor Eelhook.* Too late now. "That one is highest. Start with it."

The clerk looked dumbfounded. Cazia slapped the outside of the quiver the scholar had just taken from her, and the woman jolted into action. She drew a dart and, leaning queasily over the crenellation, shot it down the side of the tower.

It went wide, skipping off the pale pink stone. Ciriam drew another, did the spell again—more shakily this time—and shot a spike over the beast's shoulder.

Cazia plucked a dart from the quiver at the girl's hip and shot it down the side of the wall, letting her frustration and anger lurk behind the carefully built mental state required for the spell. It struck the beast's shoulder, sinking into its torso so deeply that it vanished.

The creature roared, and for a moment, she thought it wouldn't fall. When it did, Cazia turned to the clerk and held out her hand.

Ciriam was about Pagesh's age and height, but where Pagesh was tanned and strong from endless days spent outside in fields, the clerk was pale and squint-eyed, with weak, bony hands. She didn't even know how to aim a dart spell properly.

But she wasn't about to give up that quiver.

"Let's go!" Treygar called. He ushered the prince onto the cart first, of course, then let Bittler, Timush, Jagia, and Col climb on. Doctor Warpoole waved at Ciriam and Cazia, and they sprinted toward the cart.

Cazia took the opportunity to pluck three more darts from Ciriam's quiver.

As they climbed into the cart, the driver screwed up his concentration and forced it upward. They swung up and out, all of them packed in elbow to knee. Timush crouched in the front corner with Jagia in his lap, both gripping the rails with white knuckles. Bittler and Col were jammed into the back, almost falling onto the driver. The doctor shrugged, squeezing Cazia into the corner; apparently, she didn't like to be crowded. Old Stoneface gave Doctor Warpoole a dark look as she settled in; clearly, he would have preferred to have someone else in her place.

The wheels of the cart passed over the crenellation just as the first of the beasts reached the top of the tower. Doctor Warpoole drew a dart from her quiver and began her spell, her hands moving faster than any spellcaster Cazia had ever seen. Ciriam followed her example, but Cazia was behind them and couldn't help.

The beast bounded to the edge of the tower, then leaped at them. Doctor Warpoole's spike struck the beast on the crown of its head, gouging its scalp but otherwise bouncing off. The clerk didn't lead the beast enough and her shot passed uselessly behind it.

The monster seemed almost is if it could fly, clawed hands reaching out, fanged jaws gaping. Cazia thought the whole world fell silent, although she knew the beast must have been roaring, and the people around her must have been screaming. She had no time to cast a spell of her own and no space to make the gestures.

The beast—with its bristling fur, impossible size, and nearly human face—was going to make it into the cart with them.

Stoneface shoved the prince aside and swept his arm backhanded at the beast's outstretched claws. He managed to batter its hands aside, preventing the monster from getting a grip on the rail, but it caught hold of his forearm instead.

The beast slammed against the side of the cart with a crash so loud, Cazia was sure the planks would shatter, then the whole thing tipped to the side.

There were screams and cries of anguish all around her—Cazia might have screamed herself, she wasn't sure. Everyone fell toward the lowered rail of the wagon, and it was only Timush's quick hands that kept Jagia in the cart.

Doctor Warpoole knelt low, keeping her center of balance below the rail. She held Ciriam down with her, but Cazia's weight nearly sent them both over the edge.

Treygar fell flat on his stomach on the edge of the railing, clearly being dragged down by the tremendous weight of the beast. The only one still standing was the driver, and that was because he had been tied into place. His face was twisted in concentration as he tried to right the cart and gain altitude.

Cazia couldn't see the beast below the level of the cart, but she heard it roar. She pulled her dart from her sleeve. She didn't think she had time to cast a full spell before the creature climbed over the rail, but she knew what to do with the sharp end of a spike.

Lar and Col reached for Stoneface to drag him back into the cart, but the old man lunged upward to throw himself over the rail.

CHAPTER FIVE

THE WEIGHT OF THE CREATURE ASTONISHED HIM. IT SLAMMED AGAINST the side to the cart with a sound Tejohn was sure signaled the death of them all, but the wood held.

Tejohn's shoulder, however, did not. Great Way, the whole city must have heard it pop. The creature's momentum dragged him down until the rail gouged deep into his dislocated armpit and the whole cart dipped like a rowboat about to capsize.

The driver must have anticipated that, because the cart didn't turn over. Tejohn felt the others fall heavily onto his back, pinning him to the rail for a moment, until the cart rocked back the other way and they fell away from him. The pain was intense. Manageable, but intense.

The beast had hold of his bracer with its right hand, then reached for a higher grip with its left, hooking its claws into his flesh below the elbow. It was climbing his arm toward the prince, its jaws gaping.

Tejohn didn't think, didn't pretend he had time to strategize, didn't waste his time on regret or resentment. He did his duty. He straightened his legs, sliding his torso over the rail. It wouldn't take much. They were already overbalanced and the monster's terrible weight would easily pull him over the edge. Fire and Fury, but his arm felt like it might tear right off. At least hitting the paving stones would be a quick death.

Tejohn would never see his children again.

There was a dizzying moment when he felt the full weight of both bodies drag him over the edge. His injured arm jerked, nearly shaking the beast free, but that didn't matter, because it was already too late, he was going over—

Hands clasped onto him, pinning him to the wooden rail. Lar planted his feet against the rim of the cart, taking hold of Tejohn's other hand. The Freewell boy slid down onto his legs.

"No!" Tejohn cried out. "No, don't—"

But other hands were grabbing him, and someone—probably the Freewell girl—cried out "Col!" as though the boy was about to fall, too. The side of the cart dipped again; the driver cried out from the strain of keeping it upright.

The Freewell boy leaned over the rail with one of the scholar's spikes in his hand. The creature pulled itself up again, its gaping fangs about to bite off Tejohn's fingers, but the boy stabbed the point of the dart into the bottom joint of the monster's thumb.

It lost its grip. With its other hand, it caught hold of a spoke as it fell. The wheel spun and the wood snapped. The creature plummeted away from the cart with an agonized roar.

The driver finally managed to tilt the cart back to fully horizontal, and they all flopped onto the floor and benches, one atop the other. Tejohn tried to keep his feet, but the prince still had hold of his good hand and they went down together. "Is everyone still here?" Lar shouted. "Did anyone fall out?"

"Pagesh isn't here," Timush said sulkily. Jagia threw her arms around Timush's neck.

Tejohn gritted his teeth, determined not to cry out as the others bumped and jostled him. His forearm may have been bloody but it was his dislocated shoulder that was truly painful. What had seemed manageable in the face of imminent death now seemed to triple in power. He rolled away from the others, laying his face against rough wood. At least his shoulder was off the floor, and no one would bump him as they tried to crawl out from under him.

"Doctor!" Lar called. "Look to Tyr Treygar."

Doctor Warpoole urged Ciriam out of the way, then she knelt beside Tejohn. She had the same flat, chilly expression she always wore. "I'm not much of a healer. The First Gift is the most complex, and unless your injuries are life-threatening, it would be safer to find a true medical scholar or a sleepstone."

"You don't need magic to yank my shoulder into the socket," Tejohn said.

Doctor Warpoole looked nonplussed, but Lar came up behind Tejohn and took hold of his shoulders. "Col, take his wrist." Lar's voice was very close behind Tejohn's ear, and it made him uncomfortable. "Don't fret, my tyr. I may not have learned healing magic, but I've certainly done this before."

The Freewell boy took hold of Tejohn's bracer. The old soldier nearly snapped at him to let go, but the prince was so close and the tyr was nearly helpless with pain. "Don't worry, my tyr," Freewell said. "This will feel like a kiss from a beautiful girl." He pulled.

Tejohn's shoulder slid back into the socket; a wild rush of pain ran through him, then subsided. Tejohn cried out but he managed not to curse or swear, so it wasn't too embarrassing. His shoulder joint felt as though it no longer fit together, but that was to be expected. With his good hand, he grabbed the Freewell boy's wrist. "Thank you."

"You're welcome. Now let's get Lar away from here."

"Yes," Tejohn grabbed the rail and pulled himself into a sitting position. "Driver, set a course to the northeast. We need to reach Fort Samsit before dark."

"No," the Freewell girl said flatly. She looked at Tejohn strangely, as though he'd just sprouted horns. "We have to rescue the princess."

Song only knew what the girl was talking about; Lar didn't have a sister. What princess?

"Fire and Fury," Lar said. "She's right."

"She's a hostage," the girl continued, "and she's the only thing keeping the Alliance from crossing the Straim in force."

The Straim. She was talking about the prince's betrothed, the little In-dregai girl. *She's a terror.*

If the Indregai Alliance marched on the empire in force, the first place they would strike would be East Ford, where Tejohn had sent his wife and children. The thought of Teberr, his youngest, being devoured by one of the Indregai serpents made his skin crawl.

But the next words he said were, "We can't risk it. We have to get the prince to safety."

Lar leaned over the edge of the cart, looking down at the city streets. Tejohn did the same. Everything was blurry to him, but he could see moving colors that had to be fleeing commoners and the bounding, purple-furred monsters chasing them from building to building. The beasts crashed through windows and doors, falling onto young and old alike. The city was full of terrified screams.

"Lar," the Freewell girl said, "Not even Peradaini spears can fight enemies on the inside and outside at once.

"Caz is right," Lar said. "Driver, change course toward Eastgate. She's in a high-peaked house on the eastern square with two chimneys in front."

Tejohn suddenly felt terribly weary. The cart was already overfull, and they had to get free of Peradain now or lose the chance forever. "My prince, you must withdraw. The princess has her own people; let them be responsible for her."

"She is betrothed to me," Lar said as the driver angled the cart eastward. "I am one of her people, and she is one of mine."

Back toward the palace, Tejohn could see several dark smudges against the sky that looked like columns of smoke. There were no scholars to suppress the fires; they had more pressing things to do.

The cart flew low and close enough to the city wall that Tejohn could just make out the soldiers stationed along the top. None carried spears or bows—had the clerk in the Scholars' Tower failed to get her message out? The beasts hadn't made it this far yet, but the streets were in a tumult. Citizens milled about, some fleeing with sacks full of possessions, others loading oxcarts with clothes and other minor treasures, others pleading for news. A crowd of thirty men and women marched toward the palace with hammers, billhooks, hatchets, and other makeshift weapons. They didn't know what was happening, but they were going to confront the threat.

Of course, the gates had been closed for the Festival. Only foot traffic was allowed through the Little Gate, and that, too, would soon be shut.

Tejohn's throat became tight. What were they doing? He wanted to shout at them to drop everything, grab their children, and *run*.

He shut his eyes and fought back a rising wave of rage and fury. Tejohn had not wanted to parade his wife and children in front of Co and the other Evening People as though his life was just another mime for them to enjoy, so he'd sent them east. But if he had not?

They would have been down in the courtyard with the rest when the portal opened. Fire and Fury, he would have lost another family, and this time, he would have seen it happen. It was simple luck that had saved their lives.

"There it is!" Lar shouted, pointing to a building on the other side of the cart.

Tejohn struggled to his feet. The pain of moving was intense and getting worse. He needed a sling.

"Are you sure this is correct?" Doctor Warpoole asked. "Everything looks so different from up here."

"I can't land on that," the driver said. Then he added, as a nervous afterthought, "My prince."

Tejohn craned his neck to look at the house. It had been constructed in the high mountain style of the southern Indregai people so the princess would feel at home, but the driver was correct. There was no flat place to set down, even if the clay tiles could support their weight. "We can't set down in the street," Tejohn said. "The people would mob us."

"No matter," Lar said. He gestured for the tether rope at the front of the cart, and the clerk uncoiled it for him automatically, as though he'd given her a command. "Just get us low enough."

The last Italga prince, dangling on a line high above the city? No. Absolutely no.

"I'll go first," the Freewell boy said.

"Then me," the Bendertuk put in.

Bittler Witt, crouching quietly in the corner, reluctantly began to stand but Lar waved him back. That boy couldn't climb down a rope, let alone climb up again. "I will go first," the prince said. "She's my betrothed. Col and Tim can come with me, but Bitt and the scholars will stay with the cart."

He dropped the rope over the side. Tejohn didn't like this at all. "My prince, you mustn't—"

"I hope you aren't offering to go in my place," Lar said with a glance at Tejohn's shoulder. The prince's tone was sharp.

"Of course not, my prince," Tejohn said, changing tactics quickly. "But we don't need to lower anyone down, just the rope. Let her grasp it and we will pull her up."

The Freewell girl leaned over the rail and shouted, "Get a ladder and send the princess up to the roof! Quickly!" The woman she was shouting at, a guard in a snow-white Alliance uniform, looked startled, then ran into the high-peaked building.

The prince nodded at Tejohn. "You make sense, my tyr. I'm just worried that they will send their entire entourage."

The white-clad woman ran back out of the house, this time with several other guards. They tilted their heads up to stare at the cart, but there was no ladder in sight.

"The roof!" the Freewell girl shouted. "Get the princess on the roof!"

Several others began to shout the same thing. The Indregai guards milled around and looked confused. People poked their heads out of the windows, looking up at the cart as it floated down toward the building. Tejohn recognized their body language and expressions: they looked like villagers gossiping about the local madmen.

One of the monsters charged into view, racing around the side of the building with the speed of a grass lion on the attack. Everyone in the cart cried out in fear and despair. In the street, there were new screams of terror.

They crowds surged toward the Little Gate as the Alliance guards threw themselves against the monster.

It was no good; the creature knocked them aside like empty cups, then ran among them, biting each of them, one after another.

A second monster charged out of another alley toward the Little Gate, and a third burst into the gate house.

"We're too late!" the driver said, his eyes wild with fear. "We're too late!" He started to raise the cart into the air.

Lar threw his leg over the rail. "Lower us to the roof! Now!"

The Freewell girl snatched four spikes out of Doctor Warpoole's quiver and handed one to Tejohn. "I don't think I have what it takes to bully him," she said.

Bullying? Clearly, the girl didn't understand what it meant to command. Tejohn took the dart in his good hand and held the point a few handwidths from the driver's belly. "What is your name?"

The calm in Tejohn's voice seemed to capture his attention. "Wimnel Farrabell, my tyr."

Both men watched the prince move below the cart and out of sight, his quiver full of darts jangling. The Freewell boy climbed on after him. Tejohn's guts were bound as tightly as a criminal bound for the gibbet but he kept his voice calm. "Farrabell, eh? The Farrabells were Sixth Festival, as I recall. Tyrs in the west?"

"It was the west then, my tyr, but it's all Waterlands now. My people were nobles, chieftains, and generals until the Battle of the Fish Pens. Stripped of our rank, my tyr, but always loyal."

Tejohn knew the story. "Loyal but not brave," Tejohn said. The Bendertuk boy went over the rail onto the rope. "With a good name to secure a safe, cushy job for you."

The driver took a deep, shaky breath. "I will do my duty, my tyr. I will."

"Then teach this girl how to operate these levers," Tejohn said, "I want someone to know how to fly the prince to safety if I have to ram this spike into your heart."

CHAPTER SIX

Cazia couldn't help it; the idea of learning to fly a cart thrilled her.

Then she saw Lar scrabble across the gray tiles and she flushed with shame. He slipped and fell to one knee but quickly regained his footing, heading toward the chimneys at the front of the building. His red coat looked almost comical, and she wished he'd chosen something that would not stand out like a rose in the grass. Col followed close behind; Timush must have been still climbing on the rope.

She couldn't look away from them. Yes, she'd just been promised a lesson in flying—*flying*—but the one person she loved most in the world, her own brother, had just rushed onto a battlefield—and he'd brought his two best friends. A strange feeling she couldn't identify filled her like wind blowing into a tent. She felt hollow and fragile, as though the next misfortune would make her pop like a bit of froth, destroying her completely.

This is the feeling that comes just before grief. You are about to see your brother murdered in front of you because he is trying to be a hero which is your fault because this was your idea. This is how you feel just before grief overwhelms you and makes you wish you could die with him.

The screams from below became more intense, distracting her. The creatures tore through the crowd, knocking people about like brooms. Each victim received a terrible bite wound, some instantly fatal but not all, as the monsters battered their way through the mob. Men, women, and children fell before them. One of the city guard pushed against the surging mob in an effort to shut the Little Gate, but there was no hope of that.

Lar scrambled toward the chimneys at the front of the house. As he moved, he started to strip off that long, gaudy coat, but it tangled on the strap of his quiver.

"Here!" Col yelled. He slid out of his gray-and-red jacket, then tossed it to the prince. Lar held it by the collar and let the hem hang over the far edge of the roof where Cazia could not see. A moment later, the two of them heaved it back up but, only now it had a girl clinging to it.

It was the Indregai princess: pale, tiny, and severe in her white house robe. Cazia knew she was a few years older than Jagia, but she looked shockingly young. The princess scrambled handily onto the peak of the roof, then began chattering at the prince, pointing back the way she'd come.

Lar did not seem not interested in taking orders. He scrambled to his feet, pulling Colchua upright with him. Timush shouted at them, waving them back toward the dangling tether, and Cazia hissed at the noise he was making. Lar practically shoved the princess toward the cart, and a renewed chorus of screams from below made her do as she was told.

An iron dart cracked the tile roof near the chimney. The sound startled Cazia, but she drew a spike from her jacket pocket without thinking about it and began to cast.

One of the creatures had dragged itself over the edge of the roof. The clerk had cast at it, missing, but Doctor Warpoole had begun a spell of her own.

"Great Way," Treygar prayed, his voice tight, "protect the prince. Keep him on your path."

Doctor Warpoole's dart flew with surprising speed, but it struck the creature low on the back, practically on its hip. Cazia did her best to lead with her own spell, just the way she had to lead the hoops during Doctor Twofin's lessons. She struck the beast on its high back below the neck. It sprawled on the tiles and tumbled down the steep roof slope.

Cazia started another spell right away. A second creature appeared at the top of the southernmost chimney. The clerk fired another dart, striking the brick just below the creature's furred hind hand. At least she was getting closer.

Cazia wasn't going to finish her spell in time, and Doctor Warpoole hadn't even started a new one yet. Lar had a quiver of his own, of course, but his back was turned. Cazia kept her hands moving, her mind falling into the necessary state, despite the fact that she knew it was futile. The only way she could avoid this awful grief would be if the creature hesitated.

It didn't. It leaped from the chimney at the prince. Cazia could feel tragedy flying at her like a volley of arrows.

Timush shouted and dove forward, throwing his shoulder into the monster's leg while it was still in mid-leap. The beast fell heavily on top of Timush. It roared in frustration, almost drowning out Timu's cry of pain, then they rolled over and slid toward the gutter. Timush kicked at the monster's broad back, trying to put some distance between them.

Col shouted, "Lar, save the princess!" before diving down the side of the roof, sliding on his belly after his friend. Cazia finished her spell, launching her dart directly into the left side of the monster's chest. Doctor Warpoole fired off a shot a moment later, stabbing through its forearm. Col caught hold of Timush's collar and clutched at the roof tiles, desperately trying to stop their momentum.

The monster braced itself against the gutter below and spun suddenly, lunging awkwardly toward the two of them. Col shouted, "NO!" and threw himself across Timush's body.

The creature bit down on Colchua's forearm.

Cazia's concentration broke and she felt a sudden flush of shame and anger as she started her spell again. Ciriam fired a dart, but she was so worried about hitting Col and Timush that she went low of the mark, skipping off the wall below the eaves. Timush kicked, hard, and the gutter broke away. The injured creature fell into the alley below, and the force of Timu's kick stole most of the momentum from his slide.

Clutching the tiles at the peak of the roof, Lar reached toward Col and Timu. Treygar leaned over the rail, muttering, "Into the cart. Into the cart," as though he could will the prince to flee, but the prince was not going to abandon his friends.

Timush struggled to get his feet under him—his face was horribly pale and his shoulder looked crooked. Col cradled his injured forearm but he was still moving quickly, helping Lar drag Timush toward the tether.

"Help the princess," Stoneface snapped, startling Cazia out of her follow-up spell. Fire and Fury, Cazia knew she would be useless if she let every sharp word break her concentration! The princess's hands had appeared on the railing. Bittler jumped up as though woken from a trance, took hold of the little girl, and hauled her over the edge.

The cart had floated away from the roof, too slowly to be immediately noticeable, but it was happening. Maybe Farrabell didn't even realize he was doing it. Cazia turned toward Stoneface and said, "We should move closer to them."

Treygar jabbed him lightly to catch his attention. "Turn the cart so the tether line is near the prince."

To his credit, the driver did so immediately. "Lower!" Lar called from below. "I need more slack."

The driver did so, fear sweat pouring down his face. Cazia leaned out over the rail and saw the prince loop the end of the tether around Timush's waist, then press Col against him. "Embrace your cousin," Lar said. "Your love will save you both." There were no more of the creatures in sight.

Col threw himself against Timush and let Lar wrap the rope around them both. "Bad enough I have to stick my arm in a monster's mouth for him. Don't make me kiss him, too." The prince grinned as he tied the knot.

Ciriam cast another dart, and this time she struck a beast on the hand as it climbed the chimney. A beast Cazia had not noticed until that moment. It lost its grip, falling out of sight.

Cazia turned to her. "How does it feel to finally hit one?" The clerk burst into tears.

"UP!" the prince called from below.

"Gently," Stoneface added, holding the point of the spike close to the driver's belly. The man moved the lever slowly but smoothly.

Cazia leaned over the rail again. Col and Timu dangled from within a knotted loop. Lar clung to the rope above them, his foot wedged into the knot. Treygar added, "Very good, Wimnel. Now take us over the wall. I want you to pick up speed without jarring the prince below."

Cazia felt a sudden pointed elbow in her kidneys. The foreign princess squeezed between her and Doctor Warpoole, moving toward Stoneface. "Man, my rescuers are not yet safe. Set down on a flat roof so we can bring them aboard."

"I am not your man," Treygar snapped at her. "And we will not be setting down *anywhere* inside the walls. Now please sit down. You do not command here."

"How dare you!" The girl's voice was high and strident. "My line goes back forty-six generations to the Chieftains of the Forty Valleys! My people—"

Cazia caught the girl by the arm. "Vilavivianna, isn't it?" The girl's name came to her at the same moment she spoke it. "Princess Vilavivianna of Goldgrass Hill? We met last midwinter at Lar's party. Do you remember me?" Cazia lowered her voice. "Let me speak honestly with you: we are not your subjects and you are twelve years old. No one is going to follow your orders. Now please let us do what we have to."

The little princess looked as if she was about to fly into a rage, but instead, she clenched her jaw and turned her back. Cazia thanked The Child for small favors, then leaned over the railing.

They floated high over the wall, beyond the mudflat hovels that clung to the city wall. Screams and panic had already reached here, and Cazia saw a large creature leap from the top of the wall onto a muddy street, then dash into the nearest building. A half dozen muddy children burst screaming through the doors, and she saw the monster knock one down and sink its teeth into the back of her thigh, then leap at another. It occurred to her that the monsters were the same color as Pagesh's lilacs and, for some absurd reason, that made everything even more terribly unfair.

"They're tasting us," Cazia said. "They bite, but since we left the palace, I haven't yet seen anyone actually eaten."

"Some creatures prefer to drag their food to a protected place to eat," Doctor Warpoole said. "In fact, it's possible that their bites are envenomed."

Horrified, Cazia spun toward the doctor. Was she suggesting Col had been poisoned and was as good as dead?

The older woman met her gaze with an expression as flat and blank as a serpent's.

On a high plaza between the mudflat slums and the Circle Way, soldiers had formed two squares. They were dressed in black and red, their spears extending far beyond their shield walls, and their cuirasses and greaves gleamed in the gentle rain.

Treygar blurted out, "That's Third Splashtown!" as though they might save the entire city. The name didn't mean anything to Cazia, but she made note of their banner, a red waterfall on a black background. The unmistakable note of hope in Stoneface's voice gave her hope as well.

Behind them, a fleet squad of unarmored soldiers ran with bows and spears, moving to line up at an angle to the two squares. Cazia noted that many of them were women, and she wished she had been permitted to practice with a spear or a bow. They were going to *fight* the invader, and she flushed with shame that she could not be down there, too.

"SHOCK LINE!" Treygar yelled down to them. "SHOCK LINE!"

After a moment's confusion at who was shouting at them, a man with a long brush along the top of his helmet—the commander, clearly—began barking orders, and the front line of spearmen braced the butts of their weapons in the cracks of the paving stones.

The cart flew over them, picking up speed. "How much farther?" Lar called from below. Cazia leaned far out and saw the prince clinging to the rope with the crook of his elbow. Her stupid, awful imagination suddenly pictured him losing his grip and falling away—pictured his expression—and she had to look away. "Timush doesn't look good," he added.

It was true. Timush was conscious but his skin was pasty. Cazia had never seen anyone go into shock, but she knew it could be as deadly as the point of a knife.

"Yes, my prince." Treygar turned to Wimnel. "Find a place to set down. We have to get those injured men off the rope and we can't drag them."

The driver glanced nervously back toward the city. "My tyr, we must find a road—"

"We can't fly all the way to Fort Samsit with the prince hanging by his fingers—"

"My tyr—"

"—And two men who risked their lives for him dying at the end of a rope like common murderers!" Cazia was startled by the note of desperation in Stoneface's voice. For a moment, he seemed to be concerned about Col and Timu.

"My tyr, trust me when I tell you that you don't want to set down here." He nodded toward the marshy grasslands around them. "The cart wheels will get stuck in the mud and the disk wouldn't be able to pull us out. We'd have to lift the cart free physically, then hover low while everyone loads on, and if we dipped too far down, we'd touch the mud and have to start again. It's something the scholars don't yet understand about this Gift, but we must set down on dry ground to take off again. I swear by Song and Monument this is the truth, Fire take me if it's not."

Cazia believed him, and by the way Tyr Treygar grimaced, she could see he did, too. A chill ran down her back. If Old Stoneface couldn't keep his stoicism, what hope did they have to preserve anything? "We'll all be Fire-taken if we don't find a safe place to set down," Treygar said.

The Eastern Way would have been a safe place to put down, but it was behind them. By the time they circled back to it, they might find it overrun by beasts. Still, Doctor Warpoole began to insist they turn about, while Tyr Treygar refused to listen.

Typical of Stoneface and the others to be arguing over who should be in charge when they should have been searching for a safe place to set down. Cazia looked out over the tall yellow grass, letting her vision go unfocused as she looked at everything and nothing. She'd always had strong eyesight, and her habit of watching the palace staff and guards without seeming to had taught her the trick of spotting the thing that doesn't fit.

The grasslands were marshy and wet, yes, but there was dry ground out there, too, if you knew how to spot it.

"We have to turn back to the south," Doctor Warpoole said again. "The flat stones of the Eastern Way—"

"There!" Cazia called, pointing to the north a bit. "Do you see the fringe of grass?"

"No," Treygar said, but he gestured toward Wimnel, ordering him to head in that direction. He leaned over the rail and called down, "A bit farther, my prince."

The fringe of grass did not mark a road, but it did hide a broken stone foundation. Wimnel looked over the rail at it and nodded. He could set down here.

He lowered the cart gently and deftly at the edge of the foundation, laying the prince and his two friends on the stony slope outside the foundation. Then he rotated and slowly settled the cart inside the shattered walls. Cazia studied the way he handled the controls.

Treygar clutched at his injured shoulder. "Doctor Warpoole, please help them inside." Bittler climbed over the rail to help.

"What is this place?" the princess asked. Her accent made her sound as though she was talking with her mouth full.

"An old storm house," Ciriam answered. "Once the grasslands were dotted with storm houses, but people don't drive okshim herds through the mud any more. At least, not on this side of the Barrier."

Lar and Bittler carried Timush into the cart, then laid him in the front. Just behind them came Doctor Warpoole and Col.

Timush looked like a waxen doll. The sight of him shocked Cazia so deeply, it felt like pain. Had tragedy managed to strike after all?

"Make room at the front!" she shouted, using her voice to relieve her tension while she elbowed Ciriam out of the way. "Squeeze in." She helped Timush settle painfully on the rough wooden floor.

"We must raise his feet," Vilavivianna said, "to get the blood back to his face."

Of course. Cazia gave the girl a grateful look, then ordered Bittler to sit at the front of the cart and allow Timush's legs to rest in his lap. He did it.

Col settled against the rail. "By your command, o Caz," he said, not unkindly. Cazia felt herself flush anyway and clamped her mouth shut. There were tingles all over her back and arms as she watched her brother, injured but alive, smile at her. Then she moved toward the back of the cart where the driver stood. Col and Timush, resting on the floor, took up a quarter of the available space.

"We are overburdened," the princess declared. "This one is not highborn or necessary, is she?"

Vilavivianna pointed at Ciriam, and she had a point. Not only was the clerk an Enemy, she had taken Cazia's quiver. Still, the thought of pitching her over the rail into the unprotected grassland made Cazia a little sick.

Lar said, "Betrothed, we are saving everyone we can. Everyone. Sit up close to Jagia and the doctors. We'll be uncomfortable, but—"

The sound of distant screaming came through the grasses. Everyone in the cart was silent as they heard the voices of men and women raised in terror and pain. The little princess turned to look up at the clerk's face, then looked down at the floor.

"My tyr?" Wimnel said.

Old Stoneface stared into the grasses as though he could see the dying soldiers through them. "Take us away from here."

CHAPTER SEVEN

SOMETHING MOVED THROUGH THE TALL GRASSES AS THEY SLOWLY ROSE into the air. Everyone was panicky for a few moments—the Freewell girl held her hands in the first position to cast a spout of flame, and both the Witt boy and the clerk squeezed their eyes shut and muttered prayers for Great Way to clear their path—but nothing happened. Tejohn slid the spike he was holding into his waistcoat pocket, wishing it was reinforced with canvas instead of just a decorative touch to please the Evening People, and took hold of the rail with his good left hand. They'd gotten away. He had done his duty.

Leaning over the rail, he looked back toward the line of spears and the fleet squad. The soldiers they'd passed was Third Splashtown, the unit he'd served in when he'd broken the guard at Pinch Hall. His unit. They'd lost so many people they'd almost been disbanded, but Tejohn himself had entreated the king to preserve their name and banner; they'd been stationed at Beddalin Hole—guard duty for Peradain, essentially—because they had earned a place of safety and prestige.

Tejohn couldn't see the black field with the blurry red smear that could only be the Splashtown waterfall banner against the yellow-green of the surrounding grasses. In fact, he couldn't see any sign of black and red. Had they already moved out? "Mister Farrabell, start toward the northeast."

"We're not going to Fort Samsit," Lar said. "Not yet."

"My prince," Tejohn said, "there's no room for anyone else."

"That isn't my plan," Lar said. "I can cast the Sixth Gift, and so can Caz." The Freewell girl jumped as if startled, then nodded. "And so can Doctor Warpoole and Doctor . . . "

"Eelhook, my prince," Ciriam said.

"You can cast that spell, can't you?"

Doctor Warpoole wore a icy expression. "It's been a while, but I'm sure we can manage."

Below, a spear of the fleet squad broke through a stand of tall grass and sprinted in their direction. Moments later, one of the beasts raced into the open and ran him down as easily as a parent catching a disobedient toddler. Tejohn could do nothing but watch the way one smear of color overtook the other and listen to the sounds they made. The Freewell girl fumbled at her pocket for one of her darts, but Doctor Warpoole stopped her with a gentle hand on the girl's wrist.

It was already too late. The beast dragged the man out of sight into the grasses. The screams made Tejohn's blood run cold.

The cart picked up speed as they headed back toward the city wall. "Higher," Tejohn said.

"Yes, my tyr," the driver said gratefully.

There were more screams as they approached the city. "My prince," Tejohn said, "what is your plan?"

Lar seemed reluctant to look away from the city ahead. "We get high, very high above the palace. We four cast the Sixth Gift in the air above the portal, dropping stone blocks onto the dais beside it. We heap the stone until no more of these things can get through!"

The Freewell girl gasped. "Yes," Doctor Warpoole said. "Yes, of course! We can do that."

Tejohn noticed a flash of red fabric on the ground below and leaned over the side.

Third Splashtown had been destroyed. He couldn't see them clearly, not from this distance, but he could see smudges of colors motionless in the yellow grasses. Six . . . no, seven of them were the purple color of the beast men, but everywhere he looked he could see black and red, motionless. The shock line had been smashed.

Even the screams were fading. Tejohn felt a familiar companion reappear within him. It had been a long time since he'd felt the rage, despair, and grief that came in the wake of an invading army, but there it was again. The queen's remarks about revisiting his pain had piqued them, but now they piled up within him like a thunderhead. Third Splashtown had been his. He wore their colors in the gym every day, and he was proud to be part of their history. Now they had been Fire-taken.

Bittler cried out, "Look!"

He wasn't pointing at the carnage below. Instead, he pointed toward the city.

Tejohn squinted into the distance, but he had no idea what he was supposed to be seeing.

"I can't see that far," Doctor Warpoole said. "What's happening?"

"There's another, larger flying cart hovered over the palace," Bittler said. "They're dropping pink granite blocks down into the courtyard below. It has to be onto the portal, don't you think?"

"What a clever plan," Lar said.

"Oh!" Bittler sounded suddenly alarmed. "The cart just rocked to the side, like a boat on a rough river. A piece of the black disk above them just flew upward like . . . like blown dandelion fluff."

"They're throwing stones," the Freewell girl said. "The beasts are throwing broken pieces of granite at the cart, breaking it apart."

"The cart is spinning now, faster and faster, as it comes apart," Bittler said. "People are falling out. They're still so high up—Fire and Fury, the cart is tumbling—they're all falling out."

"Grateful am I," the Freewell girl prayed, "to be permitted to travel The Way."

"Turn us around, Farrabell," Tejohn said quietly. "Right now."

Lar did not argue. No one did. They didn't even talk to each other. They just hunched low in the cart, gripping tightly to the rails if they were near enough, and let Tejohn be the one to order a retreat.

There was no space for Tejohn to sit, and he wouldn't have asked for it if there was. He stood near the driver and leaned against the high back of the cart, the knots of the driver's safety harness digging into his back. Tejohn had no idea why the benches and railing didn't come with harnesses themselves; if they had, those scholars might have . . . but never mind. He'd never ridden in a cart before, so he didn't know a lot about it.

The Bendertuk boy had color in his face again, but he was obviously in great pain. If Tejohn had to guess, he would have said the boy's collarbone was broken, but there was nothing to do for him but get him to a sleepstone or, if he was lucky, a medical scholar.

The Freewell boy was holding up better, but maybe that was because his injury was easier to manage. His sister had torn scraps from the hem of her dress to bandage him, but she'd done an amateur job of it and the blood was still flowing. Tejohn wished he had both hands so he could redo the job himself.

As for himself, Tejohn wasn't holding up well and he knew it. His old knee injury ached painfully, but that was dwarfed by the agony of his shoulder. The ball and socket felt as though they were swelling to the size of a human head. His spear arm. He didn't like to think about it, but that was his spear arm. The longer he waited for treatment, the worse it would heal; his knee had taught him that, if nothing else could.

"Lost," Doctor Warpoole suddenly said. Her voice was full of sorrow but her expression was blank and deadly. "Peradain, the Morning City, and everything we were trying to build there. Music, theater, culture, empire . . . Great Way, the *writing*. All Fire-taken now. All lost."

"Monument sustain me," Lar said. "Just when I thought dirges were going out of style."

No one laughed, but the Freewell boy managed a smile and his younger sister gave Doctor Warpoole a nasty look. The scholar-administrator turned her gaze outward toward the passing scenery and kept her silence.

But Tejohn could not ignore the effect her words had on him. *All lost.* If he could no longer raise a sword or hold a spear, what use was he?

He had a lot of time to consider it. Flying carts weren't quick, but they could build speed over a long flight, and soon the wind and drizzle whipped their faces as though they were standing in a gale. The prince and the Freewell boy made an effort to hide their discomfort, but Tejohn could tell they were all cold, wet, and miserable.

But no one asked to slow their retreat. They passed over farm houses and tiny villages, sometimes clustered around high, dry paths and sometimes narrow canals, but no one suggested they stop to warn the commoners there. Tejohn had been one of them once. He knew villager folk didn't matter. Only the prince did.

After a short while, Jagia began to cry. Then the Witt boy did the same, then the Freewell girl, the Bendertuk boy, and finally the driver. The Freewell boy laid a comforting hand on his sister's shoulder, but she seemed to take no comfort in it.

He glanced sharply at Doctor Warpoole and her clerk. Both of their cheeks were wet, of course, because of the rain, but the scholar administrator maintained her composure, while the younger woman could not conceal her quivering lip. It was nothing, he told himself. Anyone would weep in this situation.

The truth was becoming clear for all of them. Their siblings, friends, spouses, even their children, assuming Farrabell and the scholars had them, were lost. Not just "music." Not "writing." Families, friends . . . People.

The queen herself had asked Tejohn for a favor just that morning and he'd refused her. King Ellifer, the man Tejohn had nearly thrown away his life to save, had been pulled down right before his eyes, and his wife with them. Kellin Pendell, the commander of the palace guard, was also gone, along with the friends who had diced and drank with them every half moon. His valet. The girl who made the stuffed buns he ate for breakfast. Sincl the performance master. Kolbi Arriya, the king's shield bearer. Doctor Twofin. The scrawny boy who collected the bowls and dishes in dining hall. The priests who swept the palace temple. The tailor who sewed the sopping wet coat he was wearing . . .

It was too much. Too many faces raced through his memory. There were too many obligations of shared kindness and duty, too many screams from the palace and the city fresh in his memory. He didn't have enough grief inside him to give them all their due. Rage, yes. He had a reservoir of that so deep it would never run dry, but not grief.

And it wasn't just the people. The Peradaini Empire had just been hollowed out the way you scrape seeds from a melon. The greatest empire the continent of Kal-Maddum had ever seen had been decapitated. As long as they held on to little Vilavivianna, the Indregai Alliance and their pet serpents would be kept at bay, but what would discourage the Durdric tribes in the western mountains? And Song only knew what Tyr Freewell and his allies would do when they heard the news.

There was more death to come. That was inevitable. And it didn't make him want to weep. It made him want to run out into the world and start the killing. *Fire and Fury*, he prayed, *grant me the strength to sweep my enemies from The Way.*

Eventually, they fell silent. Vilavivianna, sitting beside the prince with his coat wrapped around her, had certainly lost family and servants, but she had not wept with the others. She only glowered at the floor. If she survived, she would grow up to be a formidable woman.

The Freewell girl reached over and gave the little girl's hand a squeeze. The princess pulled away reflexively, as though offended. Then, after a moment's thought, she lunged forward and took hold of the Freewell girl's hand in both of hers.

No one spoke. They all huddled low, except Tejohn and the driver, and endured the wind and rain.

Eventually, they reached the River Juntusal. Tejohn had crossed it twice a year on the Eastern Way, but he hadn't been this far north since the prince's tour of the empire when he was fourteen. Even if they flew low enough for him to look around, he couldn't expect to see anything familiar; even this far north, rivers changed directions every few years, destroying some farms and creating new ones.

Still, it was wide and deep, being the source of much of the lake and marshland from Peradain down to Rivershelf. The driver turned the cart in a more northerly direction to roughly follow the course of the river.

"Is this wide enough, do you think?" Lar asked. "The creatures didn't strike me as ship builders. Do you think they'll be stopped at the banks of the river?"

"We could never be so lucky," the Freewell boy answered, and Tejohn couldn't help but nod in agreement.

They continued north. Eventually the grassy marshes turned to dry ground. Trees became more common. Orchards had been planted near the river, and there were even short piers here and there. And so many little scattered houses. Who would warn the farmers and fisherfolk? They were people just like Tejohn's wife and children, and just like his father: commoners. He thought again about slowing enough to shout down to them, to warn them to flee across the Juntusal, but no. The only heir of King Ellifer needed to be taken to safety, so common folk just like his wife and children would have to fend for themselves.

Tejohn soon realized the cart was slowing, and tried not to show his relief.

They reached Fort Samsit and the Southern Barrier just as the sun went down. They had passed out of the rainstorm in late afternoon, but even though the cart had slowed, the wind had become fiercer. The two young girls suffered the worst of it, of course, but the others did their best to comfort them.

The fort itself sat well back from the forests ringing the base of the mountain range. It was wedged into a cleft in the mountains, blocking the entrance to a narrow pass where the mountains on either side were nearly vertical. The front of the fort was a hundred feet high, built of scholar-created stone blocks that stood out pink against the black mountain behind it. It was a sheer and foreboding structure, and it was only possible because of the Sixth Gift.

The driver angled the cart hard to the east, skimming across the sharp front of the range. Dense tree foliage passed beneath them, then a sizable village at the bend of the river. Tejohn thought he should be able to see people, too, but it appeared to be deserted. For a moment, he thought the creatures might have already attacked here, but then he saw the setting sun catch plumes of smoke from the chimneys, and he decided there would have been more chaos below.

Doctor Warpoole turned to the driver. "Is there a reason you have turned away from our destination? Perhaps you've forgotten that we need food, warmth, and dry clothes."

"Not to mention sleepstones for the injured," the Freewell girl snapped.

The driver cleared his throat. "I'm sorry. My prince, I'm sorry, but we're still going too fast. I've been slowing the cart for most of the afternoon, but I misjudged the distance to Fort Samsit. The Ways have markers on them, you see, but cross-country trips are more complicated. More dangerous."

"Can't you at least take us into the pass," Doctor Warpoole asked, "and out of this wind? You can fly over the fort, I assume?"

"Through the pass?" the driver said, his tone incredulous. "At night? I won't do it."

Lar waved a weary hand at him. "I hardly think the pass would be less windy. Do what you must."

They circled the river and village long past nightfall, slowly reducing their speed.

Tejohn had never been one to fear darkness. As a boy, he'd done farm work after the sun had gone down. As a soldier, he'd camped, patrolled, and fought at night. But now, speeding through the air in this cart with nothing to mark his position but the watchfires on the walls of the fort, he felt a raw, clutching terror. Death would be sudden and ugly if the driver misjudged the distance to the cliffs, and there was nothing he could do about it but pray.

Eventually, the cart slowed so much, Tejohn thought he could have jogged along beneath it. The driver turned toward the watchfires and the cart moved toward them as slowly as doddering old man.

The driver cleared his throat again. "I'm sorry, my prince. Doctor. We'll be landing soon."

The mountains around them were invisible in the night, and the fires along the walls of the fort, and inside as well, made it look like a lonely island floating in a void.

Tejohn decided he didn't like flying; it made him feel dramatic.

The driver gently lowered the cart into the courtyard.

Soldiers in round steel helms and breastplates formed along one wall, spears lowered. A gigantic man with a red plume in his helm called out in a deep, booming voice, "Halt and identify yourselves!"

"Lar Italga," the prince said as he stood, "prince of Peradain and heir to the Throne of Skulls." Doctor Warpoole was about to speak, but Tejohn waved his hand to silence her.

The big man seemed startled by that, but he still had his duty. He scowled at them from beneath his oversized brow. "Where is your banner?"

The prince didn't know what to say to that, but the driver spoke up immediately. "Fire take me! In all the panic, I completely forgot! The palace has banners for the carts to fly so they can be identified as they land inside the fort. After what happened at Fort Piskatook—"

Tejohn suddenly felt terribly weary. "Points high, captain," he said, "The commander here is still Ranlin Gerrit, isn't he? We've known each other for many years. Tell him Tyr Treygar is here. Quickly now, we have injured."

"I'm sorry, Tyr Treygar." The captain repeated the name as though it was the boldest lie he'd ever heard. "But without the banner, the commander will not—DO NOT MOVE YOUR HANDS!"

Chapter Eight

A WAVE OF GOOSE BUMPS RAN DOWN CAZIA'S BACK. HAD SHE REALLY escaped the creatures in the city just to have a spear point rammed into her belly? She wasn't even sure who had moved.

Col stirred himself but she waved for him to keep still. The soldiers were leaning forward, their knuckles white on the hafts, their faces strangely blank. Cazia knew that one stupid decision by anyone in the cart could end all their lives. She imagined sharpened metal stabbing into her stomach, splitting her skin; would the blades feel cold against her insides?

"At ease, captain!" The voice came from a window in the central tower. A middle-aged man in a steel cap leaned out and waved the spears back. He was smiling behind his bristling beard. "That is Tyr Treygar in the flesh, although I don't recognize the others."

The captain did not put up his weapon. "Commander—"

"I know what you're going to say, captain, but I'm coming down anyway." He stepped back out of view.

Stoneface glanced sharply at the two scholars. "Hands at your sides, everyone, until I—and only I—give leave for you to move. My prince—"

"I understand, my tyr," Lar said. "You can not give me an order, but I charge you to deal with this situation with as little stabbing as possible."

Treygar nodded, looking relieved.

It took some time for the commander to appear. Doctor Warpoole began to give instructions to Ciriam on how she wanted her room prepared, treating the girl like a servant. Cazia had an unbearable urge to fidget and she suddenly realized that the driver would probably stay at the fortress for a short rest and a meal, then take off again. She, almost certainly, would be staying much longer. Since the doctor was already talking, that was apparently allowed. Her hands carefully pressed against her thighs, she turned to the driver and said, "You still haven't done what Tyr Treygar asked of you."

He looked confused for a moment. Stoneface also seemed a little nonplussed at first, but he caught up quickly. "Teach her."

The driver glanced at Doctor Warpoole as though expecting her to cancel Treygar's order. Cazia suddenly wondered if the scholars—or even the throne—had ordered the cart drivers to secrecy. Her skin tingled at the idea of learning forbidden knowledge.

Doctor Warpoole said, "I don't think—"

"Tell her," Stoneface said again. He had put the dart away somewhere and needed his only good hand to hold onto the rail. He looked pale and exhausted, but there was something undeniable in his tone.

Lar said, "If Tyr Treygar gives you an order, take it as though it comes directly from me. He speaks for me."

Cazia suddenly realized that this was a moment when everything might fall apart, and she had accidentally created it. If Doctor Warpoole defied Lar in the next few moments, anyone might. If she suddenly decided the scholars would support some other tyr, what could Lar do about it? Pressing her hands against her dress, Cazia felt the spikes against her forearm. If the scholar-administrator said the wrong thing . . .

It didn't happen. The driver licked his lips nervously and said, "The levers—"

"I understand the levers," Cazia said. "I've been watching. Is there more to it?"

"Yes, well . . . The color orange—a bright orange. The feeling of stepping into a deep puddle unexpectedly with your left foot. A square where the right side breaks midline and collapses into an isosceles triangle."

Was he making fun of her? Those were mental preparations for a spell. "What about hand movements?"

"There aren't any," the driver said. "It's not a spell."

Cazia almost called him a liar. The hand motions and mental preparations were both components of spellcasting, but to use one without the other . . .

The heavy oak door at the base of the tower swung open with the agonized groan of unwaxed wooden hinges and the commander strode through with a half dozen archers and twice that many spears. He wore full steel, with a long sword at his hip and a tall curved shield over his back. His face was partly obscured by that bristling black-and-gray beard, but it was tanned on the left side and pale pink on the right. Burn scars. *A scholar did that to him.* The thought made Cazia nervous.

The captain sidestepped to put himself between the commander and the cart, but the commander said, "At ease, captain. I know Tyr Treygar, and now I recognize the prince as well. Do you remember me, my prince?"

"I do," Lar said. "Commander Gerrit, yes? Ranlin Gerrit? Three years ago, you visited the gym and tried to teach me to wield a spear. You said that if I'd been a recruit in your unit, you'd have had me whipped for laziness."

Commander Gerrit nodded, then turned to Treygar. "The Festival is today, Tejohn. What brings you out for a pleasure tour?"

"War."

That got them all up and moving. Stewards rushed from the tower to bring warm blankets and escort the wounded to the medical chamber. Old Stoneface waved off a scholar with a medical shield stitched into his robe, and her brother did the same. "They'll want me there," Col said to the doddering old scholar scowling at his bandages. "I've seen the enemy up close."

Cazia, realizing the stewards intended to wrap her up tightly and escort her someplace comfortable and far from the prince, rushed to her brother's side and slipped under his arm. "Hold on to me," she whispered. "I'm coming, too."

Col grabbed a fistful of her wet sleeve, and a steward draped a woolen blanket over both of them. Her brother leaned on her as if he needed her.

They followed Lar, the commander, and Tyr Treygar into the tower and up the stairs. Timush had been laid out on a blanket, with three stewards taking a corner and Bittler holding the fourth. Cazia knew Bitt would make sure their friend was cared for.

Doctor Warpoole lingered in the courtyard, squabbling with Vilavivianna about whether she was permitted to follow the prince. They were attracting a lot of attention, which was to Cazia's benefit.

"What do you think is going to happen up there?" she whispered.

"I think we're going to ruin their day," Col answered.

Stoneface trudged up the stairs like a man going to his own execution. He was clearly exhausted and in great pain, but he kept going. Cazia had always thought of him as one of her most dangerous Enemies, but now she wasn't sure what to think.

At the top of the tower were an attendant's chamber and a council room. Commander Gerrit opened the council door to admit Lar, then glanced back at Cazia and her brother, as if noticing them for the first time. Gerrit turned toward the captain of the guard. "Admit the prince and Tyr Treygar."

Cazia was about to protest that she had already climbed *all those stairs* when Lar said, "And my cousins." He glanced back at them. "I want them there."

"Admit Freewells to my council room!" Gerrit exclaimed. "My prince—"

"Ranlin," Stoneface interrupted. "They've proven themselves. More than."

Cazia was honestly startled by that. Old Treygar saying something nice about her? She thought she might fall over from the shock of it. Gripping her brother more tightly, they went into the room together.

The captain stayed outside and shut the doors with a startling bang. The tower room was small, but she should have expected that. This wasn't the palace, after all.

There were two guards inside the room, both wearing short swords and holding platter-sized shields. Cazia knew the parts of their armor and weaponry had their own names, and if this war continued, she was sure she'd have a chance to learn them. Beside the commander was a pair of stewards, each holding a stylus and wax tablet. A single wool tapestry hung on the wall, looking like a crude blanket. There was no fire in the fireplace but the oil lamps had been lit.

Cazia Freewell, daughter of a traitor, was attending a royal council. Amazing. This was what she'd longed for, and she finally had her chance. She was torn between a desire to avoid attracting attention and saying something so brilliant that Lar kept her at his side always.

Lar pulled out a chair for Col to sit and Cazia helped him settle in. Stoneface wearily dragged a chair away from the table. When he had settled in, he tenderly laid his injured arm on his lap.

"Tejohn," the commander said. "We should summon a medical scholar for you."

"That would confuse and delay things. After we've done our work, I'll go down to a sleepstone."

"The longer you wait—"

"Ranlin, I was not exaggerating when I told you the empire is at war. The Morning City has been overrun and destroyed, and the King and Queen are both dead."

"Dead?" Gerrit collapsed into the chair at the head of the table. Cazia looked to Lar and saw his expression on his pale face was stern. "How?"

Tyr Treygar briefly told the story of the attack through the portal, the retreat to the Scholars' Tower, the rescue of the princess, and the flight across the marshes. He did not go into detail, but neither did he stint on praise for Timush's or Colchua's bravery, and her own, too, even though all she'd done was cast spells from the safety of the cart.

When he finished, Gerrit said, "The Evening People attacked us! I never would have thought—"

"These aren't the Evening People," Lar interjected. "These aren't people at all."

Her brother raised his injured arm and peeled back Cazia's clumsy bandage. "No person bites like this."

Gerrit did not seem moved by sight. "It sounds to me as if they unleashed these creatures on us. Yes? Consider the potency and will of the Evening People. Do you think they could have been conquered by beasts, even ones as deadly as you describe?"

Lar rubbed his face. "I agree. It hardly seems possible."

Gerrit sighed. "To be honest, I'm not surprised; we have lied to them for generations. We knew the day might come when they discovered the truth and turned on us. We've talked about this before, Tejohn."

"We have. It's a common conversation in some circles. But I don't want to assume that's what has happened simply because we've been waiting for it."

"Let me know if a better theory ever shows its face, because I don't think it will. How many were there?"

"I don't know." Tyr Treygar wiped sweat from the end of his long nose. Could pain make a person sweat? Cazia was afraid she was going to learn a lot of unpleasant things very soon. Treygar continued, "They were charging through so fast. How many were on the other side to come through in the first rush? Did the scholars manage to block the whole of the portal before their cart was knocked out of the sky? If so, how long before the creatures dig it out? I'll tell you something: they are fast and they are strong. You need a squad of men to handle one or two of them."

"Truly?"

"They're as large as bears," Col said, "but faster. I hunted bear in the Furrows with Kellin Pendell. Bears are strong and fast, but these are swifter and more economical in their movements, and they feel denser. Like a big cat."

"But they look like men."

"If men had hands where their feet should be," Lar said. "And fur. And fangs."

"So they're animals," Gerrit said. "It sounds like what you need is a hunting party, not an army."

"What we need is information," Lar said. "How can we defeat this enemy without knowing more about it? What happened on the other side of the portal? Is there another way to get through it to seek out the Evening People and discover why they did this, if it was indeed their plan? Can we close the portal early?"

Those words made Cazia's damp skin prickle. *Yes,* she wanted to shout. *Yes, this is exactly right.*

But Commander Gerrit scowled and shook his head. "The best way to learn about an enemy is to ram a spear into his belly and watch how he dies. If the spear misses, then the sword, or the torch. We learn best through battle. I'm sorry, my prince, but this is the honest fact of it."

In a low voice, Stoneface said, "You are not addressing a prince, Ranlin."

Gerrit opened his mouth, then shut it. Lar was standing, so the commander stood and bowed low. "Forgive me, my king, but these old gears spin slowly; that's why I'm hunkered down in this fortress rather than out in the field, commanding troops. But you have my service, and my loyalty, too, for whatever good it will do you. I swear on it, just as I swore to your father."

"Thank you, Commander Gerrit. I will not officially be the king until I am crowned, but until then—and after—I welcome honest counsel."

"May I offer more?"

"Please do, and reclaim your seat."

"I'll stand, thank you, my king. You should sit while your men stand, and you must command them, not ask with a *please* or an *if you would*. No one will believe you a strong king unless you actually rule over them. If you would retain the throne, you must use the power it grants."

Col's hand tightened on Cazia's arm and Tyr Treygar pushed back his chair to stand, his mouth twisted with embarrassment. Lar waved at him to stay where he was. "You make sense, commander, but those injured while protecting me may rest in my presence."

"What do you mean, *retain the throne*?" her brother asked, his voice sharp.

"Scholar, priest, trader, explorer," Gerrit said, "these are the occupations of princes, of younger brothers who will never perch upon a throne. The Tyrs pledge their armies and turn over their taxes to warrior-kings, and even then they do it grudgingly, with the knowledge that they must pay or face the king's spears. That's how your father nearly died." Gerrit stared at Lar intently. "Freewell had sent only half his summer duty, and King Ellifer stopped at Kirlik Witt's lands to commandeer a few extra fleet squads when he suddenly found himself surrounded by spear points. Luckily, Freewell wanted to use his own marriage to your Aunt Ulia to claim the throne for himself and his children, and she forbade his murder."

Cazia had heard this story from Lar years ago—no one else would even speak of it.

Lar said, "My father spared Freewell's life, too, in the end."

The commander and Stoneface looked at each other, and Cazia knew there was a history there that even Lar didn't understand. "For his reasons," Gerrit continued, "he did, although Freewell fights on the Durdric Frontier now, standing off near-constant raids. But my point is that my father rode to the King's defense because he respected the man. Yes, he'd sworn an oath to the throne. Yes, Freewell had raided Gerrit and Finstel lands along with his Witt and Bendertuk allies." He glanced at Tejohn as he said this, but Stoneface stared resolutely at the tabletop. "Yes, Freewell would have been the worst king since Edrl Spearshaker. But would the Holvos, Grimwoods, and Redmudds have mustered for a scholar? In this world of Indregai serpents, sea giants and mountain raiders, I do not think so."

"Sibilan was a scholar-king," Lar said quietly.

"Sibilan Italga reigned for three years before he lost his head, which was longer than anyone expected."

"Sibilan the Scholar fell from a tower, didn't he?" Cazia asked. "I know the song. He learned how to turn the flat stone spell into a building stone, then he built a tower . . . " The way they were staring at her made her realize she was being foolish and she felt herself flush. So much for saying something that would impress them all, although she wasn't sure what she'd gotten wrong. "It would have worked in peacetime," she said, changing course. "The tyrs would have accepted him as king if it had secured peace in the east."

"King Ellifer thought so, too," Treygar said. "That was his gamble."

"Can't we just replace the tyrs who refuse to take an oath of loyalty?" Col asked. "Including my father?"

Treygar shook his head. "It's not as easy as that. A tyr is more than just a boy with an inheritance. He has relationships. The commander of his troop will be his closest friend, and his spymaster will be a beloved cousin. The master coin collector will have found a place in his tyrship's retinue for his two eldest children, and the harbormaster will love him like a long-lost brother. If he's a clever tyr, at least, and if they're still alive after a few years, it's because they're clever. It's as easy to execute and replace a well-established tyr as it is to publicly murder a man and hope that all his dearest friends will accept you in his place. You must first turn his people against him, or replace them all afterward."

Cazia glanced at her brother. It had never occurred to her that he would not be welcomed as the new Tyr Freewell, when the time came.

"And there are some who will question Ellifer's death," Gerrit said. That was met with silence. "Not me, my king. I have known Tejohn since before Pinch Hall, and his word is good enough for me, even in a matter such as this. But it won't do for everyone. There are many who will be unwilling to muster troops and swear an oath based on this story."

"They are welcome to visit Peradain to see for themselves," Lar said bitterly.

"Many will. It will help that you have brought your cousins with you."

Cazia sighed bitterly. "Am I still a hostage?"

"Yes," Stoneface said, "Both of you have proven your loyalty beyond any doubt, as far as I'm concerned, but your father hasn't. Tyr Freewell knows that his children love the prince—I'm sorry, my king—his children love King Lar, and that you love them in return. But he also knew that Ellifer Italga would have dropped their heads onto the roof of his house if he had sent so much as a scout onto another tyr's lands."

"I don't . . . " Col couldn't finish the sentence, whatever he wanted to say. "It's not clear why I'm still alive. I know my father has no love for me or Caz, and I don't see how our lives could hold him in check all these years."

"It's not love," Gerrit said. "I've met your father several times—I may have spent more time with him than you have—and I don't think he's capable of love. But causing your executions would be a tremendous blow to his authority. After all, he's nothing more than an ambitious commoner who earned King Ghrund's favor, all those years ago. His own people already think Song shows him no favor, and if his own children were Fire-taken, someone would see to it that he was, too, to placate Fury."

"It's to the king and queen's credit that they did not stage something that would have given his people cause to remove him." Treygar said. "But we need the hostages to remain hostages still, and we need the tyrs to believe their children are in danger."

Or they will turn on the Italgas was the unspoken truth there. Cazia felt sick to her stomach.

"We still have to warn them," Lar said. "Loyal to the throne or not. I'm king to all of them." There was something bitter about the way he said it, and Cazia wasn't the only one to notice.

Gerrit nodded. "I will make my mirror available to you immediately, my king. And I recommend that you have each Tyr's child with you when you give your warning; their word will give credibility to your story."

It would also remind the tyrs that their children were still held hostage, Cazia knew.

"I saw the Bendertuk boy being carried away," Gerrit said. "And the Witt was with him. Where is the Simblin girl?"

For some reason, they all looked at Cazia. Was she supposed to look after the little girls and the grown women, too? "She didn't make it."

"That's bad," the commander said. "Rolvo Simblin is the roughest, least honorable of them all. He's practically half sea-giant himself. Still, he's the farthest from Peradain, so we will have time to prepare if he marches against the king."

"Prepare what?" Lar said. He spoke as if he was half strangled. "Peradain is gone, and the king's armies . . . Tyr Treygar, what of the king's army?"

Stoneface answered as though he was confessing to a crime he had long kept secret. "A full tenth was inside the city, disarmed, so they could compete in the games. They were the cream at the rim of the pitcher. There were five hundred or so militia fighters inside the city as well. Another thousand would have been stationed at each of the outer forts: the southern, northeastern, and northwestern holdfasts. Third Splashtown was a fifth of the strength of the northeastern, and they were utterly destroyed."

"Third Splashtown is gone?" Gerrit sounded shocked.

"In minutes," Col said. "Short minutes."

Cazia realized she was holding her breath. Peradain was gone, and when it vanished, so did the power and authority that protected them all. That power had been such a part of her life that it had been invisible to her, but now, with nothing but a burning, overrun city down in the grasslands, Lar had nothing left to protect him. The same name that had safeguarded him for his whole life now made him a target for any tyr who wanted a crown of his own.

She felt as though she'd been cast out into a storm to fend for herself. How could they restore that power? Yes, the society she'd grown up in had been full of Enemies, but this was Lar's *life* they were talking about. This was everything. The emptiness she perceived in the world was like a collapse of a city wall or the destruction of an army. How could they feel safe again? How could they bring it all back?

"I suspect there is little chance that I have any troops at all," Lar said quietly. "And I'm not sure troops can even address the problem. The creatures are enchanted; the one advantage of being a scholar is that you recognize magic when you get close enough. Their entire bodies are suffused with it." He took a deep breath. "That's why I intend to travel to Tempest Pass."

"My king—!" Stoneface said.

"I know what you're going to say," Lar told him. "My father died in the face of the enemy, and what did I do? Ran away. That's how the tyrs will see things, yes? And now, instead of rallying support and leading a force to retake the city, I'm fleeing to the far end of the empire to talk with a hermit scholar."

Stoneface nodded to show that Lar had understood. "The tyrs will be expecting certain behavior from their king."

Cazia stood beside Lar. "That's because they don't expect enough," she said defensively.

Lar laid a gentle hand on her shoulder. "Living among the tyrs while they gather their armies, I would have only the authority they were willing to grant me. And I would have to be constantly on the lookout for the edge of a tall tower so I didn't end up like Sibilan the Scholar." He gave Cazia a sly, sideways look. "But my uncle is at Tempest Pass, and he's been studying portal magic all of his life. I expect he will be able to examine the spells holding this creature together. With the Scholars' Tower at the palace fallen, he is probably the last theoretical scholar in the empire. The rest are clerks, builders, miners, and healers. I don't think spears are going to hold this tide back, any more than serpents or mountain men will."

Gerrit made an unhappy face. "Spears built this empire, my king."

"Magic built this empire," Lar responded. He leaned forward and tapped his index finger on the table for emphasis. "The Gifts of the Evening People gave our spears an advantage over every other tribe's spears. Healing, clean water, healthy crops, building stones, breaking stones: the empire would not exist without those spells. I don't say this to denigrate the brave soldiers who have fought and died for us; they deserve our respect. But so do the scholars. In fact, our next council should include Doctor Warpoole; see that she is made welcome. The empire has always relied on its scholars; we just don't like to admit it."

Gerrit and Treygar looked at each other mournfully. Cazia wanted to believe they were simply unhappy to hear that their new king planned to force them to share power with the scholars, but she knew there was more to it than that.

Lar wasn't finished. "We've conferred enough. We must inform the tyrs without further delay. Commander, have your steward show me to your mirror; you will want to ready the fort's defense. My Tyr Treygar . . . "

Stoneface stood out of the chair. "My king."

"Go to the sleepstones. The sooner you are healed, the sooner we can start our trip. Col, go with him. Caz can stand with me when we talk to your father, but I'll want you beside me for our journey."

Cazia's brother shook his head as he stood. "That's a blessing." His voice sounded odd. "Won't you need all of us to stay here as hostages?"

Lar looked guiltily at Cazia. "My father may have wanted twice the in-surance against yours, but times are stretched. I think I can only afford one."

Cazia couldn't hold it in. "That's not fair! You're going to visit Tempest Pass without me? Your uncle is the most famous scholar in the world!" Lar had promised to take her to visit him someday. Why should her brother, who knew nothing of magic, be the one to go?

"Nothing is fair, Caz."

The look on Lar's face made her flush with embarrassment. If she wanted to stay close to Lar while he was king, she'd have to control herself better. She was going to have to grow up. "I'm sorry, my king."

"You can still visit when this is all over." He said it almost as though he believed it. "

"In the meantime," Cazia said, trying to recover herself, "please com-mand Doctor Warpoole to answer my questions. She did something odd back at the tower and I think we need to know what it was."

Lar nodded. "If it turns out to be important, let me know. And I hope you understand how glad I am that you'll be safe here, inside this fortress."

The tall steward opened the door for the king, who led the way into the waiting room. Cazia hung back, well aware that she was a fifteen-year-old girl—a hostage—and Stoneface, the commander, and even her brother were more important than she was. Apparently.

When she did step through the doorway, she heard Lar say, " . . . answer her questions as though they were coming from me."

Doctor Warpoole gave Cazia a flat, unreadable look. "Yes, my king."

Col squeezed her hand. "I'll make my own way to the sleepstones, Caz. Make sure Father believes we're still hostages."

Her brother shuffled slowly down the stairs, leaving her alone with the scholar.

Doctor Warpoole's eyes were wide and bright. "The king says you have questions for me?" Her voice was brittle and it put Cazia on edge. But the administrator would just have to swallow her pride; Cazia had the king's support.

"I saw the spell you cast on the top of the Scholars' Tower—the green mist you sent down through the trap door? I know that spell wasn't one of the Thirteen Gifts, and I—"

Doctor Warpoole slapped Cazia's face. Hard.

CHAPTER NINE

THE MEDICAL CHAMBER WAS NOT IN THE LOWEST LEVEL OF THE FORT, but it was close. Tejohn had to stumble down long flights of stairs to reach them. How did men with leg or back injuries manage?

The sleepstones themselves were marble slabs broad and long enough to accommodate the empire's largest soldiers with some room to spare. Each had been enchanted with a healing spell that would persist for years—as many as ten, if it was not often used. The hunched, portly woman who met him at the entrance and examined his wounds wore a scholar's robe with a medical patch. He glanced at her cheeks and saw they were dry.

"Can you cast a healing spell, doctor?" Tejohn asked. A direct spell worked much more quickly than a sleepstone.

"This way to the beds, my tyr" was all she said in return. She held out a gray robe made of coarse wool.

Frustrating. Tejohn sat on the edge of the nearest bed and carefully changed into the robe. The Bendertuk boy was unconscious on the next slab but the Freewell boy had not yet arrived.

"Do you have any old injuries, my tyr?"

Tejohn thought again of those long flights of stairs. "Knee aches," he said, touching it with his good hand. He had no idea why she would ask; he'd been badly cut in one of his first battles, and by the time his turn on the sleepstone came, it had begun to heal naturally. It often twinged in sour weather, and Peradain was infamous for its rain clouds.

He noticed a slender iron needle in the scholar's hand as she gently directed him to lie back. The sleepstone pulled him down into slumber.

He awoke with a start. His mouth was parched and his throat dry. The scholar gave him a tiny cup full of purified water. Tejohn drank it and demanded more. The little woman took her time returning with another tiny cup almost brimming over, and by the third or fourth, he realized she was deliberately making him wait between each drink. "Bring the pitcher."

"Small sips, my tyr. That's safest."

The process continued until Tejohn had had enough. A boy brought him a piss pot to use. The gouges on his forearm had not healed shut and he still couldn't use his wrenched arm. "How long?"

"Hardly any time at all, my tyr," the scholar answered. "Please lie down."

The Bendertuk boy was still there but Freewell was not. Had he come and gone already? Had the prince—*the king*; he must break that habit—ordered him to be healed quickly with a direct spell while Tejohn himself suffered this slow, uncomfortable process?

It didn't matter. If the new king didn't favor him, there was nothing he could do about it except prove himself all over again. He noticed a spot of blood on the front of his bad knee. It took a moment for him to recognize that it was the size of the scholar's iron needle.

He lay down as he was bid. "Next time I wake," he told the scholar, "I want to see marching armor laid out for me, along with a sword, shield, and kit. See to it."

"Yes, my tyr. Now please rest."

Tejohn's thoughts were already slipping away.

When he woke the next time, he was not nearly so thirsty. Tejohn sat up quickly, pleased to feel rested and well. The gouges on his arm had healed completely; only thin white scars were left. He could move his shoulder freely and without pain. There was no swelling at all.

He slid off the bed and looked around the room. The lantern burned low, but his eyes were well adjusted. The Bendertuk boy was still sleeping. His color was good, although his lips were white and dry. He would be waking for some water of his own soon. Again, there was no sign of Colchua Freewell. As he went to the pot, he noticed a marching kit laid out on a table.

After he relieved himself and slowly drank his fill, he examined the armor. It was steel and of good quality, which did not surprise him at all. Ranlin would never offer shoddy equipment to a friend and a tyr of the empire, even though some of his men were still wearing bronze. As long as Lar received equal quality or better, Tejohn was satisfied.

First he strapped on his greaves, then the flannels, then the boots, the skirt and fringe, then finally the cuirass. Even the helm fit him; the felt underpadding was thick around the sides of his narrow skull and guard did not squash his oversized nose. Maybe Ranlin had the armorer take his measure while he was unconscious. Best of all, the helm came to a simple blunt point at the top. Tejohn thought the tall brushes that had become so popular among officer classes were silly and dangerous. Yes, they impressed barmaids, but one errant blow could knock a helm askew, blinding a soldier. Not that it was his place to criticize the generals who allowed them.

The only disappointing thing was that the shield and cloak bore the green-and-brown Four Rivers emblem of the Gerrits rather than the black and red of the Third Splashtown armor he'd left in Peradain. He was proud of those colors and was keenly aware that it was possible that no one would ever wear them again. Still, he would make do.

Tejohn inspected the sword next. Like Ranlin's, it was longer than a common soldier's, with a blade that was three hand-lengths rather than two. The dagger was old but well made. The hilts didn't match, of course, but he wasn't marching in parade. He strapped them to his hip and wondered where he would find himself a sturdy spear.

He went up the stairs, past the drab scholar's office and the hunched little woman working there. "My tyr," she said, hurrying toward him, but Tejohn brushed by. Presumably, the scholar could cast a healing spell—she wouldn't have the patch otherwise—but while Tejohn couldn't order her to cast it, he didn't have to be pleased about the time he'd lost sleeping.

Out in the courtyard, Tejohn saw the sun striking the peaks on the western side of the pass. It was morning, but was it the next morning? Had it been two days? Three? He needed to find—

Tejohn stopped short. There, at the far end of the courtyard, was a temple. Yes, he needed to report to Lar as soon as possible, but it had been more than a month since he had prayed properly. What hope did they have if they didn't pay their respects to the gods?

He strode across the yard, slinging his shield on his back and removing his helm. The entrance was a short passageway in which the walls had been carved to resemble a round tunnel—an Eleventh Festival style that he didn't care for, but aesthetics weren't important. He bowed his head at the entrance. "Grateful am I to be permitted to travel The Way."

He strode into the main chamber, which had a traditional layout for a fort or holdfast. In the center of the room was a marble statue of Fury in his Soldier avatar, painted in the Gerrit Four Rivers colors. Instead of a sword, he held a stone lamp.

Tejohn noted that lamp—little more than a bowl, really—held oil and wick but had not been lit. He looked around for a priest; none were in evidence. Maybe they were still at breakfast. Nevertheless, it was bad luck to neglect Fire in a time of war.

He knelt at the feet of The Soldier and prayed for guidance in battle and guidance in his passage on The Way. Fury was the god of humans and human action, and he was traditionally the second to receive praise and prayer, after the Great Way itself.

After that, Tejohn entreated Fire to sweep his enemies from The Way but pass him by. He did his best not to look up at the unlit lamp; the priests insisted that the gods heard prayers in a swamp or a latrine just as well as in the temple. Still, it seemed disrespectful to ask favors when they couldn't even trouble themselves to light a Fire-taken lamp.

Then he had a choice of which chapel to visit, and which god to entreat. One didn't ask the Little Spinner to turn more slowly, so he wouldn't pray there. Not yet, anyway. And it had always seemed arrogant to him to pray to Song for deeds yet undone, although few others seemed to share his opinion.

Instead, he went into the chapel for Monument. He knelt before the marble obelisk, chipped on one side but enduring, and prayed for the strength to preserve the Italga line, the empire, and whatever goodness and happiness could be found within its borders. War against the beasts would be difficult enough, but if civil war broke out as well, Fire might take the entire empire from The Way. Tejohn prayed, fervently, for the strength to remain himself, to protect his king, and to protect his empire. To withstand. Only then did he dare to pray, as fervently as he could, for the safety of his wife and children.

Maybe it was his imagination, but he was sure he felt Monument's blessing.

When he finished, he went into the main chamber again. He'd intended to leave, but Wimnel Farrabell emerged from the Song chapel. He was haggard and red-eyed, as though he'd been awake all night.

"My tyr," he said, startled. "I'm sorry to intrude—"

"You are not intruding. The temple is open to all." Tejohn noted his rumpled clothes. "Have you been keeping vigil all night?"

The man rubbed his face. "I can not sleep. I left family behind, my tyr. My wife, my children . . . I'm sorry. I know I shouldn't discuss such things. But I wanted Song to remember them, to . . . "

Farrabell seemed to run out of things to say. Tejohn understood. "If you have finished your prayers, try to sleep. We will need you soon, I think."

The driver nodded and moved toward the exit. Tejohn passed him and went into the Song chapel. There was no statuary here, of course, no lute or drum or harp. Song was a god of sound and memory, and if there was one thing these Eleventh Festival designers did correctly, it was to not represent him at all. Tejohn knelt and—briefly, because there was much to do—thanked Song for remembering those who had already fallen.

The temple exit was also carved like a tunnel, and he paused again inside. "Grateful am I to be permitted to travel The Way." The first and last prayer at every temple was to the greatest of the gods, The Great Way, through whom all were born, lived, and died, if they were lucky enough to be permitted to stay on the path.

Back in the courtyard, he saw more bustle than before. A pair of priests, brooms in hand, jogged toward the temple to do their daily sweeping. Servants, soldiers, and clerks hustled toward the Great Hall and Tejohn followed them, hoping to find the king breaking his fast.

He wasn't there, but one whiff of the morning meal made him light-headed. He hadn't eaten in some time, apparently, and so he grabbed the nearest steward and demanded breakfast.

At the upper end of the hall, Doctor Warpoole sat alone. He turned away before she could catch his eye. Tejohn had no desire to speak with her.

At the nearest table sat the captain of the guard, the one who'd held a spear on him when they'd landed their cart. Tejohn grabbed a chair from a nearby table and sat beside him.

"My tyr," the captain said, turning pale. "I—I should apologize for the way I acted—"

"Never apologize for doing your duty, captain. What is your name?"

"It's not one you will have heard before, my tyr. We're a Fourteenth Festival family; my father still has okshim hair on his clothes. I am Reglis Singalan."

The young man seemed to be scowling again, but Tejohn suspected it was a natural resting expression for him. "Fourteenth Festival? You've done well for yourself, becoming a captain so soon after joining the empire."

Reglis nodded to acknowledge the compliment. "My people are mostly still servants, herders, and farmers. I was lucky enough to be born broad of shoulder and long of leg, so I was, let's say, *encouraged* to take up the shield. And I'm glad of it."

Tejohn liked him already. "How long has it been since we arrived?"

"Three days and four nights, my tyr."

Fire and Fury, that was too long. "What news?"

"None that I know, my tyr, only rumors."

"What rumors, then?"

Reglis rubbed his beard, then shrugged. "Few of the tyrs took the prince's story at face value, so they sent ten flying carts to check out the city. Three didn't make it back, but the ones that did told quite a tale. The city has been burned and largely abandoned. Some grunts still hunt there, but most have moved outward, spreading like a stain on wet linen. The bulk of them seem to be headed south, toward the coastal cities. Few have been sighted in the north. Everything beyond that is rumor and fear-mongering tall tales."

Grunts? Is that what people were calling the beasts now?

The steward set a platter in front of Tejohn: apricots, rice balls, and roasted mutton. It was better fare than the rank and file would get, but it was his due as a tyr. "Thank you, captain."

After he finished his meal, Tejohn strode into the yard. Lar would have been given the finest room available and if they had wine in the fort he would still be abed. Time to rouse him.

A group of soldiers walked by, wooden practice swords in their hands. Tejohn addressed the nearest. "Soldier, how do I get to the commander's tower from here?"

The man looked as though just asking the question was cause for arrest, but a fat-faced young man at the back of the group spoke up before anyone else could. "My tyr, the commander is there." He pointed to the top of the south wall. They were too far away for Tejohn to see, but he saw no reason to point that out. "The quickest way is a flight of stairs just on the other side of the temple. You can't see it from here, but I'll show you the way if you like."

"That won't be necessary." Tejohn started toward the temple, hearing them murmur behind him. The fat-faced one would be telling them his name by now, and he wanted to be well away from that conversation.

On the wall, the southerly wind pulled at his hair and shield. It was chilly down in the fort, but above the protection of the walls, the incessant wind out of the Sweeps was sour and damp. His kit should have included a heavier woolen cloak.

Ranlin stood before a knot of six guards, looking irritated and dissatisfied. Bittler Witt and Cazia Freewell were also there, and the way the guards surrounded them made it clear they were in custody.

Tejohn walked toward them quickly. As young men, he had been a foot soldier and Ranlin Gerrit his captain, but now that he was a tyr—even a tyr without holdings—their roles were reversed. "Is there a problem, commander?"

"Yes, Tyr Treygar. Colchua Freewell is missing. He'd been acting strange. Last night, he left his quarters and hadn't been seen since."

"He hasn't left the fort!" the Freewell girl insisted, her tone annoyed. "He would never abandon Lar."

"His wound," Witt said. "It was bothering him. He couldn't sleep."

Tejohn was startled. Hadn't he gone to the sleepstones? "I assume you're conducting a search."

Ranlin nodded. "Yes, my tyr. It was the first order I gave."

Tejohn turned back to Witt and Freewell. During the flight from the city, they'd seemed committed to the king; could he have misjudged them? Tejohn had been born to a farming family. He wasn't accustomed to intrigue. "Is the king safe?"

Cazia Freewell gave him a sour, disappointed look. "Col would never hurt Lar. Never."

Tejohn looked down at the girl. *Stoneface*, she had called him; it had surprised him at first, but although he knew she meant it as an insult, he liked the name. Better to be like Monument and show no emotions than reveal the true feelings of one who is little more than a former farmboy with a knack for killing.

"He has to ask," Ranlin said. "It's his duty to think of the king first in all things. But look for yourself, Tejohn. The king is in the yard, sparring."

Tejohn grunted in surprise. Lar Italga, sparring? He stepped to the inner edge of the wall and turned toward the circle of sparring men just below.

Great Way, there was the prince; Tejohn recognized him immediately by the way he hunched down behind his shield, a habit Tejohn could never get him to break. He faced off against a burly fellow close to his own height, and their shields clashed against each other. Lar was getting the worst of it, but he wasn't slacking and he wasn't trying to make a joke of it.

"I'm sorry, my friend," Ranlin said from close behind him. "If I'd known the king had planned to train at sword and shield, I'd have found him a private space and a private tutor until you returned."

The burly guard caught the king's shield and pulled it away, a maneuver Tejohn had tried to teach many times. The guard's sword thrust toward the king's belly, and Tejohn's heart seemed to stop. But it was just a practice sword—a stick, really—and the man didn't come near enough to connect. Lar had tried to counter the attack, but while his move had been exactly correct, he didn't have the strength or speed to make it work.

The same fat-faced guard who had given Tejohn directions stepped into the sparring circle to address the king. Apparently, he was Tejohn's substitute, and though Tejohn longed to hear what they were saying, they were much too far away. Judging by his demonstration, he wanted Lar to start his counter much sooner. Lar said something in return, and all the men in the circle laughed long and hard.

"It's fine," Tejohn said, thinking that he was looking down at his replacement. Should he have laughed along with the prince? Would that have made him a better teacher? It was painful to think so. "I'm pleased to see the king so dedicated. And the men seem to like him."

"He has won them over," Ranlin said. "Me, too. His mind is quick and strong. If only his body was, too."

Tejohn watched the prince prepare for another round with the burly guard. That would come in time, if Fire spared him.

"What is that?" Cazia Freewell said. She pointed toward the eastern peaks.

Tejohn peered upward, squinting to see what she was indicating. Ranlin blurted, "Fire and Fury," and some of the others made small exclamations as well. Tejohn felt a surge of irritation; his eyesight had never been exceptional, but the eastern peaks were close, almost directly above the fort, and there was no reason he couldn't—

There. He saw something dark brown move against the darker background of the mountain. Could it have been a bird? Tejohn was unsure how far away it was and couldn't fairly judge its size.

"How big do you think that raptor is?" Cazia Freewell asked.

"Too, too big," Ranlin answered.

Then, as if it realized it was being watched, the bird spread its wings and took to the air.

Tejohn couldn't help himself. He gasped in surprise and his sword was in his hand before he realized he wanted it, even though a small, rational voice in his head insisted bows and spears would be more useful.

But the raptor wasn't hunting. It angled northward, tail feathers spread in a fan as it floated slowly against the headwind toward the Sweeps. Fire and Fury, it looked like a hawk, but its wingspan must have equaled six men lying crown to heel. At least.

Tejohn kept his voice low and his attention on the huge bird. "Ranlin, my friend, have you ever seen a raptor that size before?"

"Never," the commander answered. "I've never even heard anyone boast of having seen such a thing."

Tejohn didn't know what to say to that. Two strange beasts appearing in the world at once?

"Commander!"

They all turned to see one of the servants running up the stairs. He was out of breath and clearly alarmed.

"What is it, Gald? Have you found Freewell?"

The servant stumbled forward as he hurried toward them. He was dirty and half starved, like most of the servants in the empire, and sweat poured down his face. He didn't look like a man with urgent news; he looked like he was running for his life. "No, commander, but we did find his coat atop the northern wall." The man spared a furtive glance at Cazia Freewell. "It was quite bloody."

"Where?" Cazia Freewell rushed toward him, but Tejohn held up his hand to stop her.

"That's not what brings you up here in such a state," he said.

"No, my tyr," Galt answered. "I've just been down in the pens. The chicken, okshim, and sheep have all been killed, commander. They've been torn apart as if by a wild animal. The keepers as well."

Ranlin turned to the nearest guard. "Toll the bell three times. I want stations before the tone dies."

Tejohn stepped to the edge of the wall. "My king!" he roared.

The men stopped sparring. Lar turned to look up at him, and perhaps sensing something in Tejohn's tone, handed his practice sword to the fat-faced fellow. He said something that made the guards laugh and bow to him as he walked toward the stairs.

A woman started screaming. Tejohn started toward the stairs. Where was the sound coming from? It was impossible to tell in this wind, but he knew he'd made a terrible error. He should have hurried to Lar immediately.

Suddenly, a servant sprinted out of the temple, screaming and waving her arms. Her rough gray tunic flapped behind her. She ran directly toward the king.

Moments later, a blue-red streak raced after her. It slammed into the woman's back, knocking her sprawling onto the yard.

Fire and Fury, it was one of the beasts, already inside the walls. Tejohn had only a glimpse of it, but it seemed smaller than the creatures he'd faced in Peradain, and darker, too. Those other beasts had fur the color of pale lilacs, but this one was dark blue with red streaks down its back. A third creature?

The beast bit down on the woman's shoulder and she screeched in terror and pain.

Tejohn leaped from the wall onto the staircase below. Too late he remembered his bad knee. If it gave out on him, he would tumble helplessly down the stairs while his king faced the creature alone.

It didn't give out. It didn't even twinge. His sword already in hand, he ran down the stairs as fast as he could go.

It wasn't fast enough. Below, the creature had already cast aside the woman and rushed directly at the king.

Chapter Ten

THE SOLDIER WHO'D TAKEN CAZIA'S QUIVER WAS SO INTENT ON LAR that he didn't notice her steal back one of her own darts. Still, even as she started the hand motions to cast the spell, she could see that the grunt would reach the king long before she finished.

A disconnected part of her mind watched Lar as the grunt charged him. She saw the surprise on his face. She saw his hesitation. Then she saw him reach for his sword and, in his panic, miss the hilt. He slapped his hand flat on his hip as he brought his shield up.

Then it was too late. The creature slammed into his shield, bowling him over. Cazia felt a surge of terror, but in the depths of her spell, it seemed almost remote. She heard the cries of the guards around her, saw Tyr Treygar sprinting forward with his sword drawn, and she knew he could never reach them in time.

The beast clawed at Lar's shield. *They're too close together for me to take this shot.* But the spell came to its finish and she flung her hands and her will forward anyway, launching the spike at the monster.

The creature bent low, biting down hard on Lar's shoulder and upper arm. The king shouted, and now that Cazia no longer had her spell to blunt her reaction, his pain tore at her. She was reaching another dart when the first one struck.

It sank deep into the grunt's side just below its arm, almost vanishing beneath the fur. The creature fell away from her and thrashed in the mud. Stoneface had almost reached it when it went still, but the old man plunged his sword in anyway, just in case. Then he turned to the king.

Unable to lay her hand on a dart, Cazia turned and realized the guard who'd taken her quiver was gone. Bittler was still there, gaping at her, but Gerrit and his guards had run for the stairs, following Tejohn toward the king.

Cazia didn't follow. The guards had their swords drawn, and were forming ranks around Lar's body. Tejohn was shouting orders, and moments later, a guard ran toward the tower, presumably for a medical scholar. Gerrit started giving orders, shoving soldiers into an orderly square, then summoned a line of spears from the hall and ordered them to advance on the temple where the grunt had come from.

In short, the yard was full of soldiers who were angry and heavily armed, and Cazia was still a hostage. She knew Gerrit and Treygar would never order her death, but it only took one pissed-off soldier with a knife to ruin her day. They were Enemies still.

Treygar squinted up at her suddenly. There was something in his expression that startled her, and she couldn't guess what he was thinking. He didn't look grateful that she'd killed the grunt, that was for sure.

"We should go," Bittler said.

They walked along the wall, circling westward away from the main part of the commotion. Cazia didn't even realize where she was going until she was halfway there. That servant, whatever his name was, had said Colchua's bloody coat had been found atop the northern wall.

Fort Samsit was one of the first forts built after the Sixth Gift had been modified to create large stone blocks. Later forts had towers that blocked the walkways, but in Samsit, the towers were set back a few feet, allowing someone to walk a complete circuit of the wall if they wanted. In their eagerness to block the mountain pass closest to Peradain, the early kings had erected the fort without perfecting the design.

The northern part of the wall was narrower than the southern, because the peaks hemmed them in, but the wall walk was very broad to allow soldiers room to maneuver. They also did not reach the same dizzying heights, because the ground was so much higher in this part of the pass.

From the gate below, a narrow road—little more than a path, really—led into the mountains, barely large enough for two carts to pass. It went nearly straight through a sloping field of tumbled black stones. Beyond that, in the far north, Cazia knew she would find the wilderness of the Sweeps.

"Do you hear that?" Bittler asked. She couldn't at first, because of the unceasing wind, but then she did: rushing water. She looked along the western edge of the pass. There. A waterfall high on the cliff face ran into a pool, and from there, it flowed down a canal dug out of the mountain rock. It might have been the source of the water for the fort, which surprised her. Didn't they have an enchanted fountain?

Water flowed off the Southern Barrier all the time—tremendous, gushing waterfalls, some hundreds of feet wide. Doctor Twofin had once bored her for an entire afternoon comparing rainfall levels with the output of the falls at Splashtown in particular and the Waterlands in general. Now that she was here, looking up at the storm clouds blowing around the peaks, she wished she'd paid more attention.

"Are you all right?" Bittler asked.

"I'm stalling because I'm afraid," Cazia said. She hadn't planned to be honest, but her words had come out that way. "I'm afraid to find Col's body. I don't want him to be dead."

"He's not. I'm sure of it."

Cazia started walking along the wall, moving quickly so Bitt wouldn't see her irritated expression. Bittler was nice enough when he wasn't trying too hard.

To her surprise, he kept up with her pretty well. "You're looking a little better today."

"Thanks," he said. "The stewards here let me eat what I want. I haven't had any stomach pains since yesterday."

He suddenly stopped walking. Cazia stopped, too, and followed his gaze.

A pair of servant girls were on their hands and knees, scrubbing the stones near the northeastern corner of the wall.

Goose bumps ran down Cazia's back and she started running toward them. Bitt did his best to keep up, but she soon outpaced him. "Stop!" she called to them. "Stop stop stop!"

The nearer of the servants paused long enough to look up at her, then went back to her work. "Sorry, miss," the woman said. She had a long face and a lilting western accent. "Chief's orders. If I don't finish the job, I'll be getting a lash."

Cazia started a spell, which the servants noticed only when it was nearly finished. They fell away from her, falling onto the wet stone in their dirty skirts, just as the fire blossomed from her hands.

The servants screamed in terror and scrambled away from her even though the flames hardly came near them at all. "There!" she said. "Now you can tell your chief, whoever that is, that I forced you to stop. Now go!"

The women turned and ran. Cazia felt a flush of embarrassment at bullying them. Yes, they were probably Enemies just like the servants at the palace, but they hadn't *done* anything to her. Not yet.

She closed her eyes and cleared her thoughts, then looked down. The wash water was a darker pink than the stones of the wall. She honestly had no idea what she could have learned by looking at the spilled blood—were there just a few drops or a huge pool?—but it was too late. The servants had already scrubbed the whole area.

A wave of vertigo ran through her but it was too swift to make her fall. Where was Colchua? Could he really be . . . gone? Just like that, with no warning at all? If he was, then the whole of the world was Cazia's Enemy.

Bitt finally caught up with her, jogging slowly and trying to catch his breath. "There," he said, peering into the bucket. "See? That hardly looks like any blood at all. If he'd been killed, he'd have lost more than that."

"Unless the grunt ate him," Cazia said, just because she didn't trust his hopeful tone. The words made the skin on her arms prickle.

"It's not like a grunt could have swallowed Col whole. Right?"

She had to concede that one. When the grunts had killed on the dais back in Peradain, they'd torn people limb from limb. Cazia shuddered at the memory of it. The thought of her older brother—so tall and so quick to smile—having his arm ripped off—

She seemed to be shuddering quite a lot lately. Those awful thoughts kept coming back to her unbidden and at the oddest times.

Never mind. She breathed deeply, trying to slow her fluttering heart. If the others could stand it, so could she.

She went back to the wall, examining the top of the battlement. There was another spot of blood the servants had missed. She braced herself against the stone and leaned out, ignoring Bittler's nervous warnings to be careful.

There was more blood on the far side of the wall. The top of the crenellation was lightly spotted, but the outside had been smeared as though with a very bloody hand.

Could Colchua have escaped from the grunt by slipping out of the fort? It would have proved Gerrit right, if not in the way he expected.

She looked down. The ground was at least sixty feet away and there was nothing but jagged rocks below.

Cazia wouldn't have safely jumped into a calm, deep lake from this height. Could Col have made it alive to the bottom if he'd been fleeing from a grunt? The answer was obvious and chilling: not without a rope.

The bloody smears looked like the fingers were pointing downward, as though he was climbing out of the fort rather than into it. Was he trying to escape? Was he going to confront a grunt climbing up the northern wall?

There was no way to know. What she did know was that her brother had been attacked, and she couldn't imagine how he could have survived.

Something ugly and awful swelled in her chest, and she felt tears brimming. Not fair. None of this was fair. Her brother didn't deserve to be thrown from a wall in the middle of the night. He didn't deserve to be murdered, not when he'd risked so much to help Lar and Vilavivianna. He'd nearly thrown his life away for a nation that treated him like a traitor, and all that was left were a bucket of pink water and a pair of dirty rags.

As if on cue, the servants came back to the top of the wall, but this time, they trailed behind a wiry little old man with wisps of white hair blowing in the wind. His clothes were threadbare, but they were clean.

"Now see here!" he said, his thin voice almost imperious. This must be the chief. Chief servant? The palace had so many servants that they were divided up by where they worked and were overseen by men and women called "whips." She supposed a fort was too small for that sort of arrangement, but she didn't much care. "You mustn't set these girls on fire! They're only trying to do their jobs!"

Cazia glanced at the servants behind him. Each of the *girls* was old enough to be her mother. "Has Commander Gerrit seen these bloodstains?"

"No, and I hope he never does! I don't appreciate pranks, you know, especially when they might earn a lash for me or my girls! This is an imperial outpost and it must be kept tidy!"

He waved at the two servants, who crept forward to take up their washrags. Cazia had no intention of setting fire to them, but Bittler grabbed her arm as though she did and dragged her away.

She wanted to start kicking them all, or create stone blocks to wall them off from the mess. If that really was her brother's blood, it might be the closest thing she would ever get to a corpse she could bury.

At the top of a flight of stairs, she sat, dropped her hands into her face, and wept. Yes, a scholar shedding tears. Fire could take anyone who tried to tell her to hold them in.

She felt Bittler settle beside her and laid his arm on her shoulder, but it was no comfort. Her brother's coat. Her brother's blood. He was the only family she had in the world that mattered to her, and now it seemed as though he was gone.

Four days before, when she had seen him climb down that tether rope onto Vilavivianna's roof, she'd felt this moment coming.

"It wasn't much blood," Bitt said. "Truly. When I was in the Bay of Stones with Timu last year, we saw a grass lion attack a farmer. We tried to save the fellow but . . . Anyway, the amount of blood around him was shocking. Really.

I think that if Col had truly been attacked and killed by a grunt on the wall, the amount of blood would have turned that bucket scarlet."

"Great Way, Bit," Cazia spluttered. "Shut up."

"I won't believe he's dead until I see his body." After that, Bittler stopped talking and let Cazia continue her weeping.

Cazia suddenly felt different, though; Bitt was right and she knew it. She slowly realized that she was crying out of fear rather than grief and the tears seemed to fade away. After a few deep breaths, she wiped her cheeks and they went down the stairs.

This end of the fort was a maze of halls and work rooms. It was just like the servants' halls in the palace, but narrower and with more turns. Bittler was sure he knew the way and got both of them lost. Cazia had to ask a steward to lead them into the yard.

Old Stoneface waved them toward him, urgently. Cazia didn't trust the way he was looking around the yard, as though expecting another attack at any moment. Her first instinct was to slip back into the hall and make her way to her room, but that would only have made him suspicious. They hurried toward him.

"Where have you been?" Treygar hissed at them.

"To the northern wall," Cazia said. "Where my brother's bloody coat was found."

Treygar's normally grim expression softened for a moment. "Of course. What did you discover?"

"Very little, thanks to the overeager servants in this place. The spot was almost completely cleaned by the time we arrived. However, I did see a bloody handprint on the outside of the wall, as though Col was trying to climb out of the fort."

"He couldn't have, not without a rope."

"I know. But if he were trying to escape a grunt, or to push it over the wall . . . ." Stoneface gave her a doubtful look and she nearly lost her temper. Better to change the subject. "Where is Lar?"

"The squad accompanied him down to the medical chamber. Now that you two are here, I think we—"

"There's our little killer!" It was Commander Gerrit, striding across the yard toward them. Earlier, he'd been scowling at Cazia with that scarred, ugly face, but now he beamed at her. "That was quite a shot you took. My best archers would not have risked it."

Cazia didn't trust his sudden change of mood. "I am not an archer. I'm a scholar."

Treygar scowled at that and peered carefully at her face. Gerrit didn't seem to care. "Still! I should offer you a watch on the walls. That's a compliment, by the way."

Cazia took a deep breath. He was trying to be nice to her, and she was responding with a stink face. Whether he was an Enemy or not, he was too powerful to antagonize without good reason. "Thank you. Lar is my cousin, my friend, and my king. I will do whatever he needs from me. Can I have my quiver back?"

"I'll see you get a bigger one." Gerrit turned to Treygar. "What did I say, Tejohn? What we need are hunters."

Treygar shook his head. "That was different from the ones who came through the portal in Peradain. It was smaller and darker, for one thing. For another . . . " He stepped aside, revealing the dead grunt on the ground behind him. Cazia couldn't help it. She gasped. "The ones in the capital didn't have these spikes on their elbows or thumbs. They didn't have the thickened hide on their backs. No stripes. No wrinkles at the brow."

"Yes, I know," Gerrit interrupted. "And they were the color of pretty purple flowers. So, what do we have here? A youngster?"

"I don't know."

"Well," Gerrit said, "I just wish you hadn't brought it here."

Cazia spun on him, startled. "There's blood on the northern wall where my brother's coat was found. Don't you think the creature came over the wall there?"

"I do not." Gerrit's face was set. "We have watches, young lady, not just inside the fort, and they are good soldiers. Careful soldiers. They would have seen a creature like this before it ever reached the walls, let alone while it was climbing them."

"What makes you sure I brought it here?" Treygar's tone wasn't offended or upset, only curious, as though they were working out an intricate puzzle together.

"Nothing has come inside these walls for the past ten days but you. You landed on a moonless night, in the center of the yard. The grunts are strong; you said so yourself. It must have clung to the bottom of the cart—by the axles, perhaps—for the trip. When you landed, it was frightened by the torches and spears, and fled across the yard."

Cazia didn't like the way that sounded. "I think we would have seen it."

"You were all looking at the captain of the guard. And why not? He attracts a lot of attention when he's waving a spear point in your face. This old fort has dozens of unused rooms and passages. The beast must have hidden itself until it could no longer deny its hunger. Perhaps it tried to make its way to the wall to escape and there met your unfortunate brother. Then, seeing the heights it would have to descend, it went straight below to the pens."

"All this would make sense if we were talking about bears or lions," Treygar said. "But not these creatures."

"In Peradain," Cazia said, "the grunts rushed forward into battle."

"Young lady," Gerrit said, "beasts of the wilderness do not *go into battle*."

His tone was so condescending that Cazia had a sudden urge to kick his iron-covered shins. A sudden memory of the grunts breaking through the scholars' wall of flame made her wince. "You weren't even there!"

Gerrit bared his teeth. "The day I need counsel from the daughter of a—"

"Commander Gerrit," Stoneface said. His voice was calm and cool, and it took Gerrit's attention just as it had taken the driver's during their flight from the city. "She has seen battle for the first time after a life in the palace. Haven't you noticed that she has the flinches?"

"What?" Cazia had no idea what they were talking about, but she was sure she didn't like it. "What do you mean?"

"Fire take me," Gerrit said. "I'm a slow-witted old fool. My apologies, young lady. I—I will be about my duties, my tyr."

Treygar nodded to him as he backed away. "Wait," Cazia said. She didn't know what they were talking about, and she feared that if she asked them to explain, they would assume she didn't understand anything. "My brother. There was blood on the outside of the wall, I swear. The creature could have come that way, couldn't it?"

"It could have, yes," Gerrit answered. Now he sounded as though he was humoring her, and that made her hate him all the more. "If we believe it slipped by the watches and scaled the wall without being seen, *and* if we believe as well that there is another portal out in the Sweeps somewhere, a new portal that we've never even heard of before." He stroked his beard. "I am sorry, young lady, but while that is possible, I think my explanation is more likely. However, I will double the watches. Is that all?"

The man's stubbornness infuriated her, but she began to wonder if her anger was stronger than it should have been. "No," Cazia said, pretending his *Is that all* was meant for her. "We still haven't found my brother's body. I think he fell outside the fort, and I would like to go out to search for him."

The commander's expression made it plain that he was about to refuse her, but he said, "Yes, but not today. We have injured and dead within the walls already, and Colchua Freewell might lie here somewhere, as yet undiscovered, in a basement chamber. We must also conduct another search in case there are more creatures. Give us a day or two to look inside before we search without."

He left without waiting for her answer.

She was about to stomp off to her room, where she could do nothing but pound her fists against her bed, when Stoneface touched her shoulder.

"Lar is below," the old man said, "at the sleepstones with the others."

"Others?"

"He was not the first one bitten, but he was the first to be put onto a sleepstone. He will be unconscious for a while, the scholar said, but when he wakes, I'm sure he will want to see you."

The kindness in his tone was so startling that she almost burst into tears. "I will be there with him."

"Good. Be sure to collect that large quiver from Commander Gerrit first. Lar also told me, as he was being carried off, that I should speak with you about Doctor Warpoole."

"Oh!" Cazia had nearly forgotten about that. She'd gone to Lar immediately after the scholar had slapped her and told him everything, but Lar had done little more than frown and thank her. Cazia hadn't seen the scholar since, although Ciriam collected a platter of food at the great hall several times a day to bring to the commander's tower.

But if Treygar wanted something from her, he was going to have to give her more than a few kind words. "What are sinches?" He looked flummoxed by that, until she said, "You told Commander Gerrit that I have them."

"Ah. Actually, it's the flinches. Sometimes when a young soldier sees a particularly horrifying fight—and they do, often—the memory of it will make them flinch involuntarily. You can see it in their face: the image comes back to them at an unexpected moment, and they close their eyes, or bare their teeth, or look away. And sometimes they become jumpy and quick to anger—"

"I'm not a flower, you know." Cazia made sure to look him in the face; there wouldn't be any watching from the side of her eye this time. "I'm not a flimsy little doll."

"I have suffered from them myself," he said in his calm, commanding way. "I was older than you by some years, but those memories have haunted me for all of my life."

"Oh," Cazia said, feeling foolish. He wasn't insulting her after all, and somehow that didn't ease her anger. Maybe he was right. Maybe she needed to keep a closer watch on herself. "I'm sorry. I didn't know. Is there anything I can do to control it?"

"The only thing that ever worked for me was to talk with friends. Friends or peers, I should say. Grief shared is grief lessened."

"Thank you. About Doctor Warpoole . . . Her loyalty to Lar is not decided. I'm not sure what she's going to ask for, but she seems to think he needs her more than she needs him."

"We'll see about that."

The way he said that made Cazia shiver. She pushed on. "Did you see the spell she cast at the top of the tower? Just before we closed the trap on the grunts?"

"No."

"Well, I'd never seen one like it. I have not been taught all thirteen of the Evening People's Gifts, but I know them by sight. The spell she cast was not a Gift."

"What's this?" Tejohn took a step closer to her, lowering his voice and glancing around as though he was afraid someone would overhear.

"It was a green mist that floated down into the tower, melting wood and flesh like water on snow. I swear to you. Her hand motions were unlike any spell I'd every seen, and I have no idea where she learned it."

Tyr Treygar's voice was barely louder than a whisper. "Are you saying she invented her own spell? That she's a *wizard*?"

Wizards were villains out of children's stories. "She doesn't seem like one. She certainly hasn't gone hollow. I've always thought it was forbidden for scholars to learn wizard spells."

Treygar's face was grim. "Do you think the scholars are holding private Festivals to trade with the Evening People in secret?"

"Through another portal?" Cazia said more sharply than she intended. "Out in the Sweeps?"

Stoneface glanced up at the cliff where they'd seen the gigantic raptor, and when he looked down again, his expression was grave. "Thank you" was all he said, but from Tyr Treygar's lips, the words sounded like a death sentence.

CHAPTER ELEVEN

B Y THE TIME THE KING FINISHED HEALING, THE DAYLIGHT WAS NEARLY spent. Another day lost, but there was little they could do about it.

Lar Italga made his appearance in the great hall for the evening meal, and Tejohn was startled to see him wearing both armor and scholar's robe. It was so similar to what Doctor Rexler had worn on that day outside Pinch Hall that for a moment, Tejohn thought the king meant to honor Rexler.

But no, the king and that dead traitor were nothing alike. Tejohn stood, as did everyone else. The soldiers down on the floor muttered as Lar strode to his place at the table, but Tejohn couldn't judge their tone. Did they disapprove?

It seemed not. Tejohn looked again at the hall floor—he hadn't noticed at first that there were a number of civilians clustered in the near corner. They were mostly farmers and bargemen by the look of them, seeking refuge behind walls in a time of war.

What's more, they seemed to be nodding and sharing hopeful looks. Lar was making a good impression here, something he'd never managed in the Morning City.

"My tyr, it is good to see your scowling face," Lar said as he sat in the empty chair beside Tejohn. Everyone else sat a moment later.

"My king, I'm glad to see you as well. I take it you are fully recovered?"

Lar lowered his voice. "I tried to convince the medical scholar to cast a healing spell on me but she wouldn't. Apparently, she is still suffering the effects of a midwinter raid. They had too many casualties for the sleepstones, and the repetitive spellcasting put her at risk."

Tejohn glanced at the king's armor and robes. There was no need to ask what she was at risk of. "I understand, my king." It suddenly occurred to Tejohn that, with the Scholars' Tower fallen, he had no idea how many medical scholars were left.

"Tomorrow, we—" Lar stopped and glanced out on the floor.

The fat-faced guard stood facing the king some distance away. By the sheepish look on his face, Tejohn knew what he would say next. "Permission to speak, my king?"

Lar smiled down at him. "My substitute weapons master! By all means, approach."

The man stepped forward, knelt on one knee—which made him vanish below the edge of the raised table—then stood again. "I am sorry to approach during your meal, my king, but the others have . . . Actually, they bullied me into asking after your health."

Tejohn felt his face grow hot. Was this common soldier questioning the king's fitness?

But before he could respond, the king laughed. "Nothing a little snoring couldn't fix. In truth, I've taken longer naps to recover from an attack by several jugs of wine."

Soldier and king laughed together. "My king," the soldier said more quietly. "The men have begun to call you The Laughing King."

Lar absent-mindedly touched the white mourning scarf around his throat. "Better that than King Fast-Breaker. That's what the beast would have made of me. But come. Get to your real question. I can see by your eyes that you are afraid to ask it."

The guard worked his lips for a moment—clearly nerves had dried his mouth. Then he said, "Was that one of them, my king? Was that one of the beasts that invaded the capital?"

This was too much. Tejohn leaned forward and glared at the man. "How long do you intend to interrogate the king?"

The man flushed, stepped back and knelt. He'd gone too far and he knew it. "Forgive me, my—"

"Tyr Treygar is correct," Lar said. "This is a question for your commanding officer, but as you have been my substitute weapons master, for the moment I believe that would be me. So! The beast you saw this morning was not one of the creatures that attacked Peradain and killed my royal parents, along with countless other good and blameless people. It was a gentle younger brother, slow of foot and weak of jaw, but not nearly as pretty. Do you understand?"

"I do, my king. Thank you, my king." He glanced nervously at Tejohn.

"Now," Lar said as a steward set a bowl of mutton soup in front of him, "since my weapons master has recovered, I no longer need a substitute. I release you. Resume your previous duties."

The guard bowed again. "Always yours, my king." He backed away, practically fleeing to his table.

Tejohn watched him closely for some sign of insolence but could detect none. "He was awfully free with your time, my king."

"True, but I think I've won him to my side. Only a million more to go, eh? But tell me, Tyr Treygar, is it true about Col? Was he killed by the beast?"

Tejohn felt a familiar sour feeling well up in him. The steward set a bowl of soup in front of him, but he suddenly wanted nothing to do with it. It was time to talk of the dead. "It would seem so, my king. I am sorry. So many of us were wrong about him, and just as he proved himself—"

"Has his body been found?"

"No. The soldiers have searched every disused corner and old storage chamber in the fort, but there has been no sign. It appears the Freewell girl was correct; he must have been dumped over the wall."

Lar's face was pale and his lips were pressed together so hard they turned white. "You may call her 'Cazia,' my Tyr. That is her name."

"My apologies, my king. Our oldest habits are the hardiest."

"I want his body found. He and Timush risked their lives when everyone believed they would betray me. I may not be able to give my parents a decent burial, but Fire take us, I can do this for my best friend."

Tejohn felt an odd thrill run through him. Lar Italga taking command? It was more than he could have hoped for. "I'll speak to the commander tonight. And I'll make sure he puts Cazia Freewell in charge of it."

"Good. Now I hereby appoint you as my shield bearer and chief counsel."

"What?" Tejohn bumped his soup bowl, sloshing half of it onto the table. "My king, you can not be serious."

"The Laughing King is always serious. That's what makes him so amusing."

"Then my first counsel is this: find someone else."

"Who?" Lar leaned close to him. "I mean this question most seriously. Who can I find? I know you dislike me, but you were willing to die for me. Who else deserves my trust?"

"Your shield bearer should be a diplomat. He should be clever, organized, and observant. I was born a farmer—"

"It's a rare farmer who earns a tyrship."

"A landless tyr."

"Even better."

Tejohn turned away and looked over the crowd. Now that the king had been served, they were eating again. But too many were glancing nervously toward the high table. Toward him.

He mastered his expression. "There must be someone more suitable."

"There are," Lar said as he lifted his bowl of soup and drank. "But they're all dead back in Peradain. If you refuse to serve, I'll have no one to turn to but Doctor Warpoole."

"My king. . . . "

"I agree. Tyr Treygar, we have an unfriendly history. This morning, I might have slain that grunt myself if I hadn't shirked your training. I recognize my error. Must I command you to put aside your completely justified anger for the greater good?"

Tejohn held himself very still. "My king, that history was erased the moment I saw your royal mother fall. I swear to you that I will serve in whatever way you require, but this should be a temporary appointment, like your fat-faced guard over there, until you find someone more skilled in diplomacy."

"Accepted." Lar lifted his bowl and drank. "Have the driver ready to take us both to Tempest Pass in the morning, along with anyone else you think we'll need. I want to bring the body of the grunt along for my uncle to examine. With the Sweeps headwinds, it will probably be a ten-day trip by cart."

Tejohn took a deep breath. "My king, as my second counsel—"

"You mean to dissuade me from this trip."

"I do. The tyrs will never pledge their spears to your cause if they believe you are in retreat."

"I can not lose what I will never have. The only tyr in the empire who will back me is sitting across from me neglecting his soup, and he can field no armies."

"But to divert for ten days—"

Lar lowered his voice. "Tyr Treygar, drink your soup while I tell you the true reason we are going to Tempest Pass. Go ahead, lift your bowl. I want our conversation to look as normal as possible. In truth, my uncle's library is not tremendously large. He has a . . . reputation. It's difficult for him to find literate assistants willing to join in his hermitage. So, while I do plan to speak with him about the portals and these creatures, in truth I'm hoping to learn a spell from him."

Tejohn felt a chill run down his back. After what Cazia Freewell had told him about Doctor Warpoole's wizard spell . . .

"Drink your soup," Lar said. "I don't want anyone seeing that expression on your face. The spell is not made by human beings, my tyr. It's not a wizard's spell. It's derived from the Fifth Gift, the water-purification spell. And it is so deadly that my father trusted only one man with it."

"His brother."

"Yes."

"What about the spell Doctor Warpoole cast at the top of the Scholars' Tower?"

Lar sighed. "I wish I'd seen it. Caz is smart and well trained, but there's an awful lot she doesn't know. She doesn't know how much work goes into researching the Gifts, or how long it took to change, say, a spell to create a flat stone for laying roads into one that creates huge granite blocks for walls and fortresses. She doesn't know how many scholars live in seclusion so that, if something should go wrong, they would be the only ones to killed."

"I'd heard rumors . . . " Tejohn wasn't sure what else to say.

"Of course. I was not kidding when I said it was scholars who built the empire. They don't just risk their lives. Why do you think no man or woman in this fortress has yet seen me, a scholar-king, shed a single tear for my royal parents? Scholars risk their sanity, their station in life, their—" He stopped himself, realizing he was wandering from the point he wanted to make. "The Fifth Gift can purify water at a distance. The variation my uncle is safeguarding can do the same to men. It can turn the insides of their skulls to water—at a distance—twenty or more at a time."

"Fire and Fury," Tejohn exclaimed. "You cannot."

"Grunts tore my royal father to pieces. Do not try to tell me what I can not do. I don't care whether it's honorable or not. I will murder these beasts by the hundreds, if I can get near enough. And if any tyr dares oppose me, I will break their squares the way I break stalks of grass under the sole of my boot. I have plans for this empire, Tyr Treygar, plans that would end much of the misery and injustice my people endure, plans I have nursed since I was a small boy. But all will come to nothing if Kal-Maddum slips out of Italga hands."

Tejohn gaped at the young king beside him. It was astonishing to hear such talk from his young pupil. *The Laughing King,* that fool had called him, but Tejohn realized he had no idea who Lar Italga truly was.

And this spell he wanted, this variation on the Fifth Gift, might have been the weapon he needed to hold onto his throne, but it made a soldier like Tejohn—and all the good men and women he'd ever served with—into useless stick figures. Irrelevancies. Could he serve a king like that?

Tejohn remembered the last moments of Doctor Rexler's life, when the wizard had launched volleys of darts into the advancing square or sprayed huge clouds of naked flame. The wizard's expression had been dull and slack and his face had been slick with tears. Not for the soldiers he was killing, no, but for whatever secret, endless grief hollowed scholars suffered. Tejohn later heard that Rexler had once been a loving husband and father, but his hunger for power had taken him too far and emptied him out.

Lar Italga was nothing like that. His face was alive with conviction, and it seemed to Tejohn that the young man had become acquainted with an old friend: the righteous urge to slaughter his enemies.

Tejohn nodded. "I'll see that we are provisioned and staffed." For one absurd moment, Tejohn imagined himself commandeering the entire Samsit garrison, but not even Ranlin Gerrit would allow that. Still, if the king did not find spears to support him, he would never sit on the Throne of Skulls again.

But there was one thing Tejohn couldn't deny: there was an undeniable thrill to seeing a leader speak with such conviction. Even someone like his former pupil could give heart to others when he had a plan and the will to carry it out. Fire and Fury, Tejohn was ready to believe they might actually succeed.

"By the way," Lar said, "my substitute sword master kept trying to get me to narrow my stance. I did better when I used your techniques, my tyr."

The king's bowl was taken away and a platter of flat bread and roasted bird set in front of him. Tejohn received his a few moments later, but he ate without pleasure. An empire with him as shield bearer and Lar Italga as scholar-king . . . He could not imagine how it would work. He spent the rest of his meal wondering what the collapse of a empire would look like, and how he could tell if it had already happened.

After his meal, Tejohn met with the commander in his chambers. Ranlin was himself in the midst of his meal, and they talked comfortably about the journey the king would take the next morning.

Then Tejohn told him who he wanted to bring with him.

"You want to trust the king to the son of a Fourteenth Festival family?"

"His parents were overthrown by Peradaini troops," Tejohn said, "and Reglis has become one himself. If he's like most new citizens, he'll be embarrassed by his father's weakness and will cleave to the strength of his new masters. His children and grandchildren will be most likely to be nostalgic for 'the old ways.'" Tejohn shrugged. "I know that's not the usual way of looking at these things—"

"Never mind," Ranlin said. "The greater portion of my objection was the difficulty in replacing him. I had planned to name him Watch Commander. Still, it will be even harder to pry that scholar away from Doctor Warpoole."

"I have a piece of sharpened iron at my hip that will sever any connection nicely. But first, we must make sure she knows the proper spells."

"Of course." Ranlin jolted in his seat. "Fire take me, Tejohn. I have not asked after your wife and children."

"It's okay, my friend. It's been years, hasn't it? I don't think you've even met them. They're safe. They were visiting family in East Ford during the Festival."

The commander clapped Tejohn's shoulder happily, shouted for his steward, then gave her a list of names to summon.

Ranlin's meal only half finished, the two friends unfolded a patterfall cloth and began setting up the pieces. Reglis was the first to arrive, and he accepted his assignment with grim satisfaction; he also had recommendations for his replacement as captain and for a woman skilled with bow and spear who could serve as scout. She knew the Sweeps well, he explained, and had excellent vision. Tejohn accepted his recommendation gratefully.

Then Doctor Warpoole arrived with Doctor Eelhook in tow. Cazia Freewell entered with them, looking confused by the summons and uncomfortable with the company. She stood some distance from the two scholars while Tejohn spoke with them.

"Doctor Eelhook." He stood and stared at her with a grim expression. "You can not cast a healing spell, can you? Can you at least create a sleepstone?"

The scholar shook her head nervously.

Doctor Warpoole spoke up, her tone bland. "Many of the storm houses at the edge of the empire have been built with sleepstones, so there should be some available if the need—"

Tejohn waved a hand at her and she fell silent with a look of irritation. "Doctor Eelhook," he continued, "can you cast a fire spell? Can you purify water?"

"Yes," she answered meekly. "I cast those every day as part of my duties."

"What about creating and crumbling stones?"

Doctor Eelhook looked uncertain about these. "I've cast them in the past. It has been a while, but I'm sure I could refamiliarize myself."

"Do so. Tonight. What about creating a translation stone?"

"No," she said simply. Doctor Warpoole looked at the floor.

"I can do that," Cazia Freewell said. "I was learning to imbue inanimate objects with Gifts, like lightstones and fountain stones."

"How many can you make?" Tejohn asked her.

"Not many. It's a difficult spell and easy to overdo. Also, the stones themselves can be dangerous."

"One will be enough, then. I'll need one by sunrise."

"I'll start right away," she said, and started toward the door.

"Don't go yet," Tejohn told her. He turned to Doctors Eelhook and Warpoole. "You understand why I'm asking these questions, don't you?"

"Because you and the king are leaving," Doctor Warpoole said. "And you want a scholar with you."

Tejohn nodded, meeting the administrator's gaze evenly. "If I had a choice, I would bring this young woman here." He pointed at Cazia. "She seems to be more scholar than either of you."

"I can read and write!" Doctor Eelhook blurted out, as though Tejohn was supposed to be impressed.

"We have always had a great many duties to perform back in the tower," Doctor Warpoole said smoothly. "This young woman has nothing to fill her time but loitering in the practice rooms." She glanced over at Cazia. "And eating."

Cazia Freewell's eyes went wide and she bared her teeth, but Tejohn held up his hand. She held back whatever remark she was about to make. Tejohn kept his voice low and steady. "She's also a child of fifteen. Doctor Warpoole, do you have any polished silver in your chambers?"

"No," she answered, her voice just as steady. "The prince forbade it."

"The king," Tejohn corrected her. "Remember that. After we leave, I'll need you to contact any scholars in the empire you can reach with the commander's mirror. Talk to them about the . . . the grunts. Confer. The king will want to hear a report from you."

"I am happy to serve."

"But you are never to use the mirror alone, under pain of death."

Doctor Warpoole's smile was bitter. "The king does not trust me, then?"

"*I* do not trust you. I would prefer that you prove me wrong."

The woman did not answer, only nodded briefly. Doctor Eelhook cleared her throat. "Excuse me," she said, "but I am not the best person . . . I would much rather remain here in the fort."

"So would I," Tejohn answered. "Go down into the courtyard and practice creating and breaking rock. Work as though your life depended on it. I will send Miss Freewell to you in time so you can practice together with darts. Doctor Warpoole, please accompany her in case she needs tutoring."

Doctor Eelhook looked miserable as she headed for the door; Doctor Warpoole followed her out, her eyes hooded. Cazia Freewell lingered, her arms folded across her chest and her lips crooked in an insolent frown.

Tejohn softened his tone when he spoke next. "You know why you can not go with us, don't you?" *Hostage.*

"Yes."

"Will you make a translation stone for me right now?"

She sighed, then removed the net of blue stones from her hair. She'd worn it at the Festival, he remembered. She cut one of the little stones with a knife from her pocket and set it on the table. Then she took a deep breath and focused.

Tejohn had seen spells cast before, of course. Even before he became a soldier, he'd seen itinerant scholars cast spells on crops and wells; he'd seen them lay foundations of temples and imperial counting houses—they were a fact of life.

But the Twelfth Gift was rare. Doctor Twofin had once explained that it operated at the edge of the Evening People's craft—they could manipulate the physical world in profound ways, but their magic could not affect the mind. This was as abstract as the Gifts could get, and that made it very challenging.

Still, during their trip, they would have to land the cart at sunset every day, and not everyone in the empire could speak Peradaini.

The entire spell took some time, and when it was finished, the stone looked no different than it had before. Cazia Freewell, however, was pale and sweaty, her eyes distant and her jaw slack. She looked almost comatose as she stood by the table, a line of drool hanging from her lip.

Ranlin gave Tejohn a nervous look, then he moved close to her. "Child?" He laid a hand on her shoulder and turned her toward him. She looked up at him vacantly—there were no tears on her face. Tejohn was never going to get past the habit of checking scholars for tears.

Ranlin glanced at Tejohn. "We should carry her to the sleepstones."

"Hold," Tejohn said. With the back of Ranlin's spoon, he mashed a bit of beet and carefully ladled a bit onto her tongue. Her lips closed over it and she swallowed hungrily. Tejohn gave her a bit more, then a bit more. Eventually, she roused herself enough that she clutched at his soup bowl and drained the remainder in one long slurp, then tore into the remains of his mutton and rice.

"I should have eaten first," she finally said, after she had nearly cleared the platter. "Stupid. Doctor Twofin said to eat first."

"It was successful, then?" Ranlin picked up the little gem.

"*Kolga honchar idangiday, bissep,*" Tejohn said.

The unscarred side of Ranlin's face flushed. "Great Way, Tejohn. There's a young girl present."

Cazia stepped away from them. "A young girl who couldn't understand a word of that, and who doesn't want to know."

Ranlin set the stone down, and Tejohn picked it up. "How long can I hold it safely?"

The girl shrugged. "Doctor Twofin said no more than an hour a day before you start talking gibberish."

Tejohn slipped it into his pocket. "Thank you, but you're not done yet. First, I need you to go to the armory for darts and quivers. One for Doctor Eelhook, and one for yourself."

"There's no point," she said. "Eelhook is useless."

"Lar Italga's life may depend on her. I don't expect miracles, but do what you can. Tomorrow, Commander Gerrit will assign some bodyguards to you so you can go outside the fort and search for your brother's body."

The girl gasped, then lunged forward and hugged Tejohn with surprising strength. When she stepped back, she rubbed the spot on her temple where she'd bumped his cuirass. "Ow."

"Thank Lar Italga," Tejohn said. "It is the king's order that his body be recovered and given a hero's funeral. I am entrusting this task to you."

"I'll see to it." She looked up at him, eyes brimming as she forced herself to smile.

"Girl," Tejohn said calmly. "Scholars can not shed tears in public. You must control yourself or lose your hands."

That ruined her happy mood, as he expected. She still left the chamber with her head high.

Ranlin stepped over to the patterfall cloth and moved his spider to the center square. Tejohn studied the positions and tipped over his throne, conceding the game. *Lar needs a shield bearer with a better head for strategy.*

He found Wimnel Farrabell sitting alone in the great hall, a half-empty bowl of wet rice and a jar of wine before him. One of the village women was playing a summery tune on a flute for the benefit of the whole hall, but Wimnel didn't seem to hear it. Tejohn ordered the man to his bed. If he couldn't sleep through the night, Tejohn promised to choke him into unconsciousness. The driver looked up at him with haggard red eyes and wearily stood from his chair, then shuffled out of the hall.

After that, Tejohn went to the armory for a stout spear and a second dagger. By the time he returned to the yard, the steward was loading food and other supplies into the cart. The grunt's corpse had been left on a wagon behind the temple to hide the smell.

He took a heavy carpet from his room and rolled the beast in it, then ordered the stewards to put it in the rear of the cart. Camping on the ground every night with a smell like that would draw bears and hill lions from all around, especially after several more days, but no matter. This was the king's will.

Tejohn then went to the commander's tower and let himself into the command room. The communication mirror at Fort Samsit was small, an oval of polished silver barely larger than his palm, but it was enough.

He laid his hand on it and spoke Moorlin Stillwater's name.

The tyr of East Ford came to the mirror quickly, almost as though he'd been anxiously waiting for news. Tejohn disappointed him by saying he had none. He only wished to speak with his wife and children.

To his credit, Tyr Stillwater had moved Tejohn's family into the holdfast as soon as he heard of the attack. It took little time at all for Laoni and the little ones to be brought into view.

"You look tired," his wife said by way of greeting. She wasn't much for sentiment and never had been. Great Way, she looked so young, especially with the little ones climbing on her. And of course, he knew what she would say next before the words came out of her mouth. "Have you been eating?"

Leave it to a baker to worry about his meals. "I have," he said, "by royal command. How are you? How are the skirmishers?"

"Noisy. I miss you," Laoni answered, absent-mindedly touching the long, dark hair that hid her scarred right ear. "Are you coming to East Ford? The rumor in the holdfast is that Lar and his betrothed are going to take refuge in the Indregai peninsula."

"I wish that were true," he said, but before he could say more, Insel and Alina pushed into view. The twins competed more than any siblings he'd ever seen; this time, they each sang a song about rivers and cakes, then demanded that Tejohn choose a favorite. He refused, as they expected, and they pretended to be heartbroken. Then Teberr climbed into view. He had learned to clap his hands together in rhythm, and father and child kept a beat for too short a time.

Eventually, one of Laoni's cousins ushered the children from the room, so they could talk. "As you can see," his wife said, "the skirmishers still baffle and distract enemy forces."

"Tomorrow, I leave on a mission for the king," Tejohn said. "It shouldn't be a long one, but things are unpredictable right now."

Laoni's dark eyes never wavered. "Will it be dangerous?" She tried to make it sound casual.

"Everything is dangerous. Listen, there's something I want you to do. You still have cousins in Beargrunt, don't you?" Beargrunt was the Indregai city on the eastern side of the Straim. It was polite to call it a sister city, but in truth, it was little more than a village.

"A few," Laoni said. "Most came west when the bridges reopened for trade."

Tejohn nodded. "Take what supplies you'll need to do some baking, and go stay with them. Make it a long visit."

"What's wrong? Are things really that bad?"

Her eyes were shining as though she was holding back tears. If she could be strong, he would be, too. "They aren't good. I expect that, in the next few days, the bridges across the Straim are going to be destroyed." There was a gasp from Laoni's side of the mirror. As he expected, someone was listening to them. "I want you to already have accommodations when the refugees begin to cross."

"There's a problem," Laoni said. Her gaze was steady, almost as if she was afraid to look at anyone else in the room with her. "I've already been questioned, more than once—"

"What?"

"Not officially," she said, her tone suggesting official questioning might happen soon. "I haven't been brought into the courts, but people are suspicious of us. They think you sent your family away from Peradain because you knew an attack was coming."

"Are you . . . " He stopped himself. Of course she wasn't joking. It hadn't even occurred to Tejohn that someone might think this, but it should have. "No one could have known about this attack."

"And yet they don't understand why you sent us away."

"Because I didn't want you to be here when the Evening People arrived!"

Laoni glanced to her left. "That's what they can't believe."

"That's because they don't know anything about the Evening People. Do people really think I wanted to parade my wife and children in front of them as though my life was yet another performance for them to enjoy? To have them stare greedily at us, and talk to us as though we were children, and . . . " Moorlin Stillwater was listening to this conversation, and who knew how many more of his retinue, too. Tejohn needed to say exactly the right thing, or his wife and children would be suspects forever. "Laoni. You are my wife and the mother of my children. You are the woman I love. I'm not going to put you on a stage in front of those arrogant dogs as if you were the happy sequel to *that Fire-taken song.*"

He thought he could see her relax slightly. Had he said the right thing? He hoped so.

"Be careful," she said.

Tejohn nearly said, *I already tried to throw myself out of a flying cart,* but he bit the words back. "I will be. Look after our skirmishers. Tell them about me."

Her mouth twisted then, as though the pain and misery she'd been holding in were suddenly too much for her. Moorlin Stillwater took her place before the mirror as she began to cry.

"My Tyr Treygar," he said. "Are things really so grim that we should send our loved ones into the frontier?"

But Tejohn wasn't in the mood to talk to him. "You know as much as I do. Maybe more. Make what preparations you believe to be wise." Then he broke the connection.

His wife and children would be safe on the far side of the Straim, serpents or no. Safer. He hoped. Great Way, his hands were shaking.

Now to his duty to the king. He spoke Challry Grimwood's name.

It took some time for a servant to summon him, but Tejohn knew he would not yet be abed. The Grimwood lands lay to the north and west of the capital, and of all the holdings near the throne, Tyr Grimwood was the only one he would call a friend.

Challry had no time for pleasantries. Yes, the beasts were attacking Grimwood lands, driving farmers and fishermen into his holdfast. The attacks seemed to be without strategy, and Grimwood's soldiers had taken to hunting the beasts like animals, without much success.

No, he had not heard anything from Beddalin Hole, Stormfast, or Long Ridge, nor did he know what had happened to the men stationed there. The conversation was interrupted on Challry's end by a messenger with urgent news, and Tejohn said his farewells to an empty mirror.

Next he spoke Linder Holvos's name and received a reply almost immediately. He was Tyr of the city of Rivershelf and all the flood lands around it. Yes, he told Tejohn, the beasts had invaded, carrying off everyone they didn't tear apart and devour. The attacks on his lands—and on the lands of the Redmudds to the west—were intensifying. Linder's own niece had been bitten and carried away.

As with Challry, he'd had no word from Beddalin Hole, Long Ridge, or

Stormfast. He also had no time to talk. He wished Tejohn a long journey upon The Way, then broke the connection.

Tejohn went to his room and lay on his cot. Second Rivershelf had been stationed at Stormfast, and Second Ironwood at Long Ridge. If those soldiers had fled the fall of Peradain, they would have returned to the tyrs who pledged them.

What he had only feared to be true was as good as confirmed. The king's spears had been wiped out. Tejohn pulled the blanket up to his chin, thinking that Lar Italga was king of a single spear. What a heartrending song that would make.

Just as Tejohn thought sleep would never come, it did.

He awoke with a start. The sun had not yet risen. Good. He gathered his kit and took an extra blanket from his room, then went down to the great hall to break his fast. The king, dressed in armor, was already there, feasting and jesting with the soldiers. Tejohn scowled at the king's new helm; it was steel, yes, but the red plume at the top was ridiculous.

Tejohn ate in silence, taking his fill. He watched as Mister Farrabell and Doctor Eelhook entered, both looking slightly lost, and ate mechanically from the platters they were given.

Shortly after sunrise, it was time to go. They climbed into the cart, and, as the driver tied himself into place, the king gestured toward a number of other tethers on the railings. Tejohn felt a surge of relief as he tied himself into place. The captain, Reglis Singalan, and a skirmisher mounted their spears on the side of the cart.

"My tyr," Reglis said, "I present Arla Grimfield, archer and scout."

She was about Tejohn's age, in her mid forties, with long ropy muscles and a blunt, puggish face. Her nose was crooked and her chin was scarred, but her eyes were bright and wide like someone who had spent her life far from the safety of stone walls. "Grimfield? Any relation to the Grimwoods?"

"Cousins, my tyr. My people fought the empire longer and harder than the Grimwoods did, so when we surrendered, there were too few of us to make a tyrship. Of course," she added hastily, "that was a long time ago. Grimfields are a Fifth Festival clan; even then we were a small one. We're mostly miners and seed farmers now."

"Why did you become a king's spear?" Tejohn asked, his voice carefully neutral.

"King's bow, if you would, my Tyr. I was raised in these mountains in a traveling mining camp. My brothers and cousins were servants to a wandering scholar looking for silver. Dig here. Dig there. Set up a forge. Tear it down. One day, the mine flooded. The water that gushed out had terrible . . . *things* in it, and I knew no one was coming skyside from there. We kids marched out of the mountains into the nearest town below. I didn't like turning the mill wheel or tanning hides, so I did what I had to do to buy my bowstring. I've spent my whole life scouting these mountains and traveling the Sweeps."

Tejohn nodded at her. "Strap yourself in."

The driver, of course, stood at the back of the cart. Lar sat on the bench in front of him, just beside the grunt's body, which the servants had loaded into the back. Tejohn took the spot directly beside the king. Doctor Eelhook sat in front of Tejohn and Reglis beside her. The front bench stayed empty; Arla stood at the rail, apparently too anxious to settle down. The scholar and the king both wore quivers of iron-tipped darts.

The food was packed at the front, but of course with the scholar along, they would not need to carry water. Packed beside Tejohn were the weapons and few tools they might need—hatchet, rope, blankets.

A line of spears stood at attention to see them off. Cazia Freewell broke through the crowd and leaned over the railing to embrace the king. "Timu?" he asked her.

"Not awake yet," she answered.

"Tell him I'll be back as soon as I can."

She nodded and stepped away. From just behind her, Vilavivianna stepped forward. Tejohn didn't recognize her at first in her woolen hat and quilted jacket.

"My betrothed," Lar said kindly. "Have you thought about my offer?"

"I have. But tell me, what will happen to me if you are killed?"

"I can't answer that. I'm sorry."

"You are the king," she said. "Command these men to send me back to my people if you do not return from this mission."

"If I do not return," Lar said, his voice low but still kind, "no command I give will have any force."

The foreign princess didn't like that, but there was nothing for her to say.

Ranlin Gerrit approached. "My king," he said to Lar. Then he turned to Tejohn. "My friend. Safe travels to you both."

Lar smiled. "Thank you, commander. Driver, ascend."

"Yes, my king," Wimnel said, and the cart floated off the stones of the yard. Tejohn looked down at the men, knowing he would probably never see any of them again. Still, Reglis and Arla aboard, the number of King Lar's spears had doubled since last night, and he'd added half as many bows. That was a trend he'd like to see continued.

As they rose, the front of the cart dipped to counter the headwind. They rose higher, passing over the hall, the commander's tower, and finally the northern wall, headed deeper into Samsit Pass.

After rounding the first bend, Arla turned around. "This is the place. Up this way." She pointed toward a cleft in the rock. The driver turned toward the peaks and started toward them, cutting west into the mountains.

Tejohn's stomach suddenly felt tight. "What is this?" he called over the wind. He laid his hand on his knife. "We are going to the Sweeps."

"It's all right, my tyr," Lar said. "I agreed to this route while you were busy with other things."

"My tyr," Arla said to him, her gaze turning several times to the dagger he had not yet drawn. "The northern end of Samsit Pass is narrow, and the winds are tricky. It's fine for marching, but carts tend to smash against the rocks like rafts in a white rapids. This route will take us through two long high valleys to a safer entrance to the Sweeps."

She sounded quite reasonable and Lar seemed content with the plan. Tejohn moved his hand away from his knife.

They rose up through the cleft into the first valley. Tejohn was startled by how stark and beautiful it was. There was clear blue water below, with a few scrub pines growing along the edge, and black rock cliffs that looked as though a giant had carved out this valley with two mighty blows with an axe. At least, that's how Tejohn imagined it, by the blurry colors he could see.

They moved slowly through the valley though they were on a pleasure cruise. The lake below had to be terribly deep and cold.

Lar said, "Looks almost good enough to dive into, doesn't it, my tyr?"

Tejohn recognized a joke when he heard one, but he had no idea how to play along, so he said the obvious thing, "I'd like to double knot your tether now, my king."

Lar laughed. Arla turned back toward them. "You wouldn't want to swim in that water, my king. Yes, it's fresh at this end of the Barrier, not salty, but it's cold enough to kill you. Besides, it has merfolk in it."

"I thought merfolk were a myth," Doctor Eelhook said.

"Pft." Arla didn't think much of that. "Camp near the water's edge and you'll learn different. One tried to drag my baby brother into the depths, but my father changed its mind with a spade. Their flesh is light and flaky if you don't overcook it."

•

It took most of the morning, but eventually, the cart came to the source of the lake, a waterfall only a bit higher than the southern walls of Fort Samsit. They passed over it and entered the next valley. The water here was shallower and moved more quickly, and the pines grew farther apart. Tejohn looked over the rail, hoping to see some sign of fish people.

"Doctor Eelhook," the king said, "ready a dart."

That startled everyone. The king was looking at something on the cliffs above, but the black disk above the cart blocked Tejohn's view. He leaned down, practically to the king's shoulder, and saw it.

It was another one of those Fire-taken birds, watching them from a cliff above. This time, Tejohn was almost close enough to get a decent look at it. Its head was the dark brown of well-tanned leather, and its chest was eggshell white with speckles on the upper left breast. Its talons were intimidating, at least the size of the blade of Tejohn's new spear, and its beak looked to be even longer than the sword at his hip.

Arla whistled in amazement. "Well, hello there, stranger."

"I don't want to see that thing get above us," Tejohn said.

"We can't go higher, my Tyr," the driver sounded nervous. "The winds—"

"Let's not worry too much yet," Lar said. "It's just watching us."

"It's a predator, my king," Arla said. "And it's big enough to carry one of us off."

"But will it bother with an entire cart?"

Arla untied her tether and fetched her bow from the back of the cart. "My king, if you give me something to hold on to, my bow and I will ride atop this disk." She jerked her thumb upward at the black-painted wood above her. She was close enough to touch it but she didn't. Tejohn understood her reluctance.

"Can't," the driver said. "I'm sorry, my king, but we can't put anything on top of the disk. We'd drop out of the sky."

Lar laughed. "That's an awfully fussy flight spell you have there, isn't it?"

"I'm sorry, my king." The driver sounded resentful. "I'm sure the scholars are . . . " His voice trailed off. Of course, the scholars were not going to do anything to improve the flight spell. A month ago, the Scholars' Tower was probably filled with people studying it; they were all dead now.

The bird watched them fly the length of the valley. Tejohn wished he had his spear in hand. The king had a plan and the conviction to see it through, but all would come to nothing if this thing moved against them while they were vulnerable in the sky.

"Scout," Tejohn said. "Do you see any others?"

"No, my tyr. Just the one."

He looked over the rail of the cart at the huge raptor. It was far away now but still seemed to be watching them.

The driver was watching the bird, too. "Watch where we're flying, Mister Farrabell," Tejohn said. The man jumped as if poked with a stick, then immediately started to gain altitude. The valley ahead of them continued to rise, and the valley floor became rockier. The stream wound this way and that, splashing among jagged rocks.

"There goes our blessing," Lar said, his voice sounding slightly odd. Tejohn turned back to see the raptor launch itself from its perch. Great Way, it was a formidable thing. Let it keep to the Sweeps, stealing okshim from herders, or snatching merfolk from the lakes. The king took a dart from his quiver. "What do you think, shield bearer? Should I kill it?"

"Yes," Tejohn said without hesitation. "If it gets close enough to hit the heart on your first try, please do."

But it stayed well out of range, then turned away and glided back toward the waterfalls and the lower lake.

Doctor Eelhook breathed a sigh of relief. "Grateful am I be permitted to remain on The Way."

"Watch for more," Tejohn snapped. "And watch for shadows to see if they're above us."

"Arla," Lar said, while everyone looked about them, "you've truly never seen one before? Never even heard rumors?"

"No, my king. There are all sorts of stories about the Southern Barrier, and even more about the Northern. Merfolk, living shadows, three-eyed goats who talk like men. Giants made of avalanche rock. Trees with roots that grab you and pull you underground. Most are fancies prospectors say to amuse and outdo each other. Some of it is even true. But giant birds? Never."

No one spoke much after that.

At midday, Doctor Eelhook passed out jerky and sour rice cake, then filled a pitcher with water for them. It tasted, as ever, of metal, but Tejohn had drunk enough of it to know there was no danger.

The sun was getting low over the peaks ahead when Tejohn called out. "How much farther until we camp?"

"Not far," Arla answered. "We need to be clear of the slow-moving water, and the pass is close. This route should shave at day off our journey, at least."

Night falls early and quickly in the mountains. The sun dipped below a peak ahead of them and the valley was shadowed beneath a twilight sky. Arla pointed toward the northern cliffs. There was a break between them, a place where the sheer walls had fallen outward. A long slope of scree lay before them, and beyond it the still-sunlit expanse of the Sweeps.

Arla pointed to a flattish stretch of solid rock. "There, driver. Do you see? No mud."

Wimnel's voice was tired and grateful. "I do, thank you." While the passengers untethered themselves, he settled gently onto it.

After a long day of sitting, Tejohn wasn't spry enough to spring over the rail, but he did manage to stand and walk about without any embarrassing groaning. The stony ground sloped down to the stream, which was shallow over broken rocks. That meant no merfolk, he hoped. To the left was a stand of thin pines, including two that had fallen.

He turned around and surveyed the slope behind him. The Sweeps, far below, were an undifferentiated blur of fading yellow. Beyond that, he knew, was the Northern Barrier, which he couldn't even make out as colored blurs in the dimming light.

Technically, all the land on this side of the Northern Barrier and west of Fort Piskatook was part of the Peradaini Empire, but it was what Amlian used to call "lightly held." The king's spears occasionally swept through, collecting taxes and reenergizing the spells on the sleepstones up here, but it was unlikely that the nomadic peoples of the Sweeps considered themselves imperial citizens.

Reglis and Arla scanned all around them but, judging by their expressions, they saw nothing worrying. Good.

Lar took the spare hatchet and went into the pines with Reglis. Tejohn caught up to them and plucked the tall red plume from the king's helm. "Your shield bearer would never take such liberties, my king, but your weapons master insists."

Lar smiled crookedly. "And it made me feel so jaunty, too."

Tejohn returned to the campsite to find Wimnel inspecting the cart in the dying light, checking the pegs and knotted ropes to make sure they were still tight. Doctor Eelhook had refilled the pitcher to wash their cups, and Arla was building a fire pit down in a shallow depression near the base of a hill, where the flames could not be seen from the Sweeps below. Whether by design or happenstance, the cart rested at the top of the depression, acting as a windbreak.

Tejohn took his spear out of the cart and walked a circuit around the campsite. All he could find was a snake resting among the rocks at the bottom of the steep slope. He decapitated it with his spear point and carried it over to the fire pit. There were pigeons near the waterline but he could not get close enough to stick them.

Reglis returned alone with the firewood, saying that the king had asked for solitude. While Doctor Eelhook lit the kindling, Tejohn stalked through the darkness toward the trees. Great Way, night had fallen quickly. Little Spinner played like a whirling top in the mountains.

Lar's voice came out of the darkness. "I wanted to be alone."

"Every man needs time to grieve, but this is a wish I can not grant, my king. In the wilderness, anything might come upon us in the darkness. My oath—"

"Bless your oath," the king said sharply, seeming to mean it as a rebuke. He strode back up the hill toward the camping ground. Tejohn followed.

Their meal was eaten in darkness and in silence. Tejohn knew it was bad for morale to let them sulk through the end of the day, but the king's mood had turned sour, and both scholar and driver were clearly exhausted. The two soldiers allowed their mood to be dictated by the others. No one volunteered to play music, and Tejohn did not dare to broach the subject, for fear they would ask to hear that song.

The stars came out and the wind howled and groaned above them. Arla had chosen their shelter well. After everyone had eaten, they sorted the watches for the night. Reglis claimed he never slept the night through and volunteered for the middle watch. Lar claimed the first, saying he would not be able to rest for some hours yet. When Arla offered to sit up in his place, or to sit with him, he snapped at her, saying he would not be coddled. She volunteered for the final watch and Tejohn resolved to take one the next night.

They began to arrange their blankets around the fire. Wimnel had already fallen asleep, his food half eaten in his lap. Apparently, flying a cart was more of a strain than it appeared.

From somewhere off in the distance there was a loud noise. Everyone but Wimnel stood, weapons drawn. For a moment, Tejohn thought it might have been an avalanche, and he stood tense beside the hill, wondering which way to run.

Nothing came. As he strained to listen, he thought the wind sounded faintly like a beating heart.

"What was that?" Doctor Eelhook asked.

Arla answered. "It sounded like a tree falling."

"No talking," Tejohn said gently. But the scout was right. It had sounded like breaking wood. Now the question was whether it had fallen naturally or if there was something out there had kicked it over.

He gripped his spear and unslung his shield. Fire take that scout and her stories of avalanche giants. What were the odds they'd come across such a creature on their first night? Tejohn forced himself to take slow breaths. No, there was almost certainly nothing out there.

"The stars are flickering," Reglis said.

They all looked up. The stars weren't just flickering, they were winking in and out, as though—

"Away!" Tejohn called. "Away from the fire!"

He grabbed the king's arm and pulled him up the southern slope of the hollow out of the firelight. Thankfully, Lar had kept his helmet on, but where was his shield?

The wind suddenly became loud, as though a sudden storm was rushing at them through a forest. Then there was a loud crash like a holdfast gate giving way.

He spun around. The campfire was bright enough to show the smashed cart behind them, all but hidden beneath the piney branches of the tree that had fallen on it.

No, not fallen. Dropped. The raptors had dropped it and destroyed their flying cart.

"My king, stay close."

Lar stood close at Tejohn's right shoulder, and Reglis took up a defensive position on the other side. Arla stood behind them, hurriedly bending her bow to string it.

He scanned the sky above, watching for signs of shapes moving against the stars, but he couldn't see anything. A tiny voice in his head whispered that the stars had only flickered, and that the tree had simply fallen from the slope above. They were only birds. How could they carry and drop something so heavy? Birds did not work in teams.

Doctor Eelhook's robe flapped as she ran down toward the stream, into the darkness. Wimnel Farrabell was nowhere to be seen. Had he stayed by the cart or been crushed with it?

Tejohn looked upward again, but he couldn't see any shadows against the starlight. He didn't believe they would retreat. Animals didn't strike and flee without capturing prey first.

Doctor Eelhook's scream echoed from out of the darkness of the valley. Fire and Fury, the creatures were flying low across the river toward them. "Shock line." Tejohn said to Reglis. Both men braced their spears.

"Stay close to me," Lar said, as though he was their bodyguard.

Out of the corner of his eye, Tejohn saw the king's hands moving, but before he could see which spell the king was casting, something rushed out of the darkness toward them.

It was so fast, Tejohn barely had time to yank his spear head upward and to the right. The raptor, moving at him as fast as a stone from a catapult, took the point directly in the center of its outstretched foot.

The spear shivered. The raptor, already angling upwards, slammed hard into Tejohn's shield with its hind claw.

He fell back onto the loose stone, hard. Stones gouged his back and bare arms as he slid sideways down the slope. Tejohn scrambled onto his knees. The king. He had to protect the king.

At the top of the rise before him, Reglis knelt before the king, his spear braced and his shield high. Tejohn shouted a warning at them, but he couldn't be heard over the cries of the bird he'd wounded. Then the king's spell finished, and a plume of fire blasted outward, lighting up the whole hillside.

Another raptor, its wings spread and its claws reaching, fluttered directly into the blue-white core of the flames. It swerved away from the king, and flapped desperately, trying to gain altitude. It swept around in a wide circle, tail feathers burning.

A third raptor swooped in, then a fourth, the plumes of fire making them turn away before they got close. Then a fifth, a sixth, Great Way, how many of these beasts would they have to kill?

There was no seventh. Tejohn scrambled toward the king, letting the shattered spear shaft fall from his hand. He drew his sword, knowing he'd have to use the point against something moving that fast, and knowing that it would probably cost his life. *Everything is dangerous.* He took up position beside Lar . . . The top of his shield had been broken off and he hadn't even noticed.

Arla came up beside him, an arrow nocked. Fire-taken archers were even slower to join the fight than spellcasters, but Tejohn swallowed that thought unspoken. "Watch behind in case they come at us from the north."

She did as she was told. Tejohn knew how little use a single arrow would be against so many foes, but they were soldiers, and soldiers fought with the weapons they had.

"I have an idea," the king said. "When I say to shut your eyes, do it."

"My king," Arla said. "If they fall upon us while—"

"Here they come," Reglis said.

Lar began a spell. "At my word," he said. Tejohn stepped forward, raised his shield, and extended the point of his sword.

Away from the fire, Tejohn's eyes had begun to adjust to the starlight; he could just barely make out blurry shapes moving against the black shadows of the valley wall.

"From the north, too!" Arla shouted. Tejohn heard her bowstring thrum. He pivoted to put his shield at the king's back. Yes, there were several coming from this side, and they were spread out so they could strike from different angles in quick succession.

This was it. "Grateful am I," Tejohn said, "to be permitted—"

"Now!" Lar shouted, and Tejohn squeezed his eyes shut. . . . *to travel The Way.*

Laoni.

There was a sound like a sudden wind, and for an instant, Tejohn could see the veins in his eyelids, red against his pink flesh. The king had cast a bright blinding light. A light spell. A modified Fourteenth Gift.

Arla cried out and so did the raptors. The beasts screamed in rage and dismay, and Tejohn heard them as they swept overhead, wings flapping.

The light faded. He opened his eyes but a pink glare obscured the starlight and the dark shapes around him. Almost immediately, he heard a heavy wet smack. Great Way, that was an ugly sound, whatever it was.

The raptors squawked as they flapped away, heading west down the length of the valley. Tejohn stared into the darkness after them, barely able to make out their shapes. They didn't seem to be circling around, but he kept his broken shield high just the same.

"Fire and Fury," Arla said, dropping to one knee. "I've been struck blind, and the last thing I saw was one of those birds swooping at me. Have they gone? Because if that was the last thing I'll ever see, I don't even want another dawn."

Lar laid a hand on her shoulder. "They're gone. But next time I give you a command, you would do well to follow it."

Arla lowered her head. "I'm sorry, my king. My training—"

"Is no excuse. Your training is a blessing, to be sure, but it's not sufficient."

Someone cried out. They started at the sound, then rushed toward the campfire. Wimnel Farrabell had still been lying by the cart when the pine tree had been dropped on it, and was now pinned beneath a pair of broken branches. They hadn't punctured his skin, but his arm was clearly broken.

Reglis took a hatchet to the branches, clearing them enough so the driver could be dragged free. Tejohn helped Arla sit by the fire and left her there, rubbing at her wide, bright eyes. If her vision didn't clear by morning, they'd have two burdens. A driver with no cart—or even two working arms to carry gear—was useless, as was a blind guide.

"Not an auspicious start, is it?" By the firelight, Tejohn could see that Lar had a crooked grin on his face. *He's smiling so he doesn't go mad.* It was good they were away from other tyrs and generals. They would never understand. Tejohn himself didn't even understand, not really.

"I've had worse, my king," Tejohn said truthfully. "We'll be able to take better stock of our situation in the daylight, but if the cart is not salvageable, we'll have to make for the next fort. Perhaps we can get another flying cart, but that's a lot to hope for. We need provisions, at least."

"Can we go through the mountains?"

"No, my king," Arla spoke up from the fire. "There are paths, of course, but they change every year due to ice and landslide. Besides, there are deadly enemies up here, the least of which are Durdric raiders."

"Durdric?" Lar said. "Not this far east, surely."

Tejohn agreed with the king, but Arla shook her head. "Not in great numbers, no, but the Durdric are a mountain people. They range all through the Southern Barrier. It would be best for us to descend to the Sweeps, as we'd originally planned. It's a less direct route, but it would still be quicker." She cleared her throat. "People disappear in these mountains."

"I wonder why," Farrabell said, cradling his arm.

Lar turned to Tejohn. "Shall we venture back into the valley to look for Doctor Eelhook?"

"I don't think there's much use, my king. I doubt we'll find a body."

"We should still try," the king said. "What if she's cowering in the dark out there?"

Tejohn had heard a great many death cries in his life, and he was sure the scholar had uttered hers. "If you wish, my king."

"Now you're humoring me." The king turned away and looked up at the mountain above them, where they'd heard the terrible smacking noise.

One of the raptors had flown straight into the cliff face. One of its wings was bent over its back, and it wasn't moving at all.

"That kill counts as yours, my king. I don't know of anyone who could claim bigger game."

Lar didn't seem pleased by that. "Game? They dropped a tree on us, Tyr Treygar, a very large tree that would certainly require teamwork to carry. Does that seem like the action of a dumb animal?"

"I've seen gulls do something similar, my king," Wimnel said. "Last summer, when I flew trips to Rivershelf and the Bay of Stones, I saw seagulls drop clams onto shore rocks to get at the meat inside."

"I've never heard of that," Lar said. "Thank you. But assuming these beasts were trying to crack the shell of a flying oyster, I can't figure why they'd bother. The meat had already climbed out and was lounging beside the fire."

"True," Tejohn said. All this talk was making him uncomfortable. He turned his back to the fire so he could watch for movement out in the darkness. The king's words had given weight to his own suspicions. The raptors had attacked as a unit and they had adapted their strategy for their second run. What if they flew to the mountainside above and dislodged a pile of rocks? Would the group be able to flee an actual avalanche? "Perhaps," Tejohn added, "our flying vehicle offended their delicate sensibilities."

"Fire and Fury," Arla said.

Reglis finally spoke up. "You talk about them as though they have intelligence."

"Yes," the king said. "We do."

Wimnel cleared his throat. "The king should name them. He killed the first one, and . . . Well, he's the king. My king, you should choose their name."

The king laughed. "How about 'Larsbane'?"

"No!" Tejohn said, startled by his own vehemence. He stalked up the hill toward the raptor, sheathing his sword and casting his shield aside as he went. The bird had struck the mountain well above the place where it had settled, but the ground beneath his feet was still steep. Tejohn caught hold of the wing stretched across its broken back and pulled, hoping to roll the body downhill.

It didn't move. He strained harder and only succeeded in plucking out a handful of huge feathers. It was too big. No matter. He changed his grip and climbed up onto the beast, crawling on his hands and knees across its back.

The body shifted under him in a vaguely sickening way. Great Way, but it had broken so many bones. Worse, it was hot—so hot, it felt feverish to his touch.

Again, no matter. As Tejohn settled on the far side of the raptor, he placed his back against the mountain and kicked at the beast with his boots. It rocked back slightly—Fire and Fury, but it was heavy—and the momentum was impaired by the wet-bag-of-sticks feel of the corpse, but the slope was steep and the beast yielded to him, flopping onto its back.

Tejohn fell on it with his dagger, slashing deep into its breast. The meat was thick and he had to tear at it to pull it open. He needed a second slash to reach bone.

"My Tyr!" Lar called. "What are you doing up there?"

"Giving this beast a worthy name," he called back. "Arla, what's your native tongue?"

"What? Peradaini, my tyr!"

"Nonsense. You speak Peradaini very well, but you trill your R's slightly. I suspect, like many servant classes, your family raised you in your own language. What is it? Don't be afraid; it will not be a strike against you, not out here and not when we return."

Arla's voice was slightly quieter when she spoke next. "I grew up speaking Chin-Chinro with my family. But they also taught me Peradaini."

"They would have to, if they were working with a scholar. Is Chin-Chinro the language of these valleys?"

"It is, my tyr, here and to the east."

Tejohn had pulled the flesh away from the breastbone. He was tempted to saw it off and throw it toward the campfire, but that would be better done by daylight. Luckily, the rib bones were broken as well, saving him some trouble. He began to rip them out one by one. "Tell me, then: how do you say 'Meal for a King' in Chin-Chinro?"

The scout had to think for a moment; obviously, it had been a long time. Tejohn pulled out two more broken rib bones and plunged his hands into the cavity. The flesh was nearly hot enough to scald, but he found the beast's heart easily enough, and he cut it free just as easily. Fire and Fury, it was almost as big as his head.

"It would have to be 'Chieftain's Portion,' my tyr," Arla said. "*Ruh-grit.*"

Tejohn clambered down the hill toward Lar. "What say you, my king? I think it sounds fine, if we stress the second syllable. 'Ruhgrit.' To you, Lar Italga, I present the heart of the monster you slew."

Lar was staring at Tejohn with wild eyes. Then, suddenly, he burst into a bright, throaty laugh. His voice rang out, echoing through the valley as though he had no fear of being heard. The king snatched the heart from Tejohn's bloody grip, and he bit down hard at the edge and tore off a chunk of wet meat.

The laughter continued as he chewed, muffled by his full mouth. He swallowed and took another bite.

Assuming they lived through this journey, the story would spread throughout the empire. King slays monstrous bird . . . No, call it an eagle. King slays monstrous eagle with his magic and devours its heart, laughing. That would give weight to the journey they were undertaking and would rally support once the boy had learned this deadly new spell. *Grateful am I to be permitted to travel The Way.* At least for a while longer. At least until they could turn the tide against the grunts.

Lar turned away from Tejohn and held up the heart for the others to see it. For a moment, the king stood between Tejohn and the campfire, and Tejohn swore he saw something sticking out from beneath the flannel under-padding of the king's cuirass. It was only a glimpse, but Tejohn could have sworn that he could see, right on Lar's shoulder where he had been bitten by the grunt, a tuft of blue fur.

Chapter Twelve

This time, Cazia had planned ahead. Instead of letting the guards drag her back into the fort for their midday meal, she had packed food. It galled her that she had to bring a *picnic* to the search for her brother's body, but it seemed to be necessary. She hadn't told her two minders until mealtime, and neither looked particularly happy. Soldiers loved hot food, and the ones sent to "help" her seemed to have little enthusiasm for anything else.

The woman was named Peraday; apparently, it was a custom in the hinterlands for citizens anxious to prove their loyalty to the empire to name their children after the Morning City. The man was named Zollik, and he had little to say about himself or any other subject. Cazia had a powerful suspicion that he imagined himself silent and irresistible, but Cazia thought he seemed like a fool.

Both were fleet squad scouts. Cazia had not expected to find a squad—even a small one—inside a fort, but Peraday explained that the fort was more than just the walls and towers. There were outposts as well, and they regularly sent patrols through the mountains.

That meant they had steel caps but not cuirasses or greaves. Their quilted jackets looked warm, but Cazia preferred her wool cloak. It kept the wind off and she could open it whenever clambering over rocks made her break out in a sweat.

Which was often. She knew her brother had been attacked on the eastern end of the north wall—that was where the servants were scrubbing his blood—but how close to the cliff face was it? She'd returned to the top of the wall to mark the spot somehow, but all bloodstains had been cleaned away, even on the outside.

So, now she was outside the wall, going by instinct and guesswork to try to judge where the attack had taken place. The guards could have helped, but they didn't. She could have asked them to, but she didn't. They obviously resented her for making them stand in the rain, and she resented their unwillingness to exert themselves at all. They only times they talked were when Peraday scolded her for climbing too far.

The climbing was the most frustrating thing of all. Of course, she'd seen the tumble of boulders from the wall, but she hadn't appreciated just how hard it would be to cross them. The black, jagged rocks lay piled against the other, some sticking straight up, some steeply angled. Within two hours, the nearly flat rocks that she could stand on comfortably had become like good friends, and the ones she had to scramble across on her hands and knees—or worse, actually climb like a fence—were bitter Enemies.

But she had no choice. Colchua's body could have fallen into any number of niches or gaps. His body hadn't been visible from up high, so she had to check each rock, searching all around it before moving on to the next.

It was tiring work, and she might have finished yesterday if the guards had been willing to scrape their hands and knees climbing the stones with her. Instead, they hopped from one friend to another, keeping close to the road, singing stupid old campaigning songs and calling for her not to stray too far.

She'd assumed that Col had fallen from the wall, but what if he'd been thrown? She'd seen grunts climbing and leaping, not to mention swinging a soldier like a cudgel. Yes, she'd spent all of yesterday searching near the wall, with no luck at all, but she wasn't going to give up. Today, she'd search farther out. And farther tomorrow, if she had to.

So, at midday when the guards called to her, she disappointed them by opening her pack and bringing out preserved apricots and rice loaves filled with scant bits of lamb. They were travel rations and quite salty, but everyone ate without complaining aloud, and Cazia made sure to refill the waterskin twice to wash it down.

Just as they were cleaning up, Peraday cleared her throat. Zollik hopped from their good friend to one closer to the road, then squatted low, watching the horizons. Cazia looked into Peraday's face and she knew she wouldn't like what the woman was about to say. Why else would Zollik pretend to give them privacy? Cazia felt her anger stirring.

"Miss Freewell," the soldier said. Her voice was much gentler than Cazia expected. "You know already that your brother isn't out here, don't you?"

Fire and Fury, she was actually pretending to be nice. "No, I *don't* know that! And maybe if you two were willing to *help me* rather than stand around leaning on your spears—"

"So, you don't know, then," Peraday interrupted. Her voice was still kind, but she would not allow Cazia to forestall what she had to say. "Zollik was right. I'm sorry, miss. I didn't want to do this."

Peraday shrugged off her pack and peeled it open. She took out a bit of gray meat wrapped in a tattered rag. It must have smelled awful, but the winds carried the scent away. "What are you doing?" she asked.

Peraday gave her a kind but implacable look, then threw the meat, rag and all, out into the rocks.

"Five years ago, the Indregai tried to storm this fort. They claim the Sweeps to the north and both the Samsit and Piskatook passes."

"By what right do they lay claim to our land?" Cazia snapped, surprising herself with the strength of her response.

"They invite okshim herders living in the Sweeps to join their alliance, then claim their lands. Not that the herders have lands in the way we understand it. They're a nomadic people, but from the Indregai perspective, that just means they can draw their marks on large parts of the map."

"But the okshim herding clans in the Sweeps are imperial citizens. They use sleepstones, pay taxes—"

"They do, Miss Freewell, when they're west of the Piskatook Pass, at least. But my point is that the Alliance—and their *serpents*—tried to storm the fort. Many brave men and women on both sides died in those three days, and not all on the road. What's more, we sometimes get spies in these rocks who have come to time the watches and study the gates."

"Why are you telling me this?"

"Look." She pointed off in the direction she'd thrown the meat. There were three crows fluttering, squawking, and fighting over it. As they watched, two more arrived.

"Oh, no." Cazia felt her stomach give a sudden twist and she thought she might give back the picnic food she'd already eaten. What was the woman trying to say?

"I'm sorry, miss. I know he was your brother. I know you loved him. But we have had many dead before these walls—sometimes after battle, sometimes after misadventure—and we have never had to search for them very hard. In truth, if he'd died here, the watch would have known about it at the first sign of daylight. The birds always tell."

Goose bumps ran all over Cazia's body. She couldn't believe it. This woman was talking about Col as though he was a piece of rotten meat! The boy who'd called, *Save the princess*, like a fairy tale hero, who had teased them about their clothes just before the Festival, who had followed Lar onto Vilavivianna's roof!

Bad enough I have to stick my hand in a monster's mouth for him . . .

Lar, save the princess.

No. It was unacceptable. Her brother was out here somewhere. He had to be. If the birds weren't tearing at his flesh it was because they *wouldn't dare*.

Cazia turned her back on the guard and bounded to the nearest Friend. She didn't care what they said. She was going to find her brother. It was the only decent thing to do.

She heard Peraday sigh.

It took no time at all to pick up her search again. There were no crows nearby except the ones Peraday had summoned. It occurred to her that Col, having been killed by the grunt, might have the grunt's smell on him. That would drive the carrion birds away, she was sure.

No need to think about that now. She kept searching, hearing the harsh cries of the crows until they were done with their snack. The late afternoon came, and she was as far east as she could go, almost to the loose stones at the foot of the cliff face.

The grunt could have thrown him here. It could have thrown him farther, maybe up into the stones on the mountainside, but she would need a flying cart to search there.

Still, there was plenty of territory to cover that didn't need a cart. She glanced out at the pass, at the dark, still rocks. The road was fringed with stiff, bristly clumps of grass, but among the tumbledown black rocks, there was nothing. No rats, no squirrels, no birds.

Cazia threw herself against the bitterest Enemy near her, scraping her fingers raw as she clung to the rough top. There was no sign of her brother beneath it; of course there wasn't. She strained her arms and shoulders, pulling herself around the edge to check the far side, sweat running down her face and back.

And burst out crying. She laid her cheek against the cool black rock, letting the tears crawl on her skin like bugs. Bad enough her brother had been killed; could that grunt have eaten him entirely? She imagined Commander Gerrit smugly declaring that Col had run off, and she made ready to hate him wildly for it.

Cazia wanted to believe her brother had run away without her—she ached to believe it—but no. He was dead. She knew it had to be true.

There was nothing to do now but go back into the fort and admit defeat.

Admit that she'd wasted everyone's time and that she was just a girl who didn't know how the world worked, and why *hadn't they just told her*?

The sun had almost reached the top of the western peaks when Cazia began climbing across the rocks toward the road. It was easier to avoid the bitter Enemies now that she wasn't searching methodically, and she quickly found herself staring at the two guards from the top of long black slab.

"I'm sorry," she said, steeling herself in case they made a nasty remark. "I'm sorry I wasted your time."

The guards exchanged a look, then Zollik bowed and excused himself, moving closer to the wall. Peraday stepped closer to Cazia and spoke in a low voice. "We are the ones who should apologize to you. Zollik and I are fourth-generation soldiers; we are accustomed to speaking only when given permission. We could not decide on a proper way to broach the subject. And we did not want to intrude on your grief."

Cazia was equally grateful for the soldier's kindness and annoyed that she'd refused to be a target for Cazia's rage and embarrassment. "I still don't know what happened to Colchua. He would not have run away without me."

Peraday gestured toward the quiver on Cazia's hip. "Can he do magic, like you?"

Cazia shook her head. "He is a warrior all the way through. Was a warrior." The words left behind a lump in her throat that made her feel sick. She turned away toward the north, looking far uphill toward the place where the twisting pass vanished between two sloping paths as though Col might have been standing out there on a barren rock. She had no target for her anger and it was turning sour inside her.

As long as she didn't start crying again. Stoneface was right; it was dangerous for scholars to grieve in public.

"May I speak freely?" Peraday said. Startled by the tone of her voice, Cazia glanced at her. When they'd first met, Cazia had assumed she was just another bully. She had a heavy jaw and brow, a bulbous nose, and a long scar across her forehead. Her blunt accent only added to the impression. Her behavior, though, had been a complete surprise. Was this kindness?

It didn't matter, because Cazia couldn't refuse her, not now. "Please do."

"My brother, he vanished. No one knows what happened to him, and what I have learned is that vanishing is more painful for those left behind. My father had a funeral. We visit his grave every year. But for my brother, there is only loss that can never come to an end, painful gossip, and futile hope. I know it's not my place, but—"

"Perra!"

Peraday and Cazia turned toward Zollik. He was standing ten paces away but was staring back up at the wall. "What is it?" Peraday called.

"The guards are not at their—"

His next words were drowned out by the staccato clang of a bronze drum. It rang in four quick tones, then four again, then again.

Peraday and Zollik ran to the northern gate. Cazia jumped from the rock and sprinted after them. "What does it mean?"

They had no time for her questions. Zollik dug his fingers into the gap and tried to pull the gate open. It was as immovable as Monument. Peraday pounded on the wood with the heel of her hand. No one unbarred the gate or answered their shouts.

"What does four tones mean?" Cazia asked again.

"Enemy inside the fort," Peraday answered. "Fire and Fury, they've already barred the gates. No one will be permitted to come or go until the foes within have been defeated."

Cazia stepped back, looking along the walls. Was there another way in? She didn't have a rope, and she stopped herself asking the guards if there was a ladder somewhere, because of course soldiers wouldn't keep a ladder outside the fort. "How do we sneak in?"

"We don't," Peraday said sharply. "The walls are too high and we'd be shot if we tried to climb."

"We should withdraw to Stinkhole Station," Zollik said. "Dark will be upon us soon and we have no torches."

"No," Cazia said. Jagia was in there, and Timush, and Bittler. Her friends. She couldn't leave them alone to face . . . "What enemy? Not another grunt. Could it be Alliance soldiers come to steal away their princess?"

Cazia knew the answer to her own question even before she finished it. She needed to stop doing that. How could they know what had happened in Peradain and where Vilavivianna had been moved in just five days? She was beginning to realize how much she disliked questions. Answers were much better. Answers told you what to do.

"I'm sorry, Miss Freewell, but we must set out for Stinkhole right away. They won't have heard the gong and word must be spread."

"Well, we don't all have to go. I do. My friends are inside, and if they're under attack, I can't just sit on a rock and eat a picnic lunch. I just can't." *You are Peradaini. You'll never risk your lives for the Witt, Bendertuk, or Simblin heirs.* "So, how do we sneak into to the fort? Don't tell me you can't; as soon as you build a wall, someone will want to climb over it. No one knows that better than I do. So, don't tell me you haven't thought about it."

"But I haven't," Peraday said.

"I have." Zollik's expression was grave. "You can't defend if you can't prepare for an attack, and I worked out a method I would use to mount the walls. I'd hoped it would earn me the captain's helm, but Reglis got it instead, and then that floor-mopper Shunkip. But I know how I'd do it."

"Peraday," Cazia said. "Why don't you spread word to . . . Stinkhole station? Is that really a name? While we slip into the fort and see what help we can offer."

"I want that," Zollik said. "I want to do it."

"Sneaking into the fort is not likely to earn you a plume, Zol." Peraday's tone was flat. "More like a hempen collar."

"I want to do it. The consequences will be on me."

"And if you get this young girl killed?"

"Hey!" Cazia objected. "This 'young girl' slays monsters."

"Go," Zollik said. "Alert the watch stations."

Peraday jogged away from the gate, heading deeper into the pass. Cazia had expected her to sprint, but maybe the stations were farther than she'd thought. She turned to Zollik. "Okay. What's your plan for breaking in?"

"The walls are highest at the gates, but lowest at the cliff face. We climb up to the cliffs above—the eastern end seems best—and start an avalanche. The stones will pile up at the base of the wall and we can descend over the rockfall directly onto the wall walk."

Cazia waited for him to say he was just joking and to start explaining his true plan. The silence played out.

"What are you gaping at?" Zollik snapped. "We do have avalanches, you know, and they have to be cleared from the walls."

"We don't have time for that! Problem two: I can't climb mountains. Do you even know how to start an avalanche, make it the right size, and not kill everyone in the fort? No. We're going to do this a better way."

She waved at him to follow her as she went east back over the broken stones. The shadow of the western peaks followed her as she hopped from one friend to another. Zollik was not quite right about the height of the walls: they were all the same straight across the pass. The difference lay in the ground. The road at the center of the pass was the lowest point, and the rocks made a shallow slope on either side until they reached the cliff faces.

"Where are you leading me?"

"To here," Cazia said, jumping to a good friend close to the wall. It seemed sturdy enough—at least, it didn't wobble when Zollik landed beside her. "Just a moment."

"You can't tunnel through," Zollik said.

"I know that."

"Behind this wall is soil and loose stone. It won't crumble and we could never dig it out, not with all the soil from above falling in."

"I know."

"We'd never get to the inner wall in time."

"Monument give me strength, would you shut up? I need a few breaths of silence."

To her surprise, he did it.

Cazia could get them over. She knew it. She was a scholar and she'd been taught a spell that would let her climb to the top.

But she couldn't just cast it once. She was going to have to cast it over and over, and Doctor Twofin had warned her what would happen if she overused spells: she'd go hollow like Doctor Whitestalk. If she was lucky, she'd only have her fingers chopped off, then be locked up in a room somewhere to answer questions about magic. If she wasn't, it would be the point of a spear or edge of a sword, just like Old Stoneface had done to Doctor Rexler.

But could she do it? Could she cast the spell enough times to get them over without going mad? What good would it do to rush to her friends' rescue if she arrived there without any human feeling left in her?

Song knew, it was a huge risk. Doctor Twofin had always kept their practice sessions short, so she had never even come close to going hollow. What's more, whenever she'd asked him how many times she could safely use a Gift, he'd lost his temper. He didn't want to tell her because he knew she would test her boundaries.

He was dead now, she thought not for the first time. She hadn't liked him very much, but she'd loved the magic he'd taught her. Did it make her a bad person to miss the lesson more than the man? Maybe, she assured herself, it was just that she had too much grief for too many people to feel more than a pang for her old teacher.

She had a choice before her: risk madness and go over this wall or huddle out here in the darkness while her last remaining friends in the world—Timush, Bit, and little Jagia—faced danger in the fort. And that wasn't any kind of choice at all.

Cazia started the Eleventh Gift, trying hard to recall all the triggers and hand motions. It was the second most common spell taught to scholars—starting a fire was first—because there were so many mines in the Southern Barrier, but Cazia hadn't practiced it often. For one thing, making stones crumble wasn't fun. For another, hostages were not encouraged to practice magic that could breach the city defenses. It was a measure of Doctor Twofin's trust for her that he taught it to her at all.

Her first attempt failed, but she could feel the incorrect hand motion she'd made as thought it was an ill-fitting glove. She cast it correctly the next time. The top half of the bitter enemy beside them crumbled, and Cazia swept the loose stones away.

It was flat enough. She hoped. She told Zollik to climb onto it, then joined him. Turning back, she cast the Sixth Gift on the Friend. It had the exact opposite effect of the stone breaker—creating a stone block rather than breaking one apart—but the spell itself was completely different—the physical gestures and mental preparations had nothing to do with each other.

But she hadn't forgotten that, either. She cast it three times to make the stack of blocks higher than the broken enemy they were standing on, then climbed onto it, letting Zollik step on behind her.

He frowned at the stone stack. Each block was as tall as his head. "You're not really planning to do it this way, are you? We'll be here all night."

"If you don't like it, you can climb a cliff face without rope in the dark, or you can chop down a tree—assuming you can find one—and fashion a ladder. Otherwise, crouch down so I can cast."

Again, he surprised her by doing what she asked. She cast the Sixth Gift twice more, then they stepped up again. She turned around, cast the spell twice, then switched.

How would it feel to be hollowed out? How would she recognize the early signs? A sudden, terrifying longing for it to happen came over her. All her shame and anger, all her concerns over Enemies, all her petty resentments would be drained away. Would that be peaceful? Had Doctor Whitestalk been glad to lose herself to magic?

More questions. She hated them.

"The wall is about five times the height of a man here. If each of the blocks is one eighth of a man, and you're making two stacks—"

"Stop talking," Cazia said. "It distracts me, and I don't want the stack to be misaligned."

Zollik fell silent, but he began counting on his fingers. Cazia tried to pretend he wasn't there. She cast the next spell, mindful that the ground was slowly receding.

Each block was as wide and long as a sizable bench—spacious enough to stand on comfortably when the ground was less than a body length away, but more and more precarious as they went higher. Cazia heard Zollik's breath slowly become harsh with fear.

They passed the halfway point to the top of the wall, then reached the three-quarter mark. Sometimes, their tower seemed to sway, but Cazia told herself it was her imagination. Zollik's face was pale and sweaty, and his hands, when he helped her onto the higher block in her hiking skirts, were cold and damp. His fear was contagious, and he was beginning to truly annoy her.

"We should stop." Zollik suddenly said.

Cazia finished the next spell, settling the new block even with the one they were standing on. "Why?"

"Because no one has challenged us. If we still had guards patrolling the wall, they should have called to us long before now. If the fort had been taken, someone would have shot an arrow into us. But this silence—"

Cazia began the mental preparation for the Sixth Gift, then began the hand motions. The next block appeared across from them, dropping onto the one below with the hard click of stone striking stone. "I wish we had silence," she said as she climbed onto the higher block. "What could have happened inside? Is there a special drill you do where you pretend the fort has been abandoned?"

"No. What if there are more grunts inside?"

"I don't care about the grunts or the fort," Cazia explained. "My friends— the ones who haven't died—are inside, and if there's something wrong, I'm going to get them out."

"I want to know what has happened," he said, as though he hadn't just been trying to convince her to run away. He climbed onto the block beside her, crouching low so she could cast over his head.

The block dropped onto the one below with the same audible noise, but immediately after, there was a low groaning sound. The stack seemed to settle toward the wall, then became still.

Zollik and Cazia looked at each other. "I've been waiting for that to happen," she said.

"We're almost within reach of the top of the wall. Two more steps up and I should be able to grab the edge." He stepped up onto the high block. It didn't groan or shift beneath him, so he put his full weight on it. It seemed stable.

He's decided to be brave. The thought startled Cazia. Was this something people could choose, suddenly, the way they picked out clothes for the day's weather? She hoped not. It was easier to be brave when she felt she had no choice.

She climbed up herself, then cast the spell twice more and stepped up onto the high block. It seemed for a moment that the stack wobbled, but that was her imagination.

At least full dark had finally fallen. She was happier that she couldn't see the jagged rocks so far below her.

Zollik must have been thinking the same thing. "No one has lit the watch lamps."

That's right. She'd forgotten the string of lights along the top of the wall when the cart had flown into the fort. "Good," she said, and cast the spell two more times.

The blocks seemed to have found a new balance. Zollik handed her his spear and stepped onto the high block. He caught the top edge of the wall easily and pulled himself up with little effort. Cazia felt a flash of envy for his casual strength, but suppressed it. After she figured out what had happened to her brother, she would start to exercise in earnest to make herself . . . something. Something more than she was.

Zollik peeked over the wall. Whatever he saw up there must have been reassuring, because he clambered quietly over the edge and out of sight. His spear was long enough that it would have shown above the wall if Cazia had carried it the proper way, so she held it sideways like a water carrier; it made her feel unsteady in the wind and darkness, not like a warrior at all. At least the rain clouds had blown away.

She expected Zollik to reappear within at the edge of the wall and lift her over, but he didn't. At first she thought he was being careful, or perhaps taunting her by making her wait—which was silly, but she couldn't help it. Expecting the worst from people had become a habit.

But that annoyance meant something important: she had not gone hollow. Doctor Twofin would never have allowed her to cast the same spell so many times in a row, but now, standing in the wind and darkness near the top of this wall, she was full of fear that she would fall, aggravation that Zollik was making her wait, determination to rescue her friends, and love for them.

She had not been hollowed at all, not even a little bit. She had certainly not gained the secret understanding that supposedly came with the overuse of magic. She'd felt the familiar emotional flatness that came with each spell, but no trace of it lingered.

Doctor Twofin had been treating her like a child. He'd *lied* to her.

Cazia fought the urge to call Zollik's name. What if he'd been captured or killed? What if a grunt had bitten his throat just as he topped the wall, taking his life silently, the way grass lions supposedly did?

She was just about to start casting the Sixth Gift until she was high enough to climb over on her own when Zollik's harsh whisper came from above. "Raise up the spear." She did. He said, "Hold on tight."

She gripped tightly as he lifted her as easily as she might lift a sack of flour. An undeniable thrill ran through her, not just because of the height and darkness, but because it was so *physical*. The feeling embarrassed and annoyed her, but she pushed it aside. There were more important things going on.

Cazia landed gracelessly on the stone wall walk, her skirts tangled. Zollik knelt beside her. "We should make our way around the wall," he whispered. "The commander's tower is at the west end of the fort. We can find out what's going on there."

"No," she said sourly. "We have to get off the wall." She couldn't see anyone on the walk or in the yard below, but the starlight was sparse and she would easily miss someone in dark clothes. "We're too easily spotted up here." The best thing to do would be to get down to the servants' quarters to listen for news, but Cazia didn't suggest it. Zollik wanted an authority figure to turn to, but authorities didn't share information unless they had to.

She took a dart from her quiver and started eastward. Zollik fell in behind her, protesting feebly. "We're more likely to run into someone down there, and the eastern yard is sectioned from the tower. Miss, let's at least go into the central yard, where the armory is." Cazia hurried so she wouldn't have to listen.

They quickly reached the top of a flight of stairs. She could see no fires, no lights, no movement below. "Where does this lead?"

"Pens and kitchen."

That meant servants would be nearby. She started down, glad to be wearing leather boots instead of the hard-soled palace sandals she'd been given in Peradain. Zollik followed her, wisely deciding to be silent for once.

There were doors at the bottom of the stairs, and they stood wide open. Cazia knelt at the entrance; it was impossibly dark inside, but the smell was so intense, it made her eyes water. She imagined piles of corpses strewn about in the darkness, but no. No, that wasn't right.

This was the pen. Of course. She knew the animals and servants killed by the grunt had been carried away. This was just the normal smell. She assumed.

The door to next building stood open, too, and it was even darker inside. There were no windows, but she could see a threadbare cot near the door; some unlucky servant had to sleep at the draftiest place, where everyone passed in and out. She listened at the entrance, heard nothing but the wind above, then slipped inside.

"No!" Zollik whispered, but then he followed her inside. "We shouldn't—"

She shushed him. They crouched in the darkness, letting their eyes get accustomed to this new, deeper darkness. Cazia knew a spell that would have created a little light to see by, but she didn't mention it, because she didn't want to argue with Zollik about why it was a bad idea. After a short pause, they carefully picked their way through the cots and rough wooden boxes where servants stored their few belongings.

"Where are we going?" Zollik demanded. His voice was barely audible.

"To the kitchens," Cazia whispered. "No matter what has happened, people will have to eat, and the kitchens will not be shut down, not until the dim hours of the morning. If Alliance troops have invaded—or my father's or anyone's—someone will be working in the kitchens."

But the kitchens were deserted. Cazia stared in stunned silence at the embers in the cook fires. A few sticks of wood were still wreathed in flames, but even the largest pots had boiled down to sludge. The place had been abandoned long ago.

"This is a bad sign," Cazia said. "An invading army would have kept the kitchens running."

"Could it be grunts?"

"Can't be," Cazia said. "The one that bit Lar clung to the bottom or our cart, supposedly, but the others . . . Even if they ran cross-country day and night, they couldn't have reached us so quickly. Beside, Lar said that most of them were heading south toward the sea." She suddenly remembered the huge bird that had passed over the fort days before. Could a flock of them have snatched everyone out of the fort? Unseen? Impossible. "It can't be grunts. Not yet."

"You are wrong," a new voice said.

Cazia shrieked in surprise as she spun around. Zollik, his spear too long to be swung around in such a crowded room, drew his sword in a single smooth motion and stepped in front of Cazia, bumping her roughly with the shield slung on his back.

From a narrow space between two cook benches, a tiny pale hand emerged. Zollik lunged forward, his sword point dipping low, but Cazia caught hold of his elbow. He pulled back as a second little hand emerged. Both were empty.

"Come out," the guard said. His voice was low and rough with fear.

Vilavivianna slipped from between the benches into the dim light of the cook fires. She held her empty hands high in surrender, but her whisper was sharp when she spoke. "Keep your voice down, girl. They hunt by sound."

"What are you doing in here?" Cazia snapped. "What happened? And don't call me *girl*."

She stared up at them for a moment. "You want to know what happened? Follow me."

The little princess led them through the kitchen to a stairway broad enough for two people to pass comfortably. She bounded lightly up the stairs, pausing only at the top to peer carefully around the landing. Cazia stayed close to her, holding her dart in one hand and laying the other across her quiver so it wouldn't rattle. Shriek or no shriek, she was going to be as silent as this little girl.

"Let me take the point," Zollik said, and Vilavivianna spun and gave him a look of raw hatred. He fell silent and kept his position at the back.

At the top of the stairs was a covered walkway that ran along the edge of the building. A crude wooden roof would keep most of the rain off, but the open sides gave them a full view of the yards below. The princess kept very low, almost on all fours, and Cazia mimicked her. She didn't look back to see what Zollik was doing.

After reaching the far corner, Vilavivianna knelt low and pointed toward the southwest. There was another yard below them—the starlight revealed that there were practice dummies and archery targets set against the walls—but only at the far end of the walkway did they see that the largest building on the southern end of the yard actually had light within.

The doors stood open, and the lights from inside flickered with orange firelight. It was the great hall, Cazia suddenly realized. She moved a little further down the walkway so she could peer through the open door.

She saw kneeling figures, their faces pressed against the stone floor. The ones nearest the door wore the gray shifts the servants had been issued. But there, beside them, was a woman in a dark robe—it took Cazia a moment to recognize it as a scholar's robe—and her curly hair was shot through with gray. Doctor Warpoole.

The Scholar Administrator lifted her face, looking through the door into the darkness as if hoping help would come. Then she turned her head toward her left, watching something move around her.

It was one of the small, blue-furred grunts. The creature circled around them, its back to the door, then moved out of sight.

Frustration fluttered in Cazia's stomach. How many people were inside? The way they were packed together suggested there were a lot, but she needed more solid than that. Where was Timush? Where were Jagia and Bittler?

Returning to her submissive posture, Doctor Warpoole moved her hand, leaving a red smear on the stone floor. She was bleeding, and as soon as Cazia realized that, she saw that the servants had been injured, too.

Why were the grunts guarding their injured prey? Maybe they bit them to mark them, like chewing the edge of a sourcake so no one else would want it. Maybe they could follow a bloody trail if someone tried to escape. Or maybe, she thought again, they were searching for a certain flavor, like the royal bloodline.

Maybe maybe maybe. She was sick of *maybe*. What she needed were definitive answers. She needed to know where the creatures came from, how they got into the fort, why they insisted on tasting everyone.

More importantly, she needed to know how she could rescue her friends from the makeshift pen they were trapped in.

The idea that Jagia—or anyone—was trapped, waiting for her turn to be torn apart and eaten, made her so furious her skin prickled. She had to find a way to free them. There were hot coals down in the kitchen to set the hall's roof aflame, and Cazia had her quiver of darts. A fire would draw them out. If there were not too many grunts, and she could target them one at a time, without them all rushing her at—

A silhouette suddenly rose over the edge of the building just beside them. Cazia was too surprised to react, and within the space of a moment, the figure had vaulted onto the walkway, standing above them.

It was a grunt, of course. It turned slowly toward them slowly as though it had noticed something odd, but the darkness was too deep to clearly see what it was. Cazia suddenly remembered the queen falling from the dais— and Lar screaming as he was bitten—and all her heroic plans deserted her. The thought that she might be next paralyzed her.

Zollik slid to his knees and, in one smooth motion, rammed his spear into the creature's guts. It gasped—a horrible, almost-human sound of surprise and despair—then roared.

Zollik stood swiftly, trying to withdraw his spear, but the grunt grabbed the haft and pulled itself toward him, growling. Cazia felt the weight of its hind foot land on her bare right calf—its toes wrapped around her like a clutching hand. She rolled over—if the thing was going to bite her, she had to see it happen—and the creature lost its footing. It snapped clumsily at Zollik's arm but missed.

Hissing in disgust, Zollik lifted the butt end of his spear. The point struck the stone walkway and the haft levered against the grunt's ribcage, lifting it off its feet. It slid backwards, a terrible death rattle escaping it. The sound made Cazia's hair stand on end. Then it slid over the edge of the roof into the yard below.

Six more grunts rushed out of the hall. At the thud of the creature hitting the ground, the beasts turned toward the spot where Cazia was hiding and roared.

"They haven't seen you," Zollik said, then ran away from the kitchens, leaping down a flight of stairs onto a lower roof, heading south. "Alarm!" he shouted again and again, as though expecting the fort to rise up to help him.

The grunts charged after him. Vilavivianna stirred, but Cazia clamped her hand down on the girl's arm to make her be still. Zollik had chosen to be brave again—for them—and calling attention to themselves would have wasted that.

Cazia peered over the edge of the building. Another grunt appeared in the doorway, looking out into the darkness after the other members of its pack. Zollik had given her the chance she needed to free the prisoners. She lifted the dart and began her spell.

A second grunt appeared in the doorway, then a third. That made nine that she could see. Where had they all come from? Cazia stopped her spell, letting it fade. She could certainly kill one, maybe two, but three? They were too fast, and her spells were too slow. Worse, there might be more inside.

The grunts were clearly anxious to join the chase, but they lingered with their prisoners. Something inside the hall drew their attention, and the creatures charged back inside, roaring challenges. Vilavivianna pushed at Cazia's arm, and Cazia agreed that it was time to go. Where before they had crossed the walkway at a crouch, this time they crawled on their bellies as quickly as they could. They'd barely gotten a quarter of the way before they heard Zollik's battle cry, then his scream.

It was too much. The danger of staying in the open took control of her, and Cazia scrambled to her knees, crawling as quietly as she could back toward the kitchens. Could she be seen from below, and was anything looking? She had to risk it; being out in the open air was unbearable.

They reached the juncture and the stairs down into the kitchen without drawing the attention of the grunts. Cazia rushed into the warm room, glad to be out of the wind and darkness, and to have stone walls between her and the creatures outside.

Vilavivianna came right behind her. "The fool!"

Cazia turned toward her, utterly flummoxed. "Who is a fool?"

"The guard! He should have taken the creature in the throat with the spear. The throat! Then it would not have been able to call the fellows."

Cazia was too startled to respond properly. The throat was a very small target, especially in the dark. He'd have been a bigger fool if he'd missed.

The princess wasn't finished. "But no, he had to stir them all up, the stupid—"

Cazia remembered Zollik's foolish plan to break into the fort, his ambition to be captain, the astonishing and thrilling strength he had shown, and she slapped the girl's face. Hard.

Vilavivianna staggered and let her hand fall to the empty knife sheath at her belt. There was no fear in her eyes when she spoke. "How dare you strike me, girl—"

Cazia slapped her again, then again, then again. By the fourth time, the arrogance and outrage had gone out of the princess's expression and, by the sixth, she actually became afraid.

"Stop," Vilavivianna said, tears on her cheeks. "They will hear. The beasts will hear us. "

"You're the one who has to stop," Cazia hissed. "I just spent two days with that man, and yes, he was a bit of a fool. But he *just gave his life to protect us.* If you can't honor that, then you can at least keep your mouth shut about it. We're all likely to be Fire-taken before sunrise, and we would be lucky to die as well as he did."

"I would rather live," the princess said petulantly.

"He felt the same way."

The girl raised her hand and touched the red spot on her cheek. "I am sorry. You are right, I'm sorry."

Stoneface wouldn't have apologized for slapping the girl, so Cazia squelched the urge. "Let's figure out what we need to do next. How can we free the others?"

Vilavivianna only sighed and began searching the shelves, looking for something to eat. At the mere thought of food, Cazia became ravenously hungry. She took a familiar-looking crock off the top shelf and, as she hoped, found pickled compote within. There was leftover wet rice and some rather bland stewed lamb beside the stove.

The princess grabbed bowls and spoons, and they retreated to a corner of the kitchen well away from the doors and below the tiny windows into the yard. The girls sat on the floor and spooned the food into the bowls. In the dim light, Cazia thought she saw the princess scowl at the rice, but she ate.

"I do not think we can free them," Vilavivianna finally said. "I have no love for imperial troops or the servants, but they are at least human beings. I would prefer not to have them feasted upon. But I do not have the strength of arms to set them free, and I do not have a gift for trickery. Do you know any useful spells? You are a wizard, after all."

"I'm a *scholar*," Cazia said quickly. "Please." They fell silent while they ate. Trickery? Cazia had played her share of pranks in the palace—leaving anonymous "love gifts" for her Enemies, sneaking into rooms to rearrange furniture, filching cakes and buns . . .

But against grunts? To free prisoners? It was like going to war with a child's play weapons. "And none of the spells I know would be much use. I could seal one of the doors with stone, but the hall has four."

"Six," the girl corrected. "And the beasts become enraged when they find a closed door. What else can you do?"

The little princess asked that question with such seeming innocence. Cazia considered snubbing her—scholars were not supposed to discuss the Gifts with anyone outside the Empire—but this was Lar's betrothed. "I can crumble stone, suppress fire, start fire, create a light to see by, shoot one of these darts, create a stone that will translate languages, purify water—"

"One moment: you can translate languages? Why have you not . . . The beasts may be speaking to each other with the grunts and roars, yes?"

"They're animals," Cazia said. "The spell doesn't work on sheep or lions or sparrows or. . . . " She suddenly remembered the Indregai kept serpents. Did the serpents speak with each other? Was that even possible?

"Is it not worth trying?" Something in the princess's tone made Cazia suspicious. Was there something she wasn't telling her?

"It is," Cazia said. "But it's a difficult spell. Let me finish my supper, and I'll see what I can do."

They ate, and after they finished, Cazia prepared a second bowl for herself. She also cast a spell to fill a pitcher with water; pickled compote was a particular favorite of hers, but it was salty.

Afterward, she felt much better. She took the net of blue stones from her hair and pulled another free. The net came apart, which made her feel strangely sad. The stones weren't particularly valuable, but they were pretty. And blue was in style this year again. In Peradain, she meant, which didn't even exist any more.

Still, there was nothing to be done about it. She had to surrender yet another thing she cared about. She called up the mental images she needed for this particular spell, then began to move her hands into the necessary positions. She had practiced some spells, like dart-casting, so often they were automatic, but this spell needed concentration and care.

When she was done, she wiped the sweat from her face with her sleeve and let Vilavivianna press a cup of water into her hand. She drank, then drank some more. When she finished, she started in on the second bowl of lamb, compote, and rice. Monument sustain her, but that spell was exhausting.

The stone lay between them. In the dim emberlight, it looked dark purple. The princess stared at it but did not touch it. "Valuska pinsh kartooskik," she said.

Cazia understood. She picked up the stone.

Vilavivianna spoke again, but this time Cazia heard "I would like to pinch it for myself."

"You can 'pinch' it, if you want," Cazia said, "but be aware that the translation might seem strange. It's very literal."

The princess did not reach for it until Cazia held it out. Only after the girl had taken it did Cazia realize that she only spoke Peradaini. Some years ago, she'd thought to study Surgish, but all she could remember of her lessons was "Grateful am I to be permitted to travel The Way."

Vilavivianna quirked her head, then smiled as she understood. Cazia tapped the floor between them and the princess set it down with less reluctance than Cazia herself had shown, when Doctor Twofin had shown her one so many years before.

"I can see that it is difficult to make," the little girl said. "But do you have the strength to make two?"

"No," Cazia said warily. Betrothed or not, sharing magic with someone outside the empire would cost her life. "Not if I want to survive the night. Besides, they're dangerous." She emptied a pouch full of mint, slipped the stone inside, then rolled it up and stuffed it into a skirt pocket. "Use it too much, and you start to speak gibberish." That wouldn't really discourage the girl from stealing it if she wanted to, but it might make her think twice.

"We need weapons and provisions," Vilavivianna said, seeming to forget the stone as soon as it was out of sight. She gestured toward the remnants of their meal. "This food is sustenance, but it will not travel without spoiling. We need to find the meatbread your soldiers carry when they campaign; it does not seem to be kept in the kitchens. Also, I had heard that the armory was near the kitchens, but I will be floated away if I can find a path to it."

"The kitchens are servants' areas," Cazia said. The princess had seemed too smart for this sort of mistake. "The armory isn't going to be connected to the hallways and workrooms they use." But Zollik had said it was in the next yard over from this one.

Before Vilavivianna could respond, a footfall squelched in the mud from somewhere beyond the door. Both froze in place, turning toward the door.

Cazia quickly, quietly drew a spike from her quiver. The metal tip made a faint scraping noise as it came free, but in the dark stone room, it sounded as loud as a blacksmith's labors.

Cazia began the hand motions for casting a dart, moving slowly so the intruder would not hear her clothes rustle, and also because, if she finished too quickly, she would have to disrupt it and start over. They could hear the grunt's heavy breathing, but where was it? Wedged as they were in a corner, they had no way to retreat. Vilavivianna could probably have wriggled through one of the windows into the yard, but Cazia would never fit.

Cazia remembered the way the queen's neck had looked as she hit the ground. Lar's mother had been trapped on that dais, just as she was trapped now, and that was all that was needed to break her concentration. She restarted the spell, moving faster this time. *The flinches*, Treygar had called it. It wasn't fair. Her stupid brain was going to get them both killed.

The spell was nearly finished, and still the creature hadn't appeared. Cazia broke it, and just as she was about to start again, Vilavivianna screamed.

Cazia nearly jumped out of her skin. A dark-furred arm had come through the window and caught hold of the girl's long braid. Vilavivianna bared her teeth in pain as the creature dragged her toward the narrow window.

Without a moment's thought, Cazia stabbed the dart into the creature's forearm. It passed between the bones and stuck through the other side. The grunt roared in pain but didn't release the braid. Instead, it pulled harder, the point of the protruding spike striking the window jamb. Vilavivianna gasped from the pain, but she didn't cry out again.

This was no good. Cazia could stab the grunt until it looked like a thorn bush, but that wasn't going to free the princess, not before more beasts arrived. She snatched a knife from the table beside her. An orange flash in the dim light told her it was copper, but that wouldn't matter if it was sharp.

Cazia slashed the little girl's braid, cutting it straight through. She felt an absurd rush of gratitude for that officious Chief Servant, or whatever he was called, for the way he ran his staff.

"The door!" Cazia said, her voice high with fear. The girl ran out of the corner as Cazia thrust the knife toward the window. As she expected, the grunt leaned into the opening, but she misjudged its position and the tip of the blade glanced off its brow above the eye.

The beast shrieked and reeled back. The door closed with a bang, and the princess hissed, "There's no latch!"

Of course there was no latch. Why would you let servants barricade themselves in with the food? Cazia pivoted toward the door and started another spell. This time, no matter what happened, she could not let her concentration falter. Vilavivianna snatched a coal spade from beside the oven and wedged it against the door and a crack in the stone floor.

The grunt continued to spit and roar at the tiny window, but other roars began to grow nearer. This was the Fire that might take them both; Cazia walled off all thought about her growing panic and focused intently on the work her mind and her hands were doing. The spell itself helped, smoothing out her emotions, flinches or not.

It worked. A block of pink granite—taller and narrower than the ones she had created outside the wall—appeared beside the door, jamming it closed. "Close the other one," Cazia said, and began her spell again. The princess hesitated, but she did it. Cazia laid another block atop the first one.

She cast the spell again, this time against the door to the stairs. The howl of the beasts became louder as the pack drew near. All of her spells were too slow, too slow! The next block of granite appeared at the base of the stairway door, jamming it shut. She turned back to the yard entrance. That was where the grunts were, and that was the door they'd try to batter down first. Three more blocks should close off that entrance.

As she cast the spell, she felt Vilavivianna's gentle hands against her skirts. Why would the girl reach for one of her darts when the kitchen was full of knives? Cazia couldn't remember what she'd done with the copper knife she'd taken from the bench, but she hoped the princess had it.

Focus. Focus on the spell. The grunts had arrived. They battered against the door and roared through the narrow windows. Cazia had never heard anything so loud in her life; not even the chaos and screaming during the attack on the palace had pressed in on her like this.

The block appeared, fitting snug against the door and lintel. At the same time, Cazia experienced another of her flinches, and Vilavivianna took something from her that most definitely wasn't a dart.

Cazia turned as the girl stepped away. She'd taken the pouch with the translation stone. The princess deftly opened it and overturned it into her palm.

Never mind that. Cazia cast the spell again, then again. The door would never swing open, not with all that granite behind it, but if the grunts tore it from its hinges, she didn't want to leave them enough room to climb over.

When she finished, she turned toward the princess. The beasts outside screamed their animal rage and frustration, but Vilavivianna was very still. Her straw-colored hair hung loose around her face, making her seem almost adult. By the emberlight, Cazia could see that her eyes were wide with shock.

Cazia took the blue stone from her and clutched it in her trembling fist. The roars from outside suddenly became words.

Blessing! Bless you! Bless you! Take you! Blessing! Blessing!

That was it. Over and over, they all said the same thing. Great Way, they were talking.

The stupid commander was wrong. The grunts weren't animals. They were something worse.

Cazia stood there, unmoving, listening to the creatures' words in utter astonishment. If they spoke words, they could think, and if they could think, what advantage did the girls have against them?

Vilavivianna slammed the nearest shutter closed and threw the bar. The bang of wood on stone shook Cazia back to herself. She slipped the stone back into its pouch and pocket, then began another spell. The grunts battered at the door behind her as though they might push the stack of granite blocks onto her from behind. Her concentration faltered but did not fail. She stacked blocks against the second door until it was completely barricaded.

"At least we will not have to look at them," Vilavivianna said, having to raise her voice over the noise from outside. "But closed doors will bring all of them here and will drive them into a frenzy."

"Good."

"Good?" The girl took a few sticks of wood and laid them on the hot embers of the stove pit, then sprinkled shavings over them. Why not? They weren't in hiding any more. "Are we establishing Fort Child, then? We build high our walls, ration our salted fruit mush, and wait for rescue?" There was a note of derision in her tone. She frowned at her cut hair and began to braid it again.

Cazia took another breath to steady her nerves. It seemed odd to say, but the firelight made her feel stronger. There was still a great deal of work to do. "We don't have to wait for rescue. We're already here. We're going to gather supplies and get out of this fort."

The princess thrust her little chin forward and nodded.

The grunts could easily have smashed the shutters but they didn't. The door was all they cared about. Cazia pulled Vilavivianna into a narrow space between two benches—she had to kick aside a wooden pail full of boiled bones to make room for them both, and for some reason, that brought on another flinch. A bad one.

The little princess laid a gentle hand on her elbow. "Are you well?"

"I'm fine," Cazia snapped. She was not going to show weakness in front of this Indregai snob. "I just need to catch my breath." She began another spell. It was difficult to focus past the jumpiness in her stomach—the meal she'd eaten didn't want to stay down—but she did it.

A block at about waist height crumbled. Cazia crouched down to peer through but there was nothing but darkness beyond. Good. If the wall had stood against the yard, they would have seen starlight. She began shoving the broken rock through the hole, making space to crawl through.

"I can fit," Vilavivianna said. "But you should break another rock to make room for you."

"I can fit, too!" Cazia snapped. "Besides, if I broke another, the whole thing might come down on us."

"Ah," was all the princess said. She wriggled through the gap like a snake.

Cazia squeezed into the hole just behind her. Her shoulders fit through comfortably, but her breasts scraped uncomfortably against the rough stone. It was embarrassing, even in this pitch dark room with no one nearby but a child who couldn't even see. A few years ago, this wouldn't have happened, but she wasn't Vilavivianna's age any more. Her hips were a tight fit as well, but she knew she could get through. It would just take a bit of time. "Do you see any windows?" she whispered.

There was no answer at first, which she didn't like. Could something have happened to the girl in the few moments—

"No," the princess finally said. Her voice faint. "There is no light at all. The darkness, it is too much. I—"

"Patience," Cazia said. She finally got her hips through, but was punished for her haste by the sound of tearing cloth. "Fire and Fury," she said as she stood in the darkness.

She cast a light spell, placing it high on the wall beside her. It was just a little glowing ball, like a self-contained sphere of moonlit fog, but their eyes were so accustomed to the dark that it looked as bright as the rising of the sun.

"We are here!" Vilavivianna said, more loudly than Cazia thought was wise. But she was right. This was the armory. It was directly next to the kitchen, but there had been no easy connection between them until Cazia had created one.

And there were no windows, but the door was standing slightly ajar.

Cazia snatched a travel cloak from a peg in the wall and threw it over the door. The walkway where Zollik had killed the grunt must have been directly above them, which meant the great hall where the creatures held their prisoners was across the yard to the left. The armory door opened inward, with the hinges on the right. If a grunt looked out of the hall doorway, it would not see into the lighted room, but it might see a shaft of light falling into the yard.

"Do you see?" Vilavivianna asked.

At first, Cazia could not. She peeked between the cloak and the door jamb, noting the light from the great hall and the uneven ground of the yard . . .

There was a dead man lying just outside the door. Even in the terrible light, they could see it was Commander Gerrit. Farther from the door, they could see silhouettes on the ground that could only be more dead bodies.

Monument, sustain me.

The girls arranged the cloak on the corner of the door, rubbing the wool against the rough granite wall so it stuck there. Eventually, they were satisfied. The door would stand open, but no light would shine through.

In the armory, both of them went for the knives first, choosing two iron blades each with good leather-wrapped handles and belt sheaths. Then Cazia crossed to the cloaks, rations, and back packs while Vilavivianna hunted among the bows and quivers for something that suited her. Cazia had no intention of taking any more weapons. Knives and darts were enough for a scholar, and her quiver was full.

She packed meatbread and gathered smallish cloaks, a pair of wooden canteens with bladder linings, and a few other odds and ends they'd need.

The whole thing suddenly seemed ridiculous. Cazia had never trekked through wilderness in her life, but to do it at night with no other company but a girl even younger than she was?

They would be eaten by a bear or a mountain cat. They would be buried in a rockslide, kidnapped by Durdric Holy Sons, or fall from a cliff. They would starve. Cazia had spent her whole life in the palace, with only the occasional trip, under guard, outside Peradain.

Vilavivianna stepped up at her shoulder and examined her pack. "Is there no needle and thread? A copper needle will do as long as we keep the green off of it. Some gut would also be useful; I know imperial troops are used to healing magic, but we will be far from sleepstones and medical scholars."

Cazia stood and surveyed the room. In the far corner, there were small leather satchels with medical symbols branded into the corner. There were copper needles inside with gut, clean cotton, and tiny glazed jars with wax stoppers. She grabbed two.

Vilavivianna had laid out a second pack and was loading them both. She'd already loaded all the provisions Cazia had set out into one of the packs, and was adding an equal amount to the other. She'd also thrown aside the black imperial cloaks Cazia had chosen, replacing them with two unmarked gray ones. Finally, she put a hatchet onto the top of each pack.

"We are young," the girl said, "and we are not strong enough to carry everything we will need. But this will have to do."

Cazia felt almost reassured to see the princess take over. "I've never done this," she said, afraid the younger girl would mock her. *This one is not highborn or necessary, is she?* "I've never gone into the wilderness without an armed guard."

Vilavivianna strapped a long knife to her belt beside her other two. On her, it looked like a short sword. "Good. You have saved my life here in this fort, and you have done everything for us with your magic. When we get beyond the walls, I will have a chance to repay your valor."

The word *valor* shocked Cazia. Valor? All she could remember was the uncontrollable anger she felt as she slapped the girl's face like a bully, her cry of surprise when Vilavivianna spoke up from between the cabinets, and her flinches.

Her expression must have showed her confusion, because the princess said, "Have I offended you again?"

"No. Not at all. Thank you."

The little girl nodded. "I have not seen armor."

She was right. What was the point of an armory if there was no armor? They peered around the room. Racks of spears and knives, jars of oil, cloaks, a whole wall of shields . . . Why was that tapestry there?

The tapestry concealed an unbarred door, and they found armor behind it. Cazia had to cast a second light spell in this smaller room. There were three rows of iron cuirasses along one wall and four racks of iron greaves on the other.

"Tyr of the Sleeping Earth," Vilavivianna said, her hands opening and closing. "So much iron, just sitting here."

Cazia almost said, *We're not going to steal from the fort,* but that would have been ridiculous. No one had given them permission to take what they already had. "We're only going to take what we need."

"Of course," the girl said without taking offense. "I am a princess of Goldgrass Hill, not a thief. Still, with just two rows of those breastplates, one could buy a whole valley in my land. But they would only weigh us down. We need boiled leather, and it must fit us or we must leave it."

Cazia did find a boiled leather vest that fit her, even if it did was tight around her chest. Vilavivianna wasn't as lucky; not even the smallest of the fleet squad armor sat comfortably on her, and she had to make do with a thick quilted jacket. "At least I will be warm," the girl said. Cazia dug through the pile until she found one her size.

After that, they found a chest full of broad-brimmed cloth hats waxed against the rain, with iron caps sewn inside them. Cazia thought they looked ridiculous, but Vilavivianna carefully wrapped up her hair to make the smallest of them fit. Maybe, if she escaped back to her own people, it would buy her a great big garden plot.

They went back to their packs. Then the princess took a sword belt from the floor beside her. "You must wear this."

Cazia didn't know a thing about swords except that you held them by the blunt end. "I don't need it." She patted her quiver of darts.

"Those will go into your pack," Vilavivianna said. "You can not wear them in the Sweeps. Not if you want to live."

Great Way, the girl was right. Even in the heart of the empire, scholars went everywhere with an armed guard. If the two young girls in the wilderness came upon a mining camp or herding clan, they might receive hospitality. But for a scholar, kidnapping and ransom was the *best* possible outcome.

"You're right," Cazia said. "But not until we're clear of the grunts. I don't know how to use a sword, and these darts are my only weapon."

"That makes sense. Let me finish packing. You must choose a spear for the journey—do not argue. You must."

The spears were back near the gap she'd created in the wall. The howling of the grunts had not lessened—did the cursed things ever tire?—in fact, it seemed to have doubled. Clearly, they were attacking both doors now.

Cazia should never have left this hole in the wall. She swept the rubble in toward her feet, and with the sound of fists bashing on stone echoing around her, she cast a new block into the wall. It didn't fit as well as it should have; she was getting better at creating stone blocks, but she had a long way to go before she'd be ready to build a wall.

Worse, the gaps made her nervous. A too-small block would not catch the grunts' attention, but little gaps with lights flickering through?

"Are we ready to go?" Vilavivianna said. "I assume we will use your stone-breaking spell to escape through the wall."

"I have something to show you," Cazia said. She led the princess to the tapestry again. Together, they stood in the doorway and looked eastward down both rooms. "Do you see it?"

"No," the girl admitted, growing impatient. "Are you taunting me or teaching me a lesson?" Her tone suggested there wasn't a lot of difference between them.

"It looks to me as though the rooms are different lengths," Cazia said.

Vilavivianna looked again. "Yes! Such a thing never occurred to me. But what does it mean?"

Cazia examined the eastern wall. She didn't find anything interesting and extinguished the light as they went back into the main room. In the far southeastern corner, the wall had no racks on it. It took Cazia a few heartbeats to find the latch, and the hidden door creaked as the wall swung inward.

She extinguished the light in the main armory, letting darkness fall over them. Only the faint glow of lightstones shone up at them. Vilavivianna rushed down the stone stairs into the tunnel, and Cazia hurried to keep up.

"This is too long to connect to the great hall, yes?" The princess seemed excited. "It must go to the commander's tower beyond. Too bad Commander Gerrit couldn't get to it."

"Let's keep our voices low. There might be ventilation pipes."

This was a safe place, Cazia realized. If they brought their rations down here, they would have light and safety for as long as their supplies held out, or until the empire retook the fort. Surely someone would try that, considering the value of the hostages?

She stopped suddenly. Vilavivianna stopped, too. "What is wrong?"

There was no rescue coming—or rather, if soldiers liberated them from Samsit, it would not be a rescue. Every tyr in the empire was probably hunting for her, and for the little princess, too. The Italgas had treated her gently—even kindly, at times—in part because of Lar and in part out of a sense of honor.

But tyrs took hostages all the time. Sometimes, they demanded ransoms or forced marriages, or just dropped people into pits and forgot to feed them. Someone who wanted leverage over the tyr her father, far away, would find her to be a very useful fulcrum.

And Vilavivianna? She would almost certainly be forced into a marriage she didn't want, and Fire take the idea of waiting for her to come of age.

Not all tyrs were ruthless Enemies, but most were. No matter how tempting, the girls couldn't hide down here. They had to get them out of the fort as soon as possible.

"Quickly," she whispered. They ran to the end of the hall, their boots gently scuffing the stone floor.

There was no stairwell at this end, only a ladder chiseled into the stone.

Cazia put her finger to her lips and started to climb. Her pack was a burden, but thankfully, the passage was wide enough for her to pass without scraping loudly against the stone.

From there, they came to a set of curving stairs. The darkness here was absolute once she passed out of sight of the stone ladder, but she had climbed the secret stair in the Scholars' Tower many times. This was no different. She crouched low, using her hands on the stairs as she went up.

Faint glimmers of light showed her the hidden doors, and she knew which she needed. At the third floor, she paused to listen and, hearing nothing, unlatched the door.

This was the commander's Far Counsel, where he kept the mirror. Cazia had never used one herself, but she had been present for the message to the tyr her father, as well as some of the other tyrs—Fire and Fury, was it really just six days ago? The one in the palace was big enough to match the weight of ten men—to make it hard to steal, Lar had said—but this one was only mounted on a thick lead base.

So, she knew what to do. She stood before it, making sure her entire face was visible in the polished silver, and said "Tyr Gerrit."

She'd worried that it wouldn't work because *Tyr* was a title, not a name, but the mirror glowed brightly anyway. After many breaths, a man's face appeared within it.

She would never have guessed he was related to the commander. He was about fifty, with a receding hairline and a gray beard that he had twisted into a dozen small braids. His eyes were narrow and cruel, and Cazia was heartsick at the idea that this was her best hope for an ally. Tyr Gerrit had fought for the king so many years ago. If he wasn't a decent man—

"What are you doing, girl? Playing? I'll have you whipped! I'm a busy—"

His voice echoed in the stone chamber. Cazia shushed him, and while that made his face turn red with anger, something in her expression convinced him to take her seriously. "Fort Samsit has been taken."

His expression didn't change. "I've heard no reports on this. Who captured it?"

"Grunts. It happened a few hours—"

"*Grunts!* Animals stormed a fort of the empire and overwhelmed two hundred spears and bows? Where is Ranlin?"

"Commander Gerrit is dead!" Cazia hissed. This was not going at all as she expected, and she wasn't sure what to say next.

Before anything came to mind, another voice came through the mirror, from a man she couldn't see, "It's a prank. No, it's a ruse to make us keep our spears behind the walls of our holdfasts. May I?"

"This is not a prank!" Cazia's voice became louder, and the princess laid a hand on her elbow to calm her. *I have the flinches,* she wanted to shout, but would that convince them the danger was real or would that make them doubt her further? One thing was certain: it would not earn her any sympathy. There was no feeling rarer among the tyrs than sympathy.

Another face moved into view. He looked somewhat younger than Tyr Gerrit and had curly black hair with a triangular face. He looked vaguely familiar to her, although his expression was, if anything, more cruel than Gerrit's. A stage actor wearing that sneer would have been mocked for overacting. "Do you know me, girl?"

"Tyr Bendertuk," she said without thinking.

"Quite correct. Where is my son, Timu?"

"I don't know." Cazia turned to Vilavivianna, but she didn't know, either. "On a sleepstone, last I saw. He was injured in the fighting when we escaped from Peradain."

Tyr Bendertuk didn't think much of that. "That's what Treygar and the prince claimed five days ago. Has he not come through yet?"

"He had broken bones," Cazia said, hating that she stammered a bit. "But I don't know where he is now. I haven't seen him since the alarm gong went off."

"So he's dead, then." Tyr Bendertuk's expression was contemptuous.

"Great Way, I hope not," Cazia said. "Timush is my *friend.* Listen to me, please: the grunts overwhelmed the guards inside the fort. I don't know how. I can hear them howling down in the courtyard, but I don't know if you can hear it, too." Bendertuk's expression didn't alter; he couldn't—or he refused to—hear the grunts outside. "They rounded up the others and are holding them in the great hall—"

"As captives?" Tyr Gerrit said from somewhere out of sight.

"*Yes.*" Cazia tried to sound as forceful as possible, but the only response was laughter. "These aren't like the ones who came through the portal at Peradain. They're different. *Listen!*"

"I've heard the story," Tyr Bendertuk said with a dismissive wave. "You weaken it by changing it midway. I'll bet Treygar abandoned my son in Peradain, just as he abandoned Rolvo's daughter. Well, tell your prince, if he's not cowering out of sight in the room with you, that he can not control me through Tyr Freewell. I will not withhold my spears just because the Italgas hold a knife to a Freewell throat, and if he thinks otherwise, he'll be Fire-taken like my heir."

"Enough," Vilavivianna said. "You have warned them. You can not make them heed."

"And who is that?" Bendertuk said. Gerrit stepped back into the frame of the mirror, gently moving Tyr Bendertuk aside.

"Yes," Gerrit said, his voice sharp with the habit of command. "Step forward and show your face."

The princess's shoulders straightened. Before Cazia could react, she stepped in front of the mirror. "I am Vilavivianna of Goldgrass Hill, daughter of—"

"I know who your father is," Tyr Gerrit said. His cruel face seemed to open just enough to show his greed. "So, you *are* there! The Italga boy hasn't married you yet, has he? Has the prince taken you to his marriage bed?"

Vilavivianna's lip curled with disgust. Cazia pulled the girl aside, sparing the princess the sight of Gerrit's open mouth. "That *Italga boy* you keep talking about isn't a prince. He's your king."

She threw a cloth across it, breaking the connection. The glow was extinguished in moments, and Cazia was startled to realize that the shutters on the south wall were open. She'd just lit up this room like a candle in a tomb.

Cazia rushed to the window and looked out. She couldn't see anything down in the unlit yard, not by starlight. The sound of the grunts had not changed. This window faced south, toward the empire, while the beasts were in the eastern yard. For once, she'd gotten lucky.

"That was what I expected." Vilavivianna's voice was small.

Cazia wasn't sure what the little girl meant. She kept staring out into the yard. In the dark, the clouds had parted enough that she could see shooting stars. How beautiful they were. "What did you say?"

Vilavivianna's voice was shaky when she repeated herself. "That was what I expected from the nobles of Peradain. You have not been; you, Cazia Freewell, have shown me kindness, have bravely saved my life, have respected me enough to strike me with your open hand when I offended you, and have trusted me enough to magic where I could see. I did not expect you."

Cazia turned away from the window. Vilavivianna was little more than a silhouette, but Cazia could see that she was trembling.

"You have been honorable with me," the princess continued, "to a degree I never expected, and so has Lar Italga and the whole royal family. But those two men, those tyrs, they are the Peradaini I believed I was coming to live among."

"Not all tyrs are like that," Cazia said without thinking about it. "Tyr Gerrit is just afraid, I think, and the king . . . " *The king was a decent man, as kings go. He's just another tyr, but with sole control of the Gifts, which is how he retains the Throne of Skulls.* "The tyrs can be hard men, but they are not wholly evil."

"Peradaini tyrs have been crossing the Straim for four generations, killing my people, looting storehouses, and burning towns in the cause of conquest. They do not have to be 'wholly' evil to be evil enough to deserve the name."

Cazia thought that was unfair, but she had no idea how to respond. King Ellifer had sent several armies into Indregai when he was younger, and King Ghrund before that. Of course, the armies would have killed people, but . . . No, Cazia didn't know how to reconcile her own vision of the empire with what Vilavivianna was saying, but she couldn't refute the girl's words, either.

"The king made assurances to my father," the princess continued. "He made assurances that I would not be raped. I agreed to cross the Straim and live in the city, to marry the prince and bear the children when I was of age, but I was not to be forced into a marriage bed before my time had come."

"Oh, no!" Cazia rushed forward and took Vilavivianna's tiny hands. They were so cold. "Oh, no, please, I . . . I don't know what to say to you."

"Say that these tyrs coming to track me down will honor King Ellifer's agreement."

Cazia wanted to reassure the princess that it would be so, but she couldn't lie. "I'm just a girl," she said. "I don't have any lands or any spears, except the one you told me to carry, but I will do everything in my power to keep that the agreement between Lar's father and yours. I will do my best to protect you."

After a moment, the princess sighed. "Thank you."

Cazia was glad that they were standing in darkness. She didn't want to see the expression on the princess's face, not when she had thanked her in that tone of voice.

The howling from outside the windows became louder. Cazia went to the window and saw lights wavering in the night sky. The shooting stars she'd seen earlier were not stars at all.

"More flying troops," Vilavivianna said, her voice flat.

Of course. How could she not have recognized them immediately? The closest was already within the walls, slowly sinking toward the yard. It was flying green Four Rivers banners—no wonder Tyr Gerrit had looked at Vilavivianna so greedily. He knew his spears were about to seize her.

A captain in full iron called for the commander and his guard to receive them. Of course, no one was nearby, but the howling of the grunts became louder and more insistent. Cazia was frozen with indecision. These were imperial soldiers like Zollik and Peraday, and after hiding and running from grunts all night, she felt a ferocious need to be surrounded by them, but she knew what that would mean for the princess.

"They are landing between us and the south gate," Vilavivianna said. "We have to make for the north gate."

The second cart did not float down to land; it swerved to the east, sweeping over the fort. The soldiers inside had already nocked arrows and drawn bows. The third cart flew high above the tower, beyond their field of vision.

"Yes," Cazia said quietly. "And we don't have much—"

Something struck the low-flying cart of archers, bursting the wooden beam connecting the front of the cart to the black disk above. The cart jolted; the soldiers within cursed or cried out, loosing arrows accidentally against the stone below.

The lamps inside the cart lit the driver's face clearly. She was an older woman, thick-bodied and pug-faced, her gray hair plaited over her wool and quilted cotton jacket. Cazia could see the concentration on her face as she tried to right the cart, but a volley of stones from below struck soldiers, splintered wood, and her.

The back of the cart jolted downward and the driver tipped over the rail backwards, only staying inside because of her safety harness. The cart began to slide down and sideways, as though it was losing traction on a muddy hill, and soldiers cursed and fumbled at the quivers on their hips as they struggled to stay inside.

"We have to go!" the princess hissed.

Cazia followed her out of the room and down the stairs. She wanted that mirror, but they could never have carried it, even in a litter.

Want want want. She kept wanting things she couldn't have. It was ridiculous and she had to break the habit. She had to be ready to discard anything.

Except her friends.

At the bottom of the stair, Vilavivianna ran to the door at the northern end of the tower. It was the servants' entrance, naturally, but Cazia didn't follow. The princess knelt beside the open door and peered into the yard. "Now is our chance."

"Not yet." Cazia ran to the broken eastern door and peeked through. This led to the great hall, a direct connection between the commander's tower and the dining and meeting hall of the fort. In fact, it opened onto the raised section at the front of the room where the tyrs and officers ate. Cazia had a momentary flinch, then leaned through the opening.

The hall was full, but as she'd hoped, most of the people were down on the main floor. Servants, farmers—whatever jobs they had—citizens sat listlessly at the tables or stretched out on the floor. Many were bloodied about the face or arms. There were no grunts in sight.

But up on the raised section, behind the high table, sat men who looked like important town officials, men dressed as riverboat captains, and most importantly, highborn hostages.

"Bitt!" Cazia tried to keep her voice low, but it seemed that everyone within twenty paces heard her. "BITT!"

Bittler looked at her with shock, then hurried to her. Timush and Jagia, their arms in slings, slept against the back wall. Bittler's shoulder was covered by a bloody bandage; he wouldn't be helping with the packs anytime soon. "What are you doing here?"

"Saving you. The beasts are all out there fighting. Why didn't you try to escape?"

"We have to stay," Bitt said, his face pale and serious. "We all agreed that we must stay."

"What are you talking about? Don't be stupid. Get Timu and Jagia. Even if the grunts lose, Tyr Gerrit plans to take us as hostages."

"We can't leave, Cazia. We all agreed. *We've been bitten.* If you're uninjured, you need to get away from us. From all of us."

"Bitt—"

"Get out!" He bared his teeth as he spoke, his voice harsh and low and entirely unexpected. He stepped forward and shoved her, hard. Cazia stumbled backwards, the weight of her pack overbalancing her. She fell onto the wooden floor with a painful knock on her elbow. "Get out before we bless you."

Cazia watched in shock as he shut the door in her face. Vilavivianna was suddenly at her shoulder, trying to pull Cazia to her feet. "We have lingered too long. Your friends will not come and I think you know why."

"I don't," Cazia said. "I honestly don't."

"The fight in the front yard will not last much longer. Let us get beyond the wall and we will discuss it."

Cazia realized there were tears in her eyes. Stupid. How could Bitt want to stay? Yes, he'd been injured, and yes, there were sleepstones at Samsit, but what good were sleepstones if you weren't safe? Why had he said he'd "bless" her?

A nasty suspicion grew inside her mind, a thought that wasn't ready to make itself known, and she knew she was not going to like it.

She and Vilavivianna paused at the entrance to the northern yard, but only for a moment. The screams, roars, and war cries from the far end of the fort were growing fewer and fainter. "We must hurry."

There was no time to creep around the edges of the yard, crouching in the shadows of the eaves. They leaned forward to let the weight of their packs fall on their backs rather than their shoulders, and they ran as fast as they could.

There were no howls, thank the luck of the Gambler, because they couldn't have outrun a grunt even without a heavy pack, but before they'd even reached the halfway point, someone shouted, "There!"

An arrow struck in the mud in front of her, and Cazia snapped the shaft with the toe of her boot as she ran over it. Another volley fell around her, and the princess began to run in an erratic, unpredictable line. Cazia did the same.

There were more shouts from behind, and she heard splintering wood and cries of pain and rage. No more arrows fell around her, and she managed to reach the gate before the little princess, who was flagging under the strain of sprinting with her pack. Cazia lifted the bar free, then pulled the bolts out of the stone wall above. Together, the two girls pushed it open—it was small, barely wider than her old room back at the palace—and the hinges were well oiled, but the wood was so thick, it took all their weight and strength to shove it wide enough to slip through.

Within two hundred paces, Vilavivianna fell into a quick walk, and Cazia gladly matched her pace. She glanced behind them but could see nothing but the light-colored stone of the fort. The starlight in the pass was welcome, especially since there could be so little of it in the grasslands and waterlands, but it was not bright enough to tell if they were being pursued or not.

"We should get as far as possible before sunrise," the princess said. She liked authority, and Cazia thought she handled it well when she wasn't trying to prove herself. "The soldiers will not fly through the pass in the dark, assuming they win the battle with a cart intact. We will need a place to hide from them, and it should be somewhere beyond the range they think we will be capable of."

That made sense. "What if the grunts take the fort back?"

The princess's response was wary. "Then we will have more time, while they spend two days, at least, with the new captives."

"Why?" Cazia asked. "Why did Bitt refuse to flee with us?"

"Your friend knows he would be a danger to you. As for the creatures themselves, they watch over the captives for the same reason a mother stands guard over the children."

In that moment, the unformed suspicion that had been growing in Cazia's mind became clear.

Fire take me. I murdered my own brother.

Chapter Thirteen

THE WAY DOWN INTO THE SWEEPS HAD NOT LOOKED DIFFICULT, BUT Tejohn had not anticipated how exhausting and nerve-wracking it would be to walk on a slope of loose stones. They shifted under every step, required a terrible level of concentration, and made it nearly impossible to watch the skies above for more ruhgrit. The body of the grunt had been left at the campsite for the crows, but they were still carrying too much. They hadn't even reached midday before Reglis fell onto his back and nearly slid over the edge of a cliff.

A trip to the far western end of the continent, which should have taken them ten days at most by flying cart, would be interminable on foot.

And they had little time, considering the king's condition.

On the other side of the Southern Barrier, the winds were generally westerly. Sometimes, they might shift northward. On occasion, if you were near a pass, you might face a southerly wind as they did when they flew out of Fort Samsit. Very rarely, a bitter, chill wind might come out of the east.

In the Sweeps, there was no variation. The winds were always out of the west, always blowing toward the east. Every cloak, every bit of blown fluff, every waving stalk of grass pointed toward the rising sun. Tejohn hated the feel of it on his face, but on this switchback trail, he hated to feel it on his pack even more, as though it was shoving him back toward his starting point. To make things worse, the air smelled sour.

They came around a switchback, starting west again. Wimnel Farrabell lagged behind, as he had all morning. He was not accustomed to marching, even without a pack, and his broken arm drained him. Tejohn felt sorry for the man, but he was not going to wait for him. Farrabell was expendable now.

Luckily, Arla's vision had returned well before dawn. "There are no bridges," she told them as they walked. "This far west, we won't encounter many fast-flowing rivers. There will be mountain streams—cold and miserable to wade through, but that's how we'll have to do it."

Tejohn could see no streams, only the tall grasses, the stones beneath his feet, and the blurry colors that marked the valley floor and mountains beyond. He knew from maps that the western end of the Sweeps was a bit more southern than the eastern, but it wasn't noticeable unless the sun was very close to the horizon. And on this side, the Southern and Northern Barriers ran nearly straight, as mountain ranges go.

Arla pointed out into the middle of the valley. "Do you see Lake Windmark below?"

She gestured out into the distance. Tejohn could not see details at this distance, but he could see a long stretch of gray, the same color as the sky.

"Yes," Reglis answered. Wimnel and Lar had barely spoken all day.

"It looks like a lake with a shore from up here, but in fact, it's much wider than it appears. Deep marshy grasses surround it on the southern side, and okshim herders give it a wide berth when they have a choice."

"Why?" Tejohn asked.

"Alligaunts, my tyr. They are thick at the western end of this valley, but some venture far to hunt. The Northern Barrier is a steeper range, with smooth cliff faces no human can scale, but that means the lake has settled in the northern side of the valley. It's only once we get to the most western part of the Sweeps that the lake will broaden across the whole of the valley and we will be unable to avoid the water's edge. If we keep high on these southern slopes, we should be safe for most of the trip."

Tejohn said, "The graveyard menagerie in the Palace of Song and Morning had an alligaunt skeleton; I've never seen a live one, but I know they are not small."

Reglis grasped his spear in both hands. "Are they so dangerous?"

"Each is stronger than a man," she answered. "They prefer to ambush their prey near water, dragging them under and drowning them. It's a nasty death, and they often hunt in a pack so that if someone rushes into the shallows to save a victim, they are taken down and torn apart, too."

A grim silence settled over the group. Tejohn, knowing they were well above the hunting range of the creature, nonetheless scanned the area around them with extra scrutiny.

"On the other hand," Arla added, "their tails are delicious."

Lar laughed at that, and Reglis joined in. Tejohn was too hungry to laugh, but he wasn't going to be the one to call for a rest.

Reglis pointed to a small cluster of twisted trees. "We should pause here for a quick meal." He spoke with the casual confidence of a young man with nothing to prove. "We're marching at a fair clip and should pace ourselves."

Everyone seemed glad when they sat in the shelter of the trees. There were gray storm clouds overhead, but the wind kept them moving and they did not release any rain. Wimnel caught up to the group by the time they had opened their packs and taken out their food. He gently eased himself onto the ground, ate half a loaf of meatbread, and fell fast asleep.

Tejohn did not like the way Lar was looking at the injured driver. "My king," he said quickly. "We can not lose more time, not for him. Tonight, we will let him sleep without taking a watch. It will help him to heal, but we must press on."

Lar nodded and looked at the ground without speaking.

Arla said, "There are small mining camps all along this part of the Sweeps. I expect we'll find one before our third day is out. We might be able to hire an okshim cart there; as you might expect, the beasts are less expensive on this side of the barrier."

Tejohn nodded. Arla had assumed leadership of the group in all but name, and that was fine with him. It pleased him to have an experienced guide. "Is there anything else we should know?"

She glanced to the northeast with a worried expression, then looked at the ground. "I think not, my tyr."

"Don't keep secrets from me, soldier. If there's a danger to the northeast we should know about, I want to hear it."

"It's nothing, my tyr." Arla licked her lips. "Nothing but old folk tales."

Lar spoke up. "Bless us with your folk wisdom."

"I . . . My king, I am at your service. This . . . The Chin-Chinro do not often speak of the Qorr Valley. It's thought to be bad luck. I myself have not thought about it for ten years or more. But last night, after the ruhgrit attacked, it came to mind again.

"There is a valley on the far side of the Northern Barrier. Legend says it is open on one side only, if cliff faces battered by crashing waves and great chunks of ice the size of the commander's tower can be called 'open.' It is secluded, blocked by high cliffs all around, but within . . . "

She didn't seem to know what to say next. Tejohn prompted her. "Here be monsters."

"Yes," she said with some finality. "Some say the alligaunts came from there, swimming around the rim of the Northern Barrier before the sea giants or water eyes arrived. The gigantic spiders that invaded Shadow Hall most certainly came from there. Those creatures devastated the herder clans before they made their way through the southern passes. My grandfather used to talk about the times of his grandfather's grandfather, when feathered toads that poisoned anything they touched flew over those peaks."

Her implication was clear. "And you think the ruhgrit have also come over those mountains. That they are the latest monster spawned in your monster valley."

"Oh, no, my Tyr." Arla seemed genuinely upset by Tejohn's words. "It is not my valley. No human can even visit it, much less claim it as their own. There were passes once, but the ancient creatures destroyed them."

"If that's true," Reglis said, "we should see less of the ruhgrit as we move farther west, out of their range."

"They're big birds," Tejohn answered. "Their hunting range is probably larger than we'd like. We will have to watch the skies above and the shrubs at our feet for a while yet."

Lar filled everyone's canteen. That was servant work, but there was no one else to do it.

When their meal was over, Reglis woke Wimnel and helped him down the trail. Arla led the way, but Tejohn deliberately delayed Lar. "My king, I would like to see your shoulder."

"That is not blessed," Lar answered with a dismissive wave. He tried to push past Tejohn toward the trail.

"No, my king." How could Tejohn keep this behavior a secret from the others? "You appointed me your shield bearer and counsel, and I can not fulfill my duties if you lie to me or keep secrets. Let me see the shoulder where you were injured. I must insist."

After a brief staring contest, Lar shifted his cuirass and pulled up his padded sleeve. The tufts of blue hair had spread, becoming a patch of bristling fur.

"This gets worse with every spell you cast, doesn't it?"

The king shook his head. "Each spell I bless slows the change but strengthens it, too. It's like when you have to hold back blessings in temple. The more you restrain yourself, the more blessed it becomes."

Tejohn's heart sank as Lar spoke. "My king, I do not understand you."

The young man became irritated. "It's like holding back a blessing. Have you never laughed, my tyr?"

"Thank you, my king. I am not a clever man." Tejohn had a odd idea. He reached into his pocket and took out the enchanted stone he'd gotten from Cazia Freewell. "What else are you experiencing, my king?"

"Blessing," Lar answered. "My stomach feels empty all the bless, even after we eat."

Fire and Fury. Tejohn had hoped the spell would change the king's words back to what he intended. Unless that's what he did intend to say. "My king, I must ask you this: Do you know that you are substituting the words *bless*, *blessing*, *blessed* for other words, every time you speak?"

Lar Italga did not respond immediately. He stared downward, mustering his concentration. With great deliberation, he said, "The creature I am becoming is saying its name. The Blessing."

"That's what they call themselves?" Tejohn asked. Lar nodded. "Fire and Fury, but I will not call them that. Never."

Arla made her way back to them. Her blunt face and wide eyes were puzzled. "My king? My tyr? Is anything wrong?"

"No," Tejohn said. He had no intention of telling them that Lar was transforming. It would have been all too easy for the others to abandon them in the Sweeps or turn their spear points against them while they slept. Lar's curse would have to remain a secret for now.

The path was easier as they went farther down the mountainside. There were fewer switchbacks and less loose stone to slip on. Late in the day, Arla spotted a mountain lion skulking among the rocks above them. Tejohn and Reglis immediately readied their spears while Arla strung her bow. Lar turned and hurried back along the path toward Wimnel, who had fallen far behind. The king took the driver's good arm, steadying him across some of the looser stones. Tejohn and the others would not slow their pace for the driver, but they certainly waited for the king.

"I'm sorry, my king. I will try to do better." To his credit, Wimnel did not whine. He might have been a coward, but he could endure hardship. Lar only nodded and stayed with him, helping him over the rougher parts of the hill. The group as a whole moved somewhat more slowly, but the driver moved faster and kept pace with them. The mountain lion, for its part, decided to search for easier prey and disappeared into the rocks uphill.

The sun was nearing the western rim of the valley when Tejohn called for Arla. "Are we down in the Sweeps yet?" he asked.

"Yes and no, my Tyr, depending on how you measure such things. Some would say we'd entered the Sweeps when we stepped onto the scree this morning. Some when we leave the mountain side. Some when we step into our first mudhole. The land is steep to the south and less steep as you go—"

Tejohn held up his hand to stop her. "I understand. Let me ask this instead: this land has been claimed by the empire, hasn't it? Disputed, but claimed, and storm houses have been built here for our subjects."

She glanced at Wimnel, showing that she understood immediately. Before the empire spread, storm houses were places of shelter. In recent times, they were more likely to have a pair of sleepstones in them. Old King Ghrund, a murderous bastard if there ever was one, had put out sleepstones for his subjects in the Sweeps to care for their ill and injured . . . and he took them away if they rebelled. The tyrs had mocked the plan at first, but no one could deny that it had created peace.

But Arla explained that there were no storm houses this far south. Some of the more productive mining camps might have one, but she couldn't say where one could be found.

"What about that?" Reglis said, scowling upslope. It was a building made of pink scholar-created stone like the palace or Fort Samsit, but partly obscured by a knot of trees.

They scrambled up the hill and discovered that it was not a storm house at all. Worse, the southern wall was gone.

"What happened here?" Reglis said as he wandered through the single room. The pink stones of the southern wall lay scattered up hill as though flung by a giant.

"It's a scholar's hut," Arla said, "abandoned about a year, by the looks of it, and picked clean."

Tejohn glanced at Lar, who looked away. Just the day before, the king had told him that some scholars lived in seclusion, studying spells, sometimes with disastrous results. Now they had found just such a place.

Still, it was good to stand behind a wall out of the wind. "Night will be on us soon."

Lar led Wimnel to the most comfortable spot behind the wall, saw that he had water and food, then silently encouraged him to sleep. In the meantime, Arla and Reglis had gathered firewood and prepared a fire, which Lar lit for them.

Reglis and Arla took flutes from their packs, but they ate their dismal provisions in silence. "My king . . . " Reglis said. "My king, I have already sworn my life, my spear, and my duty to you, but . . . I've never seen . . . That man, a servant to the throne, was injured and you, his king, gave him your support."

Arla interrupted. "I, too, am astonished."

Tejohn shifted slightly, letting his hand fall on his sword. The captain and the guide had laid their weapons behind them, just within reach, but they still had knives. If they were about to declare him unfit, Tejohn would hear both of their death-rattles.

"My king," Reglis continued, his deep-set eyes so shadowed that Tejohn could not see them at all. "I will be your most loyal servant, not just in oath but in thought and deed."

"Reglis speaks for me as well," Arla said, her wide eyes still and calm. "although I had not expected him to."

"And me," Wimnel said from his dark corner. "Although my service is worth little."

Lar did not answer right away. Instead, he looked down at the fire, concentrating hard on what he had to say.

"My king?" Reglis asked.

"Tell. Them." Lar finally said.

"My king—" Tejohn began to protest, but Lar's expression silenced him. Tejohn sighed. The king understood his people better than Tejohn ever had, and it was time to trust him, a little.

He addressed Reglis and Arla directly. Wimnel was no soldier, and was not a concern. "The grunt that bit the king before we left was once a man. In fact, it was Colchua Freewell."

"Freewell!' Arla spat.

"Once, I would have agreed with you," Tejohn said. "I have no love for the Freewells. But Colchua was bitten while defending his king. What no one realized at the time was that the bite cursed him. It transformed him into a grunt."

There was an appalled silence. Reglis and Arla both glanced nervously at the king.

"Yes," Tejohn said. "The king has also been cursed."

"When did you know?" Wimnel said from the corner.

Tejohn wanted to strike him for asking a question, but he remembered Lar and the substitute swordmaster. He was the king's counsel now and would have to act with the king's wisdom. "Last night," he said, his voice more snappish than he'd planned.

"When will the transformation complete?" Reglis asked stonily.

Lar shook his head. "Not. Tonight."

Arla turned to Tejohn, her expression grim. "That's why you hoped to find a sleepstone," she said. "Not for the driver, but for the king."

Lar shook his head again. "Wouldn't." There was a long pause before he managed to say "Work."

"Nonetheless," Tejohn said. "We three will keep watch tonight, in shifts. King Lar must sleep—no, do not protest. You are as exhausted as the driver. The king does not expect to—change tonight, but we must watch him while we watch over him."

"If I change," Lar said, forcing the words to come out, "bless me. Kill. Me. Bless, blessing blessed *bless*."

The king bit the back of his hand to stop the words coming. No one spoke for a while, until Tejohn broke the silence. "Yes, my king."

In the morning, they ate again. The king was ravenous but finally forced himself to stop after a double portion. Tejohn, Arla, and Reglis loaded their packs in silence. The king stood a bit apart from the others as they filed out of the building; Tejohn could see Reglis and Arla were uneasy.

Then Wimnel offered the king a bundle wrapped in black cloth. "I saved half of my rations for you, my king."

Lar took them gratefully and, after a moment's hesitation, put them in his pocket. Then he took Wimnel's good arm and helped him navigate a dry streambed back down the trail.

They made better progress than the previous day, if only because the way was less steep. At Tejohn's command, Arla scouted well ahead. By mid-morning, she'd returned with troubling news.

Tejohn followed her along the path, jogging lightly to keep up. The king and Wimnel were in no condition to hurry, so Reglis stayed behind with them.

"There," Arla said as she crawled to the crest of a hill. "Do you see?"

"I can not see far," Tejohn said, "but it looks like a small village down there. I can see a stripe of pink that must be a scholar-created wall."

"Not a village," she responded. "A mining camp. They are flying a Finstel banner."

The Finstels were loyal to the Italga family. Tejohn had been born and raised on Finstel lands, and he'd been a Finstel subject. Splashtown was the Finstel city, in fact. They had risked much for King Ellifer, and been handsomely rewarded with the service of the king's scholars. "Do you think they will have a sleepstone down there?"

"A camp that size? I would expect so." Tejohn's heart leaped. Lar Italga might not think a sleepstone would fight his curse, but Tejohn intended to try. Who else did they have who could learn Ghoron Italga's spell and lead Peradaini troops against the grunts?

He started to scramble to his feet, but the guide grabbed his arm and pulled him flat beside her. "My Tyr, before you rush down there, can you see the loaded cart out in the yard? Near the gate?"

"No." Tejohn did not care about a loaded cart. They had little time to save the king, and he didn't want to waste any of it.

"It's small," she said as though reassuring him. "That cart is a Durdric design, my Tyr. Little more than a wheelbarrow. I think the camp, and its sleepstone, are in enemy hands."

CHAPTER FOURTEEN

THEY KEPT GOING UNTIL SUNRISE. CAZIA WANTED TO STOP WELL before, but she did not say anything, and Vilavivianna insisted, urging her on. Cazia convinced herself that Peraday was somewhere out here, holed up in a lookout's blind. Or something. It hadn't occurred to her to ask where the guard could be found later, and now she was angry with herself about it.

I killed Colchua.

They heard no howls from grunts and saw no carts pass overhead. The sky turned bright blue without any sign of the sun. The two girls made good progress by the reflected light. Cazia thought she should say something to the little princess walking ahead of her, but she knew the first word that came out of her mouth would result in a flood of tears. Her brother was dead and it was her fault.

She'd felt such pride after she'd done it. *I am not an archer. I'm a scholar.* Fire take her for an arrogant fool.

But of course, Col had been attacking Lar, and her brother would never have chosen to do that on his own. The beast had taken over. The curse. Probably, her brother would have *wanted* to be killed rather than attack his best friend and king, but no, no, no, she couldn't think that way. She couldn't even approach that thought. She had killed Colchua—had swept him from The Way as though she herself were Fire—and she wasn't going to pretend it had been a favor.

They walked along quietly. Eventually, tears did flow down Cazia's face, but the princess didn't look back, and she probably didn't know what they might mean, anyway.

It wasn't enough. She owed her brother more than a few silent tears—he deserved more—but she didn't have it in her. She was too exhausted and frightened to fall to the ground and wail; it would have been a performance. Who would have been her audience? This little foreign princess wouldn't care.

Those same thoughts churned all morning until they reached the crest of the pass, where the land began to slope down to the Sweeps, when Vila-vivianna asked to stop.

They clambered uphill out of the path, taking shelter behind an outcropping of rock. As she unslung her pack, Cazia was startled to see an arrow sticking out of it. She broke the shaft and threw it away, then hunted for the arrow head among her things.

The copper point had struck her canteen, passing completely through the wood and skin and protruding into her blanket. Luckily, she hadn't filled it yet, or all her things would be wet.

Vilavivianna was looking at her with wide eyes. *You could have died,* her expression seemed to say. Cazia felt goose bumps run down her back. She could have died. Would her quilted jacket and leather vest have stopped the arrow? She looked again at the punctured wood and shuddered. Fury had favored her last night, although it would have been true justice if she had taken the arrow in the neck and died.

Grateful am I to be permitted to travel The Way.

Her prayers brought no comfort, leaving her feeling odd and hollow. It was as though she had stolen Colchua's place in the world. Cazia squeezed the little princess's hand and laid out her blanket. She lay down without eating and fell into terrible dreams.

They slept for a few hours, waking only when the sun peeked over the eastern peaks and shone on their faces. They ate hurriedly. Cazia filled Vila-vivianna's canteen several times, until both had their fill and she had a full canteen to carry. The little princess seemed to have questions, but they set out in silence.

The trail down the far side of the pass was rockier than the southern side, and in some places, it was steep enough that they had to take switchback trails. Cazia looked ahead down the slope. She could see the narrow space where the mountains opened up and the Sweeps began. She had never been there, of course, but she had always been intensely curious about it. Would they see alligaunts? She'd heard they swam through the lakes, trailing water vines and fallen leaves, and she thought that would be a wonderful thing to see . . . from a safe distance. The alligaunt skeleton back in Ellifer's graveyard menagerie had given her nightmares when she was small.

She wished her old self—the one that had not yet committed murder—was taking this trip. She would have enjoyed it more.

Vilavivianna spoke only occasionally, and only on the subject of flying carts. Would one catch up to them? Would they be taken alive, even if they ran or fought back?

Cazia promised that she would count her steps and look behind at every tenth one. A cart would come up on them quickly, she explained, and only by checking continually, all day long, would she be able to see it in time.

That mollified the princess somewhat, and they fell into a pattern of walking and glancing back. By midafternoon, Cazia realized that the top of the pass would have been a perfect place for Peraday's lookout post, but she'd forgotten to search for her, or even to call her name. Turning around now, she could see nothing along the mountain cliffs that suggested a lookout station, and she certainly couldn't see a glint from a steel cap.

If Peraday had been stationed there, she would have seen the fleeing girls. Either she was not there or she wanted nothing to do with Cazia. So be it.

The sun moved beyond the western peaks, then the shadows swept up the mountainside. The sky was nearly dark when Vilavivianna decided they needed to stop for the night.

"I was hoping we could make it to the Sweeps tonight," Cazia said.

"It is too far," the princess answered. "It's easy to misjudge distances in the mountains. Besides, we will not have starlight like last night, see?"

She was right. The sky was gray with clouds blowing in from the Sweeps. It didn't look like rain, but there would be little light.

They found a flat, dry spot behind an outcropping of rock. "I wish we had wood for a fire," Vilavivianna said. "I wonder why so little grows here."

"I wish we didn't have to walk so far." Cazia arranged their blankets.

The little princess smiled. "We have not walked far at all," she said. "My mother told me that the Southern and Northern Barriers are very narrow ranges, nothing at all like the Seahook mountains in southeastern Indrega. I once spent fifteen days walking through a pass to visit another clan's sea house."

"Fifteen days!" Cazia thought it sounded like punishment. She took out a small loaf of meatbread and broke it in half, handing the little girl the slightly smaller portion.

"My uncle Nezzeriskos of Beargrunt thinks the Northern and Southern Barriers were once a single range, and that some great power swept all those peaks and rocks away, splitting the mountains and creating the Sweeps."

Cazia didn't like the sound of that. "What could do that? The wind?"

"A great worm, perhaps? A powerful magic? A godly being with a godly plow and a godly urge to plant some beets?"

They both laughed. "Godly beets," Cazia said. "Or a godly urge to plant alligaunts and herding peoples." Their shared laugh had startled her; it felt good. She silently offered an apology to her brother's memory.

"My mother says that alligaunts are demons who must be destroyed at every opportunity."

"I've only ever seen bones in the palace," Cazia said, hoping to keep their conversation light. "Never a live one."

"Let us hope it stays that way."

They ate in silence for a short while. Finally, Cazia asked the question that had been bothering her all day. "Where are we going? We're fleeing the grunts, yes, but where are we fleeing to?"

Vilavivianna set her chunk of meatbread on the cloth wrapping. "This is very dense and salty."

Cazia shrugged. She didn't think it was particularly salty, but she felt reasonably full. She wrapped their food and put it away. Best to make their provisions last.

Finally, Vilavivianna said, "Where do you want to go?"

"Tempest Pass," Cazia said immediately. "I want to join Lar in his quest, but that's impossible."

"We could never catch up to them on foot," Vilavivianna said. "Not only is the way very dangerous, they would be long gone by the time we arrived. My mother says one should never travel the Sweeps without a guide."

"I supposed we could go to another fort. Piskatook is closest, isn't it?"

The princess gave Cazia a wary look. "Would I be safe there?"

"We could disguise ourselves," Cazia said. "Take jobs somewhere, blend in until Lar finds a way to fix all this trouble."

"Become servants? Put ourselves under the care of a master? Who could order us to marry any other servants he liked?"

Cazia didn't like that idea, either. In fact, for a young woman in the empire with no name, she had few options: servitude, military service, religious seclusion, marriage, and . . . What? Open a hat shop? What she needed was to find another Scholars' Tower.

But where could she find one outside the palace and Tempest Pass? That was the whole point of building the towers. The king kept tight control of the scholars and their Gifts. "I don't know," Cazia admitted. *Col would have known.*

Vilavivianna shrugged. She did not look up from the bootlace she was trying to unknot. "We do not have to decide until we reach the end of the pass."

Cazia thought about it for a moment. "A giant worm, huh?"

Vilavivianna laughed. "It sounds like raving, I know. My uncle was an interesting man: he was a great warrior and singer. Often, when he told me stories, I could not tell if he was joking or telling the truth." After a moment, she said, "He was there, in the house in Peradain. He was the one who boosted me to the roof to Lar. I assume he is dead now."

"Maybe not," Cazia said. "By the time the grunts had reached the far end of the city, they had stopped killing and started simply biting people. Perhaps he has been transformed, like my brother."

"Then he is dead."

"I'm sorry."

"I am sorry, too. I know what happened to your brother, and what you had to do. Would it be a comfort to you if I said I think you did the heroic thing?"

"No," Cazia said, more sharply than she intended. She sighed. "No, I don't see it that way."

"I have wanted to say words of comfort to you all day, but I did not know what would be appropriate."

"I'm sorry," Cazia said. The princess could seem so formal and rigid, it was easy to forget that she was still a little girl. "Thank you very much. The truth is, we left my best friend behind in Peradain, and my brother is dead, and the others are back at Fort Samsit, waiting for their curses to take control of them—" And Lar, too. All day, she had been reliving the memory of her dart striking her brother, but she had been so focused on her own guilt that she hadn't even considered the king.

Fire and Fury. He'd been bitten the same day as the people who had just taken Samsit. He must have transformed by now.

Cazia tried to imagine the scene: Lar sprouting fur and fangs inside the cart while it sped above the treetops. The driver panicking. The soldiers drawing their weapons. Tyr Treygar . . .

Could she imagine Old Stoneface surviving a situation like that? It was possible—he was supposed to be a talented killer—but could he stand against a grunt, especially when it was the cursed king he had sworn to serve? Would he be torn by duty or would he relish the chance to gut his troublesome student?

The possibilities swirled in her head like leaves in a whirlwind; she couldn't even think about that now. She remembered Bittler shoving her and telling her to get out.

"That's all of them," Cazia said. "I lived as a hostage in the palace, surrounded by people all the time, but there were only six who didn't treat me as an enemy. Now they're all gone."

Vilavivianna laid her hand gently on Cazia's cheek. "I am fortunate. My parents are still across the Straim with my brothers and sisters. But many of my loved ones lived in that tall house in Peradain. My uncle, the wife, nine cousins—one of my cousins was only four months old. What will these grunts do to a tiny baby? Nip them lightly or devour them whole? This is something I wish to know. I also had friends I had known my whole life living with me in that house. And my honor guard."

Cazia had absolutely no idea what to say, and to her horror, she heard the words "It sounds crowded" come out of her mouth.

The little princess laughed and began to cry. Cazia knelt beside her and held her close. A stone jabbed painfully into her knee, but she did not move until Vilavivianna leaned away.

"I am sorry," the girl said, recovering her composure.

"I've been crying, too," Cazia said.

"I thought I had my fill of it in my room back in Samsit."

"Oh, no," Cazia said. She remembered how long the Italgas had grieved when Lar's younger brother died. "No, it's going to take longer than that."

"Well, that is inconvenient." They both laughed again.

Cazia took the princess's blankets and held them up. Vilavivianna lay down on her pad and Cazia covered her. Then Cazia stretched out beside her so they were nose to nose. "Tell me about Indrega."

"It is very beautiful," Vilavivianna said. "I had hoped to take my husband to see it someday, when the time came, but I do not think it will happen soon. We have trees and deep forests, and grass that is nearly blue."

"I would like to see that someday myself."

"We have mountains as well, but they are older than these. More rounded, with boqs and rabbits among the trees, and astonishing views. I do not mean to say that Peradain is not a beautiful land. The wind in the grasses makes a lovely sound, and I did enjoy the days we spent sailing on Deep Stone Lake."

"But it's not home."

"No," the girl said. "I can not walk through the deep forest here, surrounded by light reflected green by the leaves. There is little snow. There are no longhouses where everyone shares the meals and the laughter. I have felt isolated since I came here."

Cazia took her hand. "What else?"

"You want me to tell you about the Indregai serpents, yes?"

"Only if you're allowed. I've heard so many things but I've never seen one."

"They are not that interesting, I am sorry to say. They are as long as two men lying heel to crown, and quite thick around the middle. They can talk—"

Cazia felt tingles run up her back. "They can?"

"Not to us," Vilavivianna added hastily. "To each other. My uncle says we have tried to decipher the mouth sounds for years without success. And they can not even understand the most basic of verbal orders from us."

Cazia thought about the translation stone in her pocket. Would the princess try to take it from her? "So you can't understand each other at all?"

"We use gesture-words. It is basic, but it works."

"And they don't . . . attack you?" Cazia regretted the question as soon as the words left her mouth. The princess had just wept over her dead friends and family, and Cazia had to ask this?

But Vilavivianna kept a steady expression, as though it was an interesting philosophical inquiry. "Of course, sometimes. The winter before I left, a lumberman was bitten in an outer camp. The arm swelled up and turned black before he died. It turned out that he had been taunting the serpent with a stick before it bit him. My uncle used to say that human beings killed more human beings than the serpents do."

Peradaini tyrs have been crossing the Straim for four generations . . .

But it wasn't another accusation, apparently, because the girl said, "I miss my mother and father the most."

"Of course," Cazia said, as though she knew how wonderful mothers and fathers could be.

"They are very funny people," the princess said. "They have to be, with the way things work in the clans. You can not order people about the way you do here. You have to try to persuade them before you call up your warriors. My uncle used to say the Indregai will follow a joke but never a command. And I miss the boots we have at home, which are much more comfortable than yours and do not make your feet sweat in the winter. And the food. And, of course, our gods are real."

Cazia felt a sudden chill. "What do you mean? The gods are the gods. Of course they're real."

"No, I mean that our gods are *real*. You have temples and you worship, but all you have are statues or songs, yes? And one of the gods is actually many gods? I confess it all seems very convoluted and confused to me."

"Fury is not 'actually many gods.' He is one god with many aspects. He's the god of all humans." In the growing darkness, Cazia could just make out the other girl's smile. "What is it?"

"He appears as The Mother, yes? And The Sister? And The Prostitute?"

Cazia took a deep breath to soothe her irritation. She herself had giggled over the idea of a male god dressed as a mother when she was small, but Doctor Twofin had scolded her sharply, explaining that it was blasphemous to judge a god the way you'd judge a man. Besides, as she'd grown older, she'd learned that the dividing line between men and women was not always as sharp as it seemed.

So Cazia did her best to pass on Doctor Twofin's lesson, trying to sound patient and mature. "If Fury was only male, he would be the god of men only. Women would have no god to intercede for them, and what an awful world that would be for us."

It didn't satisfy Vilavivianna the way it had Cazia. "But why Fury? Why is he not called Kindness, or Love, or Laughter?"

"That was one of the first questions I asked my tutors."

Vilavivianna's voice began to slow in the darkness as sleep came for her. "What did they answer?"

"Fury feels fury because he is the only god who can feel any emotion at all."

"Hmph."

"Our priests teach us that the gods other people worship are just aspects of Fury."

"Oh, I do not think so," the princess said in her sleepy voice. "There is nothing human about Boskorul. He delivers us the whales we cut up for oil after we offer him our sacrifices."

"Do you mean animal sacrifices?" Cazia asked, hoping the girl was not about to admit that she *murdered* people in an attempt to please an aspect of Fury. Would Fury even accept that sort of worship? She supposed he would, if it was a human thing to do.

"Oh, no," Vilavivianna answered. "We give him part of our yearly harvest. We just float it out to sea for him to consume. He is a sea god, not human at all. And there's Kelvijinian, the god of the land, Tyr of the Sleeping Earth, in your language. He is not human either, although he does have a face and a great big nose almost as big as your Scholars' Tower. Boskorul is scary, but

Kelvijinian is nice. I met him when I was five, and he told me I was very pretty."

The little princess trailed off into sleep, and Cazia bit her own knuckle, trying to suppress a laugh. She tried to picture the Little Spinner, a being so vast it filled the spaces between the stars—it *was* the spaces between the stars, and all the stars themselves, and the very concept of stars—complimenting a little girl's dress.

It was absurd, obviously, but it would be rude to laugh. Cazia couldn't help but like the princess and wished she had half the girl's confidence.

What's more, Vilavivianna had people she loved in this world, and she had someplace she could go. Cazia envied her that, too.

That night, she dreamed her friends had captured her and dragged her to Indregai, where a grunt the size of a mountain waited to devour her.

In the morning, Vilavivianna insisted Cazia hide her quiver in her pack. They would be crossing into the Sweeps soon, and there was no telling what they would find. Cazia reluctantly complied.

Once they were back on the path, she looked up and down the pass. The sky was just lightening and they wouldn't see the sun for hours, but she could see enough to know that no one was chasing her. Not grunts. Not soldiers.

At mid day, they stopped for a short while. Cazia apologized to Vilavivianna for the saltiness of the food, but the little girl only shrugged. Travel foods were not meant to be delicious, only filling.

When their meal was partway done, Cazia said, "Vilavivianna, I would like to ask you a favor. In Peradain, all my friends called me 'Caz.'" The little princess sat stiffly, as though she was about to be punished. "Would you mind calling me Caz? As a friend?"

The girl's lower lip quivered slightly. "If you would call me Viv or Ivy, as my cousins once did. I would very much like for us to be friends."

They smiled at each other, and Cazia's heart felt full. In fact, she felt near to crying, which was silly. All this sorrow was making her much too sensitive.

As they hiked, the road passed beneath two cliffs that came so close, she could have thrown a stone from the base of one to the other. The winds whipped and swirled around the rugged outcroppings, and just beyond it, the path widened, the way a river widens as it nears the ocean. It became steep as well.

Cazia looked out into the valley ahead of her, marveling at the expanse of it. The Northern Barrier was vivid in the afternoon light, and she knew it wasn't as close as it appeared, even though it seemed only a few days' journey. Below that was a long narrow lake tucked against the base of the cliff, and closer still was a deep green slope of tall grasses, all bending toward the east under the constant pressure of that famous, unceasing wind. The plants were much less yellow than the grasses around Peradain, and more beautiful because of it.

She could see streams, too, dozens of them, that flowed away from her. At the edge of the grasslands below, the low, fading sun illuminated little splashes of red and white—clusters of tiny flowers growing from the rocks.

So beautiful. It looked like a place where you could run for hours and never see another human being. Pagesh should have seen this. She loved the outdoors, loved cataloging and sketching plants, then finding out their names. Pagesh should have lived long enough to see this.

Vilavivianna . . . Ivy started down the eastern edge of the slope. Good. Fort Piskatook was the sensible destination. They would head eastward along the Southern Barrier, then turn into the next pass. Cazia would first find a way to make herself useful to the commander there. Yes, she was just a girl, but she was a scholar, too. From there, she could arrange for Ivy to go home. Piskatook stood on the Peradaini side of the Straim, and it would be only logical for the local commander to see her safely across to her own people. Better that than start yet another war.

Ivy was moving at a fast clip now, practically hopping down the stony road. Cazia almost called to her to pace herself—they had many more days of travel left—but she didn't. Something about the way the girl hurried made her anxious.

She glanced to the left, looking westward now that they were nearly beyond the edge of the Southern Barrier. Somewhere out there in the shadowed peaks far beyond the grass and marshes of the west was Tempest Pass, where Ghoron Italga studied magic in exile.

Lar must have already transformed. She glanced westward. Somewhere far out there was Tempest Pass. Could Lar be there right now, without having transformed? He had spent hours on a sleepstone after he'd been bitten. Was it possible the scholar's magic cured him? Questions. Always questions.

What she needed was a flying cart. If Lar's quest failed, who would continue it—whatever it was—if not her?

She followed Ivy down the slope toward the broken-off edge of the rock—in some places, it really did look as though the valley had been carved out of the mountains. Cazia wasn't spry enough to keep up, but she tried. The princess came to the edge of a high rock spur, then stopped, as though she had come to a precipice.

Then she cried out in sorrow and sprinted forward, out of sight. Cazia rushed after her.

Ivy was running toward a large encampment spread across the grasslands below. Cazia's thoughts rushed ahead of her body: How many people could live in such a sprawl of tents? Five hundred? More?

But it was clear there was no one living there now. Many of the white tents had collapsed, the cook fires had gone out, and supply carts set up in the center of the camp had been crushed by gigantic tree trunks.

Cazia looked at the mountainside next to the camp but could see no sign of an avalanche, or of any other trees that might have fallen from above. Besides, wouldn't a falling tree have smashed the tents between the carts and the mountainside, not shred them apart?

Ivy was still running forward, shrugging off her pack. Cazia raced after her; she would have called her back, but what if Durdric raiders had done this and were still down there, picking through the loot? Cazia's spear wasn't going to be much use. She had to grab hold of the girl and pull her away before she was noticed.

A fallen banner lay broken against the rocks. Cazia didn't recognize it: there were no rivers, mountains, waves . . . none of the usual symbols. It was just a tall, narrow, fringed white cloth the same color as the tents.

Beside the nearest tent, she found deep gouges in the dirt. She heard buzzing flies. A trunk had been smashed open, spilling a pair of bronze hatchets and a pile of white clothes onto the ground.

She'd seen uniforms like those at Ivy's home in Peradain. This was an Alliance outpost, deep into the Peradaini part of the Sweeps.

This was an invasion.

"Hohwahl!" the princess called. Cazia could hear her running between the tents, looking for survivors. So much for pulling her away unnoticed.

"Don't shout!" Cazia yelled to her, as she ran between the tents, dodging around a large rock. "There could be—"

The words stuck in Cazia's throat. She came around the rock and found herself a hand width away from the head of a huge serpent.

She shrieked and leaped away, but of course it was already dead. The rock had fallen on it, killing it instantly, she was sure. She leaned a little closer. The black-and-brown head was bigger than she expected, even larger than her own. The fangs were as long as her middle finger but more slender, and there was a red frill at the back of the skull.

Shudders ran the length of her body. *Don't step on one of those fangs.* She moved to the next tent, then the next one.

The cloth had been shredded as if by swords, and there were deep gouges in the earth all around them. Cazia expected to find bodies in the mud or in the tents, but in truth, she found very few.

In the tattered, windblown remains of a tent, she found the princess crouching among dolls, leather balls, and long sticks carved into a bowl at one end.

"This was the children's tent," she said. "Children slept, ate, and played together. What kind of soldiers would do this?"

She gestured toward a broken chest. It was awash in red. Cazia felt woozy for a moment. Did that come from one person? A child? Bitt was right; the amount of blood in a body was shocking.

Vilavivianna sobbed. "I did not think even the Peradaini would stoop so low."

Cazia went to a row of trunks along one side of the tent. Folded cots lay behind them; no one had opened or searched them.

"No soldiers did this." Cazia met the girl's accusatory gaze with stubborn stoicism. "Where are the bodies? Where did the trees come from? The rocks? Do you think someone like Zollik could heft a tree trunk over his head and hurl it across a camp?"

The princess stood and looked around again. "Where *are* the bodies?"

Cazia opened the nearest trunk. It was full of white clothes. Jackets. The next held pants. The next held boots in every style. "Here you go," she said, her voice sounding flat. "Now your feet won't have to sweat next winter."

The little girl didn't say anything as Cazia left the tattered tent. She wandered through the wreckage. There was a great deal of blood, but she could only find a few bodies. Most had been crushed beneath something—four women had been sheltering beneath the carts when the tree landed on them—but one man had been slashed straight down his belly and shoulder blades, then had fallen amid some tattered cloth. Whoever had struck him down must have lost track of him there.

Cazia knelt beside him. The cut appeared to have been made by a very dull sword. The crumpled bronze point of the man's spear had dried blood on it. She couldn't look at his face, but his hair was the same pale yellow as Ivy's.

There were flies buzzing around him, of course. Peraday had been right; wild animals did not leave the dead in peace. Cazia began to walk through the compound methodically, counting the swarms.

Vilavivianna approached. Her expression was apologetic but her words were not. "I would like to take the time to bury them, if you please."

"What does that matter to me?" Cazia snapped. "What were you planning, *princess*? Why did you even bother to ask me where I wanted to go when you obviously knew they were here all along? Was I supposed to be fooled into thinking I would get to decide for myself, right up until the moment you took me hostage?" Cazia's voice broke, as though she was going to start crying, and that made her even more furious.

"Hostage?" Vilavivianna looked shocked. "How could you say that?"

"Because you lied to me! You know I'm a scholar and I'm forbidden to go beyond the borders of the empire! It would cost me my life!"

"No one here would have harmed you!" Vilavivianna shouted, sounding close to tears.

"Of course you wouldn't hurt your captive scholar. Not when you had so much to learn from her! I can't believe you pretended—" And that was all she could say. She couldn't finish that sentence. "You spoiled, stuck-up little . . . " She didn't want to finish that sentence, either.

"I would have protected you!" the princess said. "That is why I told you to put your quiver in your pack! I was never going to tell anyone what you could do, even though it would have—a lot of Alliance lives would be saved if we knew magic, too. But I would not ever! You saved my life!"

"Well why didn't you just tell me?"

"Because you would not have come!"

"OF COURSE NOT!"

Tears began to run down the princess's face. "You would have insisted we leave by the southern gate, even with all the fighting there. We would have been captured or killed—maybe even bitten. I'm sorry I did not tell you everything, but I can not believe you think I would betray you."

"Maybe you wanted what was best for us. Maybe you did. But if you trick me into doing what you want, I'm not going to trust you. You understand that, don't you? Why would you even ask me where I wanted to go if you were going to take me here anyway?"

"So I could arrange an armed escort to take you there."

They stared at each other for a few moments, letting the wind whip their hair in their faces. Vilavivianna was clearly ready to cry, but her lower lip was stuck out defiantly, and her thin brows were wrinkled over her nose. She looked adorable, despite everything, and Cazia felt a flush of shame that she'd ever slapped that pale cheek. Part of her even wanted to give the girl a hug and apologize.

She couldn't. That would have been giving in, and the world was too dangerous to let this little princess play tricks on her. Worse, what she said made a sort of sense, and that made it even more important to stand firm. If she gave in now, she'd never stop.

"Elah!"

It was a man's voice, and he was shouting loud enough to be heard over the wind. Cazia's first instinct was to flee to the back of the camp, maybe try to find a hiding place or a way to sneak across the open ground between the tents and the pass, but the princess turned and ran toward the voice.

"Elah!" Ivy shouted, her voice high and thin.

Cazia ran after her, holding on to her iron-lined hat with one hand. They stopped at the edge of the camp and saw three men and four women crossing the grassy meadow toward them. The men had long hair and beards, and they carried the longest spears Cazia had ever seen, while the women stood well back, bows in hand. How accurate could those bows be in this wind? Cazia didn't want to find out.

She slipped her hand into her pocket and touched the smooth blue stone. When the man spoke next, she heard him say, "Greetings, half-grown devil. Are your parents free for parlay?"

Ivy replied, in the man's language, "By the right of discovery, we claim this treasure for our clans and ourselves."

The man was startled, then he sighed and looked toward the skies. The two men with him laughed as though he'd been played for a fool. The women lowered their bows and scowled. They looked like they'd been cheated out of a meal.

"Devils!" the man shouted. He held his spear in both hands and advanced on them. "Throw aside your spears or be declared enemies!"

Ivy turned to Cazia. "Do as I do." She let her spear fall to the ground. Cazia did the same.

To the east, Cazia saw a long, broad, dark form move through the grasses. It was an okshim herd bound for the west, and these people were part of a herding clan. "Will they kill us?"

Ivy's lips were a think bloodless line. "They are not supposed to."

Chapter Fifteen

"Are there no guards?" Tejohn asked.

Arla slipped off her steel cap and looked over the crest of the hill. "Not that I can see, my tyr, but if their numbers were few they could watch from inside that low tower."

"I must make a confession to you, guide: I am not exaggerating when I say I can not see a tower. I can barely make out the line of pink that marks the wall of the camp."

"Ah." She slid down the hill and began to draw in the dirt with the pommel of her knife. "This is the wall. Here is the gate. Both are about a man and a half tall. This looks to be where they warehouse their ores. Beside it is the low tower, which is only a bit higher than the wall but looks very modern—there are narrow slits for arrows and the top is crenellated. Another low building on the near side is probably the barracks. In a medium-sized camp like this, the servants, guards, and scholars—I assume they have one if not more—will probably have separate rooms in one building. This is the location of the cart I mentioned. And over here is the mine entrance."

"And we are here?" Tejohn added a dot outside of her circle.

Arla erased it and moved it farther away. "I would say here, my tyr. The ground is relatively flat to the north and west. This hill right here is as close as we could get to them without a day's detour."

"Unless we tried to come at them from the south, where the mountain is."

"I would not recommend engaging Durdric fighters on a steep, uneven mountainside, my tyr. Not unless we outnumbered them sufficiently to make them retreat."

"But you believe there will be a sleepstone in one of those buildings?"

"Tyr Finstel sacrificed much when he diverted the Witt, Bendertuk, and Simblin troops. His lands, towns—"

"Arla, my sight may be short but my memory is long."

"Yes, my tyr. My apologies, my tyr. My point is that his mines are productive and well stocked. One that has grown to this size will be busy, and busy mines have accidents."

It made sense. It would take a long time to replace injured workers, but with a sleepstone, they could be healed in a few days, if not hours.

"My tyr, may I ask a question?"

Her brow was furrowed and the crinkle lines around her eyes were deep. She had to work up some courage for the question she wanted to ask, and Tejohn couldn't deny her. "If it's quick."

"Just how short is your vision?"

She wanted to know if he was a liability. No surprise. "So short that I have only held a bow once, and it was taken from me before I could loose a single arrow. So short that I was turned away by Splashtown First when I was a boy. So short that people mistake my inability to see the strength of my enemies for bravery."

It was the only jest Tejohn told, and he used to tell it to make friends with other spears. It worked here, too; Arla laughed.

"Yes, my tyr. How do you want to proceed?"

"Under cover of darkness," he answered. "Keep watch. If you see the gates open, alert me. I'll have provisions brought to you. We will need your input on the strategy we come up with."

"Yes, my tyr," she said as Tejohn slipped back toward the rest of the group.

It took very little time to explain the situation to the others, who had settled themselves down to their mid day meal. Lar devoured his meatbread like a starving man, but spit out the bits of apricot and onion. He seemed to be paying little attention to Tejohn's description of the camp.

Reglis and Wimnel listened with great intent. "I can command men," Reglis said, frowning. "But I have never been trained in strategy."

"Neither have the imperial generals," Tejohn said. "They just copy each other. Put that aside for now. We must wait for nightfall, then try to take possession of their sleepstone for the king."

Wimnel absent-mindedly touched his broken arm. "How can I help?"

"Even if you were healthy, I'd tell you to stay well back with the king. You haven't been trained for this."

"Soon," the king said. He sat hunched over and tense, as though expecting a whipping. He began moving his hands in front of his knees, and a trickle of clear water appeared just beyond his fingers. "Soon."

"I'm sorry, my king. We will do our best."

"What if nightfall takes too long to come?" Reglis said. "I am willing to risk a charge during daylight, if the king requires it."

"With so few?" Wimnel said weakly.

"Yes," Reglis said. His scowl had deepened and his big, scarred knuckles whitened on the shaft of his spear as though he intended to throttle it. "As a diversion, if need be."

Tejohn spoke in a low, calm voice, willing the young soldier to settle down. "I'll keep that in mind if it's necessary."

Reglis took a deep breath but it wasn't enough to ease his mind. "What if we can not take the camp? Or there is no sleepstone within?"

"Kill. Me." Lar's voice was low and harsh. "Bless the bl—Blessings—" The king ground his teeth, unable to speak further without saying nonsense.

Wimnel laid his good hand on Lar's shoulder. "It won't come to that." He offered the rest of his ration to the king, who tore into it.

Tejohn did his best to keep his face impassive. "No man will ever call me *kingkiller*. We will do what we must to serve the throne, and we will succeed. Reglis, how are your eyes?"

"Strong, my tyr."

"Take off your cap and join Arla. I want your best estimate of the enemy's strength."

The big man nodded and crept forward along the path. Tejohn sat near the king. Lar had curled himself up into a ball, his knees under his chin, his hands clasped in front of his shins. Once in a while, he would begin the arcane movements that would cause water to trickle from his hands into the dirt at his feet, or sometimes cause a nearby rock to crumble. The spells delayed the change, he'd told them, but it what would happen when it could no longer be held back?

Tejohn held his spear in his lap, point aimed at Lar. Once the king transformed, would Tejohn still owe loyalty and service to him, or would he be nothing more than another grunt? Tejohn hoped he would never have to make that choice.

The king bared his teeth as though he was suffering from terrible stomach pain. Suddenly, he looked very like a young soldier Tejohn had known twenty-four years before, when he was a young soldier himself. The two of them had been cut off from their square somewhere south of Deep Stone

Lake. Tejohn had been uninjured, but the other spear—barely older than a boy—had taken an arrow in the guts. They'd stayed up all night talking in low whispers. They'd been strangers, but by the time the fellow died at dawn, they knew each other quite well.

Now Tejohn couldn't remember the young man's name. That night had changed Tejohn's view of the world—of soldiers, war, and heroism—but although he could recall the man's round, moonlit face as he gritted his teeth against the pain, refusing to cry out and give away their position, Tejohn could not recall his name.

Song forgive me. He deserved better.

The day faded slowly. Tejohn could not see the mountains clearly, but he could see their colors as the sunset light filled the valley. Everything became beautiful, like a multicolored fog, and he wondered how it seemed to those whose vision was sharp. The king spent most of that time casting spells, slowly exhausting himself without ever standing off the ground.

The western end of the valley still had a faint glow of pink when Reglis returned.

"Arla and I agree that there are at least twelve fighters."

"Fire and Fury." Tejohn was good with a spear and especially with his sword, but three against "at least" twelve would never work, even if their enemies were not behind a wall. "Have any good news?"

The young man shrugged. "They're drinking."

Tejohn clapped Reglis's shoulder and returned to Arla's position. Of course, he still couldn't see the camp, especially since the slow-fading day had suddenly become twilight, but he could see a fire going in the courtyard.

"My tyr," Arla said. "There are six men around the fire, and each has their own jug. Sometimes, another man will join them, and he carries two jugs, which he shares. The Durdric like their drink."

"Guards?"

"Two have been summoned to watch, my tyr. One on the wall near us, one on the far side. The near one keeps a jug that he sneaks drinks from. The other is too far to be certain."

Tejohn sighed with relief. "A well-stocked wine cellar will even the odds a bit, in time."

They crouched together at the base of the hill, Arla giving a running description of the fighters' actions: when they wavered on their feet, when they staggered away to empty their bladders, when they fell into fistfights. It was the last one that interested Tejohn the most. He demanded to know how many men came to watch, how clumsily they fought, and who celebrated by tipping back a jug. Even from their place at the dip of the hill, they could hear the drinking songs.

Eventually, the Durdric lay upon the ground or staggered away from the fire, and the songs died away. Had midnight come? Tejohn was not good at judging the hour of the night. He and Arla began to discuss how she could best approach the camp and take out the guards with her bow.

Finally, Lar surprised them all by creeping up to their forward position. "Bless—" he said, then, after much struggle, forced himself to say "Now."

"My king," Tejohn said, "if we give them another hour, I think—"

But Lar had already taken a dart from his quiver. He stepped to the top of the hill, exposing himself to the guards below. His hands were already in motion.

Tejohn waved a hand at Reglis, stopping him from grabbing hold of the king and dragging him out of sight. They were too far to take this shot, of course they were, but Lar was still the king, Fire take them, and his will was law.

The spell went off, and the dart sped away from them at tremendous speed. It sounded faster than anything Tejohn had ever heard in his life.

"Hit," Arla said. She lay across the top of the hill beside the king, staring below.

"Which way did he fall?" Tejohn whispered.

"Forward," she answered. "Out of the camp. That was the near guard."

Lar was already casting again. When he finished, this second dart sped away from them with that same hissing, rushing sound.

"Hit again," Arla said. "Great Way, I've never seen such a shot in my life. A second hit. The far guard has fallen onto the walkway at the top of the wall. I don't see anyone moving in the camp in response."

Tejohn put on his steel cap. "Let's start killing."

Tejohn saw Arla and Reglis fall in behind him, each holding their bow and spear. Wimnel took Lar's sleeve and urged him to stay. Good.

No one called the alarm as they ran down the trail. No one shot arrows at them or waved signal fires. They reached the gate without incident and found it shut.

Reglis lowered his big shoulder as though he was about to throw his massive body against the gate, but Tejohn held up a hand to stop him. The doors did not meet exactly in the center, and Tejohn pressed his eye against the gap. He couldn't see well, but the fire burning in the yard was bright against the darkness. He bent low, peering through the gap, until he saw the bar holding the gates together.

Fire and Fury, he had been hoping the Durdric had broken the bar without repairing it. No matter. He took Regis by the shoulders and steered him to the place the wall met the gate. "Hands braced on the wall," he whispered, and the young captain did so.

He turned to Arla. "Over the top, quietly, without raising the alarm. Open the gate for us." He spoke to both of them. "I don't want to hear a single sound until every enemy is dead. This is not a test of honor, arms, and skill, understand? Tonight, we are assassins."

Reglis sighed as though he'd lifted a heavy burden, but Arla only nodded and let Tejohn boost her onto the captain's back. She peeked over the top of the gate, then slid over. Tejohn wished she'd taken longer to look over the scene, but she freed the bolt and slid it back.

Reglis followed Tejohn inside. Their boots scraped against the loose rock scattered over the yard, but in the Sweeps, the noise of the wind overwhelmed all.

Finstel corpses lay carelessly piled beside the eastern wall: guards, servants, civilians all mingled together. He could see no children—a tiny, unexpected kindness—and the corpses appeared to have been butchered. Most of them had been killed by the same downward stroke, probably while kneeling. Probably executed after they'd tried to surrender.

Stretched out by the fire were seven more bodies, all with two or three jugs beside them, and all snoring loudly. They wore goatskin robes and had seashells woven into their beards. Arla watched Tejohn carefully. Reglis was just a few steps behind.

Tejohn knew what they needed. He passed his spear to his shield hand, drew his three-hands-long sword and chopped hard across the throat of the nearest man.

He died without even a gurgle. As if given permission, Reglis cut the throat of the man beside him and Arla slid quietly into the barracks, drawing her knife.

It might not have worked if not for the continuous roar of the wind and the emptied jugs of wine. The men by the fire died quickly, and Arla killed twice as many while they slept in the darkness of the barrack rooms.

The far end of the yard by the water tables was already littered with bodies, most of them wearing the rags of servant laborers, but some in the unadorned gear of civilian guards. Reglis found a separate room at the south end of the barracks with a dead man on the threshold. The man wore scholar's robes.

Tejohn stepped over the dead man and scanned the interior of the room, which was lit by a glowing stone. The sleepstone was there, along with piles of trunks and baskets and a gurgling water pipe that ran from the ceiling through the floor.

But there were no fighters, so Tejohn moved across the yard. The animal pens—covered recently with a makeshift roof—contained only animals, but the doors to the warehouse had been broken down, and while there were no lights inside, Tejohn could hear the snores of two men. He took his time, let his eyes adjust to this new level of darkness, then slit both of their throats.

Arla and Regis met him at the doorway to the warehouse. Regis was breathing heavily through his mouth, but Arla seemed almost to glide through the darkness. In the moonlight, her bloody hands looked black.

Tejohn understood what she felt; he, too, was full of the thrill of *taking*. It was not a happy feeling. He would never share it with Laoni or their kids, but it made him feel huge and powerful.

"The tower is last," Tejohn whispered. "The tower door is open and looks to be unguarded. We can see firelight inside, but no silhouettes. Not yet. Am I right, guide?" She nodded. "We'll finish this in there."

Arla nodded her head, her wide eyes shining in the moonlight. Reglis shrugged his shoulders. "My tyr," he whispered, hefting his spear. "I will enter first."

Tejohn took his spear from him and laid it on the stony ground beside his own. "You'll follow me, and be sharp about it. Guide, nock an arrow and keep close."

Tejohn leaned away from the warehouse and peered at the tower windows. The upper floor was dark, but light flickered behind the open door. Tejohn hurried forward, the thrill of killing already fading. He lifted his shield high and held his sword close to his chest, point forward.

The entryway was deep, of course, as deep as the thickness of the stone walls. Tejohn came to the edge of the inner chamber, and the hair on the back of his neck stood up.

He leaped into the room, sensing the downward stroke of the man on his right before he could see it. The man shouted to give power to his blow, but his hammer struck nothing but the granite floor.

Tejohn swung backhanded at him, biting deep at the spot where his neck and skull met. The man's war shout ended abruptly and he crumpled to the floor.

But Tejohn didn't wait to see what became of him, because there were two more men behind the dying man. They each held their weapons high, and Tejohn made note of the stone axes they held, their body language, the half-drunken wildness in their eyes.

His body already knew what to do: he charged at the man on the right, sidestepped his downward stroke, and buried the point of his sword in the man's guts. The man on the left was stepping forward, but Tejohn knew the enemy's stroke would come too late.

Everyone was too late, as far as Tejohn was concerned. Everyone moved slower than he did and they always had, in every fight he'd ever been in. His years of training—and of teaching—in the gym had kept him sharp, but his speed and strength were something he had been born with. The Durdric had been wise to attack from his shieldless side, but it would not be enough.

Tejohn raised his shield to catch the stroke of the axe before it reached its full power. The blade cut through the metal rim, splitting the shield down the center. Tejohn pivoted, nearly wrenching the weapon from the man's grip.

It was wedged tight. The man released it—he had an odd little round shield on his left, little larger than his head—but Tejohn was already well into his downward stroke. His too-long sword struck deep into the side of the Durdric's neck, cutting down into his chest.

The man made a terrible gurgling noise as the blood ran into his lungs. Tejohn wrenched his sword free and pivoted to face the rest of the room. A fourth Durdric with a short spear retreated from the other side of the door, keeping Reglis at bay with quick, short thrusts. He backed toward the stairs, but his terrified expression made it clear he did not expect to survive.

Reglis lunged toward him then stepped back. Arla rushed into the center of the room and shot him in the chest. As the arrow went in, the spearman froze, as warriors always did, a grimace of pain and despair coming over his face. Reglis did not know enough to press his advantage, but it was only a few more breaths before he knocked the man down with his shield and slipped the point of his sword between his ribs. The Durdric died screaming.

Arla had another arrow nocked by then, but the enemies were all dead or dying. She and Reglis looked at Tejohn with a new sort of respect.

Tejohn didn't like it. Yes, he was skilled at killing. He was a weapons instructor to the king, Song knew. What did they expect? What's more, the thrill of taking had turned sour and chilled beneath the weight of so many corpses. "Check the upper floor and the roof."

The third man he'd killed had died on his side, facing the fire. Tejohn knelt beside him. He wore a leather vest with wooden plates sewn into it. His axe head had been made of flint. It was sharp enough but too brittle for a long battle.

And there, on the man's beard, was a seashell. Tejohn lifted it with bloody fingers. The Durdric were mountain people, traveling from their lands through the high, narrow valleys of the Southern Barrier. Where did they trade for shells? And why? Stories said they used the shells as coin . . . in fact, they hated all metal and mining, for some reason. Tejohn had never understood why.

Footsteps on the stair behind him made him turn. "There's no one up there," Arla announced. She and Reglis seemed almost disappointed.

"Arla, take a burning brand from the fire and get up on that wall. We need to signal the king to come down. Reglis, go with her in case we missed someone. Bar the gate once the king is inside."

They left. Tejohn retrieved his spear and headed for the room with the sleepstone. He dragged the scholar into the yard and went inside.

There was something about this room that wasn't right. Setting aside his spear and shield, he laid his hand against the burbling pipe, feeling the cold mountain water running through it. It disappeared into the floor behind some baskets.

Undisturbed baskets, in fact. The chests along two walls had been broken apart, their contents strewn everywhere—blankets, leggings, underclothes, anything. But directly behind the sleepstone was a stack of woven baskets that had been opened but not otherwise disturbed.

They were empty, of course, but had the Durdric found them this way? He tried to lift the nearest one and discovered it was pegged to the wooden floor.

Of course! The water, the scholar's corpse, the false baskets . . . Tejohn searched the floor until he found a board with a metal ring attached. He lifted it, and a hidden trap door opened, revealing a deep pit carved into the stone below.

They were called "treasure rooms," but they weren't meant for gold or jewels. Treasure rooms hid people, especially children and spouses of tyrs, wealthy merchants, and other nobles. The scholar had been killed while fleeing to a hiding place where he could wait for the invaders to gather what they wanted to steal and move on.

This one was nearly twenty feet deep, and the water that trickled through drained out of a hole in the floor, probably emerging farther downslope. A folding ladder hung off the near side.

Reglis and Arla rushed through the doorway, carrying Lar between them. "Get his cuirass off," Tejohn ordered. They worked at the straps of the king's armor as Tejohn eased the young man's helmet off.

Lar's face was swollen and distorted, and he was panting like a dog. His shoulders were slumped forward, his hands frozen like a bird's talons. Tejohn suddenly couldn't breathe for a couple of moments. *Great Way, keep him on the path. We need him.*

While Reglis fumbled with the straps of the king's cuirass, Lar grabbed Tejohn's hand in both of his own. He couldn't move his fingers, but he managed to press something small, like a pebble, into Tejohn's palm.

Then the cuirass finally came off. Blood had soaked through the king's padded flannel underarmor shirt, but before Tejohn could find the source, more began to pour from both nostrils. *Fire and Fury,* the boy was dying in front of his eyes. Tejohn shoved Lar back onto the bed of the sleepstone. The king cried out, blood foaming out of his mouth.

The young man sprawled on the slab, and Tejohn stepped back. Reglis stared wide-eyed, his fists clenched protectively under his big square chin. Arla stood in the doorway looking as though she was ready to run a race. Just behind her, Wimnel stared ashen-faced at the spreading flow of blood.

Tejohn turned back to Lar. He'd known this young man since he was old enough to swing a stick. *Great Way, please let this Gift heal my king.*

Instead, he watched his king die.

The flesh around Lar's face burst open, pushed outward by another skull growing beneath it. The king grabbed hold of his own skin and hair and pulled it downward like a cloth mask, revealing bloody blue fur beneath. Then he devoured it.

Then the creature jammed its fingers in its mouth and bit down, scraping the flesh off its own knuckles like moss from a stone.

"Great Way," Wimnel said. "Great Way Great Way Great Way protect him. Protect our king."

I failed him. I was sure the sleepstone would work but I failed. The creature did not fall into a slumber, the way human patients did, but it was still helpless in mid-transformation. The grunt was helpless.

Tejohn didn't touch his weapons. He couldn't use his sword or knife against Lar. He just couldn't. He took up his shield.

The creature tore Lar's bloody shirt in two, exposing skin split over bloody fur. *Great Way,* the thing was *huge.*

"No!" Tejohn shouted. He didn't even know what he was refusing, or why he was saying it, but the word would not be denied. "NO!"

He jammed the bottom of the shield under Lar's . . . *the creature's* body, then lifted and shoved. Reglis leaped forward to join him in the final push, rolling the thing's surprising bulk off the sleepstone.

The grunt's hip struck the edge of the pit, then it tumbled out of sight.

Tejohn raced around the edge of the sleepstone and grabbed at the ladder, throwing it across the room.

Down below, the creature seemed groggy. It had landed awkwardly and now lay stretched on the stone floor, its leg twisted under it. It groaned, rolled over, and trembled as its leg slowly untwisted itself. In the space of six or seven breaths, the beast shook its broken leg as though it was a rumpled wet blanket, then stood upright upon it. The grunt stared up at Tejohn, its leg already fully healed. It roared and leaped upward.

Too deep. The grunt tried to gouge its claws into the wall but unlike in Peradain, there were no joins between blocks where it could find purchase, and the pit was too deep for it to catch the lip.

This was not the king. This was not Lar Italga. Not anymore. "Fire and Fury," Tejohn whispered. "What are we facing here?"

It leaped again, then again, its dark eyes wild with hunger. It came close enough to the top that Tejohn could have lain flat on the floor and caught it by the wrist, but that distance was enough. It was trapped.

When the grunt jumped again, Lar's torn robes fell away from it, revealing the last of the king's bloody flesh lying among the cloth. The last of the Italga line was gone. Destroyed. Tejohn had been the king's bodyguard, weapons master, and shield bearer, but he had been powerless to prevent it.

He was overwhelmed at once by his abject failure and by the knowledge that his life's path had brought him to a place that no one could have expected. "Grateful am I to be permitted to travel The Way."

After a few more moments, the beast stopped leaping at him. It crouched at the bottom of the pit, staring upward, as it plucked the king's the bloody flesh from the ground and ate it greedily.

Lar had made jokes at Tejohn's expense at every opportunity, had shirked every exercise, had rolled his eyes at every correction. The king had been right; Tejohn hadn't liked him—he certainly hadn't loved him—but he'd sworn to serve him. Had sworn to be his shield bearer. And now this.

Tejohn felt as empty as a the air outside. The world was blowing through him, but he held no thought, no will. If he had faded into nothingness in that moment, it would have seemed a perfectly logical consequence of his failure. Instead, he persisted, for no reason at all except that the gods could not trouble themselves to burn him from the path.

The beast roared at Tejohn again. There was something odd about the way it was looking at him. Did it remember the man it had once been? Could it recognize its old teacher?

Tejohn reached into his pocket and touched the little blue translation stone Cazia Freewell had made for him.

The beast opened its mouth, but this time Tejohn heard it say, "Blessing! BLESS YOU! Blessing!"

Fire and Fury. The king had not been turned into a wild beast; he had become something else. Something insane and vicious.

But he was still the king. If the creature in that pit had wits enough to speak at all, then there might still be a bit of Lar Italga within it. And Tejohn could not give up on him. Not now or ever.

Tejohn turned away from the pit and stalked through the door. Arla stood just outside, an arrow half drawn from the quiver on her hip. "My tyr, should I . . . ?"

"No," he said. Reglis and Wimnel both looked at him uncertainly. He turned away and marched across the darkness toward the dying fire.

The nearest corpse looked a little thin, so he grabbed hold of the fatter one nearby and dragged him across the yard. The body was still warm but Tejohn pushed that thought away; he was a servant of the Throne of Skulls. Surely, someone somewhere had done worse than this.

He ignored the others' astonished expressions as he dragged the corpse into the lit room. He peeled off the dead man's leather vest, then his boots, then his belt. There were a half-full pouch, a string of shells around one wrist, and a lump of amber on a leather thong around his neck. Tejohn cast them all into the corner.

"My tyr . . . " Reglis said from behind him.

Something in that voice made Tejohn's hair stand on end. He stood and turned in one motion, his hand on his sword. "What is it, Captain?" He wished he had his shield, but he'd seen Reglis fight and didn't think it would be necessary.

Reglis had to raise his voice to be heard over Lar's roaring. "My tyr, these men are our fallen enemies. We should treat them the way we'd hope to be treated. I hope you don't plan to—"

"Hold out your hand." Reglis hesitated a moment, but he did it. "Don't drop this," Tejohn said, then placed the stone into the man's palm.

Reglis cried out in shock and horror; he recoiled so violently he would have dropped the stone if Tejohn hadn't held onto him.

"Scout!" Tejohn shouted. "Come in here!" Tejohn took the enchanted stone away from him as Reglis staggered back. Arla entered warily. Tejohn held up the blue stone. "This is a translation stone. Do you know how it works?"

Arla shook her head. Tejohn took her wrist and held the stone against her palm. Her eyes went wide with surprise.

"Do you understand?" Tejohn said. "He says the same thing over and over, but *he is speaking.* Lar Italga's mind may have been overthrown but he still exists. Our king is not dead."

Tejohn lifted the naked corpse and threw him into the pit. Immediately, the beast fell upon it, tearing the meat from the bones.

Wimnel came forward, his hand outstretched. "My tyr, may I?"

He took the stone with a strange, serene expression, then moved to the lip of the pit, staring down at the butchery.

Reglis wiped sweat from his face. "Still, my tyr, these are our enemies. We should bury them, not feed them to . . . to that thing in the pit."

"There are animals in the pen," Arla added. She still looked like she'd been stunned.

"No," Tejohn said. "The animals are going to be for the one who remains here, in this compound, taking care of our king."

Chapter Sixteen

"I WILL STAY," WIMNEL SAID. HE STEPPED FORWARD AND HANDED Tejohn the stone. "The king asked me to take his life today. It was hard for him to speak, but he asked me to strike him down. I refused, and promised to care for him."

Tejohn looked the man over. Loyal but not brave, he had thought; the man seemed likely to redeem the Farrabell name, if they survived long enough for anyone but Song to learn of it. "What if the king escapes his prison?"

"I'll see that he does not."

Arla wasn't impressed by that. "What if he does anyway?"

"Then I will die. Or I will be transformed and run through the wilderness beside him. But I will do everything I can to avoid that day."

Tejohn nodded to him. "I will take this as an oath." Wimnel nodded in confirmation.

Tejohn strode into the yard. There were so many dead here, but most would be rotten before it was time for the king to feed again. He plunged his spear into every corpse by the fire, then into every Finstel servant and guard piled by the water tables. He did not find any living enemies hiding among the dead.

Then there was the mine itself. Could more Durdric fighters be hiding inside?

At the top of the camp, just beside the mine entrance, they discovered a structure Tejohn had never seen before. It had been built against the cliffside above the level of the wall, and it consisted of a stone furnace, now cold, with a clay cone above it. Was this the crucible where Sweeps steel was made? A tiny bit of dust blew out of the bottom of the cone.

Tejohn struck his sword against it. "Come out!" he shouted. "Come out or be cut apart."

A slender, filthy bare foot stepped down onto the furnace. A young woman climbed out. She wore the rags common for servants, but they were even more caked with dirt than her leg. She had a sallow face and sad, sunken eyes.

"Bring her."

They all returned to the lower room of the commander's tower. Tejohn put some more wood on the fire so it would not burn out. When he turned around, the others stood in a circle around the servant. She stared at the floor.

"What crime brought on your debt?" he asked.

"No crime, sir," she answered quickly. She bared her forearms; her only tattoo was an arrow on her left wrist. "I'm a debt child," she continued, as if he didn't know what that arrow meant. "My mother stole sourcakes when she was a girl—to feed her family after the Witts burned our lands, she said. She was caught and sentenced to fifteen years. Me and my brother were supposed to buy her freedom partway, but she died first. My father was a fisherman who had his boat stolen and had to sell himself into service to avoid starvation."

Debt children. Convicted criminals turned over their own children to work off their crimes, and there was no time limit for the service of a debt child. They worked until they died—or were set free, which Tejohn heard happened quite often. It was one of the more unsavory aspects of the imperial economy, but there was nothing he could do about it. "Who is your master?"

"Doctor Ansabish," she answered. "He's Fire-taken."

Which meant that she might be set free, if the Finstels were feeling generous. "I'm claiming your debt."

She gasped and looked up at him in panic. "But only a tyr can—"

"My name is Tyr Tejohn Treygar, and your dead master's debt is now mine. Do you understand?"

She was already looking back down at the floor. Her voice had the same flat tone. "Yes, master."

Tejohn looked around at the corpses. "Best to keep busy," he said. "The soldiers and I will need to wash the blood from our hands. Bring bowls of fresh water to the fire to warm. Clean yourself up as well."

"Yes, master." She turned and hurried out into the yard.

"This one looks the paunchiest," Tejohn said, pointing to the man Reglis had killed. "Help me carry him to the pit. Then we'll move these others out, too."

Reglis took the corpse's legs and they carried him across the yard and laid him beside the sleepstone. The other three were left out beside the fire. Tejohn glanced over at the pen again; there were sheep, pigs, and a few chickens, too. But a roof on an animal pen?

Then he remembered the ruhgrit, and the hasty roof made more sense.

When they returned to the tower, the servant had already set bowls of water by the fire, but they were not warm. "We sleep here, with the doors barred." He turned to the servant as he scrubbed at his hands. "What is your name?"

"Passlar," she answered, her face toward the floor.

"Passlar, having done me this service"—he gestured toward the water bowls—"I declare your debt to me paid. You are a free citizen of the empire."

She looked up at him, startled, then glanced at the others as if expecting them to break out laughing at his joke. Arla stared at the young woman intently.

Reglis said, "My tyr, how will Wimnel manage alone? The work involved—"

"Wimnel Farrabell is an adult," Tejohn snapped. "I lived most of my life without someone to mop my floors for me; he can do the same. We will provision ourselves and clean our own kits. Clear?"

"Yes, my tyr."

"Passlar, what is your family name?"

"Breakrock, my Tyr. My mother didn't live long enough to tell me my true name."

"That makes it inconvenient. I'd hoped to lead you across the Southern Barrier to reunite you with your relatives, and to serve as a witness to the crimes committed here." And to convince the Finstels that they should feel a bit of gratitude toward him.

"Yes, my tyr. Inconvenient."

He almost snapped at her, but Fire and Fury, she was right. It had been a stupid thing to say, and she was a free citizen now. She was entitled to a little criticism—as long as she didn't sign on to the military.

"Miss Breakrock, I apologize for being so thoughtless. If you come here, I will cut the debt tattoo from your wrist."

As he drew his knife, Arla spoke up sharply. "My tyr. May I have the honor? I have done this before and had it done to me." She showed her own wrist, but whatever scars she bore were too faint to see in the light of the fire.

"Wash your hands first," Tejohn said, putting his knife away. "And see that

she is washed, receives warm clothes, and takes her turn on the sleepstone."
Arla rushed to the fire and began to wash. Reglis joined her.

"My tyr!" Wimnel said. "I have been waiting—"

"You'll get it," Tejohn told him. "But a broken bone will take days to heal,
while a patch of new skin will grow back before sunrise." He turned to Arla.
"Remember this: the creature in the pit is not to be discussed, nor harmed,
nor released. It is my captive."

"Yes, my tyr." Arla and Passlar hurried out into the yard.

Tejohn ordered Reglis and Wimnel to wait by the fire, then went upstairs
to investigate the upper part of the tower. His soldiers had searched it, but he
was still anxious, half expecting a Durdric fighter to leap from a wardrobe.

But there was nothing in the wardrobe, not even clothes. Someone had
already searched through it, throwing the clothes across the floor and feather
bed. The clay chamber pot was stinking full.

Happily, the weapons displayed on the walls—though covered with
dust—were of good quality.

They had a long trip ahead of them, and Tejohn intended to re-provision
out of the Durdric packs and the Finstel storehouse. He'd hoped to return the
servant to her family to establish that she was of the Finstel clan, then rely on
her testimony before the Tyr's seat to win his friendship. After all, he had just
recaptured a Finstel mine from enemies of the empire. Even if the Finstels
were unwilling to fly him to Tempest Pass, that would be worth something.

He considered, once again, ordering Reglis to remain in the camp and
bringing Wimnel through the pass. If Finstel refused to help them fly to
Tempest Pass, having a driver of his own would make it easier to "commandeer" one.

Of course, showing up with a driver of his own would arouse suspicion,
and stealing a cart was practically an act of war. As far as Tejohn was concerned, it was better to act honorably and expect honorable treatment in
return, and for those who didn't act honorably, there was always the point
of a spear.

Once he had a new flying cart, Great Way willing, he would travel to
Tempest Pass to speak with the king's uncle. Of course, at this point, the king's
uncle could conceivably make a claim for the Throne of Skulls himself, if he
was mad enough to want it. Tejohn hoped he wouldn't. If the scholar prince
could restore Lar to himself, they would return here. If he could not, they
would . . . Who could learn the deadly spell the king had hoped to use against
the grunts? Possibly Cazia Freewell could be trusted with it, and Tejohn was

well aware of how much the world had turned on its head that he was even thinking such a thought.

Barring that, Tejohn himself might be forced to learn . . . No. No that would never do. He was a soldier. If he was going to kill twenty men, he would do it with steel, not by waggling his fingers in the air.

Thinking of the Freewell girl again made him touch the pocket where he had put her translation stone, and he was surprised to discover a second object there. What did he have in his pocket?

He drew out both items. One was the stone that Cazia Freewell had made for him, of course. The other was a silver ring.

For the life of him, Tejohn had no idea where he had gotten it. He'd never owned a ring in his life. He looked at the face; the design had a small drum in the center with a circle around it.

It was the prince's ring. Tejohn suddenly remembered Lar at the edge of the sleepstone, pressing something into his hands, although in the panic of the moment Tejohn did not remember pocketing it. This was the Italga seal. The king's ring was probably still on the dais back in Peradain, but the prince's ring—

By giving Tejohn his ring, Lar had made him regent. It had only happened five times before, always when the king died before his eldest was of age. Lar had no children, of course, and his uncle had no ring of his own. Should Tejohn pass it to Cazia Freewell or Jagia Italga, even though queens who were not permitted to sit upon the throne? To Lar's uncle, a man Tejohn did not know at all? Or should he rule the empire himself, passing it to his own children?

The wind howled through the darkness, rattling the shutters. Fire and Fury, but the never-ending sound of it was enough to drive him mad. How did anyone *think* with this constant noise and pressure? He was glad to be indoors again. What's more, judging by the bed and fine cloth strewn about the floor, he was going to sleep in comfort tonight.

There was another room set off from the chambers. It held a desk, a stack of wax tablets, and a shelf of scrolls. Tejohn didn't pay them much attention.

He climbed the next flight of stairs up to the roof. He supposed it gave a commanding view of the area, but it would have been wasted on him even in daylight. The fire the Durdric had built in the middle of the yard was little more than glowing red embers now, and that was just about all Tejohn could see. Not even the stars were visible.

Now he bore the last Italga ring. He'd gone from being a landless tyr to the regent of the entire empire. For the life of him, he could not imagine a situation in which he would not lose his head for brandishing this ring.

He went back down into the bedchamber and found Arla standing stiffly beside the door, waiting for him. "Is it done?"

"Yes, my tyr," she said. Her gaze was fixed on him in a way that made him uneasy. The scout did not seem to be threatening him, but her wide eyes shone in the glow of the lightstone. "She was nervous about using the sleepstone with the king there—"

"Understandable. And don't call him 'the king' again. It might not be the death of him, but it will certainly be the death of you."

If his threat affected her, she did not show it. She didn't even blink. "I apologize, my tyr. She overcame her fear and is healing now. The incisions I made should heal before dawn. My tyr, do you plan to bring her with us?"

Tejohn took off his helmet and set it on top of the wardrobe. "She is not a servant any longer, and she is not a soldier. I can refuse to take her along, but I can not order her to go. Not unless you want to prod her at the tip of a knife."

"I would not like that, my tyr."

"So, she can come with us if she wants to make herself useful to us. Or she can stay here to assist Mister Farrabell. Or she can strike out on her own."

"That is a generous definition of the relationship between a tyr and his subjects."

"A man with nothing to lose can afford to be brave. A tyr without lands or taxes can afford to be generous. Find a place to sleep for the night. We still have much to do."

She nodded and went downstairs. Tejohn examined the three shields on the wall. All were heavy and solid enough for campaigning, but two had old-fashioned single-grip handles—a design that was out of date before Tejohn was born. The third was sensibly designed, and even had a small spike on the bottom. He'd owned a few like it. The spike was supposed to be jabbed into an enemy's foot during a shield-on-shield push, but Tejohn always forgot it was there in the crush of battle.

Best of all, the shield carried the insignia of Second Splashtown. It wasn't *quite* his old unit, but it felt good to hold it nonetheless.

He stripped off his armor and underpadding, then climbed into the feather bed. It was the softest mattress he had ever slept on and he fell instantly into dreams.

He woke late. Passlar had made a thin rice soup for their breakfast. In fact, she seemed to be keeping herself busy cleaning their kits and preparing foods for them as a show of gratitude. Tejohn asked to inspect her wrist and she showed it readily. Arla had made her cuts carefully. Even though Tejohn knew where to look, he couldn't see any trace of the old tattoo. He nodded his approval and gestured for her to sit with them. She did, and she ate greedily.

Reglis seemed uncomfortable with her and excused himself to take a watch atop the tower. Wimnel had already lain down on the sleepstone.

After eating, Tejohn cut the clothes off the paunchy corpse and dropped him into the pit. As he feared, the king had devoured the first man down to his bones. He glanced over at Wimnel's sleeping form, wondering if he would have the stomach to do the same. The grunt ate just as greedily as Passlar had.

Next, Tejohn went into the yard. Arla assured him there were no ruhgrit above, so he wandered freely through the camp. There were no tools in sight. The Durdric had thrown the metal tools and weapons into the mine. Tejohn fetched the largest hammer he could see, then returned to the forge and smashed it to dust.

Sweeps steel was the best metal in the world, and no Durdric, Indregai, or okshim herder should be allowed to see how it was made. Someday, he knew, Alliance soldiers would battle imperial troops with their own version of Sweeps steel, but it would not be because he failed to act when he had the chance.

They did a quick survey of the mine, too. There was nothing inside but the tools, a wheelbarrow, and a string of lightstones. Tejohn put the stones in his pack.

They re-provisioned from the warehouse, loading up on meatbread and filling canteens with a thin yellow tea that Arla boiled up. It made Tejohn nervous to be traveling through the wilderness without a scholar to create clean water for them, but the Sweeps had almost as many streams as the Waterlands did. Among the many dangers they would face, dying of thirst was surely the least of it, even if their guide insisted that many of the streams were poisonous or brackish.

"My tyr!" Arla sounded panicked. Tejohn went to the doorway and looked out.

In the center of the yard, a ruhgrit had landed beside one of the corpses. It gripped the dead man in a talon, then hopped into the air, beating its wings furiously to gain altitude. A second landed, then a third.

Arla had already strung her bow and nocked an arrow. "My tyr, should I?"

"Where are Reglis and Passlar?"

"In the tower."

Tejohn nodded. "If one of the ruhgrit attacks someone living or goes for the pen, take your shot. If they just want to carry off corpses and save us some shovel work, let them."

She nodded back. It wasn't the proper way to address a tyr, but this wasn't a time to stand on formalities. They watched the creatures swoop down and snatch up corpses on the wing. They did not try to break open the pen.

When they were gone, Arla unstrung her bow. She and Tejohn checked their packs one more time, then went to the tower.

Passlar waited for them beside the fireplace in the bottom floor of the tower. "The birds are called 'ruhgrit,'" Tejohn told her. He might as well start spreading the story now. "They're gone for the moment. But the smell of these corpses will draw lions into the compound. Will you be coming with us through the pass to Splashtown?"

She seemed confused for a moment. It occurred to Tejohn that no one had ever asked her what she wanted, ever. When she answered, her tone was firm. "No. Never."

She trilled her Rs just like Arla, which meant she was Chin-Chinro. Where would she go if not back into the empire? Life in the wilderness was dangerous if you didn't have a clan to protect you. "Will you stay long enough to assist Wimnel? Take the bodies out of the compound, drive off any lions, that sort of thing, at least until he wakes? I can pay you for your work, of course."

"You don't have to pay me," she said. "I owe my freedom to you. I—"

"Nonsense. If you truly owed me anything, you'd still be my servant, so be careful how you talk. I was a farmer once, you know. My own brother was a servant in the Finstel holdfast because he got into a drunken fistfight. He died there. My own wife was a debt child once. You should be careful when you speak about debt."

"Thank you, my Tyr," she said carefully, her gaze directed toward the floor. "If you please, I will take my payment from the camp. Two steel knives should serve."

In Tejohn's grandfather's time, a steel knife was a gift for a king. The world changed quickly. "Fair enough. Take the bodies out into the orchard where they can fertilize the trees. Have clean water ready for Wimnel if he needs it. When he wakes, take your knives and go or stay as you will."

"Yes, my tyr." There was a coolness to her tone that Tejohn wasn't sure how to read. When he'd settled her debt, he'd expected gratitude, possibly even a pledge of her loyalty, freely given. Instead, she seemed chilly to him and anxious to be out of his presence. So be it. She was free now and could hate anyone she liked for any reason.

It was traditional for a journey to start at dawn, but Tejohn didn't have much interest in tradition. They set out after the midday meal and were well away from the compound by the time night fell.

They camped in a low, tree-lined place out of the wind. Tejohn hoped the branches would discourage the ruhgrit. Arla started their evening fire with a flint and a tiny piece of steel, a technique Tejohn had never seen before. He studied the method carefully; it was certainly an improvement over twirling a stick.

That night, there was little talk around the campfire. Tejohn had never been a brilliant judge of human nature, but he could see there was a problem, and that Reglis was at its center.

"I have never sat at so many silent campfires as this trip," Tejohn said. "Have we lost the will to sing?"

Reglis did not look up. "It's because of you, my tyr," Arla said. "You are the man who wrote 'River Overrunning,' who made the Evening People weep like children. We are all too self-conscious to play or sing in front of you."

"Fire and Fury, I'm the worst singer in the world. Scout, I know you have an instrument in your pack. Fetch it. We're going to have music after we eat."

"Yes, my tyr," she said hesitantly.

"Reglis," Tejohn said, spooning another mouthful of mush from his bowl, "this is the best jerk stick stew I've ever eaten. "

The young captain's look of surprise made his massive brow wrinkle. "Really?"

"No. What's troubling you?"

Reglis looked at Arla, then Tejohn, then down at his bowl. Tejohn didn't have the patience for this. "Come on, soldier. Your tyr is ordering you to unburden yourself. If you have a complaint, I want to hear it."

Reglis set his half-full bowl on the ground in front of him and laid his hands on his knees. "If you order it, my Tyr, I will. When I left my family to take up a spear, my father told me the empire would turn me into a butcher. We argued for many hours, and I insisted that I would fight with honor."

Tejohn had expected this. "But you have not."

"Last night, no, I did not. I was a butcher, and today I discovered I was butchering those men to fill ruhgrit bellies."

Tejohn nodded. Reglis's glowering expression was as stoic as he could make it, but Arla's gaze was utterly flat, as emotional as Monument. "First of all," Tejohn said, "this is all imperial land—Italga land, in fact—even if"—he glanced at Arla—"the people here don't realize it. So, every meal the ruhgrit take from those corpses is a meal they won't have to make out of a living person."

Reglis nodded and picked up his bowl again. He began to eat.

Tejohn kept talking. "As for honor, warriors win honor. Soldiers win wars. The Indregai are warriors. The Durdric are warriors. They win battles sometimes, yes, and they like fights that will show their prowess. Soldiers hate fair fights. Soldiers take every advantage the way a starving child snatches food from a cart. And I'll tell you this: you will meet many more old soldiers than old warriors."

"Is that why we do this?" Reglis responded. "To grow old?"

"I'm about twice your age," Arla put in, "and I didn't get that way by giving my enemies a fair chance. Putting an arrow in my enemy's back suits me, and if I die in the field, that's how I expect it will happen."

"How long until you muster out?" Tejohn asked.

"I could have taken my ribbon two years ago," she said. "But for what? A plot of rice paddy I could hunch over day after day? It's not like I have children who could inherit from me. I was born in this skinny strip of mountain and I have no plan to leave. As soon as the king gives out ribbons for prospecting, I'll take one. Until then, I'm one of Gerrit's bows."

Tejohn nodded. "I have a wife and children back in the world."

"The wife who was once a debt child, my tyr?" Arla interrupted.

"The very one," he said, his tone careful. "I may be willing to die—and never see them again—in the defense of my king, but not to give a pack of Durdric raiders a fair chance. We fight when we are commanded to fight," Tejohn said. "We take every advantage and show no mercy unless mercy itself is an advantage. Our honor comes in the way we die, not in the way we fight. "

They ate in silence for a while. Reglis did not seem mollified, but his manner had changed. Tejohn had never been very good at reading people. The best he could do was bull forward and hope he was not making new enemies.

When the food was finished, he set the bowl on the ground. "Happy songs only tonight. Peradain has fallen and the king is hidden away. The only thing keeping the Tyrs in line is honor and tradition, by which I mean they are utterly unrestrained. I expect honest warfare to find us soon enough."

CHAPTER SEVENTEEN

THE MEN TOOK THEIR SPEARS AWAY BUT DID NOT KILL THEM. NO ONE asked for their knives or packs, so Cazia had hope that they wouldn't be robbed and murdered.

"How did you know to say that?" Cazia asked.

"A story my uncle told. An awful lot of what I know comes from stories about other people's lives."

"And you speak their language?" Cazia had not let go of her translation stone.

"No," Vilavivianna answered, giving Cazia an odd look. "They speak mine."

Three women came out of the tall grass, bows slung over their shoulders. Their long spears, like the men's, were tipped with sharpened copper. The shafts were so thin, they wobbled. "Outwitted you, did they, Kell?" They sounded like they were teasing him, but there were no smiles on their faces.

"They are devils," the man answered. "We should make—"

"You will make to shut up," the oldest of the women answered. She was tall, lean, and obviously strong, with a lot of gray in her hair. "They are just young girl-devils. What ho, youngsters! What brings you here?"

That was Peradaini. Vilavivianna answered quickly. "We sought safety among my people."

The men and women looked over the ruined camp, their faces grim. "There is no safety to be made in the Sweeps. Not any more. "

The gray-haired woman introduced herself as Hent. Scowling, she asked, politely and in Peradaini, if the girls would parlay with their clan chief.

She's addressing me, Cazia realized. Of course she was. Cazia was the elder. Did they think Vilavivianna was her younger sister? Her owner? All the warriors but Hent glared at the girls with undisguised hate.

Well, if there was one thing Cazia knew, it was how to talk to Enemies. After glancing at their confiscated spears—and noting the greedy way the warriors studied the iron blades—she and Ivy followed Hent across the grasses.

Cazia had seen okshim in Peradain of course, but never more than four together. This was the real thing: a full herd. Just like in the city, they clustered together, their bodies touching side to side. The largest stood at the far front like the tip of an arrow or a flock of migrating birds. The animals that behind it were progressively smaller toward the center of the herd where the youngest ones clustered, then toward the edges and rear she saw more large ones. Cazia tried to estimate their numbers and guessed there must be more than a thousand, possibly as many as two.

In the midst of the herd stood a tall wagon. It was built of dark wood, complete with huge wooden wheels and a fluttering green pennant affixed to a tall pole bent by the steady wind.

Behind that was a second wagon, then a third. Neither of these had windows or shutters, and the last held racks of spears, small round shields, and two young men with strung bows.

They approached the herd at about the center. They were far from the front, but the adults at the edges were huge, much bigger than the beasts she'd seen in the city. Their fur was also more yellow than the mottled brown and gray of city animals, and had added streaks of black.

Cazia approached warily, remembering the warnings the master of the pen had given her long ago. Their fur was soft and their ears long, but they could kick hard to the side with those large, flat feet, and their horny soles could pulp flesh and bone. And while they rarely bit, the curling round horns above their eyes were almost as dangerous as their kicks.

"Have you crossed the top of the herd before?" Hent asked.

"Never," Cazia answered.

The woman grunted. "I will boost you. Kell, make to bring them to the Chief's wagon. Try not to be the fool about it."

Kell scowled, then hopped easily onto the back of the nearest okshim. Hent lifted Vilavivianna by the hips—the girl yelped at her unexpected touch—and set her atop the nearest animal. The princess spread her stance by bracing her foot against another okshim. Hent held her hand while she steadied herself.

"Ready?" the woman asked in a tone that suggested the only acceptable answer was *yes*.

Vilavivianna nodded, her gaze downward. Hent let go. The princess managed to lurch unsteadily from one flat back to the next without falling. Kell did not offer to help.

Hent turned to Cazia and knelt on one knee. "You are too big to lift."

Cazia didn't detect any nastiness in the woman's tone but she assumed it was there anyway. Not that she could argue the point. Hent slapped her knee, indicating that Cazia should step there.

Well aware of her muddy boots, Cazia tore up a clump of tall grass then laid it over the flat part of Hent's thigh before she stepped on it. Let her make nasty comments. Cazia would prove she was above all that.

Walking across the back of the okshim was not as difficult as she'd expected, even with her heavy pack. They weren't conveniently flat, like a palace corridor, but they were flattish—certainly not as rugged as the broken stones north of Fort Samsit. Even better, the animals bore her weight without staggering or shuffling around.

There were gaps, though. Near the tails and around the heads there were spaces where she could fall, and she didn't want to imagine herself trapped down there under those big, hard, heavy feet.

Kell hopped lightly from back to back, never stepping on an animal in front of its shoulders or at the joint of the tail, and the girls followed his example. Once again, Cazia was struck by the oddity of her situation. Who could have foreseen her here, in this moment, hopping across the backs of an okshim herd far out in the wilderness? How Colchua would have laughed.

Ivy had learned so much from her uncle's stories, and now they were living one. Unfortunately, there was no one left to tell it to.

She stopped and looked across the top of the herd. It looked like a single huge animal with many legs and backbones, huffing and snorting. She glanced back at the muddy bootprints she'd made on their downy fur.

Grateful am I to be permitted to travel The Way.

The wagon wheels were very tall and very wide, probably to help them through muddy ground. There was also a stout hide-covered frame around the wheels. That, presumably, let them roll along in the middle of the herd, okshim pressing on all sides, without . . . What? Splitting apart and fleeing? Attacking?

The three wagons were hitched together and the front was pulled by reins attached to eight—no, ten different yoked okshim, the largest animals near the front of the herd. The lead animal was unburdened.

Cazia hopped onto the bumper of the first wagon, then followed the princess to the rear. The wagon walls were made of rough planks covered with pitch, but the roof was heavy cloth. Kell mounted his spear in a rack, knocked on the flimsy door, then opened it without waiting for a response.

Cazia and Ivy followed him inside, standing close together. An older woman, square like a stone block with a head of steel-gray hair and narrow, suspicious eyes, scowled at them. The wispy hair growing from her upper lip and chin was as long as Cazia's middle finger. Ivy bowed politely to her, but the woman just sat on her stool, frowning.

Cazia had met her type before. The palace was full of dour, judgmental old women. Standing across from her was almost soothing, like being back home.

Kell said something to the old woman in his rough-sounding language. Cazia reached toward her pocket to touch the translation stone, but Ivy stopped her by clasping her hand. The princess acted as if she was afraid, but her grip had no urgency. Cazia understood: Don't give them a reason to search your pockets.

The old woman gestured. "Sit, honored guests." Her accent was harsh but at least she wasn't calling them devils. She gestured toward a set of cushions by the wall. Cazia and Ivy shrugged off their packs and sat. The old woman wore a strip of boiled leather over her head like a bonnet, so Cazia gladly left her hat on. She knew that if she took it off, the herders might see the iron cap inside and take it from her.

Kell stood by the door, his hand near the copper hatchet at his waist. The old woman sat opposite the two girls, then took a crude iron pot from beneath a heavy cloth.

"You will have tea," she said, pouring tepid brown water into three horn cups. It occurred to Cazia that, among these people, an iron pot would be a sign of wealth and privilege. Not even King Ellifer had iron equipment in his kitchens. Iron for his soldiers and blacksmiths, yes, but never for his servants.

Ivy accepted the cup. "Thank you." Cazia did the same. She'd never had tea before. It was grassy and sour, but she managed to swallow it all without grimacing. Ivy winced at the first sip and set the full cup on the floor. Kids.

"I don't like it either," the old woman said, "but it is clean enough to make drink, and it is part of the life of my people, so while I dislike the flavor, I also love it with my spirit entire." The old woman downed her own tea in one gulp, then wiped her lips and mustache dry. "We are the Ozzhuack clan. I'm clan chief, Mahz."

"I'm Vilavivianna, of Goldgrass Hill."

Mahz snorted. "You're far from home, aren't you? And what about you?"

"My name is . . . " She was tempted to make something up, but Fire take that idea. She was herself. "My name is Cazia Freewell."

The old woman glared at her. "You hesitate as though the name should mean something to me, but I have never heard of your clan. I have never even heard of the name like yours. Cazia." She pronounced it *Kye-zerra.*

"It's a Surgish name."

"I have never heard of the Surgish." Her tone made it clear that whatever she hadn't heard of wasn't worth knowing. There was another knock and the door opened. This time, it was Hent and the two younger women who had accompanied her. They all crowded in by the door. The youngest of them had red eyes and a puffy face as though she'd been crying. Mahz paid them no attention. "Now, about your claim to my property—"

Ivy interrupted immediately. "We have made no claim to your property. We have only claimed our own."

Mahz slammed her cup on the floor with a loud bang. "Do not make to trifle with me, child!"

"Do *not* call me child!" the princess answered, her tone sharp. The warriors by the door gasped in surprise at her response, but Ivy was too indignant to notice. "Your man spoke first. He had the chance to claim the camp, if he intended to do so, but instead he inquired after my mommy and daddy."

Mahz shot a baleful look at Kell, who kept his face stoic even as he flushed red. "You penalize his good manners."

"I adhere to tradition," the little girl said, her chin held high.

Mahz didn't like that. She scowled and poured herself more tea. "You adhere to our tradition. You take what is ours and make to twist it to your own ends. Do not pretend you Indregai are any better than *her kind.*" She gestured toward Cazia with her cup, slopping tea on the floor. Cazia did not react as it splashed against her legs. "Telling me you are Surgish when I can see perfectly well that you wear Peradaini jackets and boots! Two little girls with iron weapons out here in the Sweeps! Just one of those spearheads is worth more than your lives put together. Am I supposed to make treat with little girls forty days after imperial troops collected their tribute?"

"Taxes, you mean," Cazia said. Let this old woman glower and threaten. Let her spit out her resentments. If she planned to execute them for a meadow full of torn canvas, Cazia wasn't going to plead or make nice. She had a little ball of ice in her stomach, right where she imagined the knives going in, and it gave her self-control. "All this land west of Piskatook Pass is claimed by the Empire, and citizens must pay their taxes. You use the sleepstones, don't you? You trade at the forts, don't you? You're part of the Empire, just like the Surgish, the Chin-Chinro, the Muddalan—"

"Pah! Stupid little devil girl, your head is empty. Yes, the Ozzhuacks make good use of your healing beds, but we know they were put there to insult us. We will not forget! And the clans will never join with your empire—or any other—unless you arrange it in the proper way."

Cazia had to ask. "What's the proper way?"

"Marriage. Let this King of Italga bring me a son or daughter for my son to marry, then we will be joined."

The idea of Lar marrying into this nomad's life was too absurd to laugh at. Cazia only said, "Oh."

"We will make to raise their grandchildren the way men and women are supposed to be brought up. Out in the wind! Tending to the beasts, killing to eat, and taking what you need to survive."

Mahz said the last part with a sinister leer. Ivy understood immediately. "If you take one scrap of cloth from that camp, one scarf, one wooden peg, you will be thieves. The camp is ours."

Mahz waved that off dismissively. "I have not decided whether I should make to honor your claim."

Ivy's hands were clenched into little fists at her side. Her frustration was building.

Cazia knew where this was going—where it had been going since Kell shouted at them to drop their spears. She looked the old woman in the eye and said, "We will fight you."

The old woman's eyes widened with anger, and for the first time, she bared her teeth. Fire and Fury, they had been filed into points.

The princess yelped in shock and terror, sliding away toward the wall. Cazia, too, heard herself gasp, but even as she stared in horror at the old woman's mouth, a small part of her knew Mahz had kept her teeth hidden so she could reveal them at just the right moment. This intimidation had been carefully planned.

"How dare you make to threaten me!" Mahz rolled onto her knees so she could look down at the girls. "I was killing devils before your mothers and fathers were squirted into the mud! If you raise one hand against us, I'll have you beaten black and blue, and if you spill the single drop of Ozzhuack blood, I will slay you myself!"

This is it, Cazia thought. The knives would be coming out now, and she didn't know any spell that could save her and Ivy. All she could do was die defiantly.

"Of course," she said, her lip quivering. Cazia hated that she was showing her fear, but Fire would take it all soon enough. "You can always judge a warrior by her enemies."

There was a moment of silence. Then Hent barked out a loud, long laugh. Kell and the other woman joined in, and Cazia could see that they all had filed their teeth down to points, too. It was ghastly.

Mahz settled back onto her cushion, scowling at Cazia. Then she glanced over at the younger warriors by the door and shook her head as if to say, *Can you believe this?*

"There was once the time," Mahz said, "when all of the clans of the Sweeps were fierce and feared. Plow-pullers and rock-breakers made to send their families to hide in the wilderness when we strode over the horizon. Then the empire came. The passes were blocked with pink stones. Alligaunts grew in strength and numbers in the west. There's little room for the free people in the world."

"We are a free people," the princess said.

"*You* might be free, little devil," Mahz answered, wagging her finger. Cazia had broken her performance, somehow, and now she seemed like an old woman with too many responsibilities and too little sleep. "Your hands are soft enough, both of you, and your chaperone does not appear to have ever gone hungry in her life."

Cazia rolled her eyes. "Great Way, spare me."

"Oh, do not complain! You will make to grow up to be quite the woman! I'm sure you will find the strong husband, the way you look. We might even find one for you here, provided you can prove you know how to work. But you do not make to understand what I am saying, children: we are being driven out. There's no place for the free people any more."

Cazia suddenly understood. "You know what happened to the camp, don't you?" She glanced over at the warriors by the door. The woman with the red-rimmed eyes hadn't laughed with the others, and now she looked as though she wanted to hug Ivy to her breast and cry again. "It's happened to you, too. That's why you're so close to the pass and the fort; you're driving your herd out of the Sweeps to escape from something, aren't you?"

"It was not my decision," Mahz said. "I would have made to stay and die out in the wind. But we have many little ones, and they deserve the chance to grow up. So, we must sell our herd and find new lands to live in."

Cazia tried not to think of little children with filed teeth. "You can't sell your herd at Fort Samsit."

"Oh? And why is this?"

No flying carts had come north through the pass. "Because it's been overrun. Peradain has been invaded by grunts . . . by monsters. The fort has been lost. If you take your people there, they will all die."

There was a long stretch of silence again, but this time, no one broke it with laughter. Mahz hissed and looked at the floor, her fists clenched at her side. Finally, Kell said, "That news is valuable to us. Thank you for making that kind gift."

Ivy looked up at Cazia. Gift? She didn't know what that meant, either.

"Of course . . . " Mahz said, her face turned toward the floor and her expression stormy. "Of course, I will repay such the gift in kind. You have corrected the error that would have ended my clan forever."

Cazia watched her carefully. Did this mean they weren't going to kill her and Ivy? It hardly seemed likely that things could have taken such a sudden turn. What had they done?

"Can we talk about the camp?" the princess asked. "I would like to make a trade, if you would be so kind."

Cazia looked at the little girl with her peripheral vision. She had suddenly become very polite, probably because she was just as flummoxed by Mahz's change in demeanor as Cazia was.

"What sort of trade?" Mahz's accent sounded rougher than before; the words were almost a growl.

"I would keep any coin found in the camp, and whatever tools or provisions Cazia and I can carry. You would get all the rest—the cloth, clothes, toys, tools, weapons, all of it. In exchange, you would help us bury the bodies."

Mahz's answer was almost listless. "We will not make to touch the serpents." Something strange was happening here, and Cazia wished she knew what it was. "That is impossible."

"If your people will dig the graves—one for each human or serpent—Cazia and I will put the serpents in." She looked up at Cazia, who nodded to her.

Mahz looked up at the ceiling. "I agree."

"Thank you," the princess said demurely. The chieftain only nodded without looking at them.

"Come," Hent said to the girls. Her tone and expression had become much softer, almost affectionate. "There is stew for you to share. We will make to eat under the stars together, and we will do it before darkness falls. Tomorrow, we will see to the dead."

Cazia and Ivy stood. The old chieftain wouldn't look at them, but that was fine. Cazia wasn't in the mood to feel sorry for Mahz.

Hent led them onto the narrow deck beyond the door. She took her long, slender spear from the rack. Cazia and Ivy's two iron-tipped spears had been placed there, too. No one objected when they took them. They followed Hent across the backs of the herd, heading north.

Ivy looked back at the camp as though she was afraid it would be gone in the morning. Cazia wished she could say something reassuring, but the truth was that there was nothing reassuring about their situation. The Ozzhuacks had let them take their spears, but Cazia half expected to be murdered during the night.

"Keep that spear tip up," Hent said. Cazia was holding her point above the horizontal, but she copied the older woman and pointed it straight up. At the edge of the herd, they leaped down into the grasses.

"This way to the food," Hent said, leading them toward the front of the herd. "You do not want to be downwind of the okshim while you are trying to eat."

The princess looked at the herd, packed so close together. "Do they step in each other's . . . messes, being so close to each other?"

"Yes," Hent answered. "When the okshim kicks you, it leaves you broken *and* filthy. They eat it, too."

"What?" The princess's face turned pale.

"It is true. The lead animals eat grass, but they can not make to digest it in one pass through. The ones in back—especially the young ones—get more value from plants that have already been through Mommy and Daddy's guts." She laughed at Ivy's expression, showing those horrifying teeth. "Do not worry. We do not make to feed our young ones the same way."

"What will we be having?" Ivy asked, her lips pursed.

"Roast okshim, mostly. More tea as well, and you had better make to drink it. It is the only clean water you are going to get."

"We will," Cazia said.

Hent gave Cazia a sidelong look. It made her uncomfortable, and she looked away, watching the older woman from the side of her eye. "You really played old Mahz in there."

Cazia wasn't sure if she was being criticized or not. It didn't seem like it, but with those teeth, everything that woman said seemed like a threat. "I don't know what you mean."

"Oh, no?" Hent gave Cazia another long look. After a moment, her sly smile showed some surprise. "You are telling the truth, yes? You really do not know what you did."

"Are you going to kill us?" Cazia asked. Hearing *yes* as an answer would have been horrifying, but not knowing was becoming unbearable. "Ever since—Kell, was it?—took our spears, I assumed you were going to kill us. But honestly, at this point, I have no idea what you're doing."

"I wish Mahz could hear you say that. No, girl, we are not making to kill you. I do not know what you are used to down in the southlands, but in the Sweeps, we prize hospitality. We have to, considering the dangers we face. That is why property and gifts are so important to us."

Ivy huffed. "Then why was your chieftain pressing us to relinquish our claim to the camp? Why did she threaten us?"

Cazia was grateful that Ivy kept using *we* and *our*, even if it was just because she needed someone older to support her claim. Hent's response was delivered in a flat tone, "We are desperate. Alligaunts have been bad enough. Grass lions we can handle. But these birds have made things impossible, may they rot from their guts. We have lost six children in the past eight days alone, and four strong warriors."

"Great Way, I didn't know." Cazia remembered the woman with the red, puffy eyes. How many more like her were there? The image of that huge raptor flying over Samsit flashed through her mind, and she shuddered. "I'm so sorry."

"We have not managed to take the single one of theirs in return. At first, we did not even know what was happening. We would wake in the morning and discover the empty flat with ripped bedclothes in the middle of the camp. Just as we figured out what was happening, we discovered the Poalo clan's cart, fully wrecked like the carts in your camp. The herd was gone, the people destroyed, their goods scattered."

"That is why you are hurrying to Fort Samsit," the princess said. "To sell the herds and the goods you have collected, and try to start a new life."

"Whatever life I can find down there," Hent answered bitterly. "What freedom does an unmarried woman have in the empire? Do you think I could find a husband with a smile like this?"

She grinned with those horrible pointed teeth, and Cazia's first instinct was to say, *No chance of that,* but after a moment's thought, she realized she had seen stranger things in the palace. "Well, not a good husband, maybe, but I'm sure you could find someone."

Hent rolled her eyes. "The real reason you took the sprint out of Mahz was by the gift you gave her."

"Kell said something about that," Cazia said. "But I don't understand. How is telling you about the problems at the fort a gift?"

"Because news is vital, and hospitality is the way of life for us. Mahz didn't expect . . . You southlanders always respond to arrogance with threats or pleas for mercy. She expected you to drink her tea and then violate her hospitality; she would have then made free to take the camp. Instead, you shared news that will save all of us and you did not even try to bargain first. You see? If someone gives to you when you are in need, you must repay them."

"Ah," Ivy said. "I think I understand. Hospitality enhances the giver and weakens the recipient. If Mahz can not return a gift of equal value, she will be in our debt, and that is a mark against the honor."

"Very good, little girl. And of course it is only made worse by the fact that we have been weakened by these attacks; Mahz is desperate for the way out, ashamed of the way she bullied you, and not only was the bargain you made so much in her favor, it was practically the act of charity itself, but she was forced to balk at the serpents and demand even better terms."

It was almost as though Hent was accusing them of manipulation. "We weren't trying to embarrass her," Cazia said, trying to hide her resentment. "We were just trying to be decent."

"We shall try to return the kindness. Believe it."

They had reached the front of the herd. There were three old men tending a fire, laying spits of meat across the flames and squabbling about the best placement of them. Six adults slept on little wooden pallets laid in the grass, while children ran in circles, playing the same chase games all small children enjoy. Two older kids were cutting grass and laying it in front of the herd, feeding the lead okshim.

A full dozen warriors, armed with spear and bow, patrolled the edges of the camp, watching the grass and the skies.

Hent led them to the fire, where she gave the old men orders in her own guttural language. Cazia wasn't sure if she should reach for her translation stone in case the words *Poison them* came up, but her moment of indecision cost her the opportunity.

Hent promised to return to talk more, then left to confer with the guards. The old cooks brought a pallet for the girls to sit on, then brought them skewers of meat, mushroom, and wild onion. Cazia didn't try to understand their language, but they were clearly competing to see whose cooking would be most pleasing.

The princess made a sour face when she accepted her skewer, but Cazia said, "Eat it and smile."

"There is a reason spoiled twelve-year-old girls do not make good diplomats," Ivy responded. "I'd almost rather have some of your salt-crusted jerky bread."

"Oh, please. It's not actually crusted with salt. And we had better accept whatever they offer us, not only so that our own provisions last. I don't want to insult them. Having them in our debt is a good thing."

"Until it goes to far and they kill us both." Ivy tried to slide a piece of meat off the skewer, but it was too hot to touch. The shortest and leanest of the old cooks leaned over her, smiling and miming that she should eat with her fingers. She smiled back and blew on the piece, then popped it into her mouth. "This is actually pretty good!"

The cook took her response as vindication and returned to the fire to taunt the others.

Ivy ate an onion next. "Even after everything Hent told you, you still do not trust them?"

I don't even trust you anymore. But Cazia couldn't say that. That was too cruel. She ate from her skewer. Ivy was right; it was delicious.

The other cooks forced them to finish two more skewers, even though they were full after the second. They also brought cups of tea, which tasted better alongside the food. When Hent returned, she conferred briefly with the cooks, then said in Peradaini, "They want to know which you liked best."

"The second," Ivy said immediately.

"Great Way," Cazia said, "if there's one thing I've learned, it's that you don't make enemies of the cooks. What would be the most diplomatic answer?"

Hent grinned crookedly. "With this bunch, the truth."

Cazia sighed. "The second."

When Hent passed this information on, there was much taunting and jeering, but Cazia could see that it was mostly friendly. Then the Ozzhuacks themselves began to line up, and the old men became too busy to compete.

Hent returned and sat on a mat beside the two girls. Almost immediately, a dark-haired boy raced forward and offered her a pair of skewers. He looked different from the other herders—darker, his hair unbound and hanging in his eyes. Cazia thought he was a year or two younger than her, and he was entirely beautiful.

Hent snatched the skewers from his hands. Her lip curled slightly as she glanced at him. Apparently, the Ozzhuacks had more contempt for their servants than even the Peradaini. Cazia watched the boy out of her peripheral vision, and although he did not look directly at her, she suspected that he wanted to.

"There is one thing I do not understand," Ivy said. "Why are you coming so far west? You know you would be welcomed into the Alliance without having to swear allegiance to tyr and king."

"Serpents," was the immediate response. "The Alliance made the terrible error when it made to join with the serpents. They will be your downfall. But that is not the only reason. Going east would have taken us closer to Qorr, which is where the birds are coming from. The farther north and east we go, the more dangerous."

"Qorr?" Cazia said. "Is that a city?"

Ivy and Hent looked at her in astonishment. "Have you never heard of the Qorr Valley?" Ivy asked. "I mean, honestly, you never have?"

Cazia felt herself flush, but she didn't give them the snappish answer they deserved. "Honestly. Do you think the birds have come from there?"

Hent spoke while she chewed a piece of dark meat. "My own cousin, one of the Hammershore, saw them flying over the peaks herself. They are the latest nightmare out of Qorr."

"Latest?" Cazia asked. "How have I never heard of this valley before?"

"I sincerely can not imagine!" Ivy said, managing to mix both surprise and pity into those five words. "The Qorr Valley lies on the far side of the Northern Barrier, far to the northeast. It is utterly sealed off, so no one in our lifetime has been there, but if something has wings—"

"Or can climb like spiders—" Hent interrupted.

"Yes," Ivy agreed. "The giant spiders that troubled our great-great-grand-fathers came from there as well. They did a lot of damage to the clans in the Sweeps and to my own people."

Hent shook her head dolefully. "We still have not recovered."

Cazia looked at them skeptically. How could this be real when she'd never even heard of it before? "But no one has ever seen this valley?"

"Not in living memory," Hent said. "The sorcerer gods of ancient times made to turn the passes into sheer cliffs. This was before the time of your empire, before your people began traveling the world, bending it at the point of the spear."

This again. Cazia wasn't interested in being made to feel guilty because her own Surgish people were part of the Peradaini empire. It's not as though she had any choice in the matter. "Wait a moment. When did the first of these attacks happen?"

Hent shrugged. "The Hammershores were attacked seven days ago."

Cazia looked at Ivy. "That's one day after the grunts stormed into Peradain." Had it really been so few days ago? It seemed another life.

The little princess sat straight up. "Do you think they're related?"

"Two different monsters appearing at practically the same time, so far apart? I'll bet it is. It might be an attack on the entire continent." An unexpected thought made her skin prickle. "Is there a portal in this secret valley of yours?"

Hent and Ivy looked at each other, then shrugged.

Night was falling. One of the guards yelped a warning, and everyone looked up. High above them, a bird floated lazily in the headwinds. Cazia thought about the quiver of darts in her backpack. An iron dart might not kill a creature of that size, but it should drive it off. However, the Ozzhuacks would discover that she was a scholar and they would . . . frankly, making a prisoner of her was the least awful thing she could imagine.

Hent told them it was time to sleep and assured them the guards would watch over them. Ivy was concerned but, as soon as Cazia laid blankets over them, she fell asleep.

Cazia could not. It wasn't only fear that the raptors might carry her off. While she had no doubt about the bravery of the Ozzhuack warriors, she was less sure they would risk themselves to protect her. No, she was more troubled by the realization that the birds had appeared at the same time as the grunts.

No one else had realized there might be a connection. No one else knew. What if there was a second portal in this Qorr Valley? Who could possibly do something about it, besides her? If she was never going to become Scholar Administrator—and that dream of comfort and privilege within the Palace of Song and Morning was dead, even if she was not truly prepared to admit it—she could be the person who sought out the truth about this instead.

She and Ivy woke in the middle of the night. There was a terrible commotion: shouting men and women, the shudder of bowstrings, and a loud crashing noise.

Cazia and Ivy clutched each other in the darkness as harsh bird cries shrieked around them, and the herd lowed miserably.

After a short time, Mahz knelt beside them, tucking their blankets under them. "No worries, children. We have driven them off tonight at very little cost. Sleep now."

In the morning, everything was made clear. The birds had attacked from downwind, unexpectedly. What's more, they'd carried a huge tree trunk, intending to smash the wagons. Kell had spotted them, and a volley of arrows shot with the wind had been enough to make them drop their weapon early, killing three older okshim at the back of the herd.

The old cooks were already butchering the meat well downwind of the alpha female.

Hent brought them more skewers of meat for breakfast. This time there were no onions or mushrooms, and the food was a bit singed. Cazia ate greedily anyway; they would have a great deal of work to do that day.

Mahz came to them as they were rolling their blankets up and putting them into their packs. "Start by dawn and accomplish much," she said. Cazia gave her a puzzled look. "It loses something when it is translated into your language. What I mean is that we have already begun to set the camp in order. You should join the crew."

They did. Four men and four women had pulled down all the tents, rolling the canvas into tight bundles. They had also found eight bodies, laying them in a tidy row along the eastern edge of the camp. The princess went to them first, walking from body to body, inspecting them as if she expected to recognize one. If she did, she hid it well.

Two of the men used picks to break up the earth, spacing their graves well apart from one another. Cazia went through the camp, looking for serpents. The Ozzhuacks wouldn't touch them, and she knew Ivy was not strong enough to move them to their graves. She alone could this do for her friend.

There were three. The first was the one she'd found beneath the rock. It took all her strength to roll it off the body. Seeing its full length, she understood the Ozzhuacks' terror of them; the serpents were terrifying on an instinctual level, and lying dead for several days hadn't improved their condition.

She had to drag the thing's carcass the length of the camp; its ruined body felt like a sack of broken sticks, but she did it, leaving it near—but not too near—the human bodies. When she went back for the second, she saw that the Ozzhuacks had moved into the space she'd just cleared, rolling up the canvas and setting out the trunks.

Ivy had changed her boots—they were lined with a fur Cazia couldn't recognize—and laid out a set of tools. She chose a bronze hammer, spade, and shovel, which Cazia set aside. Ivy loaded her pack with disks of damp flatbread that smelled like cheap wine; she was irritatingly pleased that she would not have to eat more meatbread.

By the end of the day, the incessant wind had folded and wrinkled the brim of Cazia's hat until most of the wax had flaked off. It would provide little protection from rain now. Ivy found a number of woolen Ergoll caps like the one she had worn at Fort Samsit, but she did not take one for herself.

The Ozzhuacks shoveled dirt into the human graves, but Cazia and Ivy had to fill in the serpents' graves by themselves. When they had finished, Ivy glared at the shovels as though she both needed and resented them.

There was also quite a bit more money than they expected. It was almost too much to carry, and Ivy held a whispered conversation with Cazia about the weight of all that copper. It would be a serious burden, but women alone could never have too much, not if they wanted to live carefully and safely.

"It's time to tell you, then," Cazia said. "I'm not going east with you to Indregai lands, and I'm not going west with the Ozzhuacks to Fort Caarilit."

Ivy's eyes widened with fear. Cazia was sure she hadn't seen that expression on the girl's face before, but that couldn't be true. The princess said, "You can't go back south!"

"No. I'm going northeast. To the Qorr Valley."

CHAPTER EIGHTEEN

OVER THE NEXT EIGHTEEN DAYS, TEJOHN AND REGLIS MADE GOOD time and traveled in comfortable silence. Arla slept by their fire and shared their meals, but during the day, she spent very little time with them, preferring to scout far ahead and range widely. On the third night, after much prodding, she confessed that she felt Tejohn's safety was in her hands. If there were enemies in the Sweeps, it would not be force of arms that would save their lives; it would be her ability to lead her companions to safety.

She was right, of course, but it made Tejohn feel helpless. He hated feeling helpless.

Reglis spoke up. "Has it been ten days since the start of the Festival?"

"Eleven," Tejohn answered. Had it really only been eleven days? So much had happened, and so many lives had been lost.

"My tyr," Reglis said. "I know it is not proper, but I can't help but wonder how many lives have been lost. Will we ever know how many have been killed or taken by The Blessing? It doesn't seem possible."

Faces flashed through Tejohn's memory: Kellin and the others teasing him about the money he'd lost at a night's game. Kolbi Arriya hurrying by in the palace corridors, wishing him a good morning in her high, chiming voice. Amlian Italga asking him to sing at the Festival. Monument sustain him, he would need a dozen years to mourn for them all. *At least my family is safe, for now.*

Eleven days. That meant the portal the Evening People used to visit Peradain would have finally vanished. How many grunts had come through? He didn't like to think about it. "Song knows," Tejohn finally said, "and sometimes I wish Song would tell us, too."

At midmorning of the nineteenth day, Arla waited for them in a small copse at a rise in the trail. They'd come upon another mining camp, but she assured Tejohn it had been abandoned in an orderly manner.

They marched down the trail in the daylight and came upon the barred doors without incident or challenge. Reglis's calls to the guard towers went unanswered, and they moved on. By nightfall, the Caarilit pass was just above them.

Tejohn would have liked to push on in the dark, but Arla warned him the way was steep and heavily forested. They would have to hike up the side of a long spur directly ahead of them before turning southeast into the pass, and that would be better done in the daylight.

He knew she was right, but it was frustrating. Their mission, doomed from the start because of The Blessing, progressed at a crawl. One night, as they sat around a well-hidden fire, Tejohn had asked Arla to keep an eye out for a new flying cart just lying around in the wilderness.

For Tejohn, the long days of walking were a time for planning. Yes, he could see the blue of the sky, the green of the trees and grasses, but beyond a couple of dozen feet, they were formless blurs to him. For someone with his extremely short vision, being outdoors for a long time was curiously like being sequestered away with his thoughts. A hundred times a day, he concluded that he would have to abandon the king's quest for this deadly spell—which seemed more like a wizard's spell than one of the Gifts, surely. A hundred times a day, he decided that his duty required him to carry through. He ached to strike out eastward toward his family, but he knew it would not be a happy reunion if he had abandoned his duty and doomed them all.

Long afternoons were spent trying to devise effective tactics Peradaini spears and bows could use against The Blessing. The problem was that the grunts were too strong and quick to fight in the field. They leaped astonishing distances, threw men around like firewood, and attacked in a fearless frenzy.

One on one, a man with a large, sturdy shield and a long spear might kill one—if he was lucky—but to do it without being bitten as well? In large groups on an open field, volleys of arrows might be effective, if the imperial archers could be trained not to aim directly at their enemy but to loose them in orderly rows like sheets of rain. Tejohn had a dim view of the chances that tactic would be happily received. Once the bows had done their work, it would fall upon a square to take on the survivors, and he wasn't enthusiastic about that.

Worse, those tactics were feasible during the daylight hours only. The best option he could come up with after dark was to fight them from within a holdfast with high walls and well-manned towers. But while that might allow human beings to kill grunts in large numbers, as a long-term strategy it was a plan for human extinction. The holdfasts simply couldn't protect and sustain a large portion of the empire, and every human left outside the walls was a potential enemy recruit.

The truth was, human soldiers weren't mobile enough to fight The Blessing on their own terms. Every engagement would be at the whim of the enemy, without the option for retreat. That meant the soldiers themselves would have to be like holdfasts, but how could they somehow transport walls and towers on a campaign? Could they wear enough armor to cover themselves completely with steel?

Tejohn couldn't quite envision how that would work, even if the units could afford the iron. In the end, his thoughts always returned to the king and his deadly spell.

The empire has always relied on its scholars; we just don't like to admit it.

As much as he hated to acknowledge it, he ended each day resolved to follow through with the king's plan: to make his way to Splashtown, where the Tyr Finstel would have to be convinced, somehow, that the fate of humankind relied on letting Tejohn borrow a cart for the trip to Tempest Pass.

From there, it meant training scholars in this new version of the Gift so they could destroy grunts at a wave of the hand. It would change warfare forever, giving hollowed-out madmen like Doctor Rexler the means to slaughter honest fighting soldiers by the hundreds, but they would have to deal with that later, after The Blessing was utterly wiped out.

If that was even possible.

There was still the hope, which was so faint Tejohn refused to speak it aloud, that Ghoron Italga, the scholar prince at Tempest Pass, might have a way to turn the grunts back into people.

That night, after Reglis and Arla had played their usual songs, Tejohn agreed to sing one, much to their surprise. Of course it wasn't "River Overrunning;" instead, he chose a song that had been old-fashioned during his campaigning days, "The Flock Wanders Far Afield."

After he finished, the two were silent. Then Reglis said, "My tyr, a newborn lamb can hold a note better than you."

They laughed, Tejohn included. But beneath that laughter, he could see the question in their expressions: how had a man with so little skill at music become so famous for a single performance?

"With luck, we'll see Caarilit tomorrow. If the commander allows, we'll use his mirror to find a tyr willing to loan us a cart for a trip to Tempest Pass. Then we can start to turn the tide against the grunts."

"It can't be soon enough," Reglis said, then added, "my tyr."

The long days of their trip—and the evenings by the campfire—had made them comfortable with each other. "Do you have someone in mind, Reglis?"

He shrugged, staring into the fire. The young man's massive brow was furrowed in anger and he stared at the flames as though he intended to punch them. "My father lived in the town south of Samsit. Lives. I meant to say 'lives.' The grunts have gotten that far by now, don't you think? He swore he would never take shelter with Peradaini soldiers . . . with all due apologies to you both."

"I need none," Arla said quickly.

"Neither do I," Tejohn said.

"He must be one of them by now," Reglis said, his voice hollow. "Along with his brothers and . . . I hate to think of it. I'd almost rather he was dead. I'm ashamed to say it, but it's true."

"That's nothing to be ashamed of," Arla said. "Monument gives us ten thousand ways to endure."

Tejohn shut his eyes. The image of Laoni fleeing in terror from a pursuing grunt, children in her arms, came to him hard. "I wish we had ten thousand and one."

Arla was watching him carefully. "My tyr, your family should be safe across the Straim, shouldn't they?"

He shrugged. "They should be across the river, and I hope it is a safe haven for them." *Everything is dangerous.* "Song knows what has happened to any of the people we knew back in the civilized world. It's possible your father had a fright powerful enough to drive him into the safety of the fort after all."

Reglis bowed his head as though accepting a compliment.

"How did you meet your wife?" Arla asked. "If it's not to forward of me to ask, my tyr."

Before this long journey, Tejohn would have bristled at such a question from one of his soldiers, but without Arla, he could not have survived in the Sweeps. He had to acknowledge an obligation to her, if a small one. It felt a bit like friendship, and friendship permitted personal questions. "It's not a story I tell often," he admitted. "A freed debt child becoming the wife of a tyr . . . "

"It sounds like a play." Reglis couldn't suppress a grin.

"A bad one." Tejohn was glad to see the young captain smile so quickly after the previous topic of conversation. Then, suddenly, he wasn't sure where to start the tale.

"Who freed her?" Arla asked, reading his hesitation.

"I did." Tejohn looked at their smiles and shrugged. "I told you it would make a bad play. But the real thing wasn't so simple. She was an Italga servant who went west to be part of the newly built Freewell holdfast. She was a babe in arms then, but when she was five, she was given to Doctor Rexler. He'd already been hollowed by then, and the things he did to his servants . . . Well, you wouldn't put it on a stage for the Evening People to see.

"But after the battle at Pinch Hall, everything was in turmoil. Tyr Free-well was still alive, and Rexler's servants would normally have gone to him, except King Ellifer forbade it, ordering him to march home without a retinue. Everyone treated the Freewell servants as though treachery was contagious. No one would take them in. Finally, they were brought to me: I was the man who slew Rexler, so his orphan servant children were presented to me as spoils of war. I ordered Laoni and her brothers to clean my boots, then declared their debt settled and set them free."

"That was kind of you," Reglis said.

Arla glanced over at him, obviously irritated. Tejohn spoke before she could respond. "No, it wasn't. At the time, I was still overcome with grief and rage. The battles were over, the war won, but I was furious that I would not be allowed to keep killing. This was three months before the Festival when I sang—I told the Performance Master I was going to do a tumbling routine; did you know? I looked fit enough and he took me at my word. That Fire-taken song was the only way to get the pain out, and no Performance Master in the world would have let me anywhere near a stage, not with my voice.

"Anyway, I didn't give a thought to a couple of orphaned servants with no family and no way to care for themselves; they could have been Fire-taken right in front of me and I wouldn't have blinked. Luckily, the priests discovered what I'd done and took them in, caring for them until they were old enough to find apprenticeships. Laoni became a baker.

"When she came to me, fourteen years later in the Palace of Song and Morning, I'm embarrassed to say I had forgotten all about her. She and her husband opened a bakery in Peradain, and—"

"Husband?" Arla said.

Tejohn spread his hands. "My wife loves me, but not as much as she loved him. He was . . . Ultimately, he was a fool. He gambled all on his charm, and eventually he lost. But they came to see me together. She had created a special red cake in my honor, to thank me for having that tattoo cut from her wrist. And I had no idea who she was."

"How was the cake?" Reglis asked.

Tejohn kept his face carefully neutral. "Extremely sweet. There's nothing an old soldier likes more than to be commemorated with something incredibly sweet and almost insubstantial." Arla and Reglis laughed, and he felt oddly pleased. "I was honored, of course, but I felt guilty, too. I began dropping by there often." Once again, he was unsure how to continue the story.

"Then," Arla continued, "the charming fool got himself knifed in a married woman's bedroom."

"It was gambling debts, actually," Tejohn corrected her. "He fell from a roof while running from casino thugs. I loaned the money to Laoni to help her settle his debt, and I kept going there for little cakes, and just to talk. Eventually . . . " He shrugged.

"My tyr, you are torturing us with your pauses," Arla said kindly. "Eventually, you realized you cared for her."

"At first, I cared for the idea of her," Tejohn admitted. "Few tyrs ever get to choose their wives, but I had no lands, wealth, or influence at court. No one wanted an alliance with me. I could do as I liked. And the truth is, I had always been known for one thing: grief. I was the man who went to war, who made the Evening People weep with a song, and who had become the first honorary tyr, all because of the way my wife and child died. I didn't want to be that person for year after grinding year, living alone in perpetual mourning. I wanted a life.

"And the more time I spent with her, the less interested I was in the idea of her and the more I liked her as a person. The Finstels frown on relationships between people with so much distance in their ages, but I didn't live in Finstel lands anymore. So, two years and a day after her husband died, we had a small ceremony in the Palace temple, a widow and widower trying again."

"That's a nice ending," Reglis said. "I like that ending."

"Sure," Tejohn said. "If you stop the story there."

"I had a younger man once," Arla said. "There were fifteen years between us, and he was as nice as you please."

"But then you found out he had another woman," Tejohn said, partly to return the charge she'd made against Laoni's first husband.

"No, I found out *I* was the other woman. I swear, I'd be Watch Commander today if I hadn't buried an arrow in his backside."

Tejohn laughed. "You were lucky he was facing away from you."

"One of us was lucky," Arla answered, "but it wasn't me."

Reglis laid his hands on his knees. "That's a thought that'll keep me up for a long while. I'll volunteer for first watch."

"Not so fast," Arla said. "It's your turn."

He sighed in a resigned way. "I nearly married. My father arranged it— that's how it worked among my people, even for the common folk. When we were children, our parents would arrange a marriage, and those two families could be friendly with each other and do business. Except that doesn't really work inside the empire. Anyway, she likes to order people about and she sings like a bleating goat. Once she learned I was taking up the spear, she convinced her father to break it off. The empire does nothing for soldiers' widows, after all."

"You took up the spear to get out marriage?" Tejohn asked.

"No," Reglis said, "but it was a happy side benefit. My father was . . . displeased, you could say. He's forbidden me to marry anyone else, and I've honored his wish. So far."

"What about your almost-bride?" Arla asked.

Reglis smiled. "She married someone else twelve days later. I understand they are very unhappy together. And my father feels . . . " That was a sentence he could not finish.

"When this is all over," Tejohn said, "we could return to Samsit and I would be willing to talk to your father about this."

Reglis seemed startled. "My tyr . . . "

"If you wish it, of course. You would know if talking to a tyr of the empire would improve things between the two of you or make them worse. But I wouldn't bully him or order him to do anything, obviously. I'd talk to him honestly about soldiers and their families. If you wish it."

"I would, my tyr." Reglis bowed his head. "If—"

"No 'if,' Captain," Tejohn's voice was calm. "There's no reason to assume the worst."

"Thank you, my tyr."

Arla smiled at him. Tejohn said, "Are you going to ask me to talk to Commander Gerrit about making you a Watch Commander?"

"No, my tyr," she said, and he believed her. "I wouldn't dream of it."

"Well, after all this"—Tejohn waved at their camp—"you both deserve a promotion. But don't think I've forgotten that you volunteered for first watch, Captain."

Tejohn settled onto his bedroll. It had felt odd to tell that story, but good, too, like correcting an old mistake. He should have trusted these two soldiers sooner. He should have been kinder.

This sense of companionship was as fragile as one of his wife's tiny cakes, he knew, but it felt good nonetheless.

The next day, they set out for the top of the spur, which took most of the morning. It was steep, slow going through thick forest, and even Tejohn was tempted to use the butt of his spear as a walking stick. The only other option, Arla assured them, was to strike out to the north and enter the spur the long way, which would take most of a day.

At the top, the trees grew sparse and the ground became hard-packed dirt with little growth. They reached the smooth, bare curve of the top of the spur and turned southeast, heading toward the pass. By the end of the day they would be sheltered within the mountain pass, and Tejohn would not have to smell the vinegar-sour winds of the Sweeps again until he returned on a Finstel cart.

"My tyr," Reglis said, and pointed toward the edge of the mountains. It was Arla, hurrying toward them with her bow strung.

She did not speak until she was close enough to speak quietly and be heard. "Troops, my Tyr, marching under a black banner."

"Can't you be more specific than that?" Tejohn asked. Half the squares in the empire used a black field. "What marking?"

"They had scouts of their own, my Tyr. I couldn't get close enough to see. But there are at least thirty spears and five scouts. Smallish shields, like a fleet squad, but they have the longest spears I've ever seen."

Tejohn scowled. Someone was getting creative with their equipment.

"They are almost certainly Finstels, my tyr," Reglis said.

The fort in Caarilit Pass ahead of them had been given to the Finstels, and every mine they'd passed had been Finstel-held. The shield Tejohn carried on his back bore a Splashtown waterfall design on a black field. But they couldn't afford to take unnecessary risks.

"Let's find cover. I want those scouts to pass right by us. When the troops come near, Arla will describe them in more detail."

They found a thick stand of trees at the edge of a steep drop-off at the side of the spur. Tejohn and Reglis lay flat on their bellies and crawled into the bushes. Arla laid leafy branches over them, nearly burying them in foliage, then wiggled in close between them. Her arm, knotted with muscle and darkened by the sun, was surprisingly soft against Tejohn's elbow.

They both shifted position to pull their limbs in.

The wind blew through the leaves. Finally, Arla hissed, "Scouts."

Tejohn did not move. He didn't need to see them; he could hear them well enough. One passed fewer than a dozen feet in front of them. Arla, lying close to the edge of the brush, stayed very still. After a hundred breaths or so, she slowly crawled backwards.

"Gray jackets, my Tyr, with small bows in hand and knives at their hips. No markings otherwise."

Gray? Tejohn didn't know of any unit that used gray as their color. Gray was bad luck. "Watch for the spears and their banner."

It didn't take long. "They're out of Splashtown."

That was what he wanted to hear. "How do they look?"

"Exhausted," she answered. "Frightened. They're doing a ragged quick-step like they've been retreating all day."

Fire and Fury. That was not what he wanted to hear. Tejohn took a deep breath and shouted, "*SPLASHTOWN!*" in the booming battlefield voice he hadn't used in years.

"That stirred them up," Arla said. "They're scrambling to form ranks."

"SPLASHTOWN! POINTS HIGH! Let's go, you two. Time to stop hiding on our bellies."

Tejohn was the first to emerge from the thicket. He gained his feet, hefted his shield high and stood his spear against his own shoulder. It was the standard posture for approaching friendly forces—spear point high—but even at this distance, he could see that the Splashtown troops were points forward behind a shield wall.

He strolled toward them casually. They were close enough to make out the colors of their shields and banners. The bright red blur above the man in front must have been the brush on his helmet. Tejohn turned slightly to walk directly towards him.

"Drop your weapons and identify yourselves!" the man with the brush shouted.

"Points high," Tejohn called back.

"Bows!" the officer called, and Tejohn could hear footsteps coming toward him from behind.

When Arla spoke, it was through clenched teeth. "My tyr?"

Tejohn didn't break stride. "You expected an arrow in the back, didn't you?"

"I guess I did. By the way, the 'captain' up ahead isn't really a captain. His sash is too long and the brush on his helmet hangs off the front."

"Thank you for that." He took a deep breath. "Acting Captain! You outnumber us ten to one and I have called for points high! You can see the emblem on my shield, can't you?"

The captain called back, his voice sounding thin in the wind. "A stolen shield, I'd wager. That emblem is three years out of date."

"I carry it," Tejohn said, "for the same reason you have attached your former captain's brush to your helmet: necessity. A Durdric axe split my old one."

"I recognize you," the captain said suddenly. "Fire and Fury, you're Tejohn Treygar. Points high!"

Startled by the sudden change, Tejohn halted. "How do you recognize me, soldier?"

"You toured the empire with the prince some years ago, my Tyr Treygar. I saw you on the parade stand. Excuse me, my tyr."

While the captain ordered his bows to reform a perimeter, Tejohn turned to Arla and Reglis. "That's an odd bit of luck," he said, feeling vaguely embarrassed.

"Not really, my Tyr," Arla said. "I recognized you as soon as I saw you."

Reglis flushed. "I did not," he admitted, scowling, "but you looked very familiar. And I heard the men laughing at me the next day because of the way I spoke to you when you landed in that cart."

Tejohn had no idea what to say to that. Long ago, he'd come to terms with the idea that his name was known all across the empire, but his face? He looked off into the Sweeps, suddenly wondering what it would be like to live out there alone.

Then he sighed and turned to the acting captain, who removed his helmet. He was a short, stocky man, and he was too young to be carrying a paunch. Tejohn said, "What's your mission, and why do you have so few spears?"

"We were heading for the mining camps," the man answered, looking a little uncomfortable. Tejohn couldn't tell if he was lying, intimidated, or embarrassed. Maybe it was all three. "To round up the people working there and escort them to safety. The first night, we were attacked by Durdric holy fighters, which wasn't serious, but then . . . " He glanced back toward the pass.

"Then what?"

"Two lines of Witt spears cut us off from the fort. The captain tried to break through with a square, but they had scholars fighting with them."

"What?" Reglis blurted out.

"At least two," the captain said. "They created stone blocks above the square, crushing the men beneath, and then they turned fire against our flank. That was yesterday. When the captain took an arrow, he gave me his brush and ordered a retreat."

"Are they in pursuit?"

"They are. Our bows took their scholars—I believe so, anyway; they hide them by dressing them like the other troops, but of course, they can't cast with shields or spears in hand—but they still outnumber us two to one. And they're between us and Fort Caarilit."

The nearby spears were close enough to overhear them. They looked exhausted and dispirited.

Arla spoke up, "My tyr, the Witt spears have not yet appeared at the mouth of the pass."

"Good. Did you see any place where we could take the high ground? Someplace narrow where our flanks would be protected?"

"I . . ." She turned back toward the hill where they'd just climbed. "In the woods near the foot of the spur, there's a reclaimed iron mine with a narrow dirt ramp. It's upstream from last night's campsite."

"It will have to do." He turned to the young man with the brush. "What's your name?"

"I am called Jolu Dellastone, Tyr Treygar."

"Jolu, I am taking command of your spears and bows. Any objection?"

He smiled. "None, my tyr."

"My first order is to take that ridiculous thing off your helmet and throw it away. No, even better, give it to me. Call in the scout that passed us by without seeing us."

The call was sent out, and the bowman returned before the metal clasps holding the brush to Jolu's helmet could be pried open. The scout was tall and lean with an ugly face. Tejohn wasn't much good at reading people, but even he could tell the man expected to be upbraided. "How much more running do you have in you?"

"My Tyr," the man answered, "I have as much as you require."

"I don't need effusive promises from an embarrassed man. I need a straight answer. How long?"

The bowman looked even more embarrassed, if that was possible. "At this pace, until nightfall," he glanced quickly at the captain, "but not much longer."

The captain had finally pried off his bright red brush. Tejohn took it from him and gave it to the scout. "That's fine. Put this on; I don't care how. Then find two more strong runners and take the banner straight down the spur. I want you to be far enough from the Witt scouts that they can not see anything but that spot of red moving against the green."

The brush would never stand on the scout's leather cap, but he took it anyway. "I will lead the enemy into the wilderness," the bowman said, "for my brothers."

Tejohn had always hated that pious crap about *brothers*. At least two of the spears were held by women, and half the bows. "I want you to draw the Witt spears down the hill, then turn them around and bring them back along the base of the spur. There's a freshwater stream for you to follow. Bring them to us."

He started off. Tejohn turned toward Jolu. "Form your spears into two columns. We're going downhill. I don't want it to look like a herd of okshim bulled through and I don't want anyone falling onto anyone else's spear."

The spears formed up and marched down into the forest. Arla lead the way, and three of the Finstel scouts remained behind to hide their trail.

With the flutter of windblown cloth, the tall scout sprinted away down the stony slope. He had two companions with him, and they were beyond Tejohn's field of vision in no time at all. He offered a silent prayer to Monument and The Great Way for their safety.

He and Reglis started down the slope.

They were going into battle. Tejohn's skin prickled with anticipation.

One of the soldiers lost his footing and slid down the dirt slope. Tejohn hopped after him and helped him off his back. His arms were bone thin, his face sallow, and his breathing ragged. This was no soldier. "What unit is this?"

The man who'd fallen was gulping too much air to answer. The man who'd been his partner—a tall, fit fellow with a tumbler's build—spoke up. "The Sixth, my tyr."

Of course, the tyrs had called up their militias.

The man lined up behind the tumbler muttered, "What's left of it."

"Fire take that talk, soldier," Tejohn snapped. "Song remembers every word and thought." Tejohn turned to the scrawny man who'd fallen. The man stared up at him strangely. "The militias—common citizens taking up arms to defend their lands—are the backbone of the empire. It's a proud tradition." He shoved the man back into his place in the column. "Try to live up to it."

As they marched away, Tejohn puzzled over the man's expression. It was common enough to see a frightened soldier, but that man had been afraid of Tejohn himself. Was his reputation so awful that the man expected to be punished for falling on a steep hill? It was the only explanation he could come up with, but he knew it didn't fit. If they survived the next few days, they'd have to think on it.

The trip down the hill was faster than the trip up, of course, but they didn't make as much time as Tejohn would have liked. They didn't reach the spot Arla had chosen until nearly dark.

The mine was partway up a cliff face, with a long dirt-and-stone ramp leading up to it. There were trees well above, but three men standing on each other's shoulders at the mouth of the mine couldn't have reached them. A pair of streams splashed through the cliffs to the south. To the north was a deer path that ran along the stream. While Jolu formed the spears at the base of the ramp, Arla led Tejohn and Reglis to the mine entrance.

Reglis glanced inside. "That's the shallowest mine I've ever seen."

"Very funny," Arla said. "It's been reclaimed, as I said, my tyr. The Durdric 'heal' wounds in the mountains by trying to fill them in, then lay that line of shells across the mouth to warn others away."

"Is this a temple to them?" Tejohn asked. Bad enough to fight Witt spears, but he didn't want a Durdric holy war at the same time.

Arla shrugged. "To them, the entire mountain range is sacred."

"My tyr," Reglis said. "Will we really be forming our square here? We'll have nowhere to retreat."

"Then we'll have to fight all the harder. Come along. Let's get ready. " He ordered a trio of soldiers into a copse of pines to collect pitch, and a squad of ten to cut down and strip a fat fir tree. Jolu organized a late meal while Arla positioned their four remaining archers.

Tejohn sat alone at their dinner meal, well apart from the others. The soldiers ate in silence, giving him furtive glances. Eventually, Tejohn waved Reglis over to him.

"Yes, my tyr?"

"Why this silence, captain? Are they so demoralized?"

"No, my tyr. The reason they don't sing is because you are here. You make them self-conscious."

"Well, after we finish here, I want you to start a song. It feels like a funeral."

"I will. Er, with your permission, my tyr, may I ask a question?"

Tejohn surprised himself; there was no flash of annoyance this time, not with this soldier. "Go ahead."

"If the scout has drawn the Witt spears to the north, why not just climb back to the pass and make for Fort Caarilit?" Reglis asked. "The way should be clear now."

"You're right, it should," Tejohn answered. "But we don't know if the fort is in friendly hands or not. If the Witts are on this side of it, I would guess not. We'll have to approach carefully, and I don't want to do that with enemy spears at our backs."

"Ah, thank you, my tyr. Is there anything else?"

"Actually, yes. How would you like to be the one who wins this battle for us?"

Half the night was gone before they were ready. The soldiers slept in shifts and dawn seemed to come late and suddenly. Tejohn himself, although he hadn't slept among soldiers before a battle in many years, woke feeling almost like a young man again.

It was nearly midday meal when they heard the sound of Witt drums echoing against the mountainside. Tejohn watched the spears form their lines at the top of the ramp, then walked among them, handing each a piece of meatbread and a cup of watered wine from a pot he himself had warmed over the fire. They were nervous, as they should be, and he did his best to let his confidence soothe them.

Flutes trilled from somewhere to the northeast. Tejohn knew that melody well. Witt soldiers had followed it into battle for generations.

"Tighten the line!" Jolu barked like a good sergeant. The spears formed up in three rows of seven, their too-long spears pointed down the ramp, their too-small shields touching side to side.

Tejohn walked behind them. He never shouted in moments like this. "I have seen many battles, and stood inside many squares. I have never, not once, served alongside giants or legendary heroes from the ruined past. Always, it has been soldiers just like you. Men and women who take up the spear and shield to defend their lands and destroy their enemies. Men and women just like you." The frightened man who had fallen on the hill stood in the center of the rearmost rank. Tejohn straightened his arm so his spear point was in line with the others. What would Laoni have thought if she could see him? What would Teberr or the twins think? "You are spears of the empire, and your courage, your will, your Fury are what will win us this day. Strength! Honor! Purpose!"

Then the Witt troops marched across the stream into the open space at the bottom of the ramp.

Their green banner and drummer marched at the front, with the flute player just behind. Children, Tejohn noted. Even at this distance, he could see that they were just children.

The spears filed in behind, falling into rows along the bottom of the ramp. They carried proper spears and tower shields like Tejohn's own. They formed up, making five ranks of ten each, with a line of four bows on each side.

Five ranks against three. Another commander might have retreated from those odds, but Tejohn had made sure there was no place to retreat.

The last of them was another child—a girl this time, by her clothes. She carried the black Splashtown banner, and threw it defiantly to the ground in front of the first rank of Witt spears.

Their captain was squat and heavily muscled, almost the twin of Jolu, although he still wore his red brush. Tejohn didn't like his swagger.

"Bring him out!" the Witt captain shouted. Two soldiers shoved a man in gray through the square, knocking him to the ground beside the Splashtown banner.

Even at this range, Tejohn could see that it was the scout who had carried off the banner and brush. Tejohn unclenched his jaw, trying to take control of the feeling that was growing within him. *He was acting under my orders . . .* No, he had to be like Monument now and endure whatever came next.

"Citizens of Splashtown!" the Witt captain shouted. It was an old insult against militia troops to call them citizens instead of soldiers. "I understand you have a *pair* of distinguished guests among you now. Hear me! I have no wish to claim your lives today. You do not have the ranks to overcome us. Throw down your weapons! We will take our prisoners away and you can return to your farms and shops in peace!"

The Splashtown ranks began to waver. Tejohn kept his voice low but he couldn't control the angry waver in it. "If you disarm before this enemy, they will slaughter you. I have fought the Witts before. They don't just want me and this scholar"—the sallow-faced man glanced suddenly at Tejohn—"they want your lands and your cities. They will make servants of your children."

Jolu stood at Tejohn's shoulder. "What response, my Tyr?"

Tejohn felt as if he stood at the edge of a precipice and had no choice but to jump. "You are a Splashtown spear and these are Finstel lands," which wasn't true, but there were no Italgas to dispute the claim. "What do you want to say to these invaders?"

"Throw down your weapons!" Jolu shouted. "All prisoners will be treated with honor!"

The Witt spears laughed. "I salute your courage!" the captain shouted back. "You are very brave with your soldiers' lives."

"Fight on!" the scout called from the ground. "FIGHT O—"

He never got the chance to finish. The captain drew his sword in one swift motion and chopped at the man's neck. The blood was bright on the ground. Then the Witt captain wiped his sword on the fallen Splashtown banner.

"That man was your prisoner!" Tejohn shouted, feeling his rage escape him like flames shooting through a hole in the roof of a burning house. His anger surged within him, transforming into that same old feeling. He'd felt the ghost of it in the mining camp, but here it was again, powerful, deadly, and almost forgotten after so many years. It felt like momentum, like the weight of a falling body or a falling blade, something dangerous and irresistible.

The militia around him were feeling it, too; he could sense it in the way they drew together and leaned forward. If the Witt captain thought that sword stroke would demoralize his enemy, he was a fool.

The Witt spears formed up and the captain took the center position. Jolu slid forward to do the same. Tejohn moved around to the northern side of the line, standing between the spears and the flanking enemy bows.

The Witts began marching, doing the stamp step every spear learns their first day. Once all of their ranks had entered the ramp, Tejohn said, "Brands."

Two spears from the rear rank chose carefully laid torches from the campfire and knelt low behind the shield wall. A volley of arrows flew toward them, but they were few and all were met with shields. The enemy lines advanced.

"Touch," he called when the spear points grew near each other. It took only moments for the pitch-smeared tunics tied to the log to catch fire. "Send." The front rank of Splashtown Six rolled the log down the ramp.

Song knew Tejohn had spent enough time with them, drilling that kick and impressing upon them the importance of rolling it correctly. It paid off; they did it perfectly. The flames roared as the log tumbled down the ramp.

"Forward!" Jolu shouted, and the spears charged behind it. They moved at double time rather than the intimidation march the Witts used. Tejohn glanced to the northern flank of the ramp again and saw that the small unit of bows were already down, feathered shafts in their backs.

The front line of the Witts staggered and loosened up. The Witt captain shouted, "Brace!" and he dropped to one knee, jamming the bottom of his shield against the ground. Immediately, the men on either side of him lunged forward to do the same, and the ragged line began to reform.

Just as the burning log struck the shields, Tejohn shouted, "Throw the oil!"

There was no oil, of course, but the Witt spears did not know that. The front two ranks fell back, falling against the spears behind them, bumping their points out of true and opening gaps in the shield wall. Just before the

Splashtown spears struck, there were screams from the back of the Witt ranks.

Tejohn followed the line down the hill. He heard men and women crying out, saw a spear point push through the back of the man in front of him, and leaped forward to take his place in the rank, even though his spear was so much shorter than the rest of the line.

There would be no pushing of shield walls today. Reglis and his tiny group had hit the enemy from behind, and the Witt square crumbled like sourcake.

"No mercy!" Jolu screamed as pushed through the Witt soldiers, striking with his long knife. The Splashtown front rank had shattered or abandoned their spears; they stabbed wildly within the Witt ranks.

The Witt casualties did not begin in earnest until the front ranks turned and fled. Several fell off the side of the ramp, their weapons shattered. Witt spears sprawled in the dirt and screamed for quarter.

"Quarter!" Tejohn roared. He didn't care much for Witt soldiers, but he wanted at least one of them to live long enough to answer his questions. Jolu took up the call, and as quickly as that, the battle was over.

The Witt captain was already dead; someone had cut his head from his shoulders. Too bad. Tejohn would have liked to hang him.

Several Splashtown spears had fallen, two were already dead, and only one of the others was likely to last out the day. Overall, it was a better outcome than they'd had any right to expect. Of the Witt soldiers, all eight of their bows were dead, and all three of their children had survived. Tejohn breathed a silent thanks to Song, Monument, and the Great Way that he would not see another dead child today.

The Splashtown soldiers lifted their weapons and shouted a cheer. Even with the hills around them to reflect the sound, their voices sounded small.

Jolu rushed up to Tejohn. "My tyr—"

Tejohn grabbed him by the shoulder and shook him. "Acting captain," he said icily, "your banner is still *lying in the dirt!*"

The man wheeled about and sprinted through the mass of bodies, many still writhing or moaning in pain. He snatched the banner out of the mud where it lay beside the scout's corpse. He lifted it, wiping mud from the red thread along the edge, then pressed it into the hand of the nearest spear. The woman accepted it, then carried it to the patch of grass where the prisoners were being gathered and held it above them.

By now, two of the wounded Witt spears had begun to shriek. They begged for healing, called for their mothers, and wept for help of any kind.

Their voices were thin and terrified, and Tejohn felt himself winding tighter and tighter with every breath.

Jolu returned. He had a shallow cut along his left cheek that was bleeding steadily. It might make a heroic scar someday. The cut on his shoulder was even shallower. "My tyr," he said, this time with less jubilation, "you were right! That log trick—"

"Was just a distraction," Tejohn interrupted. "Something to keep their attention while we hit their flank. Bring up that scholar of yours."

Jolu's mouth fell open, then he shut it again. "My Tyr, we have no—"

But the sallow-faced man had been standing nearby, and he spoke up at the same time. "Yes, my tyr. How can I serve you?"

Tejohn turned to him. "Do you know healing magic?"

The man spread his hands apologetically. "I was only a mining scholar, my tyr."

Tejohn grabbed hold of the man's cuirass and shook him, almost throwing him to the dirt. "You will be Fire-taken yet if you give me another evasive answer. Do you know healing magic?"

"No, my tyr. I can only do spells useful in a mining camp."

"What are they?" Tejohn asked. Jolu's eyes were wide and shining, but his expression was carefully neutral. He did not interrupt.

"The Third, Fifth, Seventh, Eleventh, and Fourteenth Gifts, my tyr. I can start fires, create water, encourage crops, shatter rock and create light."

"Encourage crops?"

"For the trees, my tyr." The man kept his face carefully turned toward the ground. "We need wood for the crucibles, and there are few forests like this in the Sweeps."

"Fine. What is your name?"

The scholar bowed. "I am Doctor Ullaroc, my tyr, originally from Rivershelf."

This man looked more like a footpad than a scholar. The urge to open his guts to the air was powerful, but Tejohn knew that was just the aftermath of battle. It would be hours before the killing urge left him. "Keep close to your bodyguards."

The man didn't seem at all surprised by this command. He only bowed and backed away.

Jolu looked embarrassed. "I apologize, my tyr, but my mission was secret."

Of course. If there was one thing he should have expected, it was this. King Ellifer had not maintained superiority over the tyrs through the armies he could field. His advantage was in his control of the scholars. Ellifer's own people kept them from falling under the tyrs' control, sometimes with a knife point, and it was the king himself who decided which holdfasts would have the spells on their sleepstones renewed, or had scholar-created roads, or flying carts.

With the king gone, the tyrs were scrambling to round up every scholar they could find, even mine workers like Ullaroc.

If Tejohn returned from Tempest Pass with a way to undo Lar's curse, they would have to devise a plan to bring the scholars under Italga control again. If they didn't, they might never remake the empire.

"My tyr!" That was Arla, calling to him from the bottom of the ramp.

From the sound of her voice, Tejohn knew immediately that Reglis had fallen in the battle. He started down the ramp. A Splashtown spear with blood all over his jacket lay forehead to forehead with a fellow soldier. Both of them grasped her dagger, its point aimed at his heart. A gut wound. The man couldn't have been more than twenty years old.

"Grateful am I," the man said, his voice fading, "to be permitted to travel The Way."

Tejohn didn't watch the knife go in. Instead, he focused on Arla and the man lying at her feet.

It was Reglis. Unlike so many others, he had already died. A knife thrust under his chin had taken him quickly.

"He killed at least eight all by himself, not counting the bows we took in the initial charge." That was a woman standing nearby. Tejohn recognized her as one of the three Reglis had taken with him for his flanking attack. There were two other spears beside her, both older men.

"At least eight," one of the men said. "No exaggeration."

Tejohn looked down at Reglis's pale, still face. His heavy brow had lost its glower. "Song knows what he did." If Tejohn ever had reason to speak with the young man's father, it would not be to make peace in the family. It would be to share grief.

Tejohn felt himself winding tighter and tighter, his old outrage coming on strong. Another good man, butchered like a pig. It wasn't *exactly* the same; he knew that. He didn't have the burning ache of his dead children inside him, the grief feeling so much like a pod that struggled to burst open but never could. It was like entering a room long kept shut, a visit to a past self that he had tried to leave behind forever. The urge to shed blood was on him again. He had a mission to accomplish for the Italga family, and he had enemies to kill.

Everything seemed so clear and simple.

Jolu was nearby. "Acting captain, what stands between us and Fort Caarilit?"

"Nothing but marching, my tyr."

Tejohn didn't like the man's self-satisfied expression. He didn't like jubilation, pride, or bravado in the aftermath of victory. They slowed everyone down. Tejohn wanted the next round of killing to have started already. "Get the shovels," he snapped. "I don't want any delay."

CHAPTER NINETEEN

CAZIA KNEW HER PLAN WOULD UPSET PEOPLE, BUT SHE DIDN'T EXPECT them to soil their skirts over it. At first, Ivy refused to believe her; the princess's insistence that None Of This Is Funny So Please Stop became infuriating. Once Cazia lost her temper and the truth sank in, the girl began to cry furiously as though Cazia had beaten her.

Ivy ran to Mahz, of all people, and demanded she force Cazia to go east into Indregai. At one point, she even reverted to the Commanding Princess routine she'd tried with Tyr Treygar and ordered Mahz to bind Cazia and throw her into the wagon.

That didn't go over any better with the Ozzhuack leader than it had with Old Stoneface, but while Mahz scolded Ivy for her manners, Hent took Cazia aside.

"Child"—she kept her voice as low as possible given the sound of the wind, and her tone was matronly—"can you be serious about this? Because I am also tempted to ask Mahz to bind you and lock you in the wagon. You do not have the way even to make to enter the valley. There is no pass through those mountains; people have searched for one for generations."

"I climb very well," Cazia answered. "And please don't call me *child*."

The old warrior seemed to be losing patience. "While you make to wander the base of the Northern Barrier, searching for the place to climb, you will be in high danger. The marshes are home to big cats and alligaunts, and every great bird leaving the valley will pass above you. You are laying out your bedroll on the lion's lap."

Cazia assumed that also sounded better in the Ozzhuack's own language. "No one else knows about this, do they? Do you think anyone has realized that the grunts and these giant eagles are connected somehow? What if this is a planned attack, not only against Peradain, but against every human being on the continent? What if some Enemy intends to keep killing us until only Song remembers we were even here?"

"That . . . That can not be so."

The memory of her dart sinking into the grunt—her own brother—flashed through her mind. Her guts suddenly felt tight and she put a sharper edge to her words than intended. "Why not? Because you wouldn't like it? And to think *you* called *me* a child."

Hent's eyes went wide with anger. Cazia glared back at her. If the warrior dared to strike her, Cazia would set her on fire, no matter what the consequences.

I have the flinches.

The woman bared her filed teeth. "We have made to be kind to you."

They'd tried to cheat and bully Ivy out of her people's belongings, but Cazia shoved that aside. It didn't matter. "You don't understand," she said. "My family are traitors. I have no lands, no clan, and the only friend I have left is that little girl over there." *I was going to be Scholar Administrator someday.* "All the people in the world that I care about have been turned into monsters, and I don't even know why."

"There is not always the reason why, *child.*"

Cazia was tempted to scorch her just for the tone of her voice, Fire take whatever might happen next. "Who's to say there are only two creatures, the grunts and the eagles? There could be something worse running loose in the west! And since I can't get there, I'm going over those mountains."

She pointed toward the Northern Barrier. Hent scowled and redirected her arm farther east. Fine, she didn't know exactly where the valley was yet, but she would find out soon enough.

"What do you expect to discover there?" Hent asked, letting some kindness back into her tone.

"Maybe nothing." That was hard to admit, but it was true. "But then we'll know that there's nothing to discover, right?"

"No, Cazia. We will not. You will be dead, and no one will learn of your news."

Of course, that was always a possibility, but Cazia wasn't entirely sure how she felt about it. She knew it could happen—she'd been surrounded by corpses all morning, and at Fort Samsit, and back in Peradain. Still, to picture herself as one of them, lying in the mud . . . It just didn't seem real. She couldn't imagine it.

What made it worse was that she knew she *ought* to be able to imagine it. She knew it was dangerous and silly to act as though no harm could touch her, especially after everything she'd seen. But there it was. Maybe Hent was right. Maybe she was a child. Soon enough, she'd be a dead child. Death would seem real enough to her then, maybe.

. . . *vanishing is more painful for those left behind.* Peraday's words came back to her suddenly and they made Cazia unbearably sad. She was about to vanish, just as that soldier's brother had, and who would miss her? Colchua and Pagesh were dead and Lar must have transformed by now. Jagia, Bit, and Timu would transform soon. Ivy was here, true, but they'd known each other for less than a month. Also, she was twelve; the princess would certainly forget her in a few years. Who was left? Her mother and father? Nothing could be more ridiculous.

She opened her pack again, taking care not to expose her quiver of darts. She doubted the Ozzhuacks would recognize their significance, but her time in the palace had taught her caution. Secrets were weapons that could be turned against her, and they required caution. She might not be able to imagine herself murdered and eaten, but she certainly knew what it was like to be found out and betrayed.

Ivy was happy with her damp bread disks, which meant Cazia carried all the remaining meatbread. Good. She would need all she could get. Water was no problem, but food was.

It didn't take long to arrange things. Cazia shouldered her pack and picked up her spear. It seemed silly to keep carrying it, but she had to keep up appearances. Besides, the butt end made a decent walking stick. Once she was well away from the others, she would strap her quiver of darts to her hip. It was startling how much she missed the feel of them.

She started walking, following the direction Hent had redirected her arm. She had passed nearly out of sight of the herd when she noticed Ivy running after her. "Cazia!" she shouted, "Please!"

Please? If the princess was going to be polite, Cazia would, too. She stopped and waited. The girl ran around in front of her and said, "Hent told me what you said."

Cazia scowled at her. "Don't tell me I'm being stupid or crazy, all right?"

"I won't," the girl said, trying to catch her breath. "I promise. Instead, I have decided to come with you."

Cazia looked down at the little girl and her bony arms. "Fire and Fury, you will not. I'm not taking you anywhere."

"Cazia, you can not go alone. You don't know the first thing about surviving in the wilderness, which I have been doing since I was a child."

"You're still a child."

"I'm aware of that, thank you. But you still need me. You can not just march across the Sweeps to the Qorr Valley!"

"Who's going to stop me?" Cazia lifted her right hand, holding her spear point skyward. "You?"

Ivy swung her own spear with all her might, striking Cazia's just behind the head. The weapon twisted and her thumb wasn't strong enough to hold on. She tried to catch it with her other hand but fumbled. The weapon clattered against the rocky ground. Cazia sighed. "Fire take me."

"The Sweeps will stop you," Ivy said. "You can't just stroll across the marshes. You wouldn't even get half way to Markwind Lake. But you don't have to. With the coin from the camp, I've hired the Ozzhuacks to take us eastward. Mahz is going to show us a waterway that will take us where we need to go. They certainly can't continue to go southwest, not when the grunts are spreading across the empire. I've convinced her that she would be more welcome in the peninsula."

"You convinced her?" Cazia was doubtful. "That quickly?"

Ivy shrugged. "It really was a lot of money."

Cazia laughed aloud at that, then went back to the camp to help finish packing. She also joined Ivy at the graves, for a last few moments of silence.

As it turned out, the longest delay came from turning the herd around. Okshim didn't like sharp changes of direction. Kell explained that they mixed up the side-by-sides—whatever that meant—and the wagon hitches weren't built for it, either. What's more, the beasts naturally migrated west as the weather grew warmer.

Mahz took the alpha cow by the nose and pulled it in a large, gentle circle. The warriors ran around the edges of the herd, swatting okshim with the blunt ends of their spears to prevent them from panicking and breaking away from the herd.

After they were pointed east again, the herd was allowed to rest. Children ran across their backs, dropping fresh-cut grass between them as a treat. While the beasts rested, warriors loaded the canvas and other goods into the warehouse wagon. When they finished, it was so full they could barely latch the door.

Cazia approached Mahz. The old woman had a tiny smile on her face. She didn't like heading eastward again, but Ivy's description of the grunts had convinced her they would be safer on the other side of the Straim. Also, the camp goods were valuable enough that they could pay their way through the pass without selling their entire herd. They would not have to give up the source of their true wealth.

What's more, Ivy had paid them in copper to deliver a message to Goldgrass Hill. It was in Ergoll, one of the Alliance tongues—apparently, the only Alliance tongue the herders spoke was Toal—and Mahz had to learn it phonetically. She'd also promised not have it translated. The message was for Ivy's parents only.

By the time the herd was ready to move again, it was almost sundown. They spent a quiet night without an attack, then set out east in the morning.

It was eleven days' walk along the stony, hard-packed edge of the Southern Barrier, Mahz explained, until they would separate. A more direct path—by which she meant the one Cazia had started on—would have crossed the marshes. It was *possible* to cross on foot, if you could tell solid earth from mud, didn't mind being soaked to your bottom at every misstep, and had the stamina of a hero out of the old tales, but the only people who ever tried it were outcasts, and they were rarely seen again.

Mahz preferred to ride on the back of an okshim herd but, she said, the girls would have to make do with a raft.

Cazia was not allowed to work during the trip. The princess explained that she had paid for this escort, and they needed only walk along—or ride atop the herd or in the wagon, if they liked.

But Cazia, who had received every meal, every stitch of clothing, and every stick of firewood from her father's most powerful enemy, suddenly felt uncomfortable. She felt she ought to contribute—not as a servant, obviously, but something. She felt unfairly singled out and pampered, as though the clan was making her last days on The Way as sweet as possible.

It was different for the princess. Every Ozzhuack approached the girl at some point in their journey to ask about the Indregai serpents. Some came two or three times, asking the same questions over and over.

Ivy reassured them with the same phrases over and over: the serpents were allies, they kept to themselves, they ate chickens and other small animals but nothing as large as a man, they only attacked when provoked. They were not big enough swallow a full-grown human, no matter what the stories said. Cazia thought the girl had more patience than any ten people, and asked her about it over an evening meal.

The princess shrugged. "They are just frightened, and it is a ruler's duty to calm the fears of the subjects."

"Oh!" Cazia said. It hadn't occurred to her that the girl was adding the

Ozzhuacks—along with their herd and whatever wealth they carried—to her own people. Great Way, she'd even given them a message to deliver to ensure they could end their journey at Goldgrass Hill, if they wanted.

"Besides," Ivy said. "It is for the good of them. It's silly for them to fear the serpents when fleeing into Peradaini lands would be a death sentence."

The princess was once again deciding what was best for other people, but at least she was persuading them rather than tricking them.

On the ninth day, they passed a granite hut with a sleepstone inside it. After some discussion, they stopped for the night so one of the children could sleep off a sprained ankle. Late on the eleventh day, the herd crested a rounded hill and started down into a marshy basin. Not just a marsh, she realized. It was a wide, shallow lake. There were small islands here and there—little more than humps, really—that a tall man could not lie across without getting his hair and heels wet, and each sprouted a bare, twisted tree, with cattails growing where the land slipped below the water. As the sun set behind them, Cazia watched the shadows of the trees stretch across the rippled surface of the water.

On the twelfth day, at the water's edge, the herd came to a tattered wooden dock. At Hent's instruction, two warriors went into the shallow water and lifted rocks from the lake bed onto the dock. Cazia wondered what odd custom she was seeing until the raft bobbed to the surface.

"Still sound!" one of the warriors called from the hip-deep water.

"Here we part," Mahz said. She gestured toward the stream flowing northward toward the long lake. "Coftin River is fresh water, not salt, so you can drink from it and shelter beneath trees at the shoreline."

"Or in them," Hent added.

"In them is always better when you're alone. Remember that alligaunts prefer fresh to salt, but will hunt in both."

"We have each other," Ivy said. "And I have traveled through the Sweeps before."

With an army, Cazia could have added, but she didn't.

As the herd began to wade through the marsh into the lake, Ozzhuacks leaped onto the okshims' back. Neither girl made a move to get onto the raft while they were in sight; Cazia didn't know why Ivy waited, but she herself didn't want Hent, Mahz, or any of the others to see her fall into the water.

As the last of the herd splashed into the shallows, they heard a whip crack. Cazia started in surprise; the herders didn't whip their okshim. She looked across the moving dark mass and saw a warrior—the young woman who had pestered Ivy the most—putting a short lash to a young girl with unkempt dark hair. Cazia's hand went to her translation stone. "How dare you!" the warrior shouted, punctuating each word with a swing of her arm. "How dare you splash mud on me!"

Just as Cazia noted the similarity between the girl and the boy who had brought the skewers to Hent on their first night, he appeared, shielding her with his body. "Leave my sister alone!"

The young warrior immediately lost her temper. She raised her lash again. The boy leaped forward and snatched it from her hand, then threw it down between the undulating backs of the okshim.

Now several other warriors rushed to the back of the herd, moving with surprising speed and assurance. They leveled their spear points at the two dark-haired servants and shouted.

The dark-haired girl lay sprawled on one of the okshim. Her brother helped her up and they retreated together toward the back of the herd, then leaped from the last of the animals, plunging into the water.

Just a pretext, Cazia realized. The Ozzhuacks worked, slept, and ate while muddy, and no one seemed to care. If that girl was being whipped, it must have been a pretext for some other reason, and if there was one thing Cazia's life had taught her to recognize, it was that.

The two of them swam through the muddy lake water, pulling themselves ashore near the long grasses. Ivy said. "We should probably—"

The girl cried out. Now that they were only a few paces away, Cazia could see that she was slightly older than her brother. She had, maybe, a year on Cazia, although of course she had spent more time working in the sun. Both looked slender and strong. Both wore their hair oiled and braided. The boy stood.

He looked directly at Cazia and Ivy—not in a hostile way—then looked all around. He was searching the landscape and the girls were just another part of it. There was nothing to see. He crouched beside his sister, stroked her hair once, then stood as if he'd made up his mind.

He stalked across the marshy ground and fell onto his knees in front of the two girls. He held up his open hands, his head bowed, and said, "Accept us as your servants, and we will care for you in the wilderness. Do not abandon us here." Great Way, he was so beautiful.

Ivy turned to Cazia. "What do you think he wants?"

He clapped his hands together, then held them up again. Ivy said something in another language, but when he didn't respond, she tried another. He looked up at them, his expression apologetic. He couldn't understand.

"Take us with you, please!" the boy said. "You do not understand me, do you? Are my gestures not enough?"

"Smile at them!" his older sister called.

"I am smiling!" he called back, and yes indeed, he was. His smile was bright and his eyes twinkled; Cazia's skin tingled when he looked at her.

The boy ran to the dock and leaped into the water beside the raft. After a quick examination, he shook it by the corner. He immediately waved the girls over, calling, "You see? This is not safe! We can help you." Cazia and Ivy stepped cautiously onto the dock to see what he was doing.

He pointed to the corner and pushed the raft back and forth in the water. The narrow logs clacked against each other—clearly, they weren't tightly lashed together.

Cazia turned to Ivy. "Still sound," she said, her tone sour. So much for Ozzhuacks repaying their kindness.

The boy pulled the raft onto the muddy bank. He said, "Let us begin," to his sister, and she followed him into the tall reeds. Within a few breaths, they had gathered enough reeds that they began twining them together. Soon, they began to wrap the raft more tightly.

He kept saying, "We can help. You will see," over and over, his tone assuring, and he smiled up as he said it.

Cazia's heart skipped. Great Way, he was *beautiful.*

She stepped back and turned away, letting go of the translation stone. What did he think of her, in her muddy hiking skirts and jacket and tangled hair? Not much, she was sure, no matter how bright his smile.

And anyway, who did he think he was, making her respond so powerfully? She could never trust someone like that.

It was near midday when they finally finished working on the raft. The timbers had been bound so tightly that they no longer knocked together or twisted.

Ivy turned to Cazia. "I do not suppose we can just leave them."

"I don't suppose we should take them, either," Cazia said, knowing very well that at the moment she sounded even more petulant than a twelve-year-old princess. "Mahz and Hent and the rest think this is suicide, but they want to go with us? I don't trust them."

"Really?" Ivy sounded honestly surprised. "Why? Did they say something alarming? Is it because they were driven away from the Ozzhuacks?"

Because he made me feel something I wasn't ready to feel. "How could I know what they said? I don't understand their language." Ivy looked a little chastened, but just a little. "I don't trust them, because we don't know anything about them! Servants aren't interchangeable, you know."

"If we do not take them," Ivy said, "they will have nowhere else to go. No clan. I am pretty sure they are Poalos, and—"

"Poalos!" The boy exclaimed. He pointed at his heart, then at his sister's heart. "Poalos."

"Yes," Ivy said. "That is right." She turned to Cazia. "Mahz said the people had been destroyed. Without a clan, how are they supposed to survive? Just the two of them?"

Cazia and Ivy made two, of course, and were even younger than the herders; such extraordinarily subtle hints weren't wasted on her. "How is that our fault?" Cazia knew she sounded peevish but she couldn't help it. "Besides, shouldn't they be married or something? Mahz offered me a husband, but not them?"

Ivy shrugged. "They are probably cousins. Among the Ergoll, if you take in your own family, you cannot marry them to make them work, so they become Men—I mean, servants."

Would the four of them really be safer than a pair? Cazia wanted to argue the point, but she couldn't think of anything that she wouldn't be embarrassed to say aloud. "Fine. But I don't trust them, Ivy." She lowered her voice. "Let's treat them like spies."

"All right, then; I will not trust them, either. Not until you do." Ivy turned to them, nodded her head once, then set her backpack on the ground. She pointed first at the pack, then the raft.

Grinning broadly, the boy leaped forward to carry their packs onto the raft.

The Poalos were too pleased to be accepted as servants. Servants in the palace—the most prestigious place in the world to work—had always seemed sullen and resigned, if not outright resentful. She hadn't blamed them for being unhappy, of course, but it was still unpleasant.

In contrast, the siblings seemed grateful and eager to please. They set Cazia's and Ivy's backpacks in the center of the raft, arranged so the girls could sit atop them. Ivy kept her spear upright and ready, so Cazia did the same. The Poalos used long poles to push away from the dock toward the okshim herd.

The princess was startled at first, but Cazia knew where they were going. The Ozzhuacks had thrown the Poalos' things from the back of the wagon, piling them beneath a tree on a muddy hump some distance away.

After the siblings had collected their things, including a copper hatchet and fishing spear, they let Ivy direct them downriver. The servants glanced at each other nervously, then obeyed.

The older sister was named Kinz, the younger brother was Alga and their shared family name was Chu. Cazia thought they were terrible names for two such beautiful people, but maybe they sounded better to their ears. Cazia wondered how her name sounded to them.

The Coftin River was lazy, broad, and shallow. Cazia stared straight ahead; Ivy was keeping watch, so she would, too.

But she also kept Kinz in her peripheral vision, watching her without seeming to. Once they were well beyond the dock and floating slowly toward the Northern Barrier, Cazia saw the older girl give her brother a quick, furtive look, and her smirking expression betrayed her.

They fell for it, that expression said.

CHAPTER TWENTY

BY THE FIFTH NIGHT, CAZIA HAD BECOME SO ACCUSTOMED TO SLEEPING in trees that she almost slept through until dawn. Progress on the river was steady but slow, and that afternoon, the Poalos had dragged the raft onto a sizable island in the middle of the river. With hand gestures, they made it clear that the mud and weeds on the eastern bank would be impossible for their raft. For once, everyone had found an almost-comfortable spot in their own tree.

Cazia was glad to be spending the night on the island. Everyone had told her to be afraid of the alligaunts but so far she hadn't even seen one. Grass lions, however, she'd seen, and more than once. Sleeping in a tree wouldn't protect her from *them*, but she hoped the water would.

Something woke her. The moon was high and bright. She shifted uncomfortably and looked around. The river lapped against the stony shore of the island, and of course she could hear the constant, never-ending sound of the wind. Fire take that wind; she didn't know how the herder clans could stand it. Had she been woken by a dream she couldn't remember now, or was it something else?

Cazia glanced over at Ivy, sleeping in the next tree. She was barely visible among the shadowed branches, but she appeared to be safe. By unspoken agreement, Kinz and Alga had chosen spots on the far side of Ivy so the little princess would be encircled. Cazia couldn't see them through the branches and shadows, but she was glad they were there.

Nothing seemed amiss. There didn't appear to be anything moving on the ground below. The new-sprouting leaves above twirled in the moonlight. On the water, tiny ripples and eddies moved like moonlit string. The banks were too far to see in this light; the farther north they'd gone, the broader and slower the river became, leaving Cazia to wonder if she would even be able to tell when the river became the lake.

It was beautiful.

She rested her head in the notch of the trunk behind her, letting her eyelids grow heavy. A wake marked the spot where a stone came too near the water's surface. She watched it for a moment, wondering at its size. Was it moving?

She saw an unexpected blur of movement and a loud splash. Darkness moved against deeper darkness, and moonlight reflected off the splashing water. Something had swooped down into the river and now flapped skyward again. She jolted out of her comfortable spot for a better look.

One of the giant eagles had just snatched something from the shallows at the edge of the island. Something big.

Cazia had been too startled to cry out when it happened but she was tempted to do it now, just on general principle. The creature that had been carried away had not struggled. The bird's sudden impact must have stunned or killed it outright. It was all too easy to imagine how an attack like that must feel. How swiftly she would go from a perfectly normal person traveling through the wilderness to a broken sack of dead flesh.

She glanced at the next tree and saw Ivy's face lit by moonlight. She stared with wide, frightened eyes.

They both looked down at the water again. More wakes betrayed someone or something swimming away from the island. Neither girl slept any more that night.

The sun came up shortly after, and Cazia was the first to climb down from her tree. Ivy strung her bow and nocked an arrow while her friend walked the length of the island, spear in hand. It only took a hundred paces or so to reach the far side—too quickly for Cazia to work the kinks out of her back and thighs. She wished she could ask the Poalos to check the tall grasses for her, but the only weapons the brother and sister had were their rafting poles, little hatchets, and the crude fishing spear they'd fashioned that first night. Cazia had no intention of surrendering her spear to them.

But there were no creatures to be found. Her bow ready, Ivy climbed down. The Poalos followed. The servants looked worried and confused, which was only made worse by the little princess's mimed explanation. The servants clearly wanted to leave immediately, but Ivy wouldn't allow it.

"One spot on this river is just as dangerous as any other," she insisted, although only Cazia showed that she understood. "And I am hungry."

The snares the Poalos had set the night before had fish in them—nasty-looking things with triangular teeth and long, fleshy "whiskers"—and while Kinz started the fire, Alga gutted and scaled breakfast.

Of course, Cazia could have lit the fire with a spell, but she wasn't ready to betray herself. It was true that, except for that one fleeting expression, the servants had done nothing to earn her distrust—in fact, it had been so long that she'd begun to doubt her memory of it—but life in the palace had taught her to be cautious.

And Alga . . . He had tried to be charming with her that first day, smiling at her and bringing her food, but Cazia had refused to look him in the eye. He'd taken the hint and left her alone since. Fire take him and the dreams she had about him.

She paced the island once more, her spear making her feel foolish, but this time, she checked for muddy prints along the shoreline. She found one: a long, deep, three-toed print. It was shaped vaguely like a maple leaf, if one of the fronds had been pulled back for a thumb, and there was a sharp claw at the end of each toe.

Worst of all, she found it on the near side of their raft, well back from the water's edge. She bent low to search for more and was surprised to discover an odd pile of stones.

It hadn't formed naturally, and it certainly hadn't been there the previous afternoon when they made camp. She knelt beside it. There were four small flat, smooth river stones of nearly equal size set beside each other with a fifth on top. To the right was a pair of stones with a third one leaning against the spot where they touched. Beside that was a pair of upright river stones leaned against each other, and there was the first, probably, a flat disk that had been pressed into the mud so it stood on edge.

On the other side of the five-stone pile was a stack of seven stones, and beyond that—

Kinz's boot swept through the piles of stones, scattering them. "Nyoo!" she said. She'd learned the word *no* in Peradaini, but she couldn't pronounce it correctly. "Nyoo nyoo!" She extended her arms and, elbows locked, opened and closed her clawed hands as though they were huge jaws filled with teeth.

Cazia stood and backed away, her spear point toward the water. Did alligaunts make those stone piles? They returned toward the center of the island, where Alga held the skewered fish over the fire.

He did not look at her, for which Cazia was both disappointed and grateful. Fire and Fury, he was annoying. Cazia slipped her hand into her pocket to take hold of her translation stone. She expected the servants to talk to each other, and she was right.

"Scowler found something beside the raft." *Scowler* was the name they had given her; she took a perverse pride in it. "A warning from the lakeboys."

"Lakeboys?" Alga almost dropped the skewer into the fire. "Already?"

"Unmistakable." She took a skewer from him and began to eat it. Gross. It was almost raw. "It used to be rare to see lakeboys so far from Low Lake, but not anymore. They wander the length and breadth of the waterways now."

"Do you think the girls understand?"

Kinz glanced at Cazia and Ivy briefly. "They do. But Scowler is determined and the Princess will follow her anywhere, even to death. Of course, if you had managed to sweet-talk her . . . "

"You should sweet-talk her," Alga snapped. "She hates me and I haven't even kissed her yet."

Cazia's hand sprang open as though it had a mind of its own, and she could no longer understand what they were saying. Not that it mattered. Each time she had tried it, she'd heard nothing worse than the usual resentment she always heard from servants who thought no one was listening.

Of course, translation stones were *supposed* to turn you into a gibbering fool if you used them too long, but so far she'd seen no sign of that. It was probably another of Doctor Twofin's lies. Her instructor had been the one person outside Lar's circle she'd actually trusted, but now . . . She didn't like to think about it.

The fish may have been the ugliest thing she'd ever seen but it tasted delicious. Ivy had some of her cracker bread with it, and Cazia ate a small bundle of meatbread. Kinz boiled a pot full of river water, and they all shared. It wasn't safe to drink straight from the river, of course, but Cazia would have liked to make some kind of fish head broth from it, at least. Unfortunately, Ivy and the Poalos had been horrified by the idea.

There were no lurking alligaunts beside the raft as they pushed off from the island. Ivy kept her bow strung and an arrow nocked. Cazia sat with her spear across her knees, watching for suspicious wakes. She would have preferred her quiver of darts, but she wasn't ready to reveal them. Not yet.

While the girls watched the water, the Poalos watched the skies. Occasionally, they would see one of the huge eagles flying to the northeast—or returning from it—but that was becoming rare during the day. They seemed to do most of their hunting at night and only appeared in large numbers around sunset. As long as the Poalos made camp early and hid their fire, the four of them would be safe in the trees. Hopefully.

Three days later, Cazia learned how to tell where the river ended and the lake began: the river narrowed between two hills and flowed over a little waterfall no taller than Ivy. The Poalos poled the raft toward the eastern shore and all four of them carried their supplies and the raft down the muddy hill. The shore was thick with three-toed prints but Kinz didn't seem particularly worried about them and Ivy thought they were several days old.

The waterfall proved to be made of flat river stones laid like unmortared bricks. It was crude compared to the stone walls of Peradain, but no one could mistake it for a natural formation. Ivy stared at it and stuck out her lower lip thoughtfully. "I wonder which clan built this." There was no one to answer.

The lake was surprisingly deep. The Poalos couldn't pole along the shore as they normally did, because in most places, the drop was too steep. Instead, they were forced to paddle with the unbladed poles, a slow and exhausting process. Cazia watched a family of yellow-striped boqs emerge from the tall grass to drink at the water's edge. She was about to suggest they abandon the raft and walk the rest of the way when a grass lion pounced on the youngest of the boqs, scattering the rest.

As they moved northward, the cliffs of the Northern Barrier loomed above them, higher with each day that went by. Hent had been right; there was no pass to take them into the Qorr Valley. For as far as Cazia could see in either direction—and her vision was excellent—the mountainside was a slick, shining wall.

It was late afternoon when they reached the far shore. The Poalos drove the raft toward a slope of loose scree and, after they'd transferred the packs, dragged it onto the rocks.

There were trees to the east, but here there were only rockfalls from above and marshy grasslands. They had no trees to sleep in tonight, and the cry of that little boq as the lion dragged it away was foremost in Cazia's mind. Behind them, the cliffs seemed to block off half of Kal-Maddum.

Fire and Fury, but it was a strange thing. The rock of the cliff looked like it had been melted until it was as smooth as a grape. There was nothing to grab hold of—not the slightest fingerhold—anywhere she could see. Cazia stepped back and looked up the cliffside. The textureless face stretched so high, she couldn't see where it ended.

Kinz approached the rock wall and hammered at it with the edge of a sharp rock she'd picked up from the scree at the water's edge. There was no damage to the wall, but the stone in her hand had faint white fracture lines at the tip.

Cazia's stomach felt heavy. Whatever she had expected, it wasn't this.

Ivy stood with her bow at the ready, arrow nocked. Alga stood close beside his sister, hatchet in hand. All were watching her.

"It's time," Cazia said. "Let's pile our supplies beside me."

Cazia set her own pack on the loose stones at the base of the cliff, then Ivy put hers beside it. When Kinz tried to set the Poalo pack beside them, Cazia waved her back.

"Ivy," she said. "I suspect that our so-called servants are about to turn against us. If they want to run away, that's fine. They can take their stuff and go. But if they attack us or try to take our packs, you'll have to put an arrow into one."

The little princess didn't like that. "They are older, faster, and stronger than we are. Sensible tactics suggest that if we expect an attack, we should strike first."

Out of the corner of her eye, Cazia saw the Poalos tense. After days of pretending, they finally gave themselves away: they understood Peradaini.

"No," Cazia said. "I don't want to fight them. I just don't want them to panic and run away with our supplies. If they want to go, let them." Cazia imagined Alga's shocked expression when the arrow went in, and her stomach did a flip-flop. "Let's try deterrence first."

"I would prefer that. I have never shot a person before, and I would not like one of these two to be . . . Never mind. I will not hesitate."

The princess's pale little face was determined. Cazia didn't doubt for a minute that she would do what was necessary. "Little sister, I'm more impressed with you every day. When I was your age, I never did anything I was supposed to."

"I have spent my whole life in the instruction of my family, especially Uncle Nezzeriskos. He taught me that being an Ergoll princess within the Indregai Alliance comes with many privileges, but many responsibilities, too. I do not want to shame his memory."

"I understand," Cazia said. "Remind me to give you a hug later." She tossed her spear to the ground and unlaced her pack. No one reacted when she took out her quiver of darts. It felt good to strap them to her hip, like saying her name aloud. She also noted, with a bit of worry, that she had to tighten the belt an extra notch to make it fit.

The Poalos only looked confused. Fine. They didn't recognize the darts. There would be no mistaking what came next.

She turned to the cliff face behind her. No ladder of stone blocks would get them over this wall; she would never be able to build something stable enough to reach the top. No matter. She planned to make a stair, not a ladder.

The first symbol appeared in her thoughts and her hands began the appropriate counter movements. Magic flowed through her, and moments later, a section of the strange featureless stone collapsed into rubble.

Both of the Poalos howled in shock and terror. Cazia couldn't believe it—they actually howled like dogs. Kinz backed away three steps, dropping to her knees. Alga joined her, and they began jabbering at each other. Cazia touched the jewel in her pocket.

" . . . for this?" Kinz said. "We travel all this way with one of the Cursed?"

Her brother leaned close to her. "By Inzu, we must destroy her."

"No!" Kinz grabbed his sleeve without looking away from Cazia. "We will not. Not ever. I don't care if she is Cursed; we will not murder the young girl in the wilderness. Worse, it would have to be two young girls, because the Princess would be the witness. Could you do it?"

Alga didn't answer immediately. "No," he said finally. "I do not like these devils very much, but I do not want to kill them. But what if they are both Cursed?"

Kinz and Cazia stared at each other. There was something in the Poalo girl's expression that Cazia liked.

Alga leaned close to his sister again. "We must take our things and go south. Mahz should know the truth."

Kinz shook her head. "Mahz said—"

"Mahz wanted us to discover where they were really going! She didn't believe they were *serious* and she never expected us to enter the Qorr Valley."

Kinz was still watching Cazia closely. "Mahz also asked us to watch over them."

"But—"

"You should go, Alga. Tell Mahz where we have gone. She will arrange the marriage you want. I will fulfill Mahz's other command: I will watch over them as best I can. Remind her, when you see her, that I have paid part of her debt. Perhaps she will be make to give you the extra head when you remake our people."

"Kinz, you must have gone wind-mad. You can not mean to scale these mountains, let alone enter Qorr, with one of the Cursed!"

In the slanting light, Kinz's eyes seemed to sparkle. "I do. In fact, I hope to convince her to teach me one or two of those curses."

"Actually," Cazia interrupted in Peradaini, "spells are really difficult to learn."

The Poalos gasped and stared at her, wide-eyed.

"Besides, you have to be born with the knack for it," Cazia lied. "And even then, some people can't manage."

Kinz stood tall and stepped forward. "How can you tell if I have this *knack?*"

Her Peradaini was heavily accented but clear. Cazia suppressed an urge to say *Nyoo! Nyoo!* at her. "Your Peradaini is not too bad."

"Thank you," Kinz said frankly. "We must learn it if we are to trade in the passes. Also, your soldiers collect smaller tribute if we object in your language. And yes, this means we deceived you, just as you deceived us. You never told us you could speak Henjzhu."

"I can't—Fire and Fury, I'm not even sure I can say Henchoo . . . Henzu, er, I don't mean to be disrespectful—but my magic can translate your words. Not all of—"

Alga stepped close to his sister. "Kinz, we must make to go." His Peradaini was not bad, either.

"Hey!" Cazia's voice echoed off the wall behind her. "Don't interrupt me!" Somehow, it was easy to be angry at him. "And don't call me *Cursed.* Herders have called me one rude name after another and I don't like it."

"To be honest," Ivy put in, "my people refer to scholars as 'Hosts' or 'The Possessed,' but I think that is silly superstition."

"So," Cazia said, "Mahz didn't believe me when I said I was going to the Qorr Valley?"

Kinz shook her head. "No one did."

"I did," Ivy said.

"And Hent did," Cazia added. "It doesn't matter. What did she promise you? Okshim?"

"Our name," Alga said. "She was going to give us enough okshim to start the Poalo clan again and let us leave with anyone who wanted to join us."

Cazia sighed. Her anger toward dwindled into a sour regret. So many people had died; she couldn't blame him for doing what he had to do to start over. Not really.

"Answer me this," Kinz said. "Why are you *really* making to go into the Qorr Valley?"

"For exactly the reason she said," Ivy answered. "She thinks we are being attacked. I have thought about it all during our trip, and I have convinced myself she is right."

"So, you two girls will make to go alone into the most dangerous part of the world—more dangerous, I'm told, than the shores of Espileth."

"Yes," Ivy said.

"I will go with you," Kinz said immediately. She turned to Alga and cut him off before he could argue. "Inzu will watch over me, or she won't. I do not want to hear you complain any more. Take the raft and go to Mahz. You are strong enough to catch up to her before she reaches Piskatook. Make to charm those two skinny girls you have your eye on. Become the Poalo; I do not care. I do not want to see you for the while."

"Kinzchu, how can you make to say these things to me?"

"Little brother, you have been spoiled your whole life, until the Ozzhuacks took you in as the laborer. Since then, you have made to do nothing but whine, plot revenge, and wink at younger girls. I love you, Algachu, but I do not want to be around you." She picked up their pack and offered it to him. "Take the raft. Make to the south. I will find you again, if I can."

Alga's face flushed red but he didn't respond. He touched the hatchet in his belt and the pouch that held the twine for his snare, then stepped back without taking the pack. He glanced at Ivy and Cazia. Clearly, there was something he wanted to say, but his sister's speech had undone him.

He sighed and hurried to the shoreline. He gave one last venomous look at Cazia, then a longer one to his sister. After that, he dragged the raft into the water and poled away.

"Will he be all right?" Ivy's hands, still clutching her little bow and arrow, were tucked close under her chin. "All alone?"

Cazia picked up her spear. "I don't really need this. If—"

Kinz waved their concerns away. "I am the one who needs the spear. Poalos spend their entire lives in the Sweeps. It does not frighten us the way it does you southlanders."

Ivy didn't seem mollified. "My uncle said that no one should ever travel alone in the Sweeps. Lions and alligaunts—"

"Princess, if you are going to make worry, save it for yourself. Although I do not know what *uligunts* are."

"It won't matter," Cazia said. She turned back to the cliff. "Are we crazy for doing all of this?"

"Yes," Kinz said, "although I am not sure how we are going to cross the mountains. Will you simply tunnel through?"

"Not without knowing what's on the other side," Cazia said. "I would feel pretty stupid if I killed us all by tunneling into the bottom of a lake. Besides, it's hard to keep good air in a tunnel like that. Miners do it but I don't know how. So I figured we'd carve a stair."

Kinz gave Cazia the same look that Tyr Gerrit had given to Ivy when he saw her through the mirror. She wanted magic of her own. Of course she did.

The plain truth was that Cazia could be executed for being an unguarded scholar among outsiders, even if she had never revealed herself to them. It went against everything Doctor Twofin had taught her. But then, Doctor Twofin had lied to her every day. He'd told her magic was dangerous, that she shouldn't cast spells over and over because it would hollow her out. She'd tested the limits he'd set for her and discovered that they were a sham.

"Like this," Cazia said. She cast the Eleventh Gift again, collapsing another part of the cliff. The broken stones rolled out, falling onto the scree around her feet. It made an indentation in the cliff large enough for the three of them to curl up together.

Cazia climbed into it, kicking out more rock, then cast the spell again, this time breaking stone high on the eastern part of the tiny cave. It collapsed and fell around Cazia's legs.

That hurt a bit. She would have preferred it if the stones were perfectly round but they weren't. The rocks had jagged edges that scraped the parts of her legs her hiking skirt didn't cover.

No matter. She cast the spell again, then again, taking care that part of her tunnel was open to the Sweeps wind. As the stones rolled down onto her, she swept some of them over the edge of the cliff to the grasslands below.

She heard Ivy's voice below. "Help me up! Help me up!" Cazia glanced back and saw the princess crawling toward her. Kinz came up close behind. The little princess's expression was bright and excited. "Do that again!"

Cazia laughed and did it again. The magic came to her just a bit more easily each time. It felt good just the way it felt good to create the stack of blocks outside the walls of Samsit.

Kinz tied their packs together and dragged them behind, her other hand holding the iron spear. Ivy unstrung her bow and tied a cloth over her quiver. Cazia glanced at the girl. "Princess, is everyone 'highborn or necessary'?"

Ivy's cheeks turned red. "Do not tease me! No one liked that woman and you know it. Besides, I was just trying to take control—do not worry! I learned my lesson."

Cazia laughed and the princess laughed with her. There was nothing funny about it, but they were together and Cazia's plan was working. They were really doing it.

When the ramp had reached the height of forty feet, Cazia told the other two to climb up close to her. Then she cast the Sixth Gift behind them, cutting off the tunnel with a large stone granite block.

"No retreat, eh?" Kinz said.

"No unwelcome visitors," Cazia answered. She pointed out to the grasslands where a pride of grass lions sat watching them.

"How long can you keep this up?" Ivy asked.

Answering that question was a capital offense. Cazia felt a sudden flush of shame and grief. How could she laugh with Ivy when so much had happened? King Lar Italga would have granted clemency for the crime she was committing, and she suddenly missed him—and Col and Pagesh—acutely.

Night was falling. They would have to stop to eat and sleep soon, and Cazia would be the one carving a safe space for them.

How long could she keep this up? Cazia knew what she'd been taught, but she didn't know the truth. "As long as I have to," she answered.

Chapter Twenty-one

THE FIRST TIME A GIANT EAGLE FLEW BY THEM, THE PRINCESS AND THE herder drew their little knives—useless against such huge creatures, obviously, but all the monster did was flap alongside the cliff wall to get a good look at them, then it flapped into the darkness, screeching.

After that, Cazia angled her tunnel deeper into the mountain. Instead of leaving one whole side open to clean, fresh air, she left only a narrow slot that barely allowed starlight in. Always, she dug upward and toward the east.

Eventually, Ivy asked to stop, so they did. Cazia broke a hole high in the tunnel for ventilation, then carved out a hollow, flat space large enough for them to sit up or lie down in. She turned a pair of roundish rocks into lightstones—a Fourteenth Festival spell that had been her first lesson in infusing magic into a solid object—and that was the end of the day. The most difficult part was pushing all the loose rock down the tunnel or out the hole in the side.

And she felt fine. Maybe a little tired and jittery, but she certainly hadn't gone hollow like Doctor Whitestalk. What had Doctor Twofin been doing with all those years of warnings? She couldn't imagine.

She woke in the middle of the night from terrible nightmares about falling endlessly through a narrow shaft, slowly starving to death, slowly dwindling to nothing. Kinz and Ivy slept soundly beside her; the wind swirled dust inside their chamber. Cazia sat in the dim light and wiped sweat from her face.

When she'd created the stone ladder into Samsit, she had cast the Sixth Gift . . . eighty times? Maybe more, maybe less. When she and Ivy had finally made camp in the pass the next morning, her dreams had been awful.

These were worse. She hadn't thought to count the number of times she'd cast the Eleventh Gift, but it might have been a hundred and fifty times. Probably not more than that. Sweat made her skin prickle, and her stomach felt leaden.

After a short while, she laughed at herself. Was this the terrible consequence that had frightened Doctor Twofin? A scary dream? She lay back down, still feeling a bit odd, and shut her eyes until she fell back to sleep.

In the morning, they started upward again. Cazia's troubled sleep left her stomach feeling like a bundle of wet rags, but she soon forgot that. The spell came more easily each time she cast it, and she began to lose herself in the gestures and mental images. The magic seemed to be flowing through her, spell after spell, and as her trance-like state deepened, she began to understand it better. Little variations in her hand movements had always created minor variations in the effects of the Gifts, but as she kept going through the morning, those effects became clearer to her, allowing her better control over the size and shape of their tunnel.

Were these the supposed special insights that hollowed scholars had? It couldn't be so. For one thing, the changes she could make to the spells were so trivial, they barely qualified as insights. For another, she certainly hadn't gone hollow.

However, her stomach continued to feel like lead, and along with her increased mastery, loneliness began to build within her. A longing for her lost home and lost friends tugged at her thoughts and made her insides flutter. *Colchua, I am so sorry.*

The Gifts eased that pain, strangely enough. The focus and energy required to make each spell work—to *go into it* in the very real way that was helping her learn control—allowed her respite from the sorrow growing in her heart. In the time between spells, when she had to clear stones away and crawl on her hands and knees up the ramp, her emotions seemed to rush at her, ever so slightly stronger each time.

It was late in the day when the others asked her to pause for a meal. Cazia did so, reluctantly. She pushed a handful of stones through the gap in the wall, letting them fall all the way down the cliff. They were high up, but she couldn't be sure how much farther they had to go.

Kinz passed a wrapped package to Ivy, who passed it to Cazia. "We will have to make to be careful with our provisions. I do not . . . Cazia, what is wrong?"

The little princess looked at Cazia's face in horror. Cazia touched her eyes, nose, and mouth. There was no disfigurement there, no weeping sores or blood, only dirt and sweat.

"Kinz!" Ivy called behind her, then crawled forward to touch Cazia's collar.

The servant squeezed beside Ivy in the tunnel. "Inzu's Grace! Cazia, what have you done to yourself?"

"Am I bleeding?" Cazia was surprised to hear her own voice, which sounded as though she'd been crying for hours. But her grief and misery had barely begun to swell up inside her. She couldn't understand why they were staring at her with such alarmed expressions. The urge to cast another spell to gentle her emotions was powerful, but she resisted.

Finally, it became too much for her. She began to sob. "My brother," she said, the words coming out in a squeak. "I loved my brother so much, and I *killed him.*"

Ivy's embrace was physically painful, but Cazia didn't shake her off. She just sobbed, and wept, and her raw grief washed over her in terrible waves.

But at the same time, she felt removed from herself, analyzing things the way she had when Mahz flashed her pointed teeth. Cazia had always been one to analyze things. She couldn't lose herself in anything, it seemed. Not even this.

Scholars should never show tears.

The tears stopped, then the embrace stopped. Cazia put on a brave expression, her skin still raw and tingling where Ivy had squeezed her. They ate, emptied their canteens, and let Cazia fill them again. When she cast the Fifth Gift to refill the canteens for later, her misery did not ease much at all, not like it had when she cast the Eleventh Gift.

She returned to her digging, still unclear why Ivy and Kinz had been so upset when they saw her face. It didn't seem important.

She continued casting the Eleventh Gift through the rest of the day, stopping only when the light faded through the thin break into the outside world. Cazia created another chamber for them to sleep in, then endured their worried looks while they ate.

Great Way, but she felt miserable, and only the Gifts could ease her pain. Exhausted, she fell asleep, and her nightmares were just as awful as the previous night's.

She woke in a terror several times. At dawn, she was parched and exhausted. Fine. A few bad dreams could make her life unpleasant after all. She drained both canteens and tried to force herself to sleep again but couldn't.

When daylight came, they ate their morning meal in uncomfortable silence. The sound of Ivy and Kinz's chewing and breathing irritated Cazia to the point that she wanted to scream.

"Cazia," the princess said, speaking as though she was addressing an irrational person, "we must turn back."

"Go right ahead." She sounded stronger than she felt.

"No, *you* must turn back! You can not do to yourself again what you did yesterday."

Cazia sighed. "No, it's all right." *It's not all right.* "I was just careless. I cast the same spell too many times in a row, and that made my emotions a little difficult to control. Today, I'll vary things a little and I'll be fine."

Both girls looked at her skeptically, but Kinz had a chillier, more analytical edge. "Have you never done something like this before?"

"I'm still in training," Cazia admitted. "I'm quite capable, but I don't know every spell yet." Adding the word *yet* seemed like fruitless hope, but she said it anyway. There was probably no one left in the world who would teach her magic.

Ivy shook her head. "We are still worried about you."

They had no right to worry about her. "What did you see last night? Why were you so upset when you saw me?"

Kinz answered as though it was a subject she had discussed with Ivy in depth while Cazia slept. "You are the girl who betrays your every thought by your expression. Do you recognize the truth of this? Your face makes lively, and everyone can know your mind in every grimace or roll of your eyes—even when you make to watch us while pretending you do not."

Cazia didn't know how to respond, so she drained the canteen instead.

"But," Kinz continued, "last night your face was utterly slack and devoid of life. You looked like the moving corpse."

Like Doctor Whitestalk.

"My cousin had a man who was kicked in the head during a fight," Ivy said. "The skull broke and he very nearly died, but after he recovered, he never really returned. The memory, the sense of humor, everything that made him who he was had all been destroyed. Cazia, last night your expression looked just like that. I thought your magic had destroyed your brain."

"Well, it didn't."

"But you looked terrible," Kinz insisted. "How much farther do you make to take us? All the way over the mountains? I like you and do not think you are Cursed. Yet. But if you do not stop, you may make yourself so!"

Cazia looked down at her hands. They were trembling slightly. What did

Kinz know? "I expected this to be hard," Cazia lied. Could they really tell what she was thinking? She looked down at her lap and kept her face still. "But I forgot that I'm supposed to vary the spells. I was just too eager. I'll go slower today. There's nothing to worry about."

"I will worry anyway," the princess said.

"We have heard you," Kinz said as though conceding the point, "but do not forget that you have made to block the tunnel behind us."

Cazia took a deep breath so she would not laugh. She'd forgotten about that.

"This is why you have not conquered us all, yes?" Kinz asked. "Your magic is powerful, but the toll it would take if you used it all the time would destroy you. This is why you can not make every crop the feast, or collapse the mountain, or build the wall to block the Sweeps." She fell silent for a moment. "We have seen your Cursed Ones at work."

Cazia wasn't sure she would like where this conversation was going. "Have you?"

"We spy on you," Ivy said blandly. "You spy on us. It is how things are."

Kinz continued. "We see your researches. We see the power of your spells, but it has been much debated among the clans and Indregai emissaries why you have not used them more, and why your people make weaker versions of the spells in inanimate objects. My own father was convinced that you were bound by the will of Inzu."

"Please," Cazia blurted out. "Until I met you, I never even heard of Inzu."

Kinz's lips pressed close together for a moment, then she said, "Then I wish for you the blessing of the one true god."

"Oh, good," Ivy interrupted. "A religious discussion. These always turn out so well in my father's councils."

Kinz looked at a spot on the ceiling. "I was just making the innocent observation."

"Well, then," Cazia said. "Here's another: I have a death sentence on me because I am here with both of you." Should this have frightened her? It didn't. "Do you understand? Scholars never travel without bodyguards, and those guards are trained to slay scholars before they fall into foreign hands. They protect imperial secrets above all else, and scholars as long as it seems feasible. What you have already learned—which is not nearly enough to cast a spell of your own—would have me dragged to the Scholars' Tower, whipped, and then hung. Or stoned to death. I'm told they sometimes kill women by stoning."

Ivy was very still and her eyes were very wide. "We know about this."

"I'm throwing my whole life away to do this," Cazia said, and as the words came out of her mouth, they gave power to the half-formed thoughts that had haunted her for days. Even if she wanted to turn back, even if there was someplace to turn back to, she couldn't.

Colchua had already died, and Pagesh, too. If there was something she could do to fight the Enemy that had claimed them, she would risk everything. How could she do anything less?

How could she do less than hollow herself out?

"Nonsense," Ivy said. "I am engaged to the Peradaini king! He *will* be restored; I believe this. And even if he were not a fair man—and you know better than I do that he is—as the queen, I would forbid any punishment against you."

Cazia spoke gently. "Little sister, even if none of this had happened and your wedding had gone as planned, I don't think you would have had the power to save my life. You would have been another hostage."

For once, Ivy did not know what to say. Kinz sighed, irritated. "This is how she sees the world. We are all made hostages to be taken."

"No," Ivy said. "She is the hostage. She has been one the entire life." Ivy leaned forward and touched Cazia's hand. It took all of Cazia's willpower to avoid snatching it away. "Big sister," the princess said, "I will follow you anywhere."

It took real force of will, but Cazia smiled at her. "Let's get ready."

Cazia turned toward the wall. The rock-breaking spell was ready in her mind, almost as if it had been waiting for her. She cast.

A large section of the wall crumbled, falling toward her in a mini-avalanche. All three of them began to cough from the dust, and Cazia realized she'd put too much power into the spell. As annoying as it was to crawl over the larger stones in her long hiking skirts, dust might choke them to death.

She began the spell again, vaguely aware that it might be polite to apologize. This time she widened the opening into the outside world. The light and fresh air was welcome and there were no eagles visible in the dawn light. She stuck her head through the gap but couldn't see how much farther she had to go. The daylight felt raw against her face, but she knew the spell would ease her discomfort.

She cast ten more times before switching to the water spell. Kinz gave her the canteen to fill, then she drank from it. She also took more time between spells, slowly sweeping the tumbling rocks around and behind her, shoving them against one side of the tunnel. Ten more spells and she created another lightstone. Ten more and she fired a broken rock out over the Sweeps like a dart.

It helped. Raw grief still surged through her between spells, but the deadening effects of casting them became fainter.

So she kept going, trying to keep careful watch over her mental state the way a shepherd watched her flock. Minute by minute, spell by spell, she couldn't detect any change in herself, but as the long day wore on, she had to admit that each spell left her feeling more dead inside. Worse, the ever-growing sense of grief and longing became so strong, it nearly overwhelmed her between spells. Casting slowly became a form of torture.

When the fading daylight shone horizontally through the gap in the wall, she realized that she was crying again. Ivy called her name and squeezed through the narrow tunnel to crawl beside her. She rubbed Cazia's cheeks with her gritty hands as though trying to revive them, then embraced her tightly.

Cazia desperately needed the girl's touch and found it unbearable at the same time. It was confining, comforting, it made her skin crawl, it made her want to scream. Worse, there was a tiny dead part of her that pondered how easy it would have been to kill them both. She could have just rolled over without breaking the embrace, carrying both of them through the narrow gap in the wall.

She wouldn't do it. Of course she wouldn't. But the thought had invaded her mind like an expeditionary force, and a tiny part of her examined the choice between killing them both or not with the same urgency that she might decide which boot to pull on first.

"Let me make a safe place to stop." Cazia cast her spell a few more times, creating another hollowed-out flat enclosure large enough for them to sit upright and stretch out. At the far end, she made sure to break through the wall slightly . . . for ventilation.

Ivy set five lightstones around the chamber. Kinz pushed stones down the slope. Cazia sat quietly against the hard, sloping wall, watching them and trying to pretend she was invisible.

When the space had been cleared and the packs opened, Kinz asked Cazia about her brother. So Cazia told them about Colchua: how he'd loved to climb—until Lar's brother had died in a fall, and he'd never climbed again—how he'd joked with them all, how competitive he was in the gym and cooperative in his lessons. How he sang. People looked up to him, but he'd always deferred to Lar. Not just because Lar was an Italga and a prince of the empire, but because Col loved him and believed in him.

Then she told them the story of the Festival in Peradain. She told them how The Blessing had appeared, suddenly overwhelming everyone. How she and her friends had fled. How Lar had insisted on rescuing his betrothed, and Cazia had supported him for fear that Vilavivianna's death would lead to war with the Alliance.

When she got to the part where Col was bitten on the rooftop, Ivy began to cry.

Cazia herself did not. She was talking about the most painful moments of her life, but they had no effect on the longing, loneliness, and sorrow swelling within her. It was almost as though those emotions belonged to someone else and had never been about her own pain at all.

She told them about the grunt in the courtyard but left out the part where the last king of Peradain had been bitten, too. It almost seemed silly to keep that secret here, especially since Ivy already knew it, but she did.

Then she told them about killing the grunt without realizing who he was. And how proud she'd felt. Thankfully, they didn't insult her intelligence by insisting she couldn't have known and it wasn't her fault. Of course she didn't know, and of course that didn't make things better.

"And now the raptors are here, those gigantic eagles." Cazia tried to sound as if nothing mattered more than this. "We have to find out if they're connected. There's no one else."

They did not speak for a little while. Finally, Kinz asked permission to sing a song, then sang it. Cazia touched her translation stone and listened to enough to realize she was singing about the wind. She passed the stone to Ivy, then lay back and let the unintelligible words wash over her.

It wasn't a terrible song but it was very simple. A child's song. Ivy went next and her song was not much better. Still, it suited her because it was a little girl's song.

After the two of them had taken turns a few times, Cazia felt a sudden urge to sing "River Overrunning," Old Stoneface's song. She had never sung it in front of him, of course, but she'd learned it years before.

So she sang it, her voice a little raw and uncertain, but her grief gave her power, and the dead feeling the spells had created gave her the detachment to control the melody. Because it was about watching helplessly while the people you loved were killed, she had to pause partway through to gather herself. When she finished, she saw Kinz and Ivy staring at her with wide, astonished eyes.

Ivy had started crying again. In her astonishment, Kinz said, "How could the people capable of such brutality also create such beautiful art?"

Our spear points command your bodies. Our songs command your hearts. But Cazia couldn't bring herself to say that. She couldn't even make herself say *Fire take you*, not after that song. Instead, she lay back and closed her eyes. It was a long time before she fell asleep, and her dreams were full of flames, and gods, and falls from terrible heights.

She woke in darkness. The other girls snored gently nearby and she could hear the wind whistling through the ventilation hole she'd made, but the magic in the lightstones had faded. When Lar had been her age, he could make lightstones that lasted a moon's cycle, but she'd never gotten the hang of it.

The urge to do more magic was powerful. She felt more tired than ever and utterly detached from her own life. Worse, she knew she would break down crying again if she just sat there doing nothing. At least if she started digging again, the magic would dull the pain.

Which would make her another kind of hostage . . . not that she had a choice.

She peered through the ventilation hole at the dark eastern sky. There was no way to tell when dawn would come. Cazia crossed her arms and scowled down at the starlit lands below. The waving grasses made it look like a stormy ocean dotted with tiny forests.

And they were high, but she still could not tell how much farther there was to go. She was hungry, too, but did nothing about it. She was in control of herself, and it felt good.

She stretched out on the floor again and tried to sleep; it was no use. She remembered the moment Pagesh had shoved Jagia into her arms, and the sight of her brother dangling from the rope at the bottom of the cart, and the way Queen Amlian had died. It should have made her break down weeping, but it didn't.

She ate, then decided to be satisfied with her current level of self-denial. She started casting her spell again.

Ivy and Kinz woke while she was pushing the rubble through the gap in the wall. They didn't complain, just sighed, ate a little bit themselves, and began to pack up their things.

Cazia went slowly, trying to find a balance between repeated castings of a single spell, rest time between spells, and variety. Soon, she switched to casting a water spell as every eighth spell, then every seventh, then she created a lightstone, a burst of fire and a fresh spray of water every fifth.

Still, as she swept the stones through the gap in the cliff, she could not hold back tears of longing.

They were not her tears, she finally understood. They were the tears of this new thing—this force—that filled her now. The magic she had been casting was living inside her head, making everything she touched feel like a slap, every sound seem like a shout. But because it didn't care, she didn't care, either. Her own suffering meant nothing. All that mattered was that she continue.

As she cast the Eleventh Gift over and over, she felt herself becoming the impossibly high precipice she'd fallen from in her dreams.

Then, suddenly, she cast her spell again and, after the rocks had fallen around her, found herself staring up at the sky.

"Ah!" She scrambled out of the hole. The thin, chilly wind was rough against her skin. The stars were still bright in the western sky, but the eastern horizon glowed orange and red. She stepped away from the hole to give Ivy room to come through, and that brought her close to the edge of the cliff.

She didn't feel any fear at all as she looked down from those awful heights. A long fall seemed perfect for . . . for something.

"You did it!" Ivy shouted. "Cazia, you are amazing. You have done what no one in fifty generations has been able to do."

"Don't touch me." The girl looked stricken and Cazia knew she had been too blunt. "I'm not ready yet."

The lie seemed to mollify her. Cazia didn't think she would ever want to be touched again, but there was no reason to say so.

She moved away from the cliff and surveyed the rocks around her. She hadn't reached the very top of the Barrier, just that first smooth cliff face. They were standing on a sloping, slate-gray rock about fifty paces wide and more than ten times that across. Cazia tried to determine if she had come close to the low point in the range that she'd been aiming for, but it was impossible to tell.

"We can not make camp here," Kinz dragged the packs out of the tunnel. "We are too exposed."

Cazia didn't see any birds in the sky or perched on the rocks around them. Ivy said, "As far as I can see, they only attack in the early part of the night. It is nearly daylight now."

Kinz shoved one of the packs at her. "If they make to nest up here, they may make a special exception for us."

Ivy nodded at the wisdom in that. Pack slung over one shoulder, she started toward the second cliff face. "This looks more like a natural formation of rocks. I think we should climb it."

Kinz was so surprised she dropped her pack. "Climb? That?"

Cazia glanced up at the rock face. It was at least a hundred feet high, and while it wasn't the same strangely smooth cliff face as below, she couldn't see how a person could safely climb it.

"Of course," Ivy insisted. "I have been climbing rocks like this since I was small."

"You are still small," Kinz answered. "And I have never climbed anything taller than the tree."

"Neither have I," Cazia said, her voice flat. "We're going to keep tunneling."

"But you can not!"

"She must," Kinz said firmly. "It is either that or we make retreat. I will not climb that rock with the loaded pack. If the fall did not kill us, the birds would."

"What birds?" Ivy demanded, her voice getting shrill. She stamped her foot. "I do not see any birds!"

Cazia couldn't bear to be near their argument. She turned away toward the open spaces of the Sweeps and saw that the rock face sloped so much, she couldn't see her tunnel. When she started back toward it, she found it was farther to her left than she'd thought.

It occurred to her that she should mark the location better so they could find it in a hurry—who knew what dangers they might have to run away from up here?

Before that thought had finished, she began to cast the Sixth Gift. It felt good and also wrong, and by the time she realized what she was doing it was already done. A broad pink block of stone squatted beside the opening to their tunnel.

Ivy and Kinz stared at Cazia with worried expressions. Their concern almost pressed against her. Like the Sweeps winds, it hurt.

"You can continue?" Kinz asked. "There would be no shame in making the return to the grasslands now. You could take some time to heal, and when you are ready, we could return."

Cazia shook her head. She felt full and empty at the same time. Was it even possible to heal from this? Had Doctor Whitestalk ever healed? But of course, she could not say that aloud. "People are dying every day." That had been important a few days before and she knew it would matter to her companions. "We can be at the top by midday."

Ivy didn't like that. "What if the other side of the mountain is impassable, too?"

Cazia had no answer for her. Instead, she selected a low space in the mountain tops above, then moved thirty or forty paces west. How many more times would she have to cast this spell? Sixty? More? She could do it if she had to.

She cast the first rock-breaking spell easily. It was almost as though it wanted to come out of her.

The broken stones poured out of the hole she'd made. Ivy and Kinz watched the skies all around as Cazia cast again.

They reached the top of the pass a little after midday, as it turned out. Cazia had to stop several times to compose herself, and the others wanted to eat. But when they broke through the side of the peak, the sun beamed almost straight down at them.

"By Inzu's breath," Kinz said. Ivy and Cazia stepped along the jagged crevice to follow her to the northern side of the mountain.

The Qorr Valley lay stretched out before them. Far to the northeast, they could just barely make out the churning ocean crashing against the massive black rock shore. It was squeezed between the easternmost reaches of the Northern Barrier and a second mountain range that ran nearly due north. The afternoon sun was still burning off wisps of ocean fog that clung to the base of the mountains, but where it was clear, they could see bright green grass and patches of thick pine forests.

"It's so green," Ivy said. "Just like home."

Far to the left, in the westernmost part of the valley, was the place the northern range met the Barrier. The fog was still thick there, but to Cazia, it looked as if the place where the ranges met had been scooped out with a giant spoon.

"I think we can get down there," Kinz said, pointing toward a nest of vines growing against the mountainside.

"Oh!" Ivy exclaimed. She pointed toward the corner of the little plateau below them. There, lying in the sun, were the bleached white bones of a massive dragon.

CHAPTER TWENTY-TWO

JOLU DELLASTONE WAS RIGHT. THERE WERE NO MORE ENEMY SPEARS TO be met on the way to Fort Caarilit. They reached the fort in the afternoon of the following day. Despite Tejohn's fears, Finstel banners, not Witt, hung from the walls. They marched down the throat of the pass through the northern gate as though returning from a triumphant campaign.

Inside, the fort was full of frantic activity. Without even seeing a smear of red on the ground, Tejohn knew there had been a battle.

As they passed through the little gate, Jolu's spears began to fall out, their spears dragging in the dirt. Tejohn clapped his fist against his shield twice; they snapped to attention and reformed their square. Jolu himself walked along the square, straightening helmets and slapping shields that sagged below parade height.

A tall woman in a ridiculous red comb marched across the field toward them. Tejohn met Arla's gaze, and together they stepped away from the unit. These were Jolu's men, and Tejohn didn't want to take any credit from the man.

"Where's your captain?" the woman snapped. The left side of her mouth was horribly scarred and she was missing part of her nose. When she opened her mouth to speak, Tejohn could see that she was missing teeth too, which made her sound as though she was talking with her mouth full. She was young, though, probably around twenty-fivefold. Her second was a trim, unremarkable man with a wax tablet and stylus.

Jolu stood at attention. "Lost in action, Watch Commander, along with his second. I was forced to take command."

The Watch Commander leaned close and lowered her voice. A small line of drool hung from her ruined lip. "So where is his comb?"

Jolu turned his face toward the dirt. "Fire take the comb!" Tejohn heard himself say before he'd had a chance to think about it. Even a day and a half after the battle, his blood was still up. "*This man brought back your spears. And Witt prisoners. But you're pressing him about a red frill?*"

She turned a murderous look toward him, her hand falling near her knife. Tejohn made sure to keep his spear at rest position. "And who do you think you are to talk to me that way, old man?"

Old? Tejohn's beard had barely begun to show any gray.

Before he could respond, her second cleared his throat and stared at Tejohn with his mouth agape. Fire and Fury, Tejohn knew what was coming next.

"Watch Commander, that's Tejohn Treygar. *Tyr* Tejohn Treygar."

The Watch Commander shot her second a nasty look, then turned back to Tejohn. Her ruined mouth twisted as though she'd stepped in something awful but she wasn't sure what it was.

"Our cart was destroyed by the ruhgrit," Tejohn said sternly, changing the subject because he didn't want to waste one breath on the stupid comb. "The king continued westward while we headed toward the pass and Caarilit. Does Coml Finstel still command here? I need to speak to him immediately."

Jolu shifted his position slightly. "My tyr, I can take you to his office."

"Nonsense," the Watch Commander said. "Look to your spears. See that they're fed." She pointed a finger at a soldier rushing by. "See that these prisoners are searched and put to work." Finally, she bowed slightly to Tejohn. "My tyr, I believe Commander Finstel is overseeing the repair to the walls. This way." They marched across the northern yard toward an inner gate. "My tyr, I apologize for asking again, but what was it that destroyed your cart?"

"A ruhgrit," Tejohn said, as though it was common knowledge. "Have you not seen the huge predator eagles that recently appeared in the Sweeps?"

"Yes, my tyr."

"We were attacked by . . . Was it five of them, scout?"

Arla sounded almost amused when she answered. "I counted six, my tyr."

Tejohn nodded. "The king slew one and drove the rest off, with a little support from us." He waved vaguely in Arla's direction.

The Watch Commander's step faltered. "Ellifer Italga slew one of those giant eagles?"

Tejohn stopped and glared at her. The second stared at them both, wide-eyed. "King Ellifer is dead," Tejohn said. "It was his son, Lar Italga, the Peradaini king, who killed the thing. Er . . . " He glanced at Arla as though he was afraid he'd said too much. "The king has not given leave for that tale to be spread around. Song knows what he's done, but I don't know how he would feel about me gossiping about it."

The Watch Commander and her second nodded. "Yes, my tyr," they said, almost in unison. "We understand completely."

Tejohn nodded. "What news?"

The Watch Commander and her second gave it to him, and it was worse than he'd thought. The grunts had spread quickly, overwhelming the smaller tyrships south of the capital. The Shooks had been overrun and destroyed mere days after Peradain fell, and the Redmudds had retreated to their islands, effectively cut off from the rest of the empire. The Holvos still held Rivershelf, but their archers were hard pressed and they were not likely to last long.

Worse, tyrs all across the empire had begun to strike at each other, using old grievances as an excuse to take new land. The empire was eating itself. The Watch Commander did not mention scholars at all.

As they strode through the fort, Tejohn made note of the scene around him. The people hurried, but there was something frantic and hopeless in them. Each yard they strode through was littered with broken spars and discarded trash. When they came to the southernmost yard, they saw the wall had been shattered and collapsed.

It gave Tejohn a brief flutter in his guts to see the gap. This was the power of a scholar put to battle, the power to collapse walls, crush soldiers, burn them alive.

"As for Peradain itself," the Watch Commander said, a note of pride in her voice, "rumor has it that the city has burned to the ground and no one within survives. Three different tyrs have sent flying carts to investigate, but only my Tyr Finstel's men brought back a prize."

"Prize? What do you mean?"

The Watch Commander seemed suddenly uncomfortable. "I do not know, my tyr. Rumor has it that more people returned from the city than went, but I can not say who they found. All I hear is gossip."

"Thank you, Watch Commander. I see Commander Finstel by the gate and will make my own introductions. I release you to your duties."

She nodded and marched back toward the north gate, her second close behind.

Arla watched them go with a smirk. "She will spread that tale about the king through the entire fort before sunset, my tyr."

"Do you think?" Tejohn said. "I expected the second to spread the tale, since I ordered her not to and she is so in love with her rules . . . "

"Her second is too meek to open his mouth. It's the ones who love rules the most who are most eager to break them. There's always a justification, if you look hard enough. The other Watch Commanders will know before you finish speaking with the commander, I'd wager, and word will spread from there. That was clever, my tyr."

Tejohn shook his head. "I won't be taking that bet, and thank you. I once told Lar Italga that I did not have cleverness in me, but in times like these, we all must be more than we were. What do you think of the situation here?"

Arla looked around, absent-mindedly running her callused fingers over her unstrung bow. "They look frantic and terrified. I hope we'll be moving on quickly. I don't like it here."

Tejohn didn't argue. He'd hoped to find a flying cart here, but only a fool would leave one in an unsecured fort.

Coml Finstel was a young man, barely over twenty-five and as lean as a knotted rope. As Tejohn and Arla approached, he marched around the edges of a work crew, screaming at them in a red-faced rage while they strapped timbers together. Obviously, they were making a crude barricade to fill the gap in the wall until a more permanent fix could be arranged. Every few strides, Coml laid into one of the workers with his lash.

Archers stood on platforms along the wall, but most faced inward, ready to shoot anyone who fled. Tejohn was close enough to see that the crew was made of those who were too young or too old to take up a spear.

Commander Finstel did not notice them as they approached, but his second did. She waited for him to take a breath, tapped his elbow, and nodded in Tejohn's direction.

If there was one place in all of the empire that Tejohn expected to find welcome, it was in Finstel lands. He had been born here, had carried a spear for Splashtown and Tyr Samper Finstel, and had made a point of befriending his son Shunzik when his father died. Not so many years ago, Coml himself had taken the trouble to introduce himself to Tejohn at one of Lar's birthday parties.

In truth, despite the oath he'd taken to the Italga family—with Samper Finstel's blessing—in his heart, he thought of himself as a Splashtown spear.

So, he expected to be greeted warmly, even by this young man he had met only once before. "Tyr Treygar," Commander Finstel said, "what a surprise it is to see you here." He was smiling as he gave his lash to his second, but it was the smile of a snarling dog. "But you bring happy news, I expect? Italga spears to support my Tyr Finstel? Perhaps a few scholars to rebuild our walls?"

Tejohn shook his head. "I can't offer you either of these things, although I know you need them. My scout and I are passing through on the way to visit your tyr. I ask only for provisions and the latest news."

"Of course!" The young commander smiled as though he was being provoked to murder. "You are an Italga spear now, so you must hurry to my cousin's holdfast to take what you need. Finstel lands are nothing more than a warehouse for the Italgas to raid, after all."

"Commander," Tejohn said, keeping his tone as civil as possible. "The entire empire is under siege, the king is doing his best to save us all, and you whine like a fishmonger over a few tin specks. The Finstels were warrior chieftains before the empire swallowed them up, and they have been warrior tyrs since. Song knows they were never *peevish*."

Coml Finstel took a deep breath, then sighed and scratched the side of his face. "My apologies, my tyr. Weariness takes command of my tongue at times. Of course, we must trade news. Why don't you and your scout take a meal in my rooms? I will finish here and—"

Shouts came from outside the fort. Coml turned and ran toward the gap in the wall, calling for his spear. Bows ran along the wall to take up their positions, and someone somewhere began to strike a gong.

Tejohn and Arla pushed forward as the work crew fled deeper into the fort. "What do you see?" Tejohn said.

Arla stepped up onto the unfinished barricade so she could look over the heads of the scrambling soldiers. "Eleven spears coming up the mudflat," she said. "Fleet squad with Splashtown colors. They're dragging one man behind them on a rope, and he's pleading to be released."

"I can hear him." Tejohn recognized the sound of a man facing a death sentence.

"Captain Dellastone!" Coml called. "What report?"

A deep voice called in response. "Two grunts, sir, down in the village, looking for victims." The man speaking had the same nose and chin as Jolu but was not nearly so thick in the middle. He wore a long red brush on his helmet. "The first fell to arrows and spears, but the second came upon us suddenly and broke through our shields."

By then, the spears had come to the barricade. They didn't try to enter. Coml pointed toward the tied-up man. Tejohn was close enough to see he was also part of the Splashtown fleet squad. "And him?"

The captain answered, "Bitten, sir."

"NO!" the man screamed. "It was a scratch from a claw! No more than that, I swear."

The commander took the man's arm and examined it. Tejohn wasn't close enough to see the injury, but he could see Coml shake his head. "Soldier, how do you want it?"

"It's a rake from a claw, I swear by Monument and Song! A scratch! Please!" Coml shook his head and drew his long knife. The injured man's voice went higher and Tejohn could see the other soldiers struggling to hold him. "Please!" he screamed, "Kelvijinian!"

Coml stabbed him once, quickly, as though trying to stop his prayer. When the man went limp, the soldiers carried him back along the mud flats. "Anyone else?"

The captain answered. "Only one," and held out his bloody forearm.

"Fire and Fury, Bayzu," the commander said. "How could you let this happen?"

The captain took off his helmet, ran his bloodied fingers through the brush, then gave it to Coml. "You always told me there would come a day when even I would not be fast enough, Commander."

"I did, didn't I? Monument sustain me. How do you want it?"

"Will you come with me to the temple, Commander? If it's time to leave the Way, I'd like to pay my respects first."

"Of course. Jolu has only just returned; I'll summon him if you like." Coml turned to walk with the man into the fort. His colorless gaze fell upon Tejohn, and he paused briefly to confer with his second. The second nodded, then bustled toward Tejohn and Arla.

"Commander Finstel offers his rooms to you in case you would like to eat and rest. He will join you after he attends his duties."

"Of course," Tejohn said.

The second nodded and started toward the tower. "This way, please. Is it true you came from Fort Samsit?"

"Yes," Tejohn said in a tone that he hoped would cut off further questioning.

"Ah" was her only answer.

They followed her into the main hall, climbed three flights of stairs to the top floor of the tower, and strode into the commander's rooms. The furniture and cushions were as fine as those in the palace, and wood had been laid for a fire. The accommodations were certainly finer than Tejohn had received at Fort Samsit.

"Please make yourselves comfortable," the second said. "I don't know how long the commander will be. I'll have the steward bring food. If you want to bathe, just step through that door there and pull the cord. The servants will know what to do." She indicated a heavy drape hanging across the far end of the room. "If you please, I have duties of my own."

"Of course," Tejohn answered. "Second . . . "

She was about to close the door behind her. "Yes, my tyr?"

"You should feed that work crew down there."

That took her by surprise. "Commander Finstel has said they would receive a meal when the work was done."

"The work is sloppy," Tejohn told her. "They're starving and their energy is flagging—even I can see it. Sneak something to them and remind them how close their enemies are. That will motivate them better than starving them."

The second kept her face very still, but Tejohn could see her weighing her contradictory orders. "Yes, my tyr," she said, and closed the door.

"Did she really offer us a bath?" Arla threw back the heavy drape to reveal a huge basin made of beaten copper.

Tejohn whistled. "The Finstel mining camps have been productive."

Arla stared down at it. "It takes a special sort of bastard to build it on the top floor of a tower, so the servants had to carry the water and firewood up all those stairs."

Tejohn felt a flush of embarrassment. He'd grown up in a one-room farmhouse, one bad harvest away from debt-servitude himself, but he hadn't even considered that.

He went to the bowl of water by the window and began to wash his face. As a landless tyr, he wasn't descended from chieftains, tyrants, or warlords. He was just a farmer with a knack for killing and more than his share of luck. A hot bath suddenly didn't seem worth the trouble.

When the food arrived, he and Arla reclined on couches and ate sticky salt rice and mashed apricots. After some prodding, she began to tell him of her childhood in the mining camps. Her clan, the Grimfields, were minor tyrs of the empire, but her family had to flee after her grandfather had made a failed bid for the tyrship. The Chin-Chinro came upon her parents' mountain hideout, killed the adults or sold them like slaves. Arla was born four months later. Tejohn had thought his own life was full of hardship, but her tales, simply told, were full of pain.

They had not yet finished when there was a knock on the door. Before Tejohn could answer, six soldiers walked into the room, their swords bared. They were accompanied by a short man with the flat, dead eyes of an eel. Instead of a sword, he held a burning torch. "Stand," he commanded. "Do as you're told and no harm will come to you."

Tejohn and Arla stood, warily. When Arla spoke, her voice came out in a hiss. "My Tyr Treygar is shield bearer to—"

"I don't care if he's the king himself. Keep silent while I do my duty." He bowed his head slightly in Tejohn's direction. "I am Watch Commander Stollik, my tyr, should you seek satisfaction at some future time. Now strip."

Tejohn glanced at Arla. Her eyes were wide and her teeth bared. She was ready to die fighting. "I know what they want," Tejohn said to her. He'd already set his cuirass and boots against the wall, so he unwrapped his padded undershirt and skirt. "They're looking for bite marks or patches of blue fur. Isn't that right?"

"You've just come from Samsit, so you have to be checked," the watch commander said. "No more talking. Just do it."

"Have some respect, man," Tejohn snapped. "At least have my scout taken to another room where she can be searched by other women—"

"The next words I speak will be the order to kill you both."

There was no doubt that he would do it, and there were too many to fight. Tejohn stripped nude. Arla, beside him, did the same. The soldiers Stollik had brought leered at her lean, muscled body.

"Turn," Stollik ordered, and they did, slowly, while the Watch Commander held the torch close enough to their bodies to singe their skin.

"Satisfied?" Tejohn said.

"Entirely." Stollik waved at his men, and they began to file out. He shut the door behind him.

Tejohn turned his back and pulled on his skirts while Arla dressed. After she had finished, he heard her gather up the last of her meal.

"If my tyr please, I'd like to finish in the little enclosed space there. Behind the curtain." She wouldn't look at him.

"Take the cushions with you."

She stripped the cushions off the couch and dropped them into the copper basin. It wasn't large enough for her to stretch out, but it would do, he supposed. She pulled the curtain closed.

Fire and Fury, the only tyr who would be treated this way was a landless one, without spears to his name. It made sense for them to check newcomers, but Coml could have handled this with courtesy, but instead, he made the deliberate insult out of it.

The Finstels had turned against the Italga family, and Tejohn had no idea why.

At no point in the night did the commander return to his own rooms to trade news with them.

In the morning, a servant woke them to say that Coml Finstel, Commander of Fort Caarilit, requested they break their fast with him.

As they crossed the yard to the hall, Arla touched Tejohn's shoulder. "My tyr," she said, pointing upward above the wall.

Tejohn could barely make out where the dark gray mountain ended and the dark gray sky began. "I hope you don't expect me to see—"

"I apologize, my Tyr. Ruhgrits. Three of them, watching."

"Then let's get inside before we attract their attention." A servant opened the mess entrance for them, her gaze never leaving the ground.

"My tyr, I must apologize," Coml said as they approached his table. He stood and bowed to them both. "Everyone who makes their way here from the south and west must be examined, else we suffer the same fate as Fort Samsit."

Arla froze in place. "What happened at Samsit?"

Coml gestured toward the chairs, smiling like a genial host. He had chosen a round wooden table for their meeting, placed on the raised dais that was the privilege of commanders and Tyrs. "Have you not heard? Samsit was overrun by grunts not twenty-five days ago. It seems that one got inside the walls, started biting people, and the curse spread. Tyr Gerrit tried to retake the fort, but their numbers were too great and he *nearly* lost one of his flying carts."

Tejohn shut his eyes. If Samsit had fallen, what hope did any of Reglis's family have? There was little chance now that Tejohn could speak with the Singalan family about their son. They'd almost certainly been burned off The Way.

Tejohn did his best to keep his expression calm. Stoneface, Cazia Freewell had called him. He could still be Stoneface. "Any survivors or escapees?"

"None," Coml said confidently. "I'm told Tyr Gerrit was furious at the death of his cousin, but it did prompt my own cousin to send me an extra squad. Not that it helped, in the end."

"How long ago did the Witts take Caarilit?"

"Five days." Coml smiled ruefully. "And I did not retake it by force, I'm embarrassed to say. I was planning a counterattack when they withdrew on their own, at speed."

"I would be willing to wager that Witts and Finstels are not sharing news."

Coml smiled more broadly. "No, my tyr. When Finstel and Witt speak on the mirrors, they do nothing but curse and threaten each other. Still, I think we all know why the Witt spears and bows withdrew."

Tejohn nodded. "If the grunts have come far enough west to attack

Finstel villagers, they must be ranging all over Witt lands."

"Our Witt spies have fallen silent, and I hope theirs in our lands have done the same. Also, they got their hands on a flying cart, somehow, which was supposed to be a gift for only Ellifer's supporters."

"King Ellifer," Tejohn corrected.

The commander nodded. "Of course, my tyr. And King Lar, I've heard."

"Of course," Tejohn said. "What plans has Finstel made?"

"Plans?" Coml seemed confused by the question. "We have destroyed every bridge across the Shelsiccan." It took Tejohn a moment to recognize that name. *Shelsiccan* was the original Finshto name for the Wayward River, which ran from Caarilit down to Deep Stone Lake and Splashtown.

"We guard the headwaters here in Caarilit," Coml continued. "But all my cousin's spears have been pulled back to his holdfast. Many of our citizens have fled there as well. As far as we know, none of the grunts have managed to cross the Shelsiccan, but it is a matter of time."

"What of the reconnaissance flights to Peradain?" Tejohn lowered his voice. "I have heard a person of great importance was rescued from the city."

"I have heard the same rumors," Coml said. He did not lower his voice to match Tejohn's. "My own mother, in the heart of power at the Finstel holdfast, has told me the rumors are not true. Yet they persist. The most common is that it was Amlian Italga herself who was rescued from the burning city and is now recuperating on cushions in my sister's house."

"No," Tejohn said flatly. "I saw Amlian Italga fall. She fought and died not thirty paces from me."

"As you say. But the rumors persist."

Tejohn was anxious to change the subject. "What of other lands and other tyrs?"

"The Redmudds have withdrawn to their islands down in the Waterlands, burning their bridges behind them. The Shooks have been overrun. The Holvos retreated into Rivershelf and were hard pressed as of a few days ago. I'm told they no longer respond to messages."

"Fire and Fury." Linder Holvos was a good man and loyal to the Italgas. Worse, unlike the Shooks and Redmudds, he had enough spears to make his support matter.

"And the same is true for Rolvo Simblin."

"What's this?" Tejohn couldn't conceal his surprise. "Simblin lands are as far from Peradain as they could be without falling into the Bescos Sea. Grunts could not have overthrown them already, could they?" *At least I won't have to explain to another mortal enemy why I abandoned his child to die in Peradain.*

"Not unless they stole a cart and overflew all the lands between. And the passes into the Simblin flats have been blocked by rockslides."

"And of course no one can spare a cart to investigate," Tejohn said.

"Just so," Coml answered. "What's more, our Tyrs and commanders have troubles enough of their own. We're facing the first incursions of grunts in our lands, and I have guards fleeing into the Sweeps when they should be on duty."

"Deserters?" Tejohn was surprised to hear it. Fleeing west through the Waterlands would make sense for imperial soldiers. The north held nothing but wilderness and the enemies who dwelled there.

Coml spread his palms. "They climb the wall and flee into the night without so much as a Fire-pass-you-by to their comrades. We're undermanned as it is. And we have no scholars with the spells to repair our walls."

Arla cleared her throat. "Commander, my Tyr Treygar, if I may . . . "

Coml scowled, but Tejohn answered first. "What is it, scout?"

"Even if the mining scholars can not create stone blocks for you out of the air, they will know how to cut them out of the mountainside and shape them with their magic. They will also know how to move the blocks into position through mundane means."

Coml inclined his head to her. "Thank you for the recommendation." His tone was slightly ironic, as though he couldn't bring himself to show real gratitude. "I shall confer with the scholars we have rescued."

Tejohn noticed the commander had used the plural. *Scholars.* So much for the king's monopoly over magic.

"But tell me," Coml said speculatively, "When were you ever in a mining camp?"

"I grew up in one, sir." Arla seemed to be making a dangerous admission.

Coml seemed thoughtful. "Your family is Durdric, then?"

"No!" Arla sounded aggrieved at the suggestion. "I'm a Grimfield, but I was born among the Chin-Chinro. Durdric Holy Sons murdered my best friend. My people and theirs kill each other on sight!"

"Ah," Coml said patiently, "It is hard for me to tell the difference. From my perspective, both drop rocks on my patrols when we venture beyond the pass."

Tejohn interrupted. "My scout has stood back to back with the king in battle, fending off the ruhgrit, when we were outnumbered and overmatched. She has proven her loyalty."

"I heard about that," Coml said, changing the subject smoothly. "Your Samsit captain told the tale to a few of my spears, and word spread. Is it true that Lar Italga drove off a flock of giant eagles with a single spell?"

"And slew one," Tejohn said.

"I admit," Coml said, "I'm surprised to hear it. I know scholars are useful in a supporting capacity to a square of spears or line of bows, but I have never thought them useful in the thick of battle.

Tejohn shut his eyes, as the memory of fire, crumbling rock, and fierce volleys of iron-tipped darts overwhelmed him. He had faced scholars on the battlefield. He didn't have the luxury of underestimating them.

Arla filled the silence by answering Coml's unasked question. "I myself saw the king bite into the beast's heart while he laughed."

"That's what Captain Dellastone reported. Huh. Now I can't help but wonder what the . . . ruhgrit's heart is like."

"Huge," Tejohn said, "and hot to the touch. Which brings up other news I must share. The ruhgrit stalk their prey in the daylight but they strike at night, in the darkness. You should double up your watch stations. It's possible that your night guards are not deserting after all."

The commander looked startled. "That's a disturbing thought." Coml turned his attention to his bowl, scooping out a few mouthfuls of roasted dark meat and sticky rice. When he looked more composed, he said, "My tyr, I must say, when I mentioned that Samsit fell, you did not seem surprised."

"I wasn't," Tejohn said. "One of the spears began to change en route."

"Ah. What did you do with your spear?"

Tejohn shrugged. "I took his head. He had become an enemy of the empire."

Coml stopped chewing for just a moment, then continued again. When he looked up from his food again, his expression had subtly changed. He had never been truly friendly, but now he looked like a man about to do battle. "Of course, my tyr. And what can I do for you?"

Tejohn had planned to ask to use the commander's mirror, but what he said instead was "All I need is a small rowboat and a few supplies for my scout and myself. I need to reach Splashtown as soon as possible on the king's errand, and I hope to take the Shelsiccan around the spur." If the commander was going to use the Finshto name, so would Tejohn.

Coml wiped the bottom of his bowl with a hunk of bread. Without looking up, he said, "You will need a few of my soldiers, I suppose?"

"No," Tejohn answered. "Your need is greater than mine. I hope."

"That is fine," Coml said. He stood and bowed. "Please accept my apologies, my tyr, for not waiting for your food to arrive. I have a barricade to oversee. If you would excuse me."

"Of course."

The commander hopped down from the dais onto the main floor of the mess. Arla leaned toward Tejohn. "Am I misreading things, or did he seemed threatened by something you said, my Tyr?"

"Watch him for me," Tejohn said. When he'd said *enemy of the empire,* Coml's insincere chilliness had turned into something else. Something Tejohn didn't like. "What is the scrawny little liar doing?"

"He's crossing the room toward the tables in the back. He's stopped to talk with the members of a fleet squad. Archers and scouts by the look of their gear. The commander's back is to us, but he's leaning down to speak to the squad leader . . . who just looked directly at us."

"Try to look bored. Now, at the squad leader's order, the rest of the squad will rush through their meals and go."

"Yes, my Tyr. That's what they're doing. Commander Finstel is with them."

"As they file out, do any of the others glance at us?"

"The squad leader again," Arla said. "And the tall woman in the back. And another dark-eyed one. Now their backs are to us and they're leaving the mess."

"Fire and Fury."

The stewards set bowls in front of them. More salty rice with apricots—the food of the common soldier.

Tejohn wasn't hungry anymore, but he'd been on too many campaigns to push the bowl away. He forced himself to eat.

"My tyr, are they our escort to Splashtown?"

Tejohn was surprised by the question. "No. They're our assassins."

"That's inconvenient." Arla picked up her bowl and began to eat with gusto. "My yr," she said when she had finished, "you called him a liar. But . . . What did I miss?"

Tejohn pushed his empty bowl away. "He asked about Samsit. He asked about the king. He asked about the ruhgrit. But he never asked what happened on the day Peradain fell."

Arla sat suddenly upright. "Great Way."

"He already knows the story, which means they did rescue someone from the city. Someone who was there when the portal opened."

There was no choice. Tejohn needed to get into the Finstel holdfast and find out who had been rescued from Peradain. He'd seen Amlian killed, but Ellifer had been lost in the confusion. Could the king still be alive?

And he needed a flying cart, still, because someone had to get to Tempest Pass.

He pushed his empty bowl away. "No sense in waiting around here. Let's give those assassins their shot."

CHAPTER TWENTY-THREE

CLIMBING DOWN WAS EASIER THAN CLIMBING UP, BECAUSE THIS SIDE of the Northern Barrier had a more rounded, weathered surface. It certainly wasn't a slick, featureless wall.

But it was still dangerous. It took the rest of the day to descend only a couple dozen feet to the plateau below.

The dragon bones were monstrous. The skull alone was as large as Mahz's wagon, and Ivy immediately announced, eyes shining, that she planned to camp inside it for the night. She crawled through the opening in the neck and assured them it was quite roomy inside.

Cazia didn't like it, but she crawled in after. The skull was larger than the chambers she'd created inside the rock, but her spellcasting had already made her feel somewhat less than real, and now she was going to spend the night inside a dead thing's head like a bad dream.

A month before, she might have objected strenuously. She might have insisted they shelter somewhere else. Instead, she rolled out her cloth and went to sleep.

Ivy woke her in the middle of the night. They could hear the beating of wings, and by the starlight coming through the eye sockets, Cazia could see that the princess's eyes were wide and terrified.

She rolled over and peered through the eye sockets. A pair of giant eagles had landed on the plateau nearby, beating their wings rhythmically. Then they began to squawk in high, harsh voices.

Kinz started out of a sound sleep, but Ivy shushed her. Had the birds spotted them? Cazia wondered if they would tear her apart to eat her—how much would that hurt?—or drop her from a height first.

Neither happened. Instead, they leaped into the air, circled higher and higher, then crossed over into the Sweeps.

The three girls held hands and lay as quietly as they could. The night winds were gentle now that they were out of the Sweeps, but that only meant they could better hear the beating of wings.

At dawn, they carefully crawled out to check the sky. There were no birds nearby, but two circled lazily over the misty place where the mountain ranges met. They were barely smudges against the gray sky; surely they wouldn't be able to spot her from so far away.

"We must be careful," Kinz said. "We can not climb down the side of the hill in open view the way we did yesterday."

Ivy came close. "We can not ask Cazia to tunnel us down. She would never survive it." The girl laid her hand on Cazia's elbow. "How do you feel?"

That was a good question. Cazia found it difficult to turn her attention inward to take stock of herself. The urge to cast a spell was growing. She felt as thin and hollow as an eggshell. Every word they spoke to her was like a shriek. Her skin burned when the wind blew across it, and it chafed where her skirts touched. She lifted the cloth to look at her legs—as much to break Ivy's touch as anything else—but there were no sores, no swelling, not even any redness there. She had magic inside her, and the magic hurt.

"I'm in pain," she admitted. There was no point in hiding it. "Not my hands, for some reason, but most every other part of me feels like I've been sunburned."

And I don't care. She couldn't bring herself to say that, not when her tears were so close to the surface again.

"You have been Cursed," Kinz said, but Cazia ignored her.

"Why do you look as though you are about to cry?" Ivy asked. She wrung her hands nervously, as though she'd done something wrong.

Cazia thought about her dreams and of falling during the climb. "Don't I have reason enough?"

"We are going to stay here for a few days," Ivy announced. "We have the rations, do we not?"

"If we stretch them," Kinz announced.

"We will. We can not climb down until we are all back to full strength. That is common sense. So, it is settled."

Kinz sighed. "You just want to camp inside the dragon skull the little longer."

"Of course!" Ivy answered, grinning suddenly. "Think of the story it would make."

The giant birds were least active around dawn, and that's when Kinz did her exploring. It was dangerous, but she insisted that she was skilled at moving through cover. Cazia suspected that as someone who had lived her whole life under the open sky, her scouting missions were more about escaping their confined space than actual reconnaissance.

In the meantime, Ivy spent a fair portion of the day digging out the dragon's teeth. She confided that she'd heard that, if they were planted like seeds in fertile soil, they would grow into new dragons.

By the third night, Cazia lied and said she was ready to continue. Kinz had been filling their canteens from a hillside stream, and there was no reason at all for her to cast a spell. Her pain had eased, but her insides still felt hollowed out. She'd felt no worry when Kinz crawled out of their shelter, no amazement when Ivy told the story of the ancestor who single-handedly slew a dragon, and no irritation when the others bickered about food or religion.

None of it meant anything to her.

It was clear that she wasn't going to get her personality back, so it was time to start down the mountainside. Ivy looked skeptical but Kinz was clearly grateful. She had found a way down, she said.

She showed it to them just before dawn. There was a vertical crevice in the side of the mountain that was choked with thick, bark-covered vines. None of them had ever seen anything like it, but the lattice was strong enough to support their weight. They could climb down through them, well out of sight of the birds overhead.

Ivy attacked it enthusiastically; Cazia struggled the most and often felt on the verge of falling. It wasn't just that her hands were weakest or that her body was heaviest, although they were. It was also that she felt weary of everything, and was bored even by the need to preserve her own life.

Fury guide me, she thought. She closed her eyes and silently repeated the prayer over and over. It was a prayer for poor people and servants, not for the children of tyrs. It was a prayer of desperation. *Fury guide me.* Fury was a god of many aspects—every kind of human being, good or evil, was contained in him, and that meant every human had Fury in them.

Cazia needed that fury. She wouldn't survive without it.

And there it was, kindled inside her like a spark of the divine. She closed her eyes and mentally fed that little light until it began to burn. Magic had scoured her empty, but it couldn't take away the touch of her god.

They stopped for food at nearly the bottom of the crevice, and Kinz began to rub Cazia's hands.

"How are you holding up?" Ivy asked.

Fury guide me. "No mountain is going to get the better of me."

At the bottom of the crevice was a tumble of rocks as large as Ivy's Peradaini house but no more vines. The eagles had taken to the air, hovering over ridges and shelves in the surrounding mountainside, but the morning mists were still thick, and the girls managed to slide down out of sight without being eaten.

Kinz moved very close to the other two girls and whispered, "Sound carries in the mists. We must be as quiet as snakes in the grass."

They nodded and began to clamber down through the rocks. The fog made it impossible to plan a route to the forest floor—soon, they couldn't see much farther than the reach of their arms. Each time Ivy cat-crept down a huge, sloping rock, she seemed to vanish into the mist. Still, they managed by trial and error.

By midmorning, the sun became hot enough to burn the fog away. The girls had to crawl under an outcropping of stone to hide. "Listen!" Kinz hissed.

They listened. As the fog retreated down the mountainside, they heard a strange tapping noise retreat within it. An eagle swooped low, almost down into the swirling mists toward the sound, but flew upward again with empty talons.

"What makes a noise like that?" Ivy whispered. "It sounds like someone drumming the fingernails on a piece of horn."

No one could answer, and they stayed under cover during the hot part of the afternoon. Cazia was uncomfortable, but also so exhausted from the climb that she fell asleep. It was well after dark when she woke to the sounds of Ivy and Kinz arguing with hissing voices over the empty canteens.

"I can fill them," Cazia said. She was parched herself, and while she knew the spell would increase her curse, she had been aching to use one of the Gifts all day. And what did it matter, anyway?

"No." Ivy answered, putting her hand on Cazia's shoulder. "There is no rush. We can go a day without water."

"My spells have gotten stronger. I could probably fill them all at once."

Kinz shook her head and stuffed the canteens into her pack. "You only have the few more in you, yes? Save them for when we are desperate."

They slept through the night, waking a few hours before dawn. They didn't wait; moonlight lit the fog well enough to cast everything in a diffuse light. Kinz tried to pretend she knew exactly which way to go, but Cazia could see that she was putting on a show. No matter.

They almost tripped over another column of woody vines, but unlike the one near the top of the mountain, this one creaked under their weight and sagged alarmingly. The tapping noises grew louder, then softer, moving closer, then farther away. Cazia imagined an old man below them so blinded by the fog that he went about tapping a cane against the rocks. The image was so absurd that she had to stop climbing and cover her mouth. The magic inside her wanted to scream with laughter.

Kinz disappeared below but Ivy paused to lay her hand on Cazia's shoulder. "Are you well?" she whispered.

I think I'm going mad. No, that wasn't something you said to a twelve-year-old girl. She shut her eyes. There was nothing absurd about their situation. Ivy and Kinz had been important to her once . . . Well, maybe not Kinz. Magic had taken that connection away, and she would never return to herself if she was not ready to fight for them. What's more, if she turned back without discovering the secrets of this valley, she would have hollowed herself out for nothing.

Fury guide me. Fury, I need your spark to protect my friends. She felt it kindle again, that tiny bit of heat that showed her god was still alive and still active within her. What magic had done to her could not be undone, not by her, but she could still fight against it. She could still *try* to remain herself.

Ivy was waiting. "I'm just getting ready," Cazia whispered, and it was almost true. "But stop paying attention to me; look out for yourself."

At the bottom of the column, they found themselves on a grass slope. Ivy immediately lay out flat against it, pressing her face among the blades to smell them. Kinz touched her shoulder and, through gestures, bid her string her bow. The tapping sound returned, and Ivy quietly did as she was told.

They could only see a dozen feet ahead of them in the mist, and the sound seemed to be coming from everywhere. By unspoken agreement, they did not speak. Cazia heard water lapping against rocks and moved toward it, idly wondering if she should feel afraid but glad that she didn't. Hent had been so certain she would die in this place . . . .

The gray silhouette of a boulder loomed in the dim mists. She moved toward it almost out of instinct simply because it was a landmark, and discovered it wasn't a boulder after all. It was a skull. It lay crooked against the ground, with a single, massive eye socket in the middle of its face. Broken tusks stuck out from the sides of its ugly mouth.

She rubbed her hands over the rough bone—were her own bones this rough? The dragon's had been smooth. Ivy came up behind her, then Kinz, but neither of them wanted to touch the skull. Maybe she should have been frightened by it, too, but instead she just found it fascinating.

Besides, they needn't be afraid of a skull. They should be afraid of whatever had killed it.

Cazia turned to them and touched her ear. After listening for a moment, they heard the faint sound of water. Great Way, they were so thirsty. They moved carefully around the bones, licking their lips.

The ground sloped downward, the air grew warmer and the mist thinner. The sun was coming up, somewhere, because the mist seemed to glow faintly. They came to a long mound of loose dirt that stood higher than their heads. It extended into the mists beyond where they could see, and they had choice but to climb over it.

On the other side, the soil became muddier and the mist thinner still. Kinz began to push the grass flat with her feet so she could step on it. Cazia found a place where stones had fallen from the mountainside above, and she walked across them until she reached the water.

Little wisps of steam rose from it, clearing away the mist nearby. Just like the heat of the day, she thought. The water was little wider than a small pond—a distance of some thirty paces—and it felt a bit scummy. It would have been nice to know why it was so warm, but she didn't see much hope of discovering that.

"I do not think it is safe to drink," Kinz whispered. Cazia figured she was right, but dipped her hands into it anyway. After days of spellcasting, moving rocks, and climbing down the rough vines, she figured the heat would feel good.

It did, actually. The warmth was soothing for all of two heartbeats, when she felt a tiny bite on the side of her hand.

"Ouch!' she exclaimed, yanking her hand back. There, stuck to the side of her hand, was a little round fish no larger than her earlobe. As she watched it drink her blood, it turned gray and died, falling into the water with a tiny splash.

The pond was full of those tiny fish. A drop of blood fell from her hand, and the fish fled from it as though it was poison.

Cazia crept back up the rocks. The injury was tiny—if it didn't get infected, there wouldn't be any problem with it. She sucked out a bit of her own blood and spit it onto the rocks.

The other girls waited for her by edge of the water. "Sorry for the noise," she whispered, "but—"

The tapping sound returned, louder than ever. All three of them turned toward the water, but they couldn't see what was making the noise. They slowly withdrew toward the mists just as the wind shifted direction, and a sour, acrid, burning stench made Cazia's nostrils tingle. A second tapping sound joined the first.

Whatever was making that noise, Cazia's outcry had caught its . . . *their* attention. She glanced at Kinz and Ivy again, both of whom were carefully retreating toward the giant skull, their gazes turned toward the sound. She wanted to cry again, although she couldn't understand why. Yes, she might have just gotten them all killed, but even that didn't seem terribly important.

Kinz was right. She had been Cursed. Magic had left her full of miseries she couldn't identify but no room for other human feelings. All she had left was a holy spark, and what good was that?

She had brought the tapping closer. It only seemed sensible that she should lead the danger, whatever it was, away from Kinz and the princess. Besides, she was genuinely curious what it could be.

Ivy had an arrow nocked, but now more than ever before, her weapon looked like a tiny thing—a toy for hunting squirrels. Cazia laid her hand on Ivy's shoulder, encouraging her to get low to ground beside the skull. Of course, Kinz had Cazia's spear.

"I'll be right back," Cazia lied. Lying was easy now. "Keep quiet."

She snatched a fistful of squarish teeth from beside the broken tusk and hurried into the mists before they could respond. She crouched behind a tree and looked back; they hadn't tried to follow her. A few days before, she would have been disappointed, but now she felt an odd satisfaction. She'd crossed the mountains to discover a secret, but now all she wanted to do was prove Hent right.

What am I doing? What is wrong with me?

She hurried into the trees, circling around the steaming pond. The trees she passed were spindly and narrow, with scorch marks low on the trunk; a fire had passed through here recently. She threw one of the teeth in the general direction of the pond.

She heard a satisfying splash, followed by a rustling of grasses. Something was moving toward her, and it sounded big.

Now would have been the time for her fear to really grow, but it didn't happen. She loitered by the tree, waiting for the creature, whatever it was, to appear out of the mists.

And she waited. Whatever it was, it wasn't in a hurry. It occurred to her that she could be just as cautious, so she moved backwards into the trees. Her feet made the grass rustle, but she didn't mind, not if it drew the thing toward her.

The fog thickened and her view of the forest around her shrank. She felt lost, cut off from the world. If she died here, her bones would lie in the grass for ages, just like the ones behind her. Not that it mattered.

Still, she couldn't help but be terribly curious how it would all turn out.

She came to a sturdy-looking oak broad enough to hide behind. Far enough. She circled it and crouched low on the bare roots, peering around the edge back the way she came. Her hand rested on the tiny quiver at her hip. It was still full.

The tapping had stopped but she could still hear the rustling of grass and bushes. She wondered, almost idly, if the thing would be too big to follow her between the trees, and whether that would be a good or a bad thing.

Except it wasn't a single large creature. What came out of the mists were five or six figures with round, helmeted heads and long spears. They were only silhouettes, but she was vaguely disappointed. She was honestly hoping to see a real dragon, or perhaps one of the one-eyed beasts.

As the warriors came closer, she realized they weren't wearing helmets after all. Their heads were just strangely shaped because they weren't human. They were as small as Ivy and even more slender. That awful acrid smell came off them in waves, and as one shifted its spear, she saw that its arm was as thin as a broomstick.

She leaned back out of view, hoping they hadn't seen her, and threw three of the disgusting gray teeth out into the mists in the opposite direction. One struck a tree trunk, making a sound like a snapping twig, and the other two rustled some unseen bushes. Behind her, she heard a pair of sharp taps and smelled a new level of awful stink; it occurred to her that they were talking to each other through their taps and scents. If only she'd thought to touch her translation stone . . .

It was too late for that now. She was already doing the hand motions to cast her fire spell. Great Way, but it felt good to do magic again after so many days. She had barely started the spell before the power behind it opened in a way she had never felt before.

The figures passed her hiding spot just as she finished. As she rolled to her feet, she saw the creatures clearly for the first time.

They were insects. Upright insects with segmented bodies wearing red sashes and ribbons over their dark red shells. They had tiny eyes like buttons, and claws over their mouths. Their attention was focused ahead of them, toward the part of the woods where she'd thrown the teeth. Cazia turned to her left—moving away from Ivy and Kinz's hiding space—and splayed her fingers.

Fire poured out of her with an intensity she'd never felt before. It wasn't like casting a spell; it felt very much like cracking open a forge and releasing the heat within. The flames touched the nearest creature just as it began to turn around, striking its chest, and the thing burst apart like a wheat berry in a campfire.

Cazia's old self would have been horrified by the gore, but now it was little more than a curious surprise as she ran forward toward the next warrior in the line. It had time to turn before the flames reached it, and the chemicals that sprayed out of the bottom of its skull caught fire. It, too, broke apart and sprayed gore across the grass.

Beyond that one were two more. Both tried to leap away, demonstrating startling strength in their legs. Cazia swept her spell to one side, catching the nearest one's lower body. It landed somewhere outside of her field of vision, but she didn't think it had survived. Her spell faded and the opening inside her, the one that had funneled so much magic, seemed to fall closed like a sleeping eye.

Cazia hadn't anticipated that her fire spell would be hot enough to burn away so much fog. She turned hard to the right just as something heavy struck the ground behind her—a spear? She didn't look back to see. There were more warriors back there, and she wanted to lead them farther into the valley away from her friends.

She changed direction several more times as she ran, but if she was dodging weapons, she couldn't hear them. The mists closed over her again and she kept moving, wondering about the odds of running into something even dangerous ahead of her.

She stumbled through a shallow stony stream, making a splash so loud that Mahz herself might have heard it. On the far bank, she stopped running and stamped among the tall grasses, mimicking as best she could the sound of her own running. It didn't seem likely that she could fool them with the same trick twice, but how smart could they be? They were bugs.

The translation stone was still lying at the bottom of her pocket, but when she touched it, she heard nothing. The warriors might have been talking to each other, but they were out of her range.

Then: "Hunt! Hunt!" She lifted her finger from the stone. It was the tapping noise. When she touched the stone again she heard "War! Hunt! Prey!"

Not exactly eloquent. She crouched low on the side of the tree; the stream was just barely in sight but the sounds were coming from downstream, to the east. She drew out one of her darts.

A whiff of that acrid scent returned, and on impulse, she touched the translation stone. Immediately, the complex scents became words.

"We will curl it for the lives it has taken."

"It crossed the stream and ran on."

"No! Hunt! Prey! It lay in wait for us once and may try once plus one."

"There it is!"

Cazia rolled to the side as a short, copper-tipped spear plunged into the tree trunk beside her.

They were flanking her the way any intelligent warriors would. She wished she knew how many there were, but the translation wasn't giving her different voices. *Fury guide me*, she thought, trying to keep her emotional detachment from stealing the urgency from her movements.

She took hold of her iron dart and, after a moment's consideration, took out three more. The spell she was planning was going to be just as strong as her flame spell—odd that her translation stone didn't feel boosted in a similar way—and she felt a connection to it that she hadn't experienced before. She recognized that she could alter the spell slightly to fire more than one dart, and she knew she would not miss.

Was this how the Gifts of the Evening People had been changed by scholars through the ages? Not just that they studied and thought about them, but that they Cursed themselves—destroyed their own personalities—to feel a closer connection to magic?

She'd consider that later, if she somehow managed to survive. Cazia started the mental and physical preparations for her spell; the space inside her began to open again, but it wasn't heat that was about to pass through her. It was kinetic force.

She leaped out from behind the tree, spell still unfinished, then dodged to the side as the warriors flung their weapons at her—smooth, dark stones this time. They threw them with great force, but they weren't close enough to hit her.

Then her spell finished, and a terrible *force* raced out of her. The iron darts shot from her hand, and each one struck a target full in the center of its body.

The darts did not plunge into the warriors like arrows so much as blast through them, blowing terrible holes in the far sides of their bodies. Cazia felt a slight pang of loss as her darts flew into the woods; iron was valuable.

Two more warriors charged at her from the other direction. These were the ones who had made the tapping noises while the others flanked her. One held a spear over its head, and in its other clawed hand, in place of a shield, it held a tall staff. Cazia dug into her quiver for an iron dart, but she knew it was too late already. They were too close for her to cast another spell, and what good was a dart—barely as long as a dagger—against a monster with a spear?

An arrow struck the side of the creature's head. It sounded like a cracking nut—which Cazia thought was extremely interesting—and the warrior collapsed into the grass.

Kinz ran down the bank across the stream, screaming, spear in hand. The insect creature turned to meet her, weapon ready.

"NO!" Cazia shouted. Kinz stopped on the near bank, her booted feet sinking into the mud. Ivy already had another arrow nocked and drawn. The insect warrior held staff and spear high. The warrior looked down the hill at Kinz, then at Ivy, then at Cazia. "I want this one to surrender."

She pointed her dart at the weapon in his hand, then pointed at the ground. She did it again with the staff.

The insect shifted its position and Cazia was sure it understood. Whether it would obey was another matter. It glanced around again uncertainly, and Cazia repeated her gesture.

It cast its staff away behind it, splashing into the water. The spear it threw in the other direction, directly into the trunk of a tree. Then it splayed its limbs wide.

"Inzu preserve us," Kinz said, wrinkling her nose. "Why does it stink like that?"

Cazia took the translation stone from her pocket. "We can only make this mistake once," the creature was saying to itself. "Once plus—" She didn't hear the rest, because she tossed the stone lightly at the creature's feet, then pointed at it with the dart.

After a moment's hesitation, the insect creature stooped and picked it up.

"Now you can understand what we say," Cazia said.

The creature collapsed in the grass as if dead.

Chapter Twenty-four

King Ellifer had made Tejohn a tyr by his own hand, an honor no one in history had ever received before, and on that day, he'd sworn to serve Peradain as well as the royal family. Whatever treachery Coml Finstel planned, Tejohn couldn't bring himself to withhold help from spears and bows of the empire—not to mention the citizens and servants they protected.

So, he sought out the commander at the barricade site to describe the grunts' ability to climb. Coml received the warning with gratitude, then offered Tejohn a few loaves from his storeroom.

The fort's supplies would soon be stretched thin, but Tejohn accepted. Coml's second fetched a handful of small, stale loaves—plain bread, not meatbread—and offered it to Arla as they came onto the dock.

The Wayward flowed out of the Southern Barrier as a tall, narrow freshwater waterfall. There was a clear pool at the base of the cliff, then a second smaller fall, and from there the Wayward began.

It had gotten its name because it flowed through mostly flat lands and had a habit of changing course every few years. What was fertile floodland one generation became a fishery the next. But no matter what changes it went through, it ended in the lowlands of Deep Stone Lake and it started alongside the mountain spur that stabbed down into Finstel lands.

Fort Caarilit stood on the eastern side of that waterway and, if the commander could be believed, protected the last bridge across the Wayward. If the grunts truly could not cross the it, Coml was the only human who could keep them out of the lands of Tejohn's forefathers. The thought made him despair.

At the docks, a grinning old man shuffled toward them. His greasy hair blew about in the wind and he moved with some difficulty, but he was clearly excited to see Tejohn.

"My Tyr Treygar!" he said with enthusiasm, shouting to be heard over the falling water. "It is my great pleasure to see you again after such a long time."

He bowed—no small feat with his hunched spine—and Tejohn took his elbow to urge him upright. "Stand tall, fellow. When did we last meet?"

"Toram Halmajil," the man said happily, a name Tejohn didn't recognize at all. "Folks nowadays try to say it was Banderfy Finstel who turned the tide of that battle, but no sir, I says to them. I was there. I saw Tejohn Treygar push right through the Bendertuk shield wall. Cut those boys up with their own knives, didn't you?"

Tejohn smiled at him. "I lost mine, and I had a better use for their little blades than they did."

"Indeed you did! So young and quick you were on that day! I was behind you when their square split apart, and I followed you into the flanks of Willim Bendertuk's own square. What a day! Too bad I couldn't join you at Pinch Hall itself," the old man looked wistful. "Them Bendertuks edged their shield with bronze in those days. On of them slammed down on my foot. Shattered so many bones, I couldn't sleep for the pain." His eyes went to the shield Tejohn carried. "Of course, everyone puts metal around their shields now."

"I took a Bendertuk shield with me to Pinch Hall," Tejohn said in a low voice.

"You did? I had no idea. Not with that lion of theirs, I hope."

"Song knows I scraped it clean," Tejohn said. "It was the ugliest shield I ever carried, but I loved that bronze rim."

"I wish I could have followed you," the old man said. "But there were others who needed the sleepstones more, and by the time I got my turn, it was all over. Of course, we were fighting mostly with Gerrit colors by then. The Finstels had already fought so many battles."

"Too many good men were lost."

"Song knows what they did." The old man held up a long pole, and Arla took it from him. "Heading down to Ussmajil?" he asked. This time, Tejohn was expecting it; the name meant *Splashtown* in the original Finshto. But the old fellow didn't wait for a response. "I didn't want to give you a little rowboat. They're too easy for an inexperienced man to tip, no offense, my tyr."

"None taken."

"Thank you kindly, my tyr. I have this little barge here. It's sized for one and a small cargo, that cargo being you and your packs. Just stay toward the center and keep near the western bank and it'll do you just fine."

Coml's second had already slipped away, heading back over the bridge toward the pink walls of Caarilit. The dockhand helped Tejohn and Arla position themselves properly, then he set their packs and Tejohn's shield in the center of the barge.

"Thank you, soldier," Tejohn said. "Tell me, what's your name?"

"Uls Ulstrik," the old fellow answered, touching his hand to his heart.

"Not the Ulstriks who grew apricot trees at the south end of Sunset Ridge?"

Uls's face became grave. "Them's cousins of mine, my Tyr. They was killed in the first days, along with so many others."

Tejohn felt a flush of shame. "Fire and Fury, what a fool I am to say such a thing." Of course the Ulstriks had been killed. Everyone at that end of the valley had been murdered, including Tejohn's own.

"My tyr," Uls answered, "if you're a fool, I hope we have ten thousand more fools just like you. The man who made Willim Bendertuk break his own spear across his knee will never seem a fool to me. Safe journey, my tyr. Keep to the west bank, and mind those Finstels."

Tejohn could not conceal his surprise. Was the fellow warning him against his own people? Those were dangerous words to say, and the fact that he'd risked them said much about his character.

Arla pushed them both away from the dock, and Uls turned and walked back beneath the bridge to his duties. Soon, he was too far away for Tejohn to see.

"My tyr," Arla said quietly, "How far do you think we should go?"

"Out of sight of the fort, I think. Coml might be arrogant, but he's not stupid enough to murder us where his soldiers might see."

Arla cleared her throat. "One thing I have learned, my tyr, is that it's never wise to bet on the intelligence of a tyr's relations. I'd be able to concentrate much better on keeping my balance if you would sling your shield on your back, just in case the commander back there gave his men Witt arrows."

That hadn't occurred to Tejohn. He slung the shield just as she suggested.

The Wayward turned eastward, then westward again. Tejohn thought the fort would be out of sight by now, but Arla did not think the cover along the banks was thick enough, and he had no choice but to trust her judgment.

After another wide turning, she pointed to a spot where the trees bent far over the water. "Over there, perhaps?"

"Western bank, scout. I'm not going to leave a barge—even one with a hole in the bottom—on the . . . What is that?"

He pointed ahead to a pale purple blur on the far eastern shore ahead of them. Arla immediately laid the pole across the barge and began to string her bow.

"Save your arrows," Tejohn said quietly, "unless it comes for us."

She nodded and finished stringing her bow. Tejohn quietly used the blunt end of his spear to keep them close to the western bank.

As they continued downstream, slowly, the lilac blur came into view. It was, just as he thought, a grunt. Not a dark blue one with a ridged back, this was one of the original invaders. He was startled once again by the size of it.

Water lapped noisily against the barge hull, catching the beast's attention. It looked up at them and roared, charging a step or two into the muddy river's edge.

Arla drew back her bow. "My tyr?"

"Not yet," Tejohn said.

The grunt splashed about in the water, then climbed back onto the shore. It couldn't float, Tejohn realized. It wanted to spread its curse, but it was not so single-minded that it could be tricked into drowning itself. It glanced around frantically, trying to find a way to get to them.

It raced downstream along the bank toward a large tree that leaned over the water, then leaped into the branches. The canopy trembled under its weight; it could not safely climb more than a few paces over the river.

The grunt stared at them, its expression intent and . . . Fire and Fury, it looked almost as though it was memorizing their faces.

It did not follow them around the next bend in the river.

"Put away your arrow," Tejohn said. "Are we far enough from the fort?"

The scout glanced behind her, then slid the arrow into the quiver at her hip. "Yes, my Tyr."

Tejohn poled them onto a marshy bank in the shelter of a pair of trees. They carried their supplies onto dry ground, then flipped the barge. It was heavier than Tejohn expected. He found a heavy rock with a narrow edge, broke through the bottom, then dropped stones into it until it sank.

For a brief, odd moment, Tejohn felt the urge to apologize to Uls. A month ago, he wouldn't have given a thought to the feelings of an old servant who was responsible for a little boat but didn't own it. "Scout, do you see a trail in the hills above?"

She scanned the rocky hill to the west. They would have to walk over or around it, but Tejohn wasn't farsighted enough to pick a path.

He relied on her, just as he relied on the fort stewards, the miners like Passlar Breakrock, the old soldiers with nowhere to turn like Uls Ulstrik. Tejohn had lived too long in the palace. He'd gotten used to living high up and, like the Italgas and landed tyrs, had stopped thinking about those he stood on.

"This way, my tyr." After a brief but difficult climb, they came upon a deer path and followed it along the rim of the spur.

Shortly before midmorning, Arla laid a hand on Tejohn's cuirass and bade him crouch behind a gray mass of bare blackberry vines. "They are there, my tyr."

She pointed out toward the Wayward. The river had angled eastward around a rocky promontory, and although Tejohn could not see what she was pointing at, he knew what she'd spotted: Coml's ambush.

It was a relief to know they'd avoided it, and he squelched the urge to come at them from behind. His old outrage—the familiar, wound-up urge to fight and then fight some more—was not as overwhelming as it had been when he was young. Arla continued up the hillside and he followed her.

Arla found a switchback trail that led to the top of the spur. Tejohn had never seen these lands before—they were all stony slopes and stands of narrow trees, but no people. They stopped for a meal, then he followed her westward. Always westward.

In late afternoon, Arla spotted a log cabin. "It looks abandoned," she said before Tejohn could even see it. As they came close, he noted the door had been broken in.

No one answered his hails. He held his shield in front of him and kept his hand on his sword as he stepped through the door, calling out more quietly and asking if someone inside needed his help.

The wind shifted as he entered the darkened room, and the smell of dead bodies washed over him.

"Fire and Fury," Arla said.

They had been a family. A man about Reglis's age, with thick arms and a heavy beard, lay by the door, his belly slit open. Farther inside lay the corpse of a woman of the same age, her stomach pierced by spears. Their two dead children lay behind her.

They had been older than Tejohn's lost child, but they still looked so small.

"This wasn't grunts," Arla said bitterly. "Could Witt spears have come so far west? Or Bendertuks so far east?"

"This family was killed by their neighbors," Tejohn said. "He came to the door with his hands empty. See? There's a Gerrit shield hanging on the wall."

"They killed him because he's a Gerrit?"

"A woodsman, I'd guess, and trapper, too. So many Finstel soldiers died a generation ago that people from other lands flooded in. They took over farms and fisheries—not the finest or most fertile, but empty properties anyway. And there was resentment. Great Way, it should not have come to this. Not to murdered children."

Arla's tone was flat. "The Finstels are purging outsiders."

"Even the little ones. This is no place for a Grimfield with a Chin-Chinro accent," Tejohn said. "We'll have to part sooner than I'd planned."

The woodsman had a fine bronze-bladed shovel hanging on the wall, so he and Arla spent the rest of the day digging a grave. Family graves were a tradition in Gerrit lands, so they dug wide and deep. They used up the rest of the daylight excavating the stony earth, arranging the bodies inside, then covering them over. Tejohn laid out the shield as a marker.

More than once, they had to stop and walk away from the work. When it was finished, they washed their hands in a bucket behind the cabin, then ate without pleasure. They lay on the ground beneath a starry sky, and Arla told Tejohn the story of how she saw her family murdered. When she was done, Tejohn shared his tale with her. It was an awful kind of communion, but it was what they had and they clung to it.

They slept in the woods some distance from the house. In the morning, Tejohn set his weapons on the cabin floor. It was hard to give up his shield and especially that oversized sword, but a fighting man had to know when to empty his hands.

"My tyr, are you sure you want us to part? You . . . "

"I can not see what is coming," Tejohn finished for her. "You're right. But I have managed before we met and will do so again. Besides, once Coml's fleet squad reports that we did not pass them on the river, Finstel spears will be hunting for the pair of us. Better to split up. Hike this spur back into the mountains. You certainly can't stay here with that accent."

"And you, my tyr?"

Tejohn shrugged off his cuirass, then unbuckled his greaves. "I was a farmer who lost everything, once. I can be that again."

"So, you're still going to Splashtown?"

"Lar Italga charged me with a mission, but I've decided to go to Ussmajil instead. Have you noticed that the locals have stopped using Peradaini names? The Finstels have rescued someone from the capital, and they have flying carts. I must speak with the former and steal the latter, and I don't think a landless tyr will be welcome in the holdfast. Still, somehow I must get to Tempest Pass. The king was sure that the key to defeating the grunts would be found there, and I intend to complete the task he set me. I suspect it is the only way the people of Kal-Maddum will survive."

Tejohn made sure Arla took the bulk of their provisions. He had only ten days' walk ahead of him, while she might be living in the wild for a long time.

He also threw aside his padded undershirt—it was too obviously a soldier's garment. In the cabin, he found a linen vest hanging on a hook. It was stained with mud and sweat but it would do. He kept his wooden-handled knife on his belt, and slipped the blue translation stone Cazia Freewell had made for him and Lar's ring into the torn lining of his boot.

He would have to get rid of both of them. Ideally, he should hide them. It was lucky that Coml's men had only searched his person and not his belongings. Either of those two items would be worth his life.

He stood before Arla. "How do I look?"

"Like a tyr. You stand like a proud man." He let his shoulders slump forward and shifted himself off balance. "Better, my Tyr."

He nodded. "You shouldn't call me that any more."

She smiled. "Then I will say, Tejohn Treygar, that it has been an honor to fight beside you."

They clasped hands. "And you, too. Great Way willing, we will meet again in peaceful times."

"Perhaps one day I will get a chance to try one of your wife's little red cakes." She shrugged her pack onto her shoulders, then started uphill toward the trees and mountains. It took very little time for her to pass out of his sight.

He found an old path that led across the spur to the west. He had no clear notion where it led, but he hoped it was the route the dead woodsman had used to take his cuttings to town.

After a short time, he came to a sharp bend in the path and paused. The trees and thickets here gave him heavy cover, and for the first time in days, he felt secure from prying eyes. It was time to get rid of the ring and translation stone. The idea that they were dangerous to carry came upon him like throwing open shutters to let the daylight in.

He stepped off the path, climbed through the thicket onto a flat, stony meadow. He pried up a squarish rock, laid the ring and translation gem beneath it, then set it back into place. With his knife, he notched the nearest tree. On his way back to the path, he marked another tree.

If Tejohn let himself be killed, the ring would likely never be found. The king would never be cured. The empire . . .

It was too much. The weight of so many secrets bore down on him. Not so long ago, he had stood on the promenade and spoken with the queen of the empire. Today, he was furtively hiding all evidence of that high state. As he returned to the path, he knew he did not walk the path like a proud man.

The town at the bottom of the spur was surrounded by a high wooden wall, and the gate was shut. Tejohn walked around it, showing his empty hands to the watchful men and women atop the wall.

In the flatlands, he came upon others making the same trip. Word about the grunts had spread, driving some to the road and others to barricade their homes. The one thing Tejohn had learned was that no matter what the danger—fire, approaching armies, anything—there were always some too stubborn to leave their land.

Many fellow refugees pulled wagons or drove okshim—one young couple had four yoked together, which probably made them the wealthiest commoners in ten days' march. It was slow going, but Tejohn kept his patience and dawdled with them. As he hoped, he was invited to camp with them as night fell.

They were all strangers to each other, and each briefly told their stories. The wealthy young couple owned a mine and a farm. The old woman with the crooked back caught and sold fish by the river. Others were wheelwrights, blacksmiths, or ferry folk. Tejohn told them he had been dismissed from the farm where he worked, and one or two others smirked in response; presumably, they assumed he was a runaway servant. He bared his wrists so they could see he had no tattoos there, but no one seemed interested.

Then they began trading rumors. This was what he'd lingered for, and they didn't disappoint. Among the dubious news they shared: The Redmudds had slain their servants and elderly to make their supplies stretch. Tyr Holvos had been so terrified of the grunts that he fled the fall of Rivershelf by boat. *On the sea.* There were many gasps at this news, and wise nods when the fisherwoman said eels dragged the ship under before they'd lost sight of the city.

The family of ferry folk considered themselves the best informed, and they shared gossip the way a tyr's wife might throw food to starving children. At the same time Peradain fell, the waters of the Bescos had erupted and sea giants strode up the Espileth, laying waste to Simblinton, they said gravely, as though they'd seen it happen themselves. After destroying the entire Simblin clan, the giants had collapsed the passes and returned to the deep.

The general consensus among the crowd was that everything had been planned, even though Tejohn thought the story sounded as authentic as a child's ghost story. The attacks were a coordinated assault against the entire empire at the command of either the sea giants, Durdric Holy Sons, Indregai warlords, or unnamed tyrs within the empire itself, depending on the lateness of the hour.

But they nearly came to blows over the description of the grunts themselves. The ferry folk claimed they were pink and white, with horns like goats. Others claimed they were dark blue and red, and the argument got heated, with the ferryman's sons waving their fists at the wealthy young couple's chief servant. Tejohn broke through the argument by saying he'd seen two kinds of grunts, then described them.

They pressed him hard with questions, and he answered very slowly. Several of the other campers wanted to hear his news more than once, and he told it, haltingly, in the same way each time. It didn't take long for them to tire of him, and they settled in to sleep.

It was troubling to hear that sea giants were moving in the west, even if it came from someone as untrustworthy as those ferry folk. Could the grunts be part of a coordinated attack against the empire? Would the sea giants range far enough to the north to impede his progress to Tempest Pass?

On the twelfth day of their journey, they came into sight of Ussmajil itself. The outermost parts of the city were surrounded by barricades so new, some of the logs still had green leaves attached. Tejohn expected to see refugees camping outside the city—there were always a few—but the flats were empty. Were they going to be turned away?

The wealthy young couple were greeted by three women wearing fine, clean linen and attended by twenty servants. They, their animals, and their servants were ushered away toward the central holdfast. The wheelwright removed a strip of red cloth from inside his robe, tied it over his biceps and, carefully not looking at anyone else in the crowd, went directly to the market square.

None of the other refugees had someone to meet them or a red cloth to tie to their upper arm. They were herded at spear point toward a long, muddy pit. Spears stood guard at the near end and, Tejohn assumed, at the far end as well. The sides of the pit were braced with more logs, and bored archers stood along the top.

"Where are you taking us?" the ferryman demanded, and received a rap from the edge of a shield to silence him.

They passed below a line of heads mounted on spears. All had rotten until they were barely recognizable as human.

A dozen refugees were penned like sheep while the blacksmith's family was brought before a bored-looking official seated at a long wooden table.

Beside him stood an overweight soldier with a tall red comb. Behind both of them stood another dozen spears.

Tejohn hung back beside the fisherwoman. "What's happening?" he asked in a low voice. "I can't see that far."

Her answer was so quiet, he almost couldn't hear it. "They're charging us for admission to the city." She shuffled her feet, glancing back toward the wooden gate as though she wanted to get back onto the road, but she didn't have the courage to leave the pen. "I don't have more than a few copper ins."

It had been a while since Tejohn had reason to think about money. It was one of the privileges of his place in the palace—he thought for the first time about the strongbox in his rooms back in the Morning City. It was heavy with silver bolds and even a few gold pinches. Right now he wasn't carrying so much as a tin speck.

The blacksmith's family was led to a second pen, their shoulders slumped. "They even took his tools," the fisherwoman said.

That was bad and they all knew it. The ferry folk were brought forward next, and the father tried to bluster through the interview, talking in a loud voice about the important news he brought from the south and how he was certain his tyrship's good fighting men would want to hear it. But when it came time to open his purse to the officials, he demanded they tell him the fee first.

For his trouble, one of the good fighting men he'd been flattering rammed a spear into his guts. While his family knelt in the mud and wailed, his body was stripped and thrown into a cart. There were no other corpses in there, but the hour was early.

The other family members—wife, sons, daughters, grandmothers—had everything of value taken from them, then they were penned with the smith. Tejohn shut his eyes and prayed that The Great Way would look after his own family and allow them to stay on the path.

Just before she was taken away, the fisherwoman took Tejohn's hand and pressed a single coin into it. "Better to have something for them to take, I think, since they're going to take everything."

It would have been an insult to refuse. "Song will remember," Tejohn said.

"The Little Spinner never slows," she said as she was led away. It was a saying he'd heard often from farm folk when he was young, but had never heard in the palace. *Everything changes.*

When it was his turn, he gave his name as Ondel Ulstrik, a farmhand from just downslope of the spur. He told them the farmers were holed up on their property and had no supplies to spare for hired men.

The official told him weapons were not permitted inside the city and took his knife. They demanded an accounting of his personal property and rolled their eyes when he held out the copper ins. Tejohn could feel the soldiers looking him over; he made sure to slump his shoulders and keep his expression slack.

"Entrance to the city will cost you two ins," the official said with a bored expression. "Those boots will cover the balance."

His boots were worth more than an ins, but he took them off without a fuss and gave them over.

The mud was cold against his bare feet. He joined the others in the second pen. No one could speak over the wailing of the ferry family—the grandmother's pleas that they be allowed to bury the man's body were ignored.

As they were led up the ramp at the far end of the pit, a pair of soldiers pressed tiny loaves of bread into their hands. They were insistent that everyone take one because Tyr Finstel wanted no starvation within his walls. Tejohn reluctantly accepted.

When they came out of the pit into a small building, they were told there was a charge of six specks for the bread. The ferryman's widow tried to pay with a silver bold she'd hidden on her person, but she was beaten and given six years of servitude for Concealing Assets.

No one else had a single speck to offer, let alone six. All of them, Tejohn included, were tattooed and sentenced to a year of servitude in the name King Shunzik Finstel, ruler of Ussmajil.

Chapter Twenty-five

"It is there, ape. Just down in that ravine."

Chik, the insect warrior they had captured, had taken to calling them *apes*. In his opinion, Cazia, Ivy, and Kinz were the ugliest creatures he'd ever seen, and he occasionally insisted that every word of their conversation was a trick being played on him by one of his people's many enemies. He was convinced the translation stone simulated their conversation, because only insect brains were complex enough to understand abstract concepts.

Kinz was so irritated by these frequent pronouncements she sometimes seemed on the verge of violence. Ivy treated the creature like one of her subjects, as if it needed nothing more than tolerant instruction.

Cazia was beyond those sorts of emotions. She felt nothing more than an intense curiosity about the creature—especially the way the small frills at the base of its skull vented one odor after another, which her blue jewel dutifully translated into a long string of boasts about himself, his queen, and the mighty empire of the Tilkilit people.

They had spent most of the day and part of the night creeping through a fog-shrouded forest with Chik guiding the way. Kinz suspected the creature was leading them in circles, but Ivy pointed out that many of the trees had a stringy red moss on the northern side. It would have made sense for Chik to take them in circles until they found another one of their patrols, but it was clear they were traveling in a straight line.

Whether he was leading them where they wanted to go was a different question. Chik claimed to be taking them to the Door in the Mountain. According to him, the eagles had come through this door, and so had he.

"This is where our scout patrols, the swiftest and most worthy, chosen by Queen Sheshoorakolm herself, Ruler of the Depths of Glory and Stone of Might, She who birthed a billion warriors, the All-Blind, All-Knowing Mother of the Tilkilit people, first made entry into this land."

He gestured toward a place where the grass gave way to scraggly bushes and the ground rose steeply into bare, stony ridges. A warm wind blew from between two of them, thinning the fog to nothing. They could not advance without coming out of the cover of the trees.

Chik kept talking. "Seventy-second into this land, Chik Strong Eyes, Bearer of Lance and Mace, Master of Secret Ways—"

"Enough," Cazia said. She was holding the blue stone and, although Chik was unable to understand her, he recognized her tone. He clicked his claws twice to indicate his contempt, then fell silent.

"He never shuts up, does he?" Kinz asked. She had held the stone for a few minutes while Cazia had taken and discarded Chik's weapons, a copper-bladed spear, a pouch of smooth, dark stones without a sling, and a flanged club worn where a human might wear a dagger. It was the only time Kinz had listened to him, and she'd refused to take the stone since.

"I think I understand," Cazia said. When did her voice get so flat? "They talk in smells, and all this information is released in a single stink. Each odor is complicated by a dozen substances, see? But for us, each piece of information has to be turned into a word and strung out in long phrases. That's why he's insulted that we shorten his name, because it's not actually shorter to him, just simplified."

"Give him the stone," Ivy said. "I will explain this to him."

"No, do not," Kinz said. "It will just give him another opportunity to tell us how superior he is."

Kinz, who had signed on to this mission as a servant, was now giving orders. It would have bothered Cazia once.

She picked up the blue stone again. In her odd state, the warrior's words seemed to echo in her head. Had she used it for an hour yet? The other girls knew to warn her if she started talking gibberish, but what if the effect came on suddenly? Would going hollow increase the danger or reduce it? Or was this another of Doctor Twofin's scare stories? So many interesting questions.

A shadow passed over the ravine floor. A raptor. Cazia and the others were well hidden among the trees, but they retreated to a dense stand anyway.

She set the stone down beside Chik; they'd already learned it wouldn't work if both of them held it at the same time. The creature picked it up with its clumsy claws, and Cazia spoke. "No names, understand? Just tell us how long you have been here and where you come from."

He set it down and she picked it up. "My people have been here for two hundred plus sixteen plus three days, although I suspect you apes will not be able to understand a number of such complexity. We fight, always, without reinforcements, and are unable to find deeper soil. Our empire—which has a name that would boggle your mammalian brains—is far to the south of here, where the weather is warmer and the soil, grass, and trees are orange. A warrior could march eastward and return years later from the west, without ever setting foot outside our empire."

Cazia repeated that and Ivy became convinced Chik came from a globe-spanning continent beyond the sea. Cazia thought it was more likely that he was lying to make himself seem important, and Kinz refused to accept that the world could be round.

It was midday. Cazia decided they shouldn't risk the translation stone any more. Kinz and Ivy slipped out of the grove to find a squirrel or something to eat, and Cazia tried to create a basic sign language with their prisoner, just as Ivy's people had with the serpents, but he had no interest in that at all.

Chik ate almost continually, taking tiny portions of crusty stuff from a pouch at its shoulder. Kinz had initially demanded he turn his rations over to them, but he warned them he could only speak if he had access to his food, and they relented.

The girls took turns standing guard over him through the night. Cazia would have liked some rope to tie his legs with, but they hadn't brought any. Chik, although smaller than Ivy, was stronger than any of them; woven grasses wouldn't do the trick.

In the middle of the night, Cazia woke to voices. Ivy was explaining the history of her bow—that it had been made for her by her mother as per family tradition. They were just shapes in the darkness, sitting as far from each other as visibility of the thinned-out fog allowed.

"What's going on?" Cazia interrupted.

"Chik doesn't understand where my bow came from," Ivy answered. "I keep telling him that the women in my family have been making them for generations, but he keeps asking who taught us."

"You're wasting your breath," Cazia said. "He's asking what non-human creature taught you. He doesn't believe *apes* are smart enough to create them, and you're never going to get past that contempt."

Chik shifted his position slightly, and Cazia knew what he was going to do before he did it. The blue jewel landed beside her in the wet dirt, and it only took a few moments for her to find it and pick it up.

"How did you apes get into this valley?" Chik asked, once again posing the question they'd agreed to never answer. "You have no wings. You have no burrowing tools. Mighty serpents make the water impassable. You certainly could not climb over the mountains with the smooth cliffs and Great Terror above." The *Great Terror* were the huge eagles.

The old Cazia would have said the Great Terror regularly let her people ride on their backs in exchange for pretty shells or something equally snide, but she'd burned that part of herself away. So instead, she tossed the jewel to him and asked him a question in return. "How did your people come to the Door in the Mountain and this valley?"

He returned the jewel and answered, "We were brought here by the Great Way."

Cazia couldn't sleep for the rest of the night.

In the dark, tears flowed down her cheeks for no reason she could understand, and they stopped for no reason, too. The alien sorrow and longing ebbed and flowed; she could do nothing but ride it out and wonder what it all meant.

Lying at the edge of the fog, Cazia saw dawn light the tops of the peaks ahead, and she woke them all. At first, Chik refused to leave the cover of the trees, but the point of Kinz's spear drove him forward. They quickly realized that he was extremely nearsighted; once they assured him there were no Great Terror nearby, he ran with them.

They found scrub and a few scattered trees in the ravines between the ridges, and hurried from one piece of cover to the next. Chik could cover ground quickly but had little stamina, so they rested often. Whenever the path reached a fork, the warrior would point one direction or another, sometimes leading them over loose rockfalls, sometimes through ravines so steep they were practically tunnels.

Cazia remembered the way the other warriors had leaped when she fought them. He could have escaped from them at any time. Why didn't he?

"Who has the jewel?" Ivy asked. They had taken shelter beneath a rocky overhang while Chik ate and rested for another sprint.

"I do," Cazia answered.

"Okay. Are we sure he is not trying to melg us?" Ivy became annoyed at the look they gave her. "Melg," she insisted. "Kinz is the one who thought of it first. Could he be trying to melg us?"

Kinz sighed. "What language are you speaking?"

"Peradaini," Ivy snapped. "And I speak it very well, thank you."

Cazia put her hand on Kinz's. "It's not her fault. Ivy, you've been talking to him too much. You're saying *melg* when you mean *trick*." Ivy's hands went to her mouth and throat. "It'll go away in a few days, if you get enough sleep. But no more holding the stone for a while."

She nodded, her lips pressed together.

"I still think he is trying to melg us," Kinz said.

Cazia didn't laugh. "I don't think he's clever enough for trickery. He hasn't even tried to escape. As arrogant and obnoxious as he is, he seems to do whatever he's told out of habit."

Chik signaled and they rounded a long rockfall and came to another, shallower overhang. Chik crouched low inside it. Still, it was not much cover, and Cazia scanned the high places all around them. They'd come very close to the base of the northern mountain range—if this wasn't the place where the ranges met, it had to be a short distance behind them. The ravine widened here, opening up into a broad slope of loose rock. She couldn't see any Great Terrors flying nearby, but the rocks were nearly the same color as their feathers. If one was perched above—

"By Inzu," Kinz said. "Have I gone wind-mad, or is that the hole in the world?"

Cazia turned toward them. Kinz, Ivy, and Chik were all looking down the rocky slope toward a collapsed spot at the base of the mountainside. She followed their gaze.

A disk of light hovered near the bottom of the rocky slope, and it was identical to the one she'd seen in the palace during the Festival.

Fury's spark, still burning within her, seemed to grow warm. She expected to see The Blessing come charging through the disk at any moment, but they didn't. It just floated there in the air, unmoving.

Tears ran down her cheeks again, but the longing within her felt different somehow. Not that it mattered.

Chik was making a terrible smell, and Kinz caught Cazia's wrist even before she realized she was reaching for her translation stone. "We can not have two of you speaking gibberish. I have hardly talked to him at all, so it is my turn." She dug the stone out of Cazia's pocket and knelt beside Chik.

The stink washed over them all. "He says that is the Door in the Mountain," Kinz told them. "He said the other side appeared inside the old storeroom one day, a magic door to new lands. His unit came through and marched up this very slope. The door stayed open for only nine days plus one—hmph. Ten days. Why can he not just say 'ten'?"

Ten days. The Festival lasted ten days because the portal in Peradain lasted that long.

"He says it changes every ten days. Now the hot dry wind blows from it.

Before, there was a poisonous smoke. Before that, snow. Sometimes creatures will come through and die choking, as though the air is poison. There is the puddle at the bottom of the hill from one such—it did not rot, just turned into the fluid that will not evaporate."

Cazia saw a little pool at the base of the slope, glinting black in the reflected light.

"Once, soon after he arrived, he says the jet of fresh water shot through. He said it was cold as glaciers and completely . . . I don't know that word. Without life. Ten days later, the water began to flow back through the hole. Many of his brothers were swept away.

"It changes constantly. Chik's people have been trapped in the valley since they arrived, and they check every ten days to see if the other side of the Door once again opens in their home. Once, they saw a landscape of wriggling worms. Once, they saw a storm of fire and lightning. Once, they could not even look through the opening, because a great eye on a stalk from a creature much too large to fit through the Door had come to peer at them.

"Then, forty days ago, the Great Terror emerged. They hunt his people, destroying their . . . I do not know that word. Riding beasts. They would drop stones or fallen trees from the sky and devour the corpses of the Bearers and Masters."

While all this about the Great Terror was important to Chik, Cazia thought it was a waste of time. "Kinz, stop him so we can ask him the question."

Kinz clicked her tongue to get Chik's attention. Then she gave him the stone.

Cazia said, "Have you seen mammals come through? They would have been larger than us, with purple fur. Have you heard of a race of peace-loving mammals called 'the Evening People'? "

Chik tried to hand the stone back to Cazia, but Kinz intercepted it. "No, he hasn't," she said. "He says the Tilkilit would have defeated enemies like those easily."

Cazia didn't know what to think. This opening obviously looked like the one in Peradain, and it connected his land to another land far away for ten days at a time, but the one in Peradain only appeared for ten days, then vanished. This one persisted, changing from place to place.

The Tilkilit had not come through at the urging of a third party, which is what would have happened if they were part of an organized attack on Kal-Maddum. But, of course, they had been here for months; it was the Great Terror who had come through at the same time as The Blessing.

But was there a connection between them? It seemed increasingly like a terrible coincidence.

She looked back at the glowing disk, and the longing in her suddenly surged. *That* was what she wanted . . . no, what the magic in her wanted. The emptiness inside her ached for that portal and she knew that, once she entered it, there would never be another tear, not for her. No more sorrow. No more longing.

"We have our answers, do we not?" Ivy said. "We wanted to discover where the giant birds came from and whether they were connected to The Blessing. I think it is pretty clear the answers are 'there' and 'no.'"

"I have to enter the Door." Cazia was as shocked to hear herself say it as the other two were to hear it. "Don't say anything right away. Just listen. Kinz is correct about one thing: the magic I've done has changed me. I have been destroyed and there's no cure."

Ivy gaped at her. "I do not understand."

"To get here, I broke every rule about magic there is. I ignored my teacher's first lesson, and to be honest, I did it on purpose, just because I hate to be told something is not allowed. But that old me is dead. I'm hollow. I'm Cursed." Cazia looked frankly at Ivy. "I can't even love anyone anymore, not even you." Ivy began to cry, and Cazia felt no response other than a mild satisfaction that she had correctly predicted the girl's response. "That part of me has been taken over by emptiness, and that emptiness is calling out to that Door the way the smell of roasting meat calls to a starving child. I'm just not strong enough to resist, even if I wanted to."

"We will make you resist," Kinz said.

"You're a servant," Cazia told her. "Mind your place."

Ivy spoke up. "I'm a princess—"

"Not my princess."

"And soon I will be a queen, wife to your own cousin—"

"None of that means anything to me now."

"Cazia, you can not do this! You came here to find answers, and you must bring them back to the outside world."

"You can bring the answers back. I have new questions to pursue."

Kinz shook her head. "You blocked the passage, remember?"

Cazia glanced down the slope at the disk. How could she explain this feeling in a way they would understand? It was a sacred urge, as though her new, ruined self had rediscovered its temple.

Maybe, Cazia thought, if she stepped through the Door in the Mountain, she would travel the Great Way and emerge from the other side as herself. Maybe she could leave her Curse inside.

At the far end of the rocky slope, a neat line of reddish-black figures marched down the slope. Cazia's hand went to her quiver and drew out an iron dart even before she recognized them as more of the Tilkilit. They fanned out in neat order, marching down the hill toward the disk, their weapons and attention directed toward the skies for the most part.

Forty days, Chik had said. The Door in the Mountain changed every ten days, so of course the Tilkilit had come to check it today.

If there had ever been a moment when Cazia could have bolted from their hiding place and reached the disk before the warriors did, that moment was already gone. She knew how strong they were, had seen them jump, and she had no illusions that her magic could handle so many, even if she'd had fog to conceal herself, which she didn't.

Better to wait. They would check the portal and retreat, probably. She could return to her temple then.

They all heard a loud, sharp tap—a Tilkilit commander giving orders, Cazia assumed—and she noticed Chik lean forward to grab a wedge-shaped rock in one clawed hand. Cazia grabbed Kinz's arm and pulled her out of the away just as Chik swung for her head.

Cazia stabbed the dart into his chest just below his arm. Her hand slipped at the impact—the weapon had no handle or hilt—but the point broke through Chik's shell and plunged deep into his flesh anyway.

Fury give me the urgency I need. Chik fell backward, his hard shell scraping along the metal dart, and a terrible plume of stink billowing out of him. Slime coated Cazia's fingers, but it didn't bother her. She threw herself onto the warrior, raising the dart for a killing stroke, when Chik snapped his jaws together twice, quickly.

The sound echoed against the cavern walls. Cazia plunged the dart into Chik's head, missing his eye but breaking through his "skull." He died instantly.

She had felt so proud when she'd killed The Blessing and she'd felt such grief after. Now she had killed a warrior up close, someone she'd spoken with, and the only effect she felt was the urge to kill again.

"He said, *Passage,*" Kinz whispered. She was still holding the blue stone. Cazia took it from her and began to creep backward toward the ravine. The warriors had turned toward their general direction, but they didn't seem to be facing them directly. Cazia knew she hadn't killed Chik quickly enough, but if the other warriors' vision was as bad as his—

She heard a short series of clicks that her jewel translated as "War! Hunt! Prey!" and the warriors at the front of the column leaped toward them.

CHAPTER TWENTY-SIX

THERE WAS NO TIME FOR CREEPING, HIDING, OR CASTING A SPELL. Cazia hissed, "Come!" and the three girls bolted out of cover and ran back up the ravine.

"They are gaining!" Ivy shouted, glancing behind her.

"Do not look back!" Kinz shouted.

"Be quiet!" Cazia snapped. Had they forgotten the Tilkilit were practically blind? They should be able to lose them in the twisted ravines.

"I remember the way," Kinz said, more quietly this time. She and Ivy took the lead, despite the fact that they were carrying weapons. Their fear of being caught urged them on, almost leaving Cazia behind.

She didn't have their survival instinct. She wasn't afraid or angry. Given a choice, she would have circled around to the portal—oh, how the empty space inside her longed for it—but that would have been suicide. She still had a chance to enter the Door in the Mountain, but first she would have to survive.

All they needed to do was put some distance between themselves and the warriors. Chik's people could sprint at astonishing speeds and could leap into a third-story window, but they had no endurance.

Luckily, the distance between the girls and the warriors had been great enough that they couldn't immediately overtake their "prey." Cazia's old self would have hated that word, but her new one found it interesting. The insides of Chik's shell had been so unappetizing; if she found a way to make a soup out of him or roasted him inside his shell, would he have become the prey?

She suddenly remembered Doctor Whitestalk back at the tower, cutting open songbirds and tasting them. Cazia wasn't there yet. Even if she couldn't feel kindness or concern any more, at least she knew that she should fake it.

"Pace yourselves," she said. "The bugs are sprinters, remember? We can keep ahead of them as long as we don't exhaust ourselves."

They all slowed a bit, for which Cazia was grateful. Better to save their energy in case they stumbled upon more warriors or, worse, one of the so-called "riding beasts."

Passage, Chik had said. For a few moments, she couldn't imagine what he'd meant. He had one warning to shout to his people, and—

Of course! Passage out of the valley. The Tilkilit were trapped here with the Great Terror, unable to move into the larger continent. They were looking for *deeper soil*, which was probably a euphemism for a decent latrine.

Kinz took a left turn, which seemed wrong to Cazia, but this wasn't the time to argue. They ran through a deep, crooked ravine Cazia didn't recognize. Tapping echoed all around them, but it was impossible to tell if it was coming from in front or behind. Then, without warning, the sound came from directly above.

Five Tilkilit warriors had crested the ridge above and a little behind them. The warriors were too high to leap all the way to the bottom of the ravine, but they bounded down the slope, spears in hand.

Ivy nocked an arrow. Kinz shuffled back with her spear, holding it upright. Cazia had already drawn five iron darts from her quiver and started her spell. The Tilkilit were coming upon them so quickly, she might not have time to get the spell off, but Great Way, it felt so right to be doing magic again.

Ivy loosed an arrow just as one of the warriors stepped off the side of the hill. The shot took it low on its torso, punching through the front of its shell and poking out the back. The creature collapsed on the hillside and struck hard against the stones. The distant, analytical part of Cazia's mind thought Ivy's arrow might not have killed it, but that impact surely had.

Then her spell finished and her five darts flew from her hands. Each punched through a warrior's torso with tremendous force, including the one Ivy had already felled. The magic felt so natural, she thought she could have shot every dart in her quiver at once without missing. She could never have done that before she Cursed herself. How envious Lar would be to see her now.

There was another series of taps from the top of the ravine. A warrior at the crest of the hill was sending a complex message to the others, but Cazia didn't bother reaching for her stone to translate it. Whatever the warrior was saying, her tactic would be the same: run.

Ivy shot an arrow at him, but at this distance, whether it hit or not was doubtful. They turned and ran along the ravine. Within a few moments, stones began to rain down from above. Cazia glanced back and saw two creatures taking stones from the pouches at their side—stones without slings, she suddenly remembered—and throwing them.

Great Way, they hit the ground around her with such force. The Tilkilit were strong enough that they didn't have to bother with slings. Cazia began to run in an uneven pattern, hopping onto one side of the ravine or the other, running down the center at varied paces. The warriors might still get lucky, but—

Kinz cried out in sudden pain, then dropped the spear and stumbled. Ivy called out Cazia's name, and they could both see immediately how she'd been injured. A stone had struck high on her back where the pack was nothing more than two layers of thin leather. Her right arm dangled uselessly.

The smart thing would have been to leave her behind. She was a liability now—actually, how many Tilkilit had she managed to kill on her own? None, as far as Cazia knew. Yes, it was nice to have someone to collect firewood, but that seemed to be all she was good for. There was no reason to die for a servant.

But Ivy ducked under Kinz's good arm and supported her. Cazia sighed. What did any of this matter, anyway? The only thing that mattered—

A shadow swept over them with the speed of a blinking eye, and sudden frantic tapping echoed through the canyons. The rain of stones stopped immediately. The Great Terror had found them. Cazia looked up but couldn't see anything except clouds and stone. Where—

Another raptor passed over them with the speed of an arrow in flight. If one of them flew the length of the ravine at that speed toward them, she would never have time to cast a spell.

She ran back and picked up Kinz's spear. It was her spear, really, but Kinz had been the one who carried it, so—She shook those thoughts off. Focus on survival. Even if she didn't have time to cast a spell, she could hold a spear upright.

Ivy didn't have the strength to hold Kinz upright for long, but the servant quickly found her feet and jogged along the bottom of the ravine.

At the next juncture, they stumbled into a widened place in the canyon floor with three paths to choose from.

"By Inzu," Kinz said, "I made us lost."

Liability. "We need to keep heading southeast," Cazia said. "Narrow ravines would be best."

"That one, then," Ivy said. "How fast can you move across that open ground?"

"Watch me." She ran across the stony ground with her left hand holding her right arm against her torso.

Cazia ran close behind the other two, looking up often to check the sky. There were birds above them, circling lazily, but the girls had not yet drawn their attention. Kinz gasped and groaned with every step, and when they reached the far side of the open area, she collapsed in the shadow of a huge overhanging boulder.

"We must get this off you." Ivy eased the backpack off Kinz's injured shoulder but it was too heavy for her to lift. Cazia didn't need to be asked. She slung it on. They couldn't leave their food or bedrolls behind, after all. It didn't seem terribly heavy, but maybe that was because they were running low on everything.

Now that Cazia had the food, it was time to decide when she would abandon Ivy and Kinz to strike out on her own. She had fourteen darts left in her quiver. She'd lost the five she shot in the ravine and one from several days before that Kinz had not been able to find. As a rough estimate, she'd seen forty warriors by the portal, with who knows how many more still behind the ridge.

Ivy's quiver held eight arrows. Not enough. Not enough.

Kinz pulled her shirt all the way up to her neck. There was a white circle over her shoulder blade, with a growing red rim around it.

"Oh, Kinz," Ivy said, dismay clear in her voice.

Sweat ran down Kinz's face. "I think I need to make the sling."

For once, Ivy was at a loss. "Finally," Cazia said, drawing her knife. "Something your uncles didn't teach you." No one had taught Cazia, either, but she'd seen it done. She plunged her knife into the hem of her skirt and cut off a long strip of cotton fabric. She wrapped it around Kinz's ribs, binding her upper arm to her side. Then she looped it around the older girl's wrist and, pulling it tight, tied it off at the back of her neck.

Cazia felt tears on her cheeks again. The others seemed to mistake it for sympathy or empathy, but the sorrow had nothing to do with her.

Shadows swooped over them, heading north and west. They had lingered too long. There was more tapping, and she took the blue stone from her pocket again. "Wizard! Capture!" were the words they said over and—

A Tilkilit warrior fell hard onto the stony ground just behind them. The sound startled them all, and as they crouched in the shadow of the boulder above, a raptor swooped down on it.

It was facing away, giving them all a view of its impressive tail feather fan. Then another bird shrieked, and the stone in Cazia's hand translated the sound.

"Don't touch the ground!"

How interesting. The huge bird scooped up the little warrior in one talon, then flapped away.

"Inzu's breath," Kinz said.

"I have bad news," Cazia said. She held up the stone. "The birds talk to each other, too."

"We must keep moving," Ivy said. Kinz rolled to her feet and, after checking the sky above them, started along the ravine again.

From somewhere nearby, they heard a tremendous crashing sound, like an avalanche. Run. Run.

The ravine curved slightly to the northeast, then, after a hundred paces, doglegged around a spur and ran back toward the west like the shaft of a spear, with no turnoffs they could see. It would lead them right back to the thick of the Tilkilit.

All three of them circled back the way they came. Two raptors swooped through the area the girls had just run through, and a swarm of stones flew upwards at them, driving them back. Cazia had already pocketed her translation stone, so she couldn't understand the staccato tapping and screeching, but she didn't care. Fire and Fury, there were a lot of warriors back there.

They couldn't double back. But if this path would take them nearer the enemy . . .

"We must continue down the ravine," Ivy said.

"No," Cazia said. "We continue eastward . . . There. We go up that rock-slide and over to the other side."

"But we will be exposed on the ridge!" the princess said.

Without further discussion, Kinz started up the rockslide, loose stones rolling behind her. She needed the head start, too, because the slope was steep enough that they all needed their hands to keep their balance, and Kinz struggled the most.

Cazia reached the top of the ridge first. There, to the east, was a beautiful green landscape, and they only had one more ridge to cross to reach it.

Fire and Fury, there were birds everywhere: twenty, at least, flying from farther out in the valley toward them.

One of them changed direction toward her. *Finally.* She tossed the spear aside and began to cast a spell just as Ivy and Kinz came up beside her.

The power built within her, easing her emptiness and soothing her false sorrow. She had secretly hoped for this when she'd started up the ridge. The empty space inside her almost tingled at the idea of casting another spell, especially something harmful.

It would be fire this time. Why waste the darts? But as she cast it, some part of her understood at a visceral level how it could be changed. She curled two of her fingers more than she was supposed to, and changed her thoughts to match.

The spell finished before the bird was in range, but she released it anyway. The flames flew from her as a bolt rather than a jet, as though she'd catapulted a pulse of burning oil.

The bolt struck the raptor full on its belly, fire washing back over its torso. It veered away, shrieking in pain and dismay in a way that Cazia didn't need a blue stone to translate. Thick black smoke trailed behind it.

Everyone will see that.

"Cazia! Come on!"

Let them fear me.

"Cazia!"

Cazia looked back at the princess, and something in her expression made the girl gasp and step back, almost toppling down the steep hill.

I promised to protect her. There was nothing inside her that cared a whit for old promises, but still. With the Tilkilit and the raptors, she had no way of getting to the portal now, and nothing to live for. If she took the girl over the mountains, Ivy's people would surely want to come back in force. That portal might give them access to the Evening People and their Gifts.

And Cazia would lead the way.

Ivy and Kinz struggled down the hill at an angle. Cazia glanced at the sky. The raptors were giving her a lot of space, swooping down into a nearby ravine in waves, swerving away from volley after volley of stones. She couldn't see Chik's people, but the fighting seemed to be closer.

She grabbed the spear and jumped down toward Ivy and Kinz. Loose stones slid from beneath her feet and she fell on her side, scraping her left leg. It didn't hurt much—in fact, the pain felt good, almost like a second spark from Fury—but it wasn't likely to inspire fear in others.

Was that what her sorrow had become? An urge to kill and be known for killing? Interesting.

The Great Terror were making a horrendous racket, and the showers of stones hitting the ground made a sound like she'd never heard before, almost like a sudden burst of rain.

As the three of them crossed the bottom of the ravine and struggled up the other side, one of those volleys of stones fell just off to their left. Cazia noted that the rocks were jagged gray stones just like the ones they were climbing over. Clearly, the warriors had run out of the special dark, smooth stones in their pouches.

"They are getting closer," Ivy gasped. Cazia stopped often to check the sky, as much because she wanted another chance to cast her new spell as out of concern for their safety.

Four of the raptors left the maze of ravines, flapping out over the forest and gaining height. Cazia couldn't see where they were going, but she heard that avalanche sound again . . . except it didn't sound like an avalanche any more.

They finally reached the last ridge. The other side was a longer, gentler slope, but it was covered with scraggly bramble and thorny vines. Reaching the misty green forest beyond wasn't going to be simple.

"Tree," Kinz said, and hobbled southward down the slope. There was a single tree growing just below the top of the ridge, lonely, twisted, and blackened by fire. Cazia and Ivy followed.

Afternoon sun had burned off enough of the fog that the treetops of the forest were visible above the upper layer. The place Chik had led them into the network of ravines was south of them now; they could see swirls of mist retreating from the warm air blowing from it.

"Oh!" Ivy exclaimed. She pointed out into the forest mists. A treetop suddenly rose up out of the fog and fell to the side. Then another one. The sound of a tremendous, crashing avalanche, which before had seemed to come from everywhere, echoed from the forest.

Something was moving out there in the fog, and this time they knew it could not be a Tilkilit squad. Whatever it was, it was big.

Kinz fell against the tree trunk, panting. She was the strongest of them, but her injury was exhausting her. Ivy, too, was flagging. Cazia knelt beside them. She realized she should have been more tired than either of them, then immediately noticed the ache in her lungs and weariness in her legs. Odd that she couldn't feel her own pain without actively thinking about it.

While they caught their breath in the shadow of the tree, Cazia tried to consider their options. The vine towers they'd used to descend into the valley were a day or two east of them, far out into the forest. Not only would they have to escape the Tilkilit to reach them, they'd have to avoid whatever was crashing around in the fog. And the protection the vines would provide from the raptors was chancy. But they certainly couldn't climb the rock face; the Great Terror would pluck them like jars of compote on a pantry shelf.

The only other option was to create another tunnel. They would be safe from the raptors, but casting that spell that many times would utterly destroy her.

Part of her wanted that.

"We have to chance the forest," Cazia said.

"I can climb," Kinz said. "Do not leave me behind. I can still make it."

Ivy clutched her hand. "Of course we won't leave you behind!"

Kinz shot a hard look at Cazia. There was no use pretending she wasn't considering it, but fine. All three would escape together, if they could. Cazia nodded.

There was another terrifying rumble, and the mists swirled to the south. Whatever it was, it was heading to block the entrance to the ravines.

Then, in the space where the warm winds blowing into the forests pushed back the fog, they saw it. The soil swelled up—looking suddenly very like the long mound of loose earth they'd climbed over—then broke apart and fell to either side. From beneath, a massive brown cylinder pushed partway out of the ground.

At first, Cazia had no idea what she was looking at. It looked almost like a stack of squat clay pots tipped on its side. It lifted up at the center, body curling as it dragged more segments out of the soil. It toppled trees, turf, and stone.

Then the near end broke free and raised up into the air.

It was a mouth. The end of it was all mouth.

The rim was surrounded by what looked to be teeth, but after a moment, Cazia realized they were moving like stubby, knuckle-less fingers grasping at the air. *They move the dirt into its mouth,* she realized. *It's a huge worm.*

The inside of the mouth reflected sunlight with a weird rainbow sheen, and fluid sloshed around in the bottom of its inflexible jaw. Insect warriors ran alongside it, many scooping stones off the ground. A few, dressed in white sashes, scaled the side of the worm in huge bounds and clung to the top like sailors balancing on a capsized boat.

"Riding beasts," Cazia said.

Chapter Twenty-seven

THE TILKILIT'S HUGE, BURROWING MONSTER WAS SIMPLY FASCINATING. Kinz fell back behind the tree, clutching at her mouth as though stifling a scream. Ivy crouched behind her, fumbling at her little quiver. Both had clearly been struck with terror at the sight of the thing, not to mention the swarm of warriors accompanying it. There must have been a hundred Tilkilit at least, with more streaming out of the forest with every breath.

But to Cazia, it was all just a curiosity. Had the worms come through the portal? They must have, and it must have been a tight fit. What did a creature like that eat? What would it be like to be devoured by that gigantic mouth? Was it just another gateway to a new world?

"Get down!" Ivy snapped, grabbing Cazia's sleeve and dragging her behind the dubious cover of a thicket.

"By Inzu," Kinz said, "we will all make to die here, just as Mahz said."

"No, we will not," Ivy said. "I have an idea."

Cazia peeked over the top of the thicket. The warriors were advancing toward the opening of the ravine, but the worm was squirming toward the hill, moving closer to the three of them as though it could sense them.

Ivy cut the hem of her hiking dress off, just as Cazia had, then sheathed her knife. She rubbed the length of cloth on Kinz's oiled braid and began to tie it behind the head of one of her arrows.

"Big sister," Ivy said, not looking up at Cazia, "do you think you could create a tiny fire? We do not need to burn down a city, just create a little candle flame."

Casting a spell was something Cazia very much wanted to do, but the power running through that hollow space inside of her was tremendously strong. Creating a tiny flame would be like cracking open a shutter in a hurricane.

Still, many things were possible. Cazia glanced again over the top of the thickets. The worm had reached the base of the hill and had started up toward them. It wasn't fast, but it was inexorable. The Tilkilit had changed direction with it, following whatever sense led the creature toward them. From the top of the ridge, Cazia hadn't been able to spot paths down through the thickets, but the warriors had. They marched upslope in two single-file lines.

She crouched back down and began making the hand movements, instinctively adjusting them to restrict the amount of magic that would pass through her. No, she realized suddenly, it wasn't instinct. The hollow space itself knew how to control her spell. It was not just a wound or a Curse; it was somehow aware. Not alive, but aware. And aching with sorrow.

That, too, was interesting. Yes, just a few days ago she would have been horrified at the idea, but she was no longer capable of that. Maybe the thing inside her, whatever it was, had planned it that way.

Spell finished, a flare shot from the space between Cazia's hands. It was small, but not as small as a candle flame. It touched the roots of the thicket and, green and damp though they were, set them aflame.

Ivy had the arrow with the oiled cloth tied to the front already nocked. She swung the trailing piece of cloth into the little jet of flame, and it caught.

The little princess immediately stood, and Cazia stood with her. Fire and Fury, the worm was already more than halfway up the hill, and it was much too big to have fit through the portal. Once again, Cazia idly wondered what Chik's people fed it.

Ivy's loosed her little arrow immediately. As it arced downward, the Tilkilit began to make frantic tapping sounds. *A child's weapon against a colossus,* Cazia thought.

Then the arrow struck the rainbow sheen in the worm's mouth just above the liquid sloshing in the bottom of its jaw. Flame immediately raced around the inside of the mouth like water spilled over a stone floor. Then it touched the pool of fluid. The mouth lit up like a bonfire.

The Tilkilit threw a volley of stones, forcing Cazia and Ivy to take cover behind the tree. Bark flew off the trunk at each impact. These were smooth, dark stones like the ones Chik had carried in his hip pouch, and Cazia wondered why they bothered when there were so many others lying around.

A spout of flame blasted through the thickets in a wave of heat and blinding light. Kinz screamed and fell to the dirt, her hair alight. Ivy leaped on her, smothering the flames with the hem of her skirt. The tree above was on fire . . . everything around them was. *The Fifth Gift is a water spell,* Cazia realized, but Kinz's oiled hair had already been smothered. Harsh, acrid smoke choked and blinded them.

Cazia stood. The worm had reared up, throwing its riders in every direction. Foot soldiers fled down the hill for the cover of the forest, but the worm rolled and thrashed, crushing many of them. Then it slammed its mouth against the side of the hill and tried to burrow; the stony, broken soil thwarted it.

Plumes of black smoke billowed from its open mouth, with more squirting out between the segments; the worm looked to be slowly coming apart. Raptors circled well above the smoke and fire. Cazia was sure that if the creature could make a sound, it would have been screaming.

The girls retreated southward along the ridge line. Kinz looked at Ivy with astonishment. "Was that the magic arrow?"

"No!" Ivy answered, equally astonished. "I never expected—"

The fifth segment behind the worm's head suddenly burst open, spraying burning fluid and meat across the stony ground. The creature collapsed. The head struck the hillside and rolled—still burning—toward the forest.

"I never expected this," Ivy said again. "I saw that rainbow sheen on the inside of the mouth and knew it was oil. I hoped to just drive it off, maybe frighten it away. I did not mean to kill it. Do you think it was in pain?"

Of course, Ivy had already shot two Tilkilit warriors, but Cazia didn't want to upset her further by pointing that out. "Look, the fire has burned away some of the thicket. Let's—"

Ivy didn't need encouragement. As she started down the hill, Cazia beat burning specks from the back of her dress.

Kinz trailed behind, but Cazia no longer minded the delay. Thanks to Ivy and Kinz, she had seen something no human had ever seen before. And to think that she had been about to abandon them.

Together they ran down the burning hillside, kicking aside blackened thickets and beating at flames and thorns that caught at their clothes. Cinders floated around them, landing on their bare arms and cheeks. They were halfway to the bottom when Cazia realized she'd left the spear on the ridge.

A change in the wind blew oily black smoke over them, and they nearly collapsed with choking. Cazia had to practically carry the princess down the hill.

A raptor swooped down into the smoke, then flapped upward with a figure in its talons. Kinz lost her balance and fell to her knees. Ivy went slack and fell beside her, still coughing. When Cazia dragged them both upright, their clothes were ashy and smoldering. Somewhere up ahead, another of the worm's segments burst open, hurling chunks of burning flesh into the air.

"Keep moving," Cazia said, her throat tight. She realized she had slowed quite a bit. Her lungs. She was choking on the smoke and not getting nearly enough air. If she didn't start paying attention to her body, it was going to kill her.

Cazia knew they had to stumble onto one of the paths the Tilkilit had used to climb the hill, eventually. The torn hem of her skirt no longer protected her shins from the cinders and thorns. Her boots were becoming painfully hot.

Then she stepped, and found no ground for her foot to fall on. The three of them slid down a steep, stony part of the hill. Kinz cried out piteously, a sound Cazia was sure would draw the raptors. Ivy lay on her stomach at the bottom of the slope, her elbows and forehead scraped bloody. Cazia went to help her up and was suddenly face to face with one of the insect warriors.

It was dead, obviously. It had been burned gray, still upright only because it had become tangled in the thicket. Interestingly, the worst burns seemed to be around the base of its skull where its speaking scents came out.

Beside the body was a deer path down the hill. Cazia helped Kinz to her feet, then led them away from the flames. Immediately, the air became cleaner. After several paces, they stopped long enough for their coughing fits to pass.

Ivy had broken her bowstring somewhere on the hill; she'd be doing no more fighting today. Her scrapes were raw but shallow—they'd already stopped bleeding—but she looked frightened and dispirited. Maybe she needed some encouragement, maybe a hug, but Cazia wasn't the one to give it.

Kinz knelt beside the princess; she looked just as weak and shaky. Cazia suspected she didn't look much better, although her own scrapes and hacking cough seemed to be someone else's problem.

The Tilkilit clicking seemed to be far away. The thicket grew higher than their heads on both sides. Cazia brushed ash and cinders from Ivy's clothes. They had seen and done amazing things together, and she would need them both as witnesses if she was going to return in force for that portal.

They moved forward, sliding down the hill in places where it grew steep. Behind them, another of the worm's segments burst, then two more in quick succession. Eagle cries filled the air. Smoke rose into the sky like twisting black towers.

A piece of burning shell fell onto the narrow path. It was as large as three butchered sheep, and the flames began to spread through the bushes on both sides. Cazia made to push through the thicket to go around.

"No!" Kinz hissed. "Hunting birds will dive at rustling grass. You will call them down upon us."

Fine. That just meant Cazia had an excuse to cast another spell.

Her water spell sent out a spray from the empty space between her hands. The fires sputtered and the black smoke became mixed with white steam, but she kept the water flowing until the only flames left were floating downhill on the tiny stream she'd created.

The spell didn't want to end, so she sprayed water onto her boots, then her skirts, then onto the other two girls to cool them. Cazia felt the magic building in the hollow space inside her the way a flooding river builds behind a dam. It seemed that it might break her apart and rush out into the world. The pressure suddenly became intense, and that dead intelligence inside her longed to break free like an infant striving to be born.

All she had to do was surrender, and she would fly apart and be no more. *Hollowed out.* The waters of her spell would wash Ivy and Kinz away—everything would be washed away, and she would never enter that portal.

The portal. Cazia pinched off the power of the Gift, letting it fade away. She wanted to enter that portal. It didn't matter if the waters washed Ivy and Kinz away, or if it gave away their position to the raptors above. The portal was everything.

The spell dwindled to nothing, and Cazia fell into the mud and wept. Ivy and Kinz knelt beside her—her spell had drenched them brow to boot—and tried to comfort her, but they didn't understand. How could they when she didn't even understand herself?

Ivy turned Cazia's face toward her own. "Cazia. Big sister. We must keep moving." She sounded as if she was trying to reason with a mad woman. *That's because she is.*

Another segment of the worm burst open, bathing them all in orange light. Something passed over them—Cazia felt the breeze but didn't see it—then a piece of shell as long as a door fell into the bushes beside the path, filling the air with a new plume of black smoke. Time to go. Cazia lifted Ivy over the blackened flesh blocking the path, then Kinz.

All three of them ran down the path, stumbling when the ground was uneven, snagging their skirts on thorns when they veered too far to one side.

Then they were clear of the smoke. They had reached the bottom of the hill and the end of the path. The stony ground ahead was bare of any cover except for a few brown weeds and charred logs. The green forest seemed very far away.

All three knelt within the cover of the thicket. It had taken Chik almost two days to lead them to this part of the valley. How were they supposed to make it back with all of his people hunting them? "We'll never make it back to our climbing vines, not with all this, assuming we could even find them. We'll have to dig through the mountains again," Cazia said. She could feel the Eleventh Gift growing inside her, and she had to clench her fists to keep from casting her spell.

"Cazia, no!" Ivy said.

They looked at her as if she'd announced she was going to drink poison. And they were right; she knew they were right. The last spell had nearly gone out of control . . . It felt as if it would kill her.

But the urge was still there, suddenly become as undeniable as starvation. She knew that when it came out of her, it would run out of her control. Could she cast a version of the Eleventh Gift strong enough to bore all the way through a mountain?

A voice inside her said *yes* but she wasn't sure she could trust it.

"Cazia," Ivy said. "You have to promise you will not cast any more spells. The strain you are putting on yourself is too much."

"And the damage you have already made to yourself—"

"I know." Cazia wiped tears from her sooty face and tried to summon up a reasonable expression. "I know I have already done too much, but I want us to get back over the mountains, and we're not going to do that without magic."

"We can," Ivy said. "Cazia—"

"Cazia is dead." Part of her wanted to feel good about finally admitting that, both to herself and to the world, but she couldn't. It wasn't even entirely true, but it would be soon. Not that it mattered.

"Have it your way, *Doctor Freewell.*" Ivy's tone was sharp and her eyes filled with tears. Did she think Cazia was trying to offend her? If they reached safety, Cazia would have to explain that she didn't care enough about the girl to insult her. "But I want you to swear to us, on your magic, that you will not cast another spell today."

Cazia looked up at the mountain looming above them to the south. She could imagine the stone-breaking spell it would take to bore a hole straight through it, could envision the changes to her hand motions and visualizations that would require.

She didn't have that kind of power, but she could channel it. She could open the hollow space inside herself and let the magic flow through.

She knew it would destroy her, but wasn't entirely sure what that meant. Would she physically die? It was possible, but the strain she'd felt when she was putting out the fire didn't seem physical.

Would she become like one of the wizards from the children's stories she'd heard all her life, creating monsters, poisoning rivers, murdering whole clans in their sleep? Would she become like Doctor Whitestalk? Like Doctor Rexler, the man Old Stoneface became famous for killing? Would she even remember her name?

Ivy and Kinz were waiting for her promise. "No."

A Tilkilit warrior suddenly landed beside them. Ivy spun toward him and lost her balance. She fell against Kinz's injured side, and together they tumbled into the thicket. Kinz cried out in pain.

Cazia snatched a dart from her quiver. Was this going to be the spell that tore her apart? It seemed to be. She began to make the necessary hand motions.

Dropping his spear, the warrior slipped his hand into the pouch at his hip and drew out one of the strange, black stones they carried there. Fire and Fury, he was too close to miss. Tilkilit warriors could throw those stones hard enough to break bones, and as he drew back his arm, she dove sideways toward the only cover available to her, Ivy and Kinz's bodies.

But she had no fear to give her movements urgency, and that made her slow. The warrior threw the stone; it struck her solidly on the thigh.

The whole world dimmed, then pain shot through her body. The hollow space inside her registered a moment of curiosity: *That was no ordinary stone; what an odd sensa—*

Then the alien hollowness inside her was ripped away, and Cazia screamed.

CHAPTER TWENTY-EIGHT

TEJOHN HAD GROWN UP ON A FARM WHERE THE WORK STARTED before first light and never really ended. He'd drilled with soldiers, marched through the night, and charged enemy squares when he was on the edge of collapse. He had drilled the prince and his friends for hours through the hottest days of summer.

But he had never worked as hard in his life as he did as a servant.

Every morning, he was woken with a sharp slap from a baton. Every day, he labored for hours in the wind and rain, wearing nothing but a cloth tied around his waist. He was fed once, at midday, usually thin rice gruel. The work continued long after darkness until he was so tired, he could barely hold his head up.

People died all around him. On his first day hauling rocks, a man collapsed on the rocky slope, spilling his basket. The overseer lashed him until his back was raw, but nothing could make the fellow respond. Tejohn watched in horror as the body was hauled away like trash . . . until a lash across his own back drove him back to work.

At first, Tejohn was determined to prove his worth. He was certain that if he worked harder than the others and did not complain, the people in charge would move him to less miserable work. He pulled baskets of broken rock out of the pits faster than anyone else. He carried them up the hill fastest. He even picked up stones that others dropped.

On his second day, the frayed basket he was raising out of the pit broke. It wasn't anything he did; the woven grasses simply tore under the weight, raining stones into the pit below. Luckily, no one was hurt.

But six of the overseers dragged Tejohn away, tied him to a post, and gave him four lashes. He did not make a sound until they finished by throwing a bucket of icy salt water onto his back.

In his soldiering days, he would have been ordered to a sleepstone, as long as there was no one else with a greater need. Instead, the overseers sent him back to the pit. For the rest of the day, he worked more slowly than anyone else.

That night, he found that one of the other servants had stolen his thin blanket, the only protection he had against the damp, chill air. As he lay shivering, a whispered voice in the darkness said, "You think you're better than us." There was so much venom in it that Tejohn was sure he would be murdered in his sleep, but he was wrong. No one was going to be merciful enough to simply kill him.

Servants were beaten when they worked too slowly. They were beaten when they hurried. They were beaten when they looked an overseer in the eye or did not meet the overseer's gaze. Talking was forbidden but silence was suspicious. They spent every day hungry, exhausted, and so parched, their heads hurt. Merchants and other townsfolk sneered at him when they weren't close enough to spit on him. Wealthy men strolled along the edges of the work yard, looking over the women working there the way Tejohn might choose a fish at a stall.

His back ached and bled. His stomach grumbled. His bare feet were covered with cuts and bruises. Once, when he slipped on a rain-slick piece of slate and bruised his knee terribly, the overseer put his boot on the back of Tejohn's neck.

He lay on the dirt, waiting for the man to decide whether to lean one way and break Tejohn's neck, or lean the other to let him live. When he'd been a tyr, Tejohn had ignored the servants. He quickly discovered that, to a servant, there was no better class of person than that.

It took six days for him to transform from a tyr of the Peradaini empire into a servant that dared not look another man in the face. He could not even risk thinking of his wife and children during the daylight hours for fear that an overseer would see him smile.

The only times they could rest—aside from their few hours in the huge, drafty warehouse where they slept—were when they were fed. Most servants sat in tight circles, and Tejohn thought they were being cliquish.

On the eighth day, as Tejohn stood in line for his bowl of gruel, he noticed a group of six young men watching them with hard, measuring glances. Tejohn knew bandits when he saw them, even when they were as half-starved as these. None were older than he had been when he went into the army.

The one standing at the front looked at Tejohn briefly, then glanced away, searching for an easier target.

He found it. The leader moved alongside an old man as he walked away with his full bowl, the whole group following. The old fellow, already shuffling like a defeated man, didn't bother to protest as the little gang forced themselves into his little circle of gray-haired servants. The young men snatched bowls of gruel from the elders to pour into their own.

After the gang moved away, they headed toward the back of the line to get the serving they were due. The old fellow hung his head low and wept. "I'm sorry," he said in a cracked voice. Luckily, there were no overseers close enough to hear him.

Shame flowed through Tejohn. Was this the empire he had served? He wanted to believe the Finstels were running amok now that the Italgas no longer stood guard over them, but he didn't believe it. Conditions might have changed somewhat in the days since the Festival, but they couldn't have become *this* terrible. This was a long-standing practice, or long-standing prejudice given free rein.

And Tejohn had fought to preserve it.

Without even thinking about it, Tejohn swallowed the rest of his gruel and disposed of his wooden bowl. He walked empty-handed back toward the food line, meeting the leader and his little gang. Their bowls were full almost to the brim; was that because they were bullies, or did the end of the line get larger portions?

"Boys," Tejohn said, his voice hoarse and thin from disuse, "you should repay those elders for the food you borrowed."

The leader of the gang smiled nastily, showing his gray teeth. "Who's going to make us, old ma—"

Tejohn punched him in the throat with all the speed and power he had left in his good right hand. With his left, he gently cradled the bowl of gruel. The leader collapsed in the dust, writhing and making choking noises. Tejohn gestured toward the old man they'd cut out of the line. He approached hesitantly and accepted the bowl of gruel warily.

Tejohn looked at the other gang members. They were just boys, but he had killed boys before. He'd killed them in uncountable numbers.

Luckily, that wasn't going to happen today. The boys turned toward him, their shoulders slumped, as though accepting him as their new leader. "Pay back those elders."

One chubby-faced boy—he must have been as new as Tejohn—spoke up. "I gave it to my mother."

As he spoke, a haggard-looking woman rushed toward them. "He didn't steal for himself," she said, breathless from the exertion. "He was worried about me. He stole for me."

Tejohn suddenly recognized her as one of the ferry folk. It had been her husband who had taken a spear to his belly. The boy's voice was dull. "I gave the food to my mother."

"I'm sorry," the mother said, her face flushed. "Quildin told us"—she gestured toward the gang leader who had stopped thrashing but was not yet dead—"this was the only way we'd survive. Great Way, I'm ashamed of what has become of our family's good name."

Tejohn turned toward the boy. "What a good lad you are to give your daily ration to your mother. Now return the food you stole."

The elders they'd robbed had already come close, and they held out their empty hands. The shortest of the boys bowed as he offered the bowl to an old woman, then he turned to Tejohn. "What will you have of us, sir? You're the leader now."

Tejohn realized the old fellow, his face carefully blank, had lingered nearby to eavesdrop. "No, I'm not," Tejohn said. "She is." He pointed at the ferry woman.

"What?" she looked stunned. "I can not—"

"These boys don't need a leader skilled at killing. They need someone with a desire to do better. You, woman, will organize things for everyone here as best you can. You ran a business once, yes?"

"The sturdiest, fastest ferry in the northern Waterlands."

"Find out how to make things better for the other servants, then make it happen. But if I find out you are stealing again"—he pointed at Quildin, who had finally died—"no one will come to your aid, either."

The old fellow chuckled. "You're forming a rival cupboard."

Tejohn looked down at him. "I don't know what that is."

The fellow turned toward the ferry woman. "Your name is Beshier, isn't it? Follow me to my section, and I'll tell you what you need to—"

"What's this!" a man shouted, startling them all. One of the overseers had come up to them from behind. His two guards, truncheons in hand, stood over Quildin. "What happened to this man?"

"He collapsed, sir," Beshier said. She didn't look the overseer in the face, but they all knew she was risking a beating by answering the man's question. "Just collapsed."

The overseer snorted and walked away.

That night, Tejohn slept under a blanket again. The next day, he discovered a piece of mutton and an apricot in the bottom of his gruel.

The work that was killing them all seemed to be busywork. They broke rock to dig pits and hauled the stones to the riverside. Every fourth day, three-quarters of the servants were taken down to the water to move the stones onto barges. That was a prized detail, because servants would occasionally contrive to step or fall into the Shelsiccan to clean themselves.

Tejohn never volunteered for that detail. They were downstream of Splashtown itself—*Ussmajil,* he had to remember not to use Peradaini names here—which meant the river was full of sewage. Some of the workers who worked the barges died later from diarrhea or infections.

Presumably, the broken stone was for the city's walls, which had been in poor repair for a generation. Even those tyrs most favored by the Italgas were not going to get scholar-built walls around their cities. Forts in the passes, yes. Around their ancestral homes and lands? Never.

But why quarry the rock as though digging one shallow well after another? Tejohn wasn't entirely certain, but he thought they were working on the old parade grounds where local athletic contests had been held and green troops practiced skirmishes and drills. He couldn't be certain, though, not only because it had been so many years since he'd marched on those grounds—and it had only been the once, when the Gerrits brought the Witt and Bendertuk banners to Splashtown in tribute to their losses in victory—but because he couldn't see any landmarks of any note, not even the Southern Barrier.

The twelfth day was another day of barge duty, and the pit workers once again found themselves lightly guarded. The most vicious of the overseers and the majority of the guards stood close watch over the waterways to prevent escape attempts. Tejohn worked down in a pit that day, a duty he hated because the air could be stifling, and was surprised to hear a human voice speak to him in a measured tone.

"You're the one who did right by old Padenwo."

Tejohn was so surprised, he dropped the stone he was lifting. The woman who had spoken to him smiled weakly; she knew the effect a human voice could have.

She was withered and lean, like anyone who had been a servant for a long time. Her face was dark from the sun and her hair streaked with gray, but Tejohn suspected that she was a few years younger than him.

"I guess I am," Tejohn said, "for what that's worth."

They did not stop working. "It's worth some extra rations, if you haven't noticed."

"I have. Are you the one I should thank? Or can you pass my thanks on to the correct person? I have been afraid to speak my gratitude aloud, to be honest."

"Today, we can risk careful speech. And you can thank the cupboard. It's off-limits to most of the refugee servants, but it's been opened to you now."

There was that word again. "What treasures can I take from this cupboard?"

"It is the meanest cupboard in the empire. You can only take what treasures a slave might have."

Tejohn loaded a few more stones, taking care to work slightly faster than his companion but not too fast. "Information, then. I would like information."

She smiled at him again, but by the time he realized he should smile back, she had turned away. "Very wise, soldier. What do you want to ask?"

Something about her tone made him cautious. This "cupboard," which was presumably a secret, illegal organization of servants, would not look kindly on prying from someone so new. In fact, if he were part of such an organization, he would arrange an interview just like this to test him, to see if he was a mole or informant.

"What are we creating here? And why?"

"Have you not seen the—" One of the ropes holding a basket wiggled like a worm and she fell silent. Tejohn followed her example and loaded a basket in sullen silence. A few breaths later, he saw the shadow of an overseer pass over them.

When the rope wiggled again, she resumed her answer. "Have you not seen the blockhouse they are building upriver?"

"I can barely make out the features of the people standing over this pit."

"Ah, I understand. The pits we're making are one of Shunzik Finstel's big plans. There are other servants following behind us, building prison houses over these pits."

"Is it true that Tyr Finstel rescued someone from Peradain? Someone important?"

"'Captured' would be a better term for it. The prisoner is being held in one of the first pits, under guard every minute of the day. And you would do well to remember that he is King Shunzik now. He has renounced the title of Tyr, rejected the very concepts of chieftains and tyrants, and crowned himself."

For a moment, Tejohn wondered if the man planned to claim the entire empire or just his own lands. But the answer was obvious: He would be king of whatever he could take and hold.

"Is the captive Ellifer Italga?"

"No," the woman answered. "There are no servants here who would have recognized him, but we would have heard talk from guards or commanders. Someone would have recognized an Italga and talked. This is someone that no one recognizes."

Someone that no one recognizes? Tejohn had no idea who that could be. Quallis, the king's valet? Kellin Pendell, the commander of the guard? Kolbi Arriya, Ellifer's shield bearer? Even Sincl, the Festival performance master? Great Way, it could be anyone.

"And what of you?"

Tejohn sighed. He didn't want to do this, but it would have been dishonorable to lie. "What I'm about to tell you could get me hanged." She didn't respond. "My name is Tejohn Treygar."

"I know that name," she said. "I would not have expected to find you here."

Tejohn only grunted in response. The basket was full. He waved to the blurry shape at the top of the pit and started to fill the one beside it. "I lived in Peradain, inside the Palace of Song and Morning, for over twenty years. If anyone will recognize the prisoner in the pit, it will be me."

Chapter Twenty-nine

THE NEXT DAY, TEJOHN FOUND HIMSELF ASSIGNED TO A NEW WORK duty. He had no idea who made the change. A servant told him to turn left at the entrance to his barracks rather than right. Beside him stood a forlorn-looking young man with a crooked nose and scratch marks on his neck. He, apparently, was taking Tejohn's place.

The woman he'd spoken to in the pit led him to his new duties, but before he could ask her name, she looked over her shoulder and said, "My name is Weshka Stokes. Everything else around here is getting its old Finshto names back, but not servants. We're not worth the bother."

She led him into a large wooden building. A stone hearth had been built in the center below the smoke hole. Tejohn couldn't help but cough slightly as he entered. There were servants everywhere, some feeding the fire, some stirring the content of bowls with wooden spoons, some slicing at butchered pigs or chickens.

The smell of roasting meat made Tejohn moan slightly; Weshka glanced at him again.

"Just be sure you understand the rules here. You never touch anything unless you've been given explicit permission, and that goes triple for the women, the children, and the food. Stealing food might get someone's aunt or mother whipped, and for that, you'd be stabbed in your sleep. As for the women and children, touch them and you'll wish you'd been killed in bed."

"The fellow with the crooked nose who took my place?"

Weshka nodded. "He thought he was so well liked that we would wag our fingers at him."

Tejohn was given a cup of grass tea. It was cold, but the young man who poured it filled the cup four more times. *Small sips, my tyr. That's safest.* Tejohn's dull, unyielding headache eased.

He was led to a group of young men and given a largish bun stuffed with roasted onion and boiled greens. He ate half. It wasn't enough, but he tried to slip it inside his ragged shirt for later.

"That's not necessary," one of the young men said. He was a handsome fellow—barely old enough to march with a spear—with wide, expressive eyes. He nodded towards Tejohn's shirt. "We'll be getting more around midday."

Tejohn felt embarrassed for some reason he couldn't really understand and ate the rest of the bun.

They spent the morning along the riverbank, collecting wood. Tejohn pulled the cart to the work site, even though he was at least twenty years older than the oldest of his co-workers. They felled trees with bronze axes, all six of them, with no one guarding them but a pair of archers who joked and laughed with each other, and kept only a casual eye on the servants. On the way back, everyone but the archers worked together to pull the cart.

After a mid day meal that consisted of some rice and boiled fat, Weshka came to him with a special job. "Do you see this trail?" She gestured toward a cart trail that ran along the main road. There was a muddy ditch between them—the road was for troops and traveling merchants. The cart trail was for servants and had a tall fringe of weeds so decent folks wouldn't have to look at them. "Take this cart of wood to the stone building at the end of this trail. Don't touch the building without permission or joke with the guards. They have important prisoners, and they're touchy. Hunch down more. You still walk like a soldier."

He nodded to her and started up the path, pulling the two-wheeled wagon behind him. *Important prisoners.* The trail was not as friendly to his injured feet as the grass had been, but it was kinder than the stones of the parade grounds.

Since he could not see very clearly anyway, he did not even try to look for the tower. He just kept his eyes on the path, avoided stones, and thought.

Tyr Finstel—he would not be calling him King Shunzik any time soon—had a flying cart, Tejohn was sure of it. He was also sure that revealing himself to his former tyr and asking to borrow it for a few days would get him thrown into a pit. Or worse.

Still, he needed to get to Tempest Pass as quickly as possible. While he was starving at his labors, the grunts were out there, making more of their kind.

The first step was to get into the holdfast somehow, which meant striking out upriver. He would have to find the cart first, then need to hire or bully someone trained to fly it. Then they would both have to escape without being opened up like a pig on a butcher's block.

The most logical place he could turn for help were the other servants, but it was too soon to ask for so much. What's more, if he failed, it would certainly cost all of them their lives.

No, better to work this out on his own: escape somehow, avoid the guard's usual methods of recapturing fleeing servants—

Fire and Fury, he didn't even know how to avoid the guards. Yet. Song knew his plan was so absurdly unlikely that it was farcical, and still it would be a month before he was ready to try it. He needed something else. He needed a way through, or he was never going to accomplish the task Lar had set for him, and there would be no one to save them all. But what?

The cart path was fairly straight, but Tejohn was startled to see it widen suddenly into a meadow. He'd come upon the tower very suddenly, and as he did, he saw Shunzik Finstel standing before him.

He did not look much different than he had at Lar's birthday, except he was wearing a black fighting tunic emblazoned with the Finstel waterfall. He had his father's pugnacious nose and rounded chin, but none of the scars.

There were four bodyguards beside him—all carrying absurdly long spears—and another eight farther back . . .

Beside the carts. There were two flying carts set on stone daises beside the tower. There were drivers standing inside, but of course, they were too far away for Tejohn to make out their faces, let alone study them for—

"You!" One of the guards marched toward him. Tejohn let his face go slack as he looked at the man—a young man, barely older than Shunzik, with a bull's neck and a scar down his cheek—then at the ground. "If you have work to do, see that it's done quickly and move on. Their tyrships do not need to be eyeballed by the likes of you."

"Keep to your position, soldier," a very familiar voice said. "Your tyr requires your attention."

Tejohn couldn't help himself. He glanced at the man who had spoken. It was Tyr Belder Gerrit. His braided beard had gone gray and his hair was nearly gone, but his eyes were still shrewd. He and Tejohn had feasted, gamed, and sparred together. Belder had laid a laurel crown on Tejohn's head himself and poured out a cup of his finest wine. Tyr Gerrit had called him friend and brother.

His gaze met Tejohn's for a long breath. *I have been discovered.*

But no. There was no spark of recognition in Tyr Gerrit's face.

Tejohn was invisible. Dressed as a servant, he was so far beneath the notice of the people he had known that they couldn't even see him.

The tyrs and their soldiers strode back to their carts. Tyr Finstel was insisting on something with a young man's impatience. Tyr Gerrit assured him there was time enough for their plans to be finished.

As Tejohn pulled the cart toward the tower gate, the guard at the front shouted at him, "You'd better have brought us enough this time. Last night was chilly!"

"I bring what I'm given to bring, sir," Tejohn said, flushing with shame as he spoke.

The guard slapped him on the side of the head, but Tejohn saw the blow coming and rolled with it. Still, he knew better than to show he hadn't been hurt; he sprawled to the side, rolling across the dried, packed dirt. The guard stood over him, the corner of his mouth turned up with satisfaction. "Who are you? Where is the usual man?"

A familiar tension ran through Tejohn's limbs. Not even days of servitude could stifle his urge to start killing. "Ondel Ulstrik, sir. I don't know about the usual man. They don't tell me anything."

"Pah. Get up!" The guard banged twice on the door, turning his back to Tejohn as he opened it.

It wasn't much of a tower. It wasn't as high or as broad as the Scholars' Tower in the palace, or even the commanders' towers in the forts. It had been built with stones of every shape and shade of gray, all held together with mortar. Tejohn didn't much trust mortar; it crumbled too easily, then what did you have? A pile of stones to mark your grave.

The lower level of the tower was lit only by a fire in the open hearth and daylight streaming in from the second floor mezzanine. Tejohn pulled his cart into the main hall. The floor was same stone slab, but it had been swept of the dried mud and loose stone that covered the servants' path. There were two guards in here, both standing bored at opposite ends of the room. In the exact center, a wooden grate was set into the floor.

Tejohn began to stack the wood into the empty wooden platform beside the hearth. What excuse could he make to get close enough to the grate to look at the person down inside? His only idea was to drop a piece of firewood so it rolled toward the center of the room, but that was too obvious.

"Bring a third of that upstairs," one of the guards said.

The stairs up to the second floor didn't bring him near the grate. Two more guards walked around the stone mezzanine, slowing as they passed their little fire. The peaked roof above was supported by four stone columns.

Tejohn wondered idly what it would take to break them, the way the ruhgrit had crushed their flying cart.

From the inner edge of the mezzanine, he looked down to the first floor, but beyond the wooden grate on the floor he could see only darkness.

Helpless frustration burned in him. Ellifer Italga could be *right down there* but Tejohn could do nothing about it. Still, it was time for a tactical retreat.

As he turned the wagon around in the narrow hall, one of the guards called, "Hey! Come over here."

The other guard said, "Kyun, not again."

Kyun ignored him. "Pull up that man's waste bucket and dump it in the hole outside."

"Kyun, that's your job."

"Watch Commander delegated it to me, and I'm delegating it to this rock-wit here. It's a rock-wit task, isn't it?"

"Kyun—"

"Yes, sir," Tejohn said, using the same slow voice he'd used among the refugees on the road. He padded out into the center of the room and crouched over the grate. It wasn't locked into place. He lifted it and set it aside.

Fire and Fury, it was deep and dark. Tejohn could see someone moving down there, but only barely. He certainly couldn't tell who it was. Here he was, right where he'd said he would need to be, and he'd still failed.

A rope was tied off to a hook set just below the rim of the pit. Tejohn pulled it up, raising a stinking bucket of waste up to his hand. He untied it, still peering down into the darkness but unable to make out the face there.

From the darkness: "My Tyr Treygar?"

Tejohn recognized that voice instantly. It was Doctor Twofin.

"Hey!" not-Kyun shouted. "No talking allowed! Fire and Fury, this is what I was talking about, Kyun!"

Tejohn backed away, holding the bucket in front of him.

"You!" not-Kyun shouted. "What did he say? Did he give you a message?"

"No, sir!" Tejohn tried to shrink himself down and appear afraid. "I don't even understand what he said."

"Tyr Treygar!" Twofin shouted out of the bottom of the pit. "Tyr Treygar, release me! I've been loyal to the Italgas, I swear! *Tyr Treygar!*"

Not-Kyun stared at Tejohn, and Tejohn gave him an empty stare right back. The other guard was directly behind him, of course, and Tejohn let his fear of a knife in the back show in his expression. After a breath or two, not-Kyun sighed bitterly and said, "Put that down and get out. And there better not be any gossip about this, or it will be your head. Kyun, why don't you do your Fire-taken job?"

Outside the tower, Tejohn saw that the flying carts were gone, and so were Tyrs Gerrit and Finstel. His head was spinning, but he knew two things: he no longer needed to find a driver, and he had to get Doctor Twofin out of that cell tonight.

Chapter Thirty

Compared to hauling stone, cutting and carrying wood was light work, but Tejohn still collapsed onto his little bunk at the end of the day. Even with his increased rations, he still hadn't had enough to eat, and he needed time to recover from the grueling days on the parade grounds.

It didn't matter. Doctor Twofin was held in that pit, and he'd called Tejohn's name. The guards might have thought he was delirious, but if they mentioned it to anyone—especially to Tyr Finstel or Tyr Gerrit—Tejohn would be discovered before the day was out. Having his head mounted on a spear outside the city was the gentlest treatment he could hope for. *We'll have nowhere to retreat.*

Tonight had to be the night, so Tejohn sat on the edge of the plank that was supposed to be a bunk, and he counted slow breaths. His stomach rumbled and his headache had returned. In fact, his head felt light—he wasn't sure he had the strength to do what he needed to do tonight, but he would try.

After he counted a thousand breaths, he slid quietly off the bunk and made his way through the dark.

"Where are you going?" a voice whispered.

"The ditch," Tejohn answered. Servants were supposed to relieve themselves in a ditch behind their barracks.

"No, you're not."

"Don't be stupid," Tejohn snapped, as angry at himself for being noticed as he was at this man he couldn't even see. "Go to sleep."

Tejohn went through the door and around to the back. He did have to drain his bladder, but when he finished, he headed for the road, not the barracks. He slumped his shoulders, shuffled his feet, and kept his head down. No one challenged him. No one cared.

The kitchens were empty and so dark, the smoke hole was nothing more than a faint dark gray circle against the black roof. He left the door open so dim last-quarter moonlight could shine inside. It took time for his eyes to adjust, but he felt his way slowly through the room. It took him several breaths to find the meat-cutting bench and the long, slender bronze knife he'd seen hanging above it. There.

No matter how comforting it was to hold a weapon again, it would be slim use against armored men with shields and iron-tipped spears. He stood in the darkness, trying to remember all the tools he'd seen that day. Had there been a platter he could use as a makeshift shield?

The door swung open and two figures rushed inside. One held a lantern high, panel open at the front to illuminate the room. Even such a weak light was enough in this darkness. Tejohn had been discovered.

But these weren't guards. He lowered the knife back and stood upright, letting the light shine on him in full. He knew who had come to meet him even before he recognized her voice.

Weshka said, "What are you doing?"

"It has to be tonight," he answered. "I know who they're keeping in that pit, and I have to get him out before morning."

"Who is it? And why?"

Tejohn glanced at Weshka's companion. He was just a silhouette, but from what Tejohn could make out, he was tall and painfully skinny, with a long fringe of hair around a bald scalp. Tejohn didn't recognize him, but he assumed this was the voice in the darkness.

A servant's treasure became less valuable the more it was shared, but Weshka was asking and he wouldn't withhold information from her. "His name is Oskol Twofin."

"My great-grandfather came out of Twofin lands," Weshka said. "So, he's some minor tyr's favorite second cousin? That makes him important?"

Tejohn shook his head. "Back in Peradain, he was the scholar who taught magic to the king."

"Fury guide us, we have another scholar-king?" Weshka's tone was bitter.

"Lar Italga is no . . . This isn't the time for this. Doctor Twofin is one of the most accomplished scholars in the empire. If Tyr Finstel turns him . . . Twofin can create blocks and translation stones. With most of the Peradaini scholars killed, Finstel could establish a new Scholars' Tower in Ussmajil and declare himself king."

"One king or another makes no difference to us," the companion said.

Weshka sighed and shut the door behind her. "But war in the Waterlands does. The tyrships to the east have already fallen to the grunts; could the others really be turning on each other?"

"They already are," Tejohn told her. "Witt spears took Fort Caarilit for a short time, and ranged throughout the Sweeps, scooping up mining scholars. Finstel soldiers only took it back when the Witt spears marched for their holdfast, probably to deal with the grunts."

"But why tonight?" Weshka asked.

"Doctor Twofin called me by name. It meant nothing to the guards, but if Tyr Finstel or Gerrit hears . . . "

"You will be tortured and executed," Weshka said.

"I still don't see how this concerns us," the companion said. Tejohn wanted to rush across the room and punch him in the throat. "We're strained enough as it is."

"Lar Italga gave me a mission," Tejohn said. "I need Doctor Twofin to complete it."

"Describe this mission."

"I can't," Tejohn said. "I swore an oath."

The companion hissed. "Every oath you've ever taken was forsworn when you became a servant and again when you entered our cupboard."

"Tejohn," Weshka said, silencing the man with a wave of her hand. "This mission of yours will hold together the Italga empire, won't it?"

"It will defeat the grunts," Tejohn said, which was a bit of an exaggeration, but he couldn't take it back. "I don't know what would hold together the empire at this point. I doubt that anything could."

"Can this Doctor Twofin do healing magic? Can he create a sleepstone for us, in secret?"

Tejohn immediately saw the wisdom in that. "No," he said. "I don't think so. I'm sorry. Medical scholars wear a special badge on their robes, and he doesn't have one."

Weshka nodded grimly, as though used to disappointment. "I will help you, but in return, someday I will come to you to ask for a favor, and you will grant it to me."

Why not? "Agreed."

She set the lantern on a work bench. "Being servants, we have heard the stories about you. Can you take all five guards? We have no armor or bows to give you, nor can we return your youth."

Tejohn would have been stung by that comment a few months ago. "I'm hopeless with a bow, but if I can get close enough and fight them one at a time, I can kill them." Or they could kill him.

"You can not use a knife from this kitchen," Weshka said. "The overseers keep track of our tools, and if you killed a guard with one of these knives, it would cost the life of every man, woman, and child who works in this room."

A small price to pay was his first thought, but he dismissed it immediately. He'd killed more men and women than he could count in battle, and he'd ordered more to take positions he knew would likely lead to their deaths. A series of faces flashed back into his memory—people he hadn't thought of in years—all of them dead because he'd ordered them to hold a particular position or mount a diversionary assault.

But they had been solders. Having lived among the servants, he couldn't toss away their lives. Not like this. He set the long bronze knife on the bench beside him.

"I can get you close, I think. Come here." Weshka led him to the back door, then pulled a folded black cloak off a shelf. The hood was large enough to hide the wearer's face, and there was a large white circle on the top.

"Sometimes," she said, "when a servant is desperate for money or food, he—or more often, she—will visit a guard post wearing this. Sometimes, she earns enough to bribe the medical scholars to let her use a sleepstone, or to acquire extra food for her child. Approach the tower wearing this and they will not make you stand and announce yourself. If you survive, it would be best if this was not found anywhere near the tower afterward."

Tejohn took it from her and threw it over his shoulders. The hood was long enough to shadow his face, but he had to crouch so the hem covered his large feet.

"Clasp it here," Weshka told him, "to hide your beard. Men are sometimes turned away. Women almost never are. Do you need food?"

"This is ridiculous," the companion said.

"Food would help."

She offered him a hunk of cold lamb that was as large as his fist. Just a few bites were enough to steady his hands and clear his head. He wrapped the rest in a piece of old linen and tucked it into his shirt in case Doctor Twofin needed it.

"Remember your promise" was all Weshka said to him as he slipped out of the kitchen onto the cart path.

The journey to the meadow, which seemed so long when he pulled a cart of firewood behind him, now seemed to take no time at all. He was so surprised to come upon the edge of the meadow that he paused there, staring at the looming, blurry shape of the tower ahead. Fire and Fury, the wind off the river was cold.

Tejohn forced himself to keep moving forward. He couldn't see how many guards were ahead of him. What if they tripled their numbers after dark?

But no, as he came close, he could see that wasn't so. There was still the one guard standing outside the entrance and two more patrolling the open second floor. All held the ridiculously long spears that seemed to be in fashion here. Jeering came from up above as Tejohn shuffled toward the guard at the gate, his body shrunk as much as possible. But inside, his desperation was churning, becoming that old feeling again. *I am going to kill you.*

"You're visiting late tonight," the guard at the gate said. "You two up there! Get back to your rounds. You'll get your turn, if you have the coin for it."

Tejohn slowed as he approached, expecting to be led into a secluded place. Instead, the guard waved him closer, toward his guard position. He had no intention of leaving his post.

"New, are you?" the guard reached up to throw back the black hood. "Let's see who—"

Tejohn punched him in the throat. The man didn't have a chance to make a sound. His hands went to his throat out of instinct, and Tejohn yanked his sword from his scabbard and plunged it deep into his armpit.

There was no way to hide the sound of a sword being drawn or an armored body falling. Tejohn grabbed the spear before it hit the ground and lifted it upright, so the tip was near the ledge of the second floor but not above it.

As expected, one of the guards leaned over the wall. He was several paces to the right of Tejohn's spear point.

"What are you fools—"

Tejohn lunged to the side, holding the spear awkwardly by the very end. There was some sort of metal ball on the back end of the shaft. A counterweight? The guard above seemed frozen for a couple of breaths as he tried to make sense of what he was seeing. Tejohn thrust upward with the spear and caught him below the chin.

He gurgled and fell backward into the tower. Someone cried, "Alarm!"

Tejohn yanked the short sword out of the guard's chest and, with all his might, stabbed it through the gate latch into the jamb. It wouldn't hold the soldiers inside for long, but he hoped it would be long enough.

The guard above leaned over the ledge with shield and spear. Tejohn jabbed upward, but the man easily deflected his spear.

Someone inside the tower yanked at the door. For a moment, Tejohn thought the sword would tear out of the wood, but it didn't. It wobbled more than he'd like, but the door held.

In the moment he looked away, the guard above struck. Only the fact that Tejohn had been trained to move constantly prevented the spear from stabbing through his collarbone. The weapon slipped between his chest and his left arm, the flat of the blade striking the side of his thigh.

"Agh," he cried, "my leg!" and began to crumple toward the ground. The guard above sneered in triumph and leaned far over the ledge to stab a second time.

Tejohn leaped upward and to the side, stabbing all the way through the guard's neck. The man made no sound at all as he slid forward, spear and shield falling nervelessly from his hands. The weighted end of Tejohn's spear wedged against the ground; the falling body bent then shivered the shaft.

Tejohn picked up the dead guard's spear and shield, then his sword. Peradaini soldiers preferred their spears, but a fight inside would be sword work, just like at the mining camp. He took up a position beside the door, then stabbed the sword into the dirt. He held the spear near the blade and crouched, swaying side to side, watching the sword in the latch waver back and forth as the men inside tried to open the door.

He was bleeding. He touched the front of his chest with his shield hand. It came away wet. It was a shallow wound, the sort that could be healed with stitches and a poultice, but it never failed to startle him to realize he'd taken an injury without feeling it.

Just as the wooden jamb around the sword began to splinter, Tejohn threw his shoulder into it. The door burst inward. The point of the sword, still protruding from the latch, struck the shield of the man who'd been pulling at the door. He raised his shield as though meeting an attack, and Tejohn stabbed low, plunging the spear tip into his inner thigh.

Blood fountained in the firelit room. The man cried out and fell back onto the stone floor. Tejohn was already spinning, bringing his shield around, when the second man stabbed at him. Tejohn deflected the attack, but his own spear twisted out of his hands.

He scrambled backward through the doorway, the guard jabbing at him as he retreated. He struck the back of his head against the doorjamb, then slipped through, knocking aside the spear point with the edge of his stolen shield.

His vision partially obscured by spots, his strength draining away, Tejohn yanked the sword out of the dirt and leaped to the side. He wasn't sure how much exertion he had left, but it would have to be enough to take on one more man. He could still feel the battle lust inside him, as irresistible as a falling blade.

The guard he'd stabbed in the leg lay moaning against the wall, trying to pinch off the blood flow. The other man stood crouched in the entrance hall, spear point facing forward. This wasn't one of the ungainly spears the others had held outside. This was the shorter spear that Tejohn had fought with in his youth, and he suppressed an absurd urge to ask the man to let him hold it one last time.

Tejohn rushed through the doorway, slamming the edge of his shield against the man's spear, batting it aside. He tripped over the spear on the ground as he advanced but managed not to fall. The guard cast his spear aside and reached for his sword, while at the same time slamming Tejohn aside with his shield.

Finally, someone who knew how to use a shield correctly. The metal rim struck painfully against Tejohn's forearm but he didn't lose his grip on his short sword. Then, both blades were bared, and the two men clashed. Their faces were lit in red by the flames in the hearth, and they could see each other. Something in Tejohn's expression must have given the guard confidence, because he suddenly grinned.

Tejohn wedged his shield against the other man's, prying it away from his torso. The guard swung overhand at Tejohn's unprotected skull, but he felt the attack coming and ducked low and to the right. The guard felt his shift in position and pivoted away from Tejohn's sword thrust.

Fire and Fury, Tejohn was fading, losing his quickness and power. Still, the guard's arm was high over his own shield, and there was another artery there—

White hot pain pierced Tejohn's low back, just above his right hip. He gasped and looked down; a spear point protruded from his lower abdomen, dark bloodstains all over his tunic.

I am dead. He didn't even have to turn around to see who had done it. The guard he'd stabbed in the leg must have stopped trying to save himself and taken up his dropped spear.

Tejohn had failed his king, he would never see his sons again, never again hear his wife's voice.

Laoni, I'm sorry. Tell them about me.

All these thoughts swirled within him as the strength ran out of his legs like water. He collapsed on the floor, cursing himself for his carelessness. Who could now go to Tempest Pass to find the spell needed to defeat the grunts? Lar never should have trusted this mission to Tejohn; this was a task for a hero of the ruined past, not an ordinary man.

The guard sneered and raised his sword. He was going to smash Tejohn's skull and Tejohn couldn't even raise his shield. He'd fallen on it, and the spear through his side acted like a brace; he couldn't roll off it.

Grateful am I to be permitted to travel The Way. But he couldn't just let himself be killed. On the guard's downstroke, Tejohn slashed at him with all his remaining strength. Parrying was for suicides, but he did manage to strike the guard on the wrist.

The man's hand came off in a shower of blood, and his falling blade bit heavily into Tejohn's cheek and ear. The guard fell back against the wall and screamed. It was the sound of a young man who knows he is about to die; Tejohn knew that sound better than the laughter of his own children.

Tejohn forced himself to roll onto his stomach, pulling himself off the point of the spear. The man behind him could have stabbed him again, but he didn't. A quick glance showed he lay unmoving on the floor; if he wasn't dead, he would be in moments.

The guard looked at the stump of his wrist and turned very, very pale. He toppled like a felled tree, striking his helmeted skull against the side of the hearthstone.

Tejohn was left alone with the sound of his own ragged breath. "Who is there?" Doctor Twofin called. "What is happening?"

Tejohn's pain felt overwhelming and his mouth was parched. It would have been easy to lie back and die. But if he did, just a few paces from the scholar's cell, his death would not just be a story of failure but of complete failure. Every life ended, Song knew that, but Tejohn didn't want the task his king had given him to die with him.

He forced himself to his knees and crawled to the grate, then yanked it away. It seemed heavier this time.

"My Tyr Treygar!" the scholar cried. "What—?"

"Shut up," Tejohn said. "I like you, Doctor Twofin, but we don't have much time. When does the next guard shift arrive?"

"Dawn."

"How do I get you out?"

"There's a rope and pulley against the wall."

There was? Tejohn squinted around the room and saw it, a wooden boom tucked away beneath the stairs. How had he missed it before?

Tejohn looked down. "Doctor, if let you out, you must swear to me that you will finish a task I set you. The King ordered me to do it, but I can not."

"Why not?"

"Because I'm about to die." Tejohn was about to die on this stone floor, in his home lands, far from his wife and children. He would never see his children again. Great Way, they were so small. How were they going to survive in this collapsed world?

Thoughts like that would do nothing but give over his last few moments of life to despair. He had to focus on the things he could control. "Doctor Twofin, Lar Italga believed his uncle, Ghoron Italga, knew a spell powerful enough to defeat the grunts. It was from the Fifth Gift and could kill dozens at range. I was supposed to bring that spell back from Tempest Pass. Before I free you, you will have to swear to go in my place."

"Go to Tempest Pass? The library there might be the largest in the world now that the Scholars' Tower—"

"Doctor, swear it while I have life in me to free you, or—"

"I swear, Tyr Treygar. I swear to complete your task."

Finally. Tejohn crawled across the floor and pulled himself upright on the pulley ropes. His vision went cloudy and he nearly fainted, but that passed after a moment. He swung the boom out over the pit and let the rope fall into the pit. He felt the rope jerk as the scholar grabbed it.

A wave of dizziness washed over him. Tejohn fell against the wall and slid to the floor. *Hold on.* His vision grew dark and it was hard to think. He reached up, grabbed the rope and pulled it toward himself. His king was trapped in a pit. Doctor Twofin was trapped in a pit. Holding this rope was important to both of them in some way, but he couldn't remember how.

"Almost there!" a frail, foolish voice called. At the same moment, the rope bucked. Someone was trying to pull it out of his hands, but no, Tejohn wouldn't allow that. He put the last of his fading strength into holding onto the rope, for no other reason than that someone wanted to take it. Why did he hurt so much?

"I made it!" the foolish voice called. "I'm free!" Someone moved across the field of Tejohn's vision and he saw an old man in black robes staring at him. *I'm dying.* The unspoken truth he'd been living with for days and days could no longer be denied. He was never going to see his family again. *Tell them about me*, he'd asked his wife, but he didn't even know if they were still alive. *I'm dying.* The words wouldn't come. His mouth was too dry and he didn't even have the strength to move his jaw. He suddenly realized his pain was gone. *I'm dying.*

"I'm so hungry! Ah!" the old man said. He rushed toward a shelf. "Bread! And meat!" he cried, and began to eat happily.

Tejohn Treygar felt the world slip away.

CHAPTER THIRTY-ONE

THERE WAS LIGHT. HE'D NEVER ACTUALLY TAKEN FIRE LITERALLY, BUT flickering orange light wavered in his vision. *I am Fire-taken after all.* The priests had always said that soldiers who died in battle weren't claimed by Fire, that they left the Great Way naturally, but here were the flames anyway.

Still, he did not burn.

"My Tyr Treygar, it's good to see you open your eyes."

"Doctor Twofin?" The scholar's voice was unmistakable. Tejohn let out a moan of despair. Both of them had left the Way, and the task Lar Italga had given him would never be finished. "Fire and Fury."

"Come along," the scholar said. "Drink this. I saved you some lamb but you'll need to eat quickly. Dawn will come soon."

It suddenly occurred to Tejohn that he was not dead after all and might yet be reunited with his family. He touched his side where the spear had gone through. There was no pain, not even a tender spot. *Grateful am I to be permitted to travel The Way.* Clearly, everything had been a terrible dream.

He was lying on the floor of the tower room, and Doctor Twofin was kneeling beside him, pressing a cup of water into his hand. Not a dream after all. "You're a medical scholar?" Tejohn asked. "But you don't wear the badge."

Doctor Twofin pressed Tejohn's elbow to make him raise the cup to his lips. Tejohn drank. "The Scholars' Tower keeps secrets from everyone, even the royal family."

Tejohn's hand fell to his hip, but he wasn't wearing a knife. He was still dressed as a servant. Doctor Twofin was backlit by the hearth and Tejohn could not make out his face.

"Drink more and then have some of this meat. You lost a lot of blood."

"How long?" Tejohn said, then drained the cup. The smell of the roast goat made his stomach grumble.

"Most of the night. I'm long out of practice—I thought I'd lost you twice. But still, with the sun comes a change of the guard and my Tyr Finstel."

"Doctor Twofin, what did they want with you? Why were you here?" Tejohn began to eat.

"They wanted me to go mad," Twofin answered. "Tyrs Finstel, Gerrit, and the others didn't know this, but what they asked would have destroyed me. Tyr Finstel wanted me to build a new Scholars' Tower within his holdfast, and he wanted it in three days. I tried to explain that pace would have driven me mad like Doctors Rexler, Breakstump, and all the other criminals and monsters in his childhood stories, but Tyr Finstel thought I was plotting against him. After I taught the spell to three of the mining scholars he brought me—"

Tejohn almost choked. "What? You can't give away the king's Gifts like that!" He forced himself to his feet.

"Tyr Treygar, *the king is dead*. Peradain has fallen. If you threw that clay cup against the wall with all your strength, you could not break it into as many pieces as the empire. What's more, my Tyr Finstel saved my life. I owed him my allegiance."

Tejohn knew it was foolish to argue, but he felt honor-bound to do so. "You owe your allegiance to the Italga family. Lar is still alive and working to defeat the invasion . . . the way a king should."

Doctor Twofin shook his head. "Lar is a clever boy with honorable instincts, but he'll only survive until the tyrs find him. He has no army, no land, no money, and no way to control the scholars. Italga rule has ended." He glanced back at the hole in the floor that Tejohn had pulled him from. "My allegiance to the Finstels is over, too. Now I will work with you, Tyr Treygar."

Tejohn finished the meat and immediately felt better. Few things pleased a soldier like a full belly. The lamb he'd hidden in his shirt had fallen out somewhere.

He went to the door and looked out. The meadow he had crossed in his black cloak was still dark, but a faint red glow shone through the trees to the east. They had to hurry.

He dragged the two dead guards into the building. None of their equipment fit him, so he dropped them, gear and all, into the cell. The one who'd stabbed him in the back had a helmet that was much too small but his padded shirt and cuirass were just large enough. The one who had collapsed when Tejohn took his hand had dented the back of his helmet, but the third, who had fallen from the mezzanine, had one that only squashed Tejohn's nose a little. He'd worn worse. Unfortunately, none of the boots would fit him.

He strapped on a sword and knife, then took up a short spear. The longer ones would probably be more inconspicuous, but he wanted a weapon he could fight with.

Great Way, shouldn't he have felt more than this? More than just a sick feeling in the pit of his stomach? Splashtown soldiers had taken him in at the bottom of his grief, had fought beside him and called him brother. They weren't Fire-taken—Tejohn wasn't arrogant enough to think that way—but they would be mourned. He wished he could find his own grief again; anything would be better than this terrible loneliness.

He took a black shield marked with the Splashtown emblem and a black cloak. "Are you ready?"

"No spells," Doctor Twofin said. "Even if I were a trained medical scholar, a healing like the one I did last night would have used me up for a days. I will come with you and help you complete your mission, but it will be some time before I can cast another spell without losing myself."

"Don't worry," Tejohn said, glad that the scholar was still sane enough to worry about going hollow. "I don't need you for a spell."

He dropped the last three dead guards into the cell and placed the wooden grill over them. Then he led the old scholar out the door.

The servants' cart path led back to the work camp. There was also, across the wide ditch, the road that followed the river. In daylight, that road would be thick with merchant carts and soldiers, but it was still empty in the dark.

Tejohn forced his way through the ditch, trying to avoid stepping on thorny vines, until he reached the slope leading up to the road. He stuffed the dead man's cloak under the roots of a tree. Then he hurried back to the tower and draped the cloak with the white circle on the hood over Doctor Twofin's shoulders. Tejohn explained that the cloak was a disguise but thought it best not to explain the significance of the circle.

They hurried to the stone dais behind the tower. Daylight was already filling the forest around them, and they needed to be under cover. They found a suitable willow tree and settled in. The sky was cloudless. It was going to be a beautiful day.

The old scholar's cheeks were dry, Tejohn noted with relief, but his expression was slack, almost like a dead man's. Obviously, it was hard to get a decent night's rest in an underground pit. With luck, he'd be up to the task ahead.

The change of the guard arrived just as sunlight touched the top of the tower. The empty guard stations and the bodies inside caused exactly the alarm Tejohn expected, and they found the hidden cloak in the ditch well before they had a chance to search near the willow.

The youngest and quickest of them was sent back to the holdfast with a message. While they waited for their tyr to arrive, the shift stood around anxiously. They assumed that the cloak meant the scholar had been taken away by the road or river, most likely heading south away from the Finstel holdfast, and having an answer they liked, they stopped their search.

Tyr Finstel's cart seemed to take a long time to arrive, but Tejohn knew that was just his impatience. The sun hadn't even touched the bottom of the mezzanine rail when the cart floated out of the north and settled onto the stone dais.

Tejohn kept the scholar well hidden while they listened to Tyr Finstel bark orders and demand explanations from the guards nearby. Only when their voices grew faint did Tejohn dare to glance around the tree trunk.

The tyrs and their guards moved out into the meadow away from the tower. They'd left behind two men to watch over the cart, and both stood with their backs to Tejohn.

Now. Tejohn slipped out from behind the tree, moving as quietly as he could. He moved close enough to the cart that his cuirass almost bumped against it, then stabbed one of the guards in the back of his neck.

The man made a sharp choking sound. Before he could fall, Tejohn had already drawn back his spear and thrust it at the other guard. The second man, who had turned in surprise toward the falling man, took the point full in the throat.

Doctor Twofin was right behind him. "I can not fly a cart, my tyr."

"It's not a spell," Tejohn set down his spear and knitted his fingers, letting the scholar step onto them for a boost. Tejohn lifted him into the cart, and Doctor Twofin immediately took hold of the controls. Tejohn clambered in after him. "The color orange—a bright orange. The feeling of stepping into a deep puddle unexpectedly with your left foot. A square where the right side breaks midline and collapses into an eye solar seas triangle."

Tejohn laid his hand over the scholar's. The old man's eyes were closed to help him concentrate, his face still slack. "I assume you meant 'isosceles,'" Twofin said, but the cart began to shudder.

His hand over the scholar's, Tejohn moved a lever. They floated straight up, quickly. Men shouted and came running, but the cart was out of their reach before they were within ten paces. A pair of spears thudded into the wheels, for all the good it did the throwers. He turned another lever for Doctor Twofin and felt the cart tilt and move off to the south.

"I'm getting the feel for this," Doctor Twofin said.

Spears below ran after them, but they were wasting their time. Tejohn wrapped a rope around the old man's midsection and began to knot it. "We need to turn around before we head for Tempest Pass. Lar Italga gave me a ring—"

"No, my tyr. I don't care to see an Italga on the Throne of Skulls, and I don't need you any more."

Tejohn had the second part of the harness already half tied, but the sound of the doctor's voice startled him. He stepped back, his hand falling to his knife out of habit.

Tears were streaming down Doctor Twofin's cheeks.

Tejohn had always been quick—quicker than anyone—but the scholar was ready for him. What's more, all he had to do was flick his wrist.

The cart wrenched sideways, angling toward the east. Tejohn fell against the edge of the rail and his body weight hurled him over. His knife clattering against the wooden floor of the cart, Tejohn caught hold of the rail, but his fingers weren't strong enough to keep hold.

A moment later, he was falling through empty air. The cart, framed by that beautiful sky, receded from him. Then something soft and heavy slammed into him.

His left leg went wild with pain, and water splashed against his face. *The river bank attacked me*, he thought. Would Laoni have thought that funny? He would never know.

The cart disappeared over the treetops. Tejohn was still unable to move when the gleaming iron spear heads came into his view.

CHAPTER THIRTY-TWO

IT WAS NIGHT WHEN CAZIA AWOKE. HER HANDS AND BACK ACHED, AND all she could see above her were pine trees shrouded in moonlit fog. Cazia needed a few moments to remember where she was.

Then it came back to her: the Qorr Valley, the Tilkilit, the stone that had struck her leg as she—

"Ivy!" The panic in her voice surprised even her. She struggled to sit upright, doing her best to ignore the pain that shot through her limbs when she moved. "Ivy, where are you?"

"Cazia?" It was Ivy's voice, coming from somewhere to her left. Cazia rolled onto her knees—her hands were tied behind her back; that was why they hurt, her feet, too—but she had to see whether the girl was all right.

"Little sister, are you hurt?" Cazia crawled toward the sound of the princess's voice on her knees, stones and twigs jabbing into her bare knees.

"Cazia?" came the voice again. "Are you . . . yourself again?"

The question startled her, but as soon as she heard it, she realized the answer. She *was* herself again. The hollow space inside her—unliving but intelligent—was gone, and so was the feeling that she might start weeping at any moment. Gone, too, was the inexplicable yearning to enter the portal, or to destroy herself by casting spells. The Tilkilit's stone had ripped the hollow from her and returned her to herself.

"I am," Cazia said, and she started crawling forward again. "Whatever they did to me with that stone—"

A Tilkilit warrior came out of the fog and held a spear point at her throat. Two more followed, aiming their weapons at her.

Fire take them. Cazia wasn't going to cower in front of them. "Have they hurt you?"

The warriors didn't plunge their weapons into her. Maybe, like Chik, they didn't believe that the apes could talk.

"No," came the answer. Cazia sagged onto the forest floor, her relief stealing all her energy. "But they have done something to Kinz. She is in some kind of cocoon—"

One of the warriors came up behind Cazia and pressed a hard, cool object against the back of her neck. A shiver ran through her and she felt something being torn from her the way a bedcover would be torn from a bed. If she hadn't been lying on the ground, she would have collapsed. *The black stone again.*

A Tilkilit set a bowl of water beside her head. Was she supposed to drink like a dog? She was tempted to curse at them, but she didn't have the strength, and she was *so parched* . . .

Ten of the little warriors came out of the swirling fog, pulling a sled behind them. It was huge, larger than any cart Cazia had ever seen, and once her water bowl was empty, Cazia was lifted bodily and laid on it beside Vilavivianna.

She was also bound with her hands behind her back but she appeared to be unhurt. At least, not hurt any more than when Cazia had last seen her. The scrapes on her head and cheek had scabbed over cleanly. The warriors dragged them across the bumpy ground. "It's good to see you," Cazia said.

Ivy looked into her face intently, searching for something. "You are really okay," she said. "You have really returned to yourself."

"Whatever they did to me, it cured me. But I can't move my fingers."

Ivy rolled away from her to display her hands. The strong, thin strands the Tilkilit had bound them with were packed around her hands like glue. They both had been bound, and very effectively, too. "Where's Kinz?"

Ivy nodded to the other side of the sled where Kinz lay completely covered by the same stuff binding Ivy's hands. Only her sleeping face showed, and if nothing else, Cazia thought her color had improved. Maybe they were healing her?

She thought again about the strange dark stones. Cazia wanted one. Fire and Fury, she wanted a thousand. What if every scholar had one? They could use the Gifts at any pace they liked, and when they began to go hollow, one touch of the stone would cure them.

Cazia closed her eyes, trying to ignore the bumping of the sled. The Tilkilit really needed someone to teach them about wheels. She thought about a simple spell, something she had cast hundreds of times. Fresh water. The forms came back to her, and so did her new, deeper understanding of them. With a change of a single shape, she could have made it salt water, with a darkening of a color it would have become as cold as a glacier.

It was all under her control. Cazia rolled over and stared at Ivy. She wanted to tell her everything, but she knew the princess wouldn't understand.

I have become a wizard without losing my soul.

The Tilkilit suddenly dropped the sled onto the uneven ground, and both girls rolled off of it. Warriors picked them up like sacks of grain and carried them up a hill of newly dug earth. Cazia felt a moment of panic as they came over the top and started down into the earth. She glanced back and saw Ivy and Kinz coming just behind. Were they all going to be buried alive?

The darkness was complete. Cazia felt herself carried deeper, but by the time it occurred to her to keep track of all the turnings, it was already too late.

They needed light. The lightstone spell came to her mind, and she thought about it critically for the first time. If she were going to cast it without using her hands, how would she do it?

No. No, it wasn't possible. Monument sustain her, she knew she could make one with minimal movements, but she needed gestures.

Not that it mattered at the moment. Her connection to the magic was gone. The Tilkilit stones had not only taken her hollowed space, they'd taken her magic, too.

Temporarily, though. They wouldn't have used one a second time if the loss of her magic was permanent.

After many turns and descents, the warrior set her down on hard-packed earth. It was still utterly dark, but Ivy cried, "Ouch!" when she was dropped beside Cazia, and the echo suggested a cavern.

Something moved in the darkness, something heavy and sharp, scraping against stone and shell. Goose bumps ran down Cazia's back. *What is in here with us?* Had they carried her all this way just to feed her to one of their worms?

Then a voice echoed inside her skull. It was harsh and furious, and it had all the warmth of an avalanche.

::Creatures,:: it said. ::You are now my property.::

To be continued in THE WAY INTO MAGIC

Author's note

In modern publishing, there is no force more powerful than word of mouth. If you liked this trilogy, please tell your friends. Write a blog post, post a review somewhere, tweet about it, even mention it during a face-to-face conversation, if people still have those.

And I don't just mean my books; tell the world about *all* the things you enjoy. Make yourself heard. Readers who share their enthusiasm are more powerful than any Hollywood marketing campaign.

Thank you.

CPSIA information can be obtained at www.ICGtesting.com
Printed in the USA
LVOW12s1929030215

425525LV00003B/260/P